CRISIS OF COMMAND

DISSONANCE

JON FRATER

DISSONANCE
©2023 Jon Frater

This book is protected under the copyright laws of the United States of America. No part of this publication may be reproduced, stored in a retrieval system, or transmitted, in any form or by any means, without the prior permission in writing of the publisher, nor be otherwise circulated in any form of binding or cover other than that in which it is published and without a similar condition including this condition being imposed on the subsequent purchaser. Any reproduction or unauthorized use of the material or artwork contained herein is prohibited without the express written permission of the authors.

Aethon Books supports the right to free expression and the value of copyright. The purpose of copyright is to encourage writers and artists to produce the creative works that enrich our culture.

The scanning, uploading, and distribution of this book without permission is a theft of the author's intellectual property. If you would like to use material from the book (other than for review purposes), please contact editor@aethonbooks.com. Thank you for your support of the author's rights.

Aethon Books
www.aethonbooks.com

Print and eBook formatting by Steve Beaulieu. Art provided by Phillip Dannels.

Published by Aethon Books LLC.

Aethon Books is not responsible for websites (or their content) that are not owned by the publisher.

This book is a work of fiction. Names, characters, places, and incidents are the product of the author's imagination or are used fictitiously. Any resemblance to actual events, locales, or persons, living or dead is coincidental.

All rights reserved.

ALSO IN SERIES

Disjunction
Dissonance
Dominion

PROLOGUE

THE HYPNOTIC FLOWS of fold-space swam past the bridge display as the scout vessel *Cyclops* drove through the final leg of its journey. The computers knew their way and the bridge countdown clock ticked down the time. They'd be home soon if the fold drive didn't explode.

"Here. This is what I wanted to show you," Cleo said.

Former Flight Admiral Sora Laakshiden of the Royal Movi Navy leaned over the railing as her hench indicated part of the engine assembly with a laser pointer. The whole system was open to the air. Sora wasn't well educated in Sleer designs, but she knew that the reactive furnaces pushed power to the fold drive which itself shared a power flow with the rest of the ship. The furnaces were now cranking out three times more power than they should be, even in the middle of fold-space. Enough to maintain the ship in mid-jump and power the maneuver drives and everything else. That wasn't supposed to work that way.

"What's the cause?"

"I think those stupid primates we took it from entered a destination that was too far out of range and they broke the damn thing," Cleo snarled. "Either that or the ship was badly assembled at the construction site and none of the inspection drones picked up on the flaw. It happens, you know. Especially with the new automated bays the Sleer build into their battle rings. But I'd rather blame the damn humans."

It was certainly possible. This Zalamb-Trool-class scout had a dense, short history. Built aboard Earth's battle ring a band of human soldiers had stolen it and used it to hide within their own outer solar system. A few of them had taken it to Great nest on a scouting cruise. They'd been pursed by Sleer destryers, the ship was damaged, and by the time her crew, their wounded Cycomm, and a host of political prisoners discovered it and gained access,

four Skreesh titans and the entirety of the remaining Sleer forces present were at each other's throats. The Sleer evacuated everyone they could and left Battle Ring Great Nest to fight a holding action. Sora's crew had come aboard the damaged scout to find a lone Sleer Defender who'd actually been a human wearing Defender battle dress and knew the medical drone well enough to perform what cures she could. Then she'd blinded the nav computer and run off with the navigator, leaving the three Movi to figure out how to pilot the vessel manually.

But sure. Blame the humans for everything. It might even be true.

"So. Recommendation?" Sora asked.

"It's overheating. I can compensate for that. It's the radiation levels that I don't like."

"Reactive furnaces aren't supposed to emit radiation at all."

Cleo's face lit up. "My point exactly. I say clear this section, get back to the bridge and drop out of fold-space. Then we can re-set the next jump after we power down and power back up. If it happens again, then we need to ditch this vessel and get something more reliable."

"That plan isn't too far removed from how we acquired this ship in the first place."

"That was different," Cleo objected. "That prison transport was breaking down and... hmm."

"I grant you we might not be able to repair it ourselves. Our passengers certainly don't seem technically minded." The twenty-odd former prisoners they'd taken off the prison barge remained aboard, in quarters on the mid decks. They stayed quiet and had access to the mess hall and freshers. The occasional scream or giggle made it past some closed doors but there was a limit to what the medical drones could do. They weren't designed to handle Cycomm psychology except for sedation.

"At least I don't think we'll need to move them. The upper decks are shielded from this... effect. And if the ship explodes, it won't matter where they are."

"You're practical, Cleo. I like that about you."

"Sellik is practical, too."

"Yes. But Sellik is a barely controlled monster." They exited the section, closed the blast door behind them, and Sora palmed the intercom. "Sellik, close all the blast doors to the engineering section and take us out of fold space."

"Just drop us out?" Sellik asked, the dismay in her voice clear.

Sora took a breath and said, "You may take the time to confirm we're not about to collide with a star or planet. Then power down the reactive furnaces to an idle and wait for us. We're coming up."

"Copy that."

Down the corridor to a wide junction and then to a lift. Cleo shuddered as the door closed. "Not a fan of Sleer design philosophy," she explained. "Too many wide-open spaces, too few people."

"But so much room to get fit." Sora spied an exposed girder

lift roof, probably paret of the life cage. She sprang up upwards, grabbed it and did a hanging crunch. Then two. Then a thid just to show the first two hadn't been accidents. She dropped down and caught her breath. "It's not meant to be anything but a fighting ship. Certainly it's not meant to be staffed by three people. Up to two hundred Defenders with all their gear. Rollers, walkers, everything."

"I'd prefer that. I'll always take a crowd over an empty—"

The universe flipped through a new dimension. Spectra flashed and time twisted and turned on itself, and their perceptions heaved as if they were both frozen in motion and still watching themselves from outside their bodies. They caught flashes of Sellik half-imprisoned in her crash couch, a puzzled expression on her face as she tried to follow orders. They heard the cries of their passengers freaking out over the already panicked state among them. And outside the ship, a hole in space-time, a wall of non-existence that turned them off their course.

The moment ended and they slowly came to themselves. Red lights replaced the standard lighting and the lift gave a harsh grinding sound. The effects lifted moment by moment and Sora staggered onto the bridge, her stomach doing flip-flops. Sellik had barely moved... but she'd turned her face away. Sora heard the sound of retching and tried not to succumb to the same urge.

"What was that?"

"A fold fault. I hate this ship!" Cleo shouted. She pulled herself into the command couch next to Sellik while Sora took her place behind them. "Status report."

Sellik dry heaved the last of her breath while Cleo took up her job. "Engines are down. Reactive furnaces are idle. We're no longer in fold space. Looks like we had just passed into Movi space as we came out of our transition."

"Good to know. Sellik, are you alive?"

A strangled cough. "For the moment."

"Excellent. Plot our position."

One more cough and Sellik got to it. "NTS-0358. It's a pulsar, about two light years from Telstan. No planets. It's used as a navigation beacon for message boats. And there are faint gravity signatures everywhere. I'd guess they're being made by M-boats or some other small vessel using warp tunnels and singularity drives."

Sora coughed out the last of her fear at the sudden change of status. "Which means there's a maintenance depot nearby."

Sellik flipped through a handful of star maps. "Nothing on the map."

Cleo sniffed. "It's a Sleer map. They wouldn't necessarily know about it."

"I would if I were them," Sellik said.

Sora said, "Fair enough. Start scanning the M-boat channels and military bands for beacons. We'll see what we find. Cleo, start experimenting with restarting the reactive furnaces and fold drive."

"That might not be possible. The fold drive is red-lined. Plenty of power for the maneuver drive, though."

"Just find that depot," Sora ordered.

"This is Bitch Fleet One calling any allied personnel. We need assistance. Please respond."

They waited. And waited. And waited. Clear scopes. The comm bands were full of chatter and quantum flux spikes. Obviously, M-boats dropped in and out of spatial transitions all over this system, so yes, there was indeed a depot for them close by. But without knowing where it was, any course they randomly chose would almost certainly be the wrong one. Worse, none of the responses she picked up were directed toward her ship.

Sora couldn't understand it. The general comm channels were usually brimming with news and chatter. "Why won't they talk to me? We couldn't have been away that long..."

"I'm not so sure," Cleo harrumphed. "I'm scanning the civilian and military bands. I'm not sure of what I'm hearing. The messages are all over the place. Call signs, fleet movement orders. Emergency departures. Attack orders." She sorted the frequencies and put them on the main display. The entire EM spectrum was awash in chaotic bursts and not mere background noise either. The whole solar system was talking to itself. "Ours is not the only distress call. I get the idea that this pulsar has been drawing a great many vessels besides M-boats to it."

"What could have changed everything in only a few weeks?"

"It wasn't a few weeks." Cleo raised her hands to the display, pulled orbital patterns out of the matrix, and highlighted them. "One good thing about a pulsar is that it's an excellent timepiece. The depot synchronizes its transmission to it, so that exact departure and arrival times can be kept. Every message has a time stamp. These are some of the most recent ones I could find. That fold fault must have been one wild ride. We're more than two years out of our groove."

"*What?*"

"Here, look for yourself." It was true. Two years one month and seventeen days since their folding away, under fire, from Great Nest. "You think it's because of us? We get convicted of spying, sent to prison, and the world goes haywire?"

"I doubt it," Sora said with a sigh. "I had friends in high places, but not so many and not so high." Not high enough to void the conviction or to sneak them out of Cycomm space anyway. "Cleo, scan for key terms. Let's see what they are talking about."

"Let's see... natural disaster... not bad. War... that's a bit more... how about death... " She hit the button and the answers flowed across the display like a river.

"Maybe we should have kept Binil."

"We didn't need Binil. This is a Sleer vessel. It's all computers and molecular circuit networks and relays. No need for a telepathic navigator."

"Except we're traveling with a wrecked Cycomm transport in our hold, plus Cycomm passengers and two Vix corpses rotting in the bridge ready room. If we encounter a Sense Op patrol—"

"We won't—we're nowhere near Haven." There was less truth there than she liked. If the kingdom was gone, or at war with itself, then arriving with former prisoners might trigger a strong response from the Cycomm Unity. The Movi admiralty had long worried about the Cycomm's desire for solitude, to keep the rest of the universe away from their home system. With an intact kingdom around them, that was easy enough to do. But with warring factions all working to carve out individual spheres of influence close to home bases, then the Cycomms might be encouraged to create a buffer zone around their home world. With their patrol cruisers equipped with skip drives, Haven's Sense Op ships could go literally anywhere in Movi space in an instant. Sora could imagine them creating one hell of a deep buffer zone around Haven.

And what of the miscreants inhabiting Marauder's Moon? Surely they were laying plans of their own, plans that would not be good for the Movi or their fellow Cycomms.

What a mess she'd blundered into!

They listened, a more three-dimensional version of the world opening around them. Tensions were already high on the

Movi home world of Movra. There hadn't been a cohesive royal court in nearly three generations. What started as a dynasty with the Sovereign Movus I had slowly but surely metastasized into a thousand-year spiral of entitlements and titles awarded for economic gain. Merchant families and assorted corporate interests worked hard to bring newly discovered worlds into their spheres of influence to increase personal, corporate, and royal wealth, and it worked. Ambitious nobles found ways to marry into the royal family, distributing the gene pool further. Add to the mix that the noble lines practiced polygamy, and soon an endless parade of royal nieces, nephews, uncles, and cousins further diluted the claim to the Vermilion Throne. Many of those who claimed noble titles were part of the Royal Movi Navy, and one such individual was Archduke Zakir Mineko.

Despite the relative lack of details, it was clear what happened: Mineko spent time putting his henches, agents, and lackeys into key positions in the royal palace and literally pulled the trigger on the royal couple, their daughter, and at least three others. In the confusion he'd taken flight aboard his flagship, the planetoid *Darak*, and claimed the throne through the right of royal blood.

In the two years since the assassination, the Sovereign's nephew, Singhir—not the man his uncle was, nor much of a leader in any capacity—was holding the kingdom's remains together. He couldn't unify the factions, though. At best, he was slowing the fragmentation— but new factions appeared almost weekly. Everyone wanted the throne, and those who couldn't figure out how to claim it directly were making deals and forming alliances.

The result was a level of chaos not seen since the first Movi-Sleer conflict fifty thousand years ago.

She didn't approve of Mineko's treachery, but she understood it. Where the royal court saw treason, he saw opportunities for advancement. It was the way of things. There were many more ambitious officers than there were command slots for them. So... accidents happened. A great many accidents. A loyal crew was worth more to a leader than the ship they flew. She looked at the two women piloting her stolen scout ship. Her crew was too small to do anything of worth now. And even if they weren't, what was the point of staying here? The royal court? The peerage? The administration? Eighteen merchant clans six tiers deep? The navy, the army, the spies—everywhere, the spies—the royal police, the defense contractors, the bureaucrats, the national education board... what was it all for? How many lives had it cost in the time she'd been away? Her time in the military, Sellik's time in the trenches, Cleo's time performing and contorting herself for wealthy twits who owned more living complexes and villas than they could ever live in. What was it all for if not to maintain some manner of continuity?

They could afford tax breaks on people who were already so rich they could spend a billion credits a day and still end up richer by the end of the year. They could afford planetoid-sized battleships and crazy multi-configuration fighters that literally had no targets and no purpose, not with the Sleer being driven from their empire by the Skreesh. The Skreesh weren't even moving through Movi space, so who was around to attack or defend against? They could afford to bail out friends of the court whenever a business investment went sour or a new industrial site needed a loan just for a while to make ends meet. And somehow, no matter how peaceful the streets in any city, their mayors always found reasons their police needed more military-style equipment and vehicles. To protect Movi. Somewhere. From someone.

It was *almost* enough to make her want to return to Great

Nest, locate some remaining officer, and find a way to ally with the humans. The short woman with the red hair. What was her name? Reagan? Something like that. Apologize for past misdeeds and work to do better in the future. Cleave to what might well be the most capable rising power in the galaxy right now.

"It was *not* for nothing," she growled, drawing her underlings' gazes. "Not if we fix it."

"If you have a plan, now would be a proper time to share it," Cleo suggested.

"Not a plan... more of a concept. Bring up a star map. Everything between Great Nest and Movra." Sora stared at the display, reaching into the hologram to pick and pinch off details like cutting holes into a wheel of cheese. "Eight hundred inhabited worlds, more than 150 naval bases, and no command and control structure worth a damn," she said. "There are nineteen naval bases between here and Movra. There must be several fleets stationed at them collectively."

Red points appeared on the map. "Here," Sellik offered, "Nineteen numbered fleets, three named fleets. Twelve reserve fleets. Nearly ten thousand ships in all."

"So, our first question is, who's winning?" Sora wondered aloud. "If I had to guess, I'd say it's the royal court or what's left of it. That means the standing navy. That means First Warlord Anterran ad-Kilsek and all his minions. That means those three named fleets are his." Named fleet were huge, designed to maintain control over whole sectors of interstellar space. A numbered fleet was a naval standard. Enough to seize control of a few systems at best. Reserve fleets were composed of obsolete vessels from earlier generations. Serviceable but useless except as cannon fodder or occupation forces.

Cleo punched keys and read the display. "His flagship is a *Sebar*-class planetoid with a full complement of troops and satellite ships. Those named fleets have nearly a thousand ships each. They run all the core systems within three hundred light years of Movra. What can you possibly offer him?"

"The thing they all want—an empty Sleer hub system where they can rest and resupply." No one said anything. Sora heard a rebuke. "Well, don't you both congratulate me at once," she groused.

"If anything, I'd call Great Nest a Sleer hub system being ravaged by Skreesh titans and resisted by the remains of a civilian fleet," Sellik murmured.

"I'm sure the Sleer remnant and those clever primates will have figured out something by now."

"That was two years ago, Sora. What if they lost? You'll be leading your very special officer and his command into a grand trap. No one will pin medals on us for that."

"That's fair. We may have to send a scout mission first."

Cleo turned around in her seat. "Sora, we have a ship of our own, which is the match of any vessel of its size in the royal navy. Yes, it needs some work, but who here doesn't? Why not ditch the prisoners and strike out for ourselves? With the kingdom in shreds, we could run rampant over any number of worlds, taking what we need and leaving the royals guessing. In six months, we can have enough to buy our own planet. But only if we do it slowly. Organically."

Sora raised a finger. "Or... we can make our alliance now and be in charge of the whole kingdom when the other factions exhaust themselves. If we're looking ahead six months, we might as well set an audacious goal for ourselves."

"I'm sure we should," Sellik said, "but I wonder if the man who put you on that prison ship is the one to enable your return to glory?"

"He tricked me because he wanted my command and I was in his way. He had a stable base of support when he betrayed me. That base is now gone. And while I know what he's likely to do, our arrival in a Sleer scout will no doubt be a surprise to him. It will leave him shaken, uncertain. He will need allies. If he thinks I can provide them... he'll have to keep me around."

It took them days to sort through the broadcast news bits. The reports were scattered, jumbled, and incoherent. The official government broadcast channel was putting out propaganda, ceaseless images and reports that their sovereign, Sovereign Movus XXXV, was in fact alive and well and visiting his mountain villa with his family. The other channels weren't as benign. There were fragmented images of fighting: beaches stormed by troops in heavy battle armor, firing high energy weapons against what they recognized as government strongholds. One clip showing a fleet of thirty spherical warships high above the palace, firing on the castle grounds, disturbed Sellik so badly that she looked at her hands until it was over. Doomsday cults sprang up on some worlds, while notoriously balkanized governments on others pulled together into unified nations. There were scenes of local politicians trying to calm their people, and a bevy of talking heads, academic experts, and military officers offering their opinions of the ensuing conflict.

Names appeared to have some meaning, depending on how often they were uttered. Archduke Mineko was the most prominent, notably because he was being accused of murdering the Sovereign and his family. Warlord Anterran ad-Kilsek, the royal family's top military officer, had two reports bearing his name. First, Mineko was trying to gain his support as the new sovereign, then, that he had launched an attack on forces loyal to Mineko in an apparent attempt to form a constituency of the noble families in order to support a elevating a known heir to the throne.

Meanwhile, there were reports about Movus's nephew, Singhir, who was the next apparent heir in the official line of succession... and who had a history of using the royal treasury to fund outrageously unprofitable merchant expeditions into Sleer space. Missena Kiln ad-Esservil ap-Somak was another who got a ton of coverage. A distant relation to the royal family and nowhere near the line of succession, her husband was the CEO of a major merchant conglomerate, and she was drawing a great deal of support from the court's rank and file. The assumption was that the bulk of the wealthy families who ran the big business centers and merchant houses just wanted things to go back to normal, and imagined that Missena was the one to make it happen. The one major flaw in their argument was her family history: her father had been convicted of treason and for the testing of a white hole device on a highly populated planet at the Movi core, resulting in the destruction of the planet and the hundred million souls who called it home. His execution was public and widely broadcast.

The final name they heard often was Honored Mother Votel Gala-Shom, a popular public figure who was known for her on-screen rages against all things royal, denouncing the family, accusing them of inflicting needless death on Movi across the kingdom. She held no fleets, but she had millions of adherents all across the kingdom. It wouldn't take much to forge them into an army if she thought it would help her secure a slice of the new world that seemed to be emerging.

Sellik shut down after a while. "Such waste. The families were all cooperating for once. It was all coming together for the first time in centuries! Wasn't there talk of reforming the court a while back?"

Sora snorted. "There's always talk of reform, but it never

seems to materialize. Just bluster, sycophancy, and backstabbing. It's a realm of long knives and short memories. Everything else is mere illusion."

"I suppose your commission won't mean much then."

"It may yet open a door or two." Sora peered at the various displays and eventually ran a finger across them. "Factions are emerging... we need to know two things. Who is winning, and who we should support."

Cleo's brows knitted together. "I thought we would side with the military."

"With Anterran... but we need to know who is supporting him. Counting ships and armies isn't enough. We need information. Find me a courier. Preferably one trying to exit the system."

Cleo got to work, deftly using her console to sweep the skies. From their vantage point above the plane of the ecliptic, they were drawing very little attention. But all the participants were focused on each other, not on *Cyclops*. "Found one. An express boat tender. It's moving quickly, so it's either just dispatched a boat or it's racing to pick one up."

"In either case it will have a data bank full of useful intelligence," Sora agreed. "Vector us toward it, all weapons active." Now that there was something constructive to do, Sora felt buoyed, vibrant, in control of herself and the universe.

"This is Flight Admiral Sora Laakshiden of the vessel *Cyclops*. Stand down and prepare for data transfer."

The display fuzzed a bit then cleared. A slender Movi face peered into his display. The captain blinked, speechless, and leaned into the camera, his face filling the display. "*Sora?*"

She blinked and took a step back. Who was this person? Clearly, he knew her. They had a history. And apparently, she'd made a deep enough impression that he remembered her. But she hadn't—

Then it clicked. "Vellus?" She clapped her hand to her mouth to keep from sputtering. Sputtering would make her look stupid and out of control. "You're supposed to be dead!" she said.

"Evidently not," he said. "I hesitated to sign my loyalty oath to the Sovereign. They took away my commission and reassigned me to transporting message boats from one end of the solar system to the other."

"I'm glad!" she blurted. This was going poorly. "I'm... glad you're not dead. I was shattered when they told me that."

"Well. That incident is behind us. And getting you booted from the command track was part of it. They said the Cycomms convicted you for espionage. What happened? Why are you in a Sleer ship? You're supposed to be warming a cell on Marauder's Moon."

"Come aboard. I'll tell you everything. And I'll need your data banks... I'm sorry."

"You know I can't—"

"Cleo, fire a shot across his bow."

Red beams grazed the forward quadrant of the tender. Sora watched how the deck bucked beneath Vellus, and heard and alarms sound in his cabin. But there were no explosions.

Vellus waved hopelessly. "Fine. You're welcome to them. Your ship might be the safest place in the whole kingdom right now."

The tender was just the wrong shape and size to fit in the scout ship's central cargo bay. They came up with a workaround, where the tender's umbilical was extended and connected to the scout's hull with a fancy adapter built by the technical robots in the larger ship's workshop. Cleo and Sellik remained on the bridge while Sora and Vellus headed below to sort through the mess.

The moment the airlock opened and she saw him, a man

she'd taught herself to live without, she rushed and embraced him, unable to keep her hands off. They kissed almost violently, then separated in a whuff of air.

"Vellus... what *happened*?"

"Depends on who you ask. The Holy Mother had been especially abrasive and strident that past few weeks. Then there was an assassination, and then Archduke Mineko went on the air all over Movra, declaring himself the leader of the new Movi Empire."

"That's ambitious."

"That's one word for it. First Warlord Anterran ordered the palace sealed and started calling for the archduke's arrest. A fleet of planetoids run by officers loyal to Mineko opened fire on the palace grounds, and Anterran sent message boats calling for every fleet he could find to come to home world immediately. A good portion of them refused, and sided with Mineko or decided to fly Missena's flag instead. Still others declared themselves neutral. And more than a few joined one of the various merchant houses as escorts. I suspect those captains will expect to be paid in wealth other than sovereign credits."

"That won't last long."

"It's lasted for over a year. Long enough for the real instigators to consolidate their forces. A third are loyal to Singhir. Anterran and Mineko have split another third between them, and the rest are biding their time, waiting to see who emerges with a clear advantage." He shrugged. "My data banks won't give you any better information than that, but they will tell you where all the various kingdom assets are. At least, where they were three days ago when the orders were recorded, and the boats sent out. What you do with it is your choice."

"What will *you* do?"

"Me? I'm a drudge who runs the hub of our interstellar communication network in this sector for the loyalist navy. The message boats have all been dispatched. I'm calling all my tenders together here. There's a sizeable war fleet on the way to Garrison Cluster to wait out the violence. We'll join them."

Garrison Cluster was a collection of naval construction and weapons testing sites deep inside Movi space, facing the Sleer border. In case of war or disaster, they would be the rallying point to organize a defense against an approaching Sleer fleet. There would be message boats and planetoids to secure them. Plus fuel, supplies, ammunition by the shipload, and enough spare parts to build new ships. Entire systems devoted to the construction, repair, and supply of Movi starships. Exactly the sort of thing that a military force would want to capture intact.

She tapped an intercom. "Cleo, how many repair drones do we have on board?"

"None. We lost them in the fight at Great Nest. But I think I can conjure one or two from the ship's workshop."

"Please do. Assign them to repairing Captain Vellus's tender. We wouldn't want him to be stranded out here."

"Obliged," he said. "How will you explain your triumphant return home to the royal navy?"

"I've given it some thought. We seem to have a choice," she said. "Ally with a spoiled royal brat, the brat's admiral, the archduke who murdered the brat's family, the daughter of a war criminal, or a religious zealot."

"I chose the admiral, and the current Sovereign. Eventually."

"Agreed. The admiral seems the best bet," Sora agreed. "Damn politics and the nobles who abuse it anyway. Sellik, put in a call to the war college and demand an audience with Warlord First Admiral Anterran ad-Kilsek."

CHAPTER 1

FIRST LIEUTENANT SIMON BROOKS' Office of Military Protocols uniform felt like a prison, his Captain's insignia like a curse. And yet, the combination, along with his Sleer military implants, put him effectively in charge of Battle Ring Great Nest.

Before he and Sara Rosenski had been conditioned by the OMP for obedience, Brooks thought life in the ring's command tower seemed almost sedate. Granted, it wasn't *his* domain or anyone else's, not really. The giant orbital ring's command tower wasn't the equal of the ones used aboard the ring orbiting the Earth. It was small, but unlike the others it was completely functional. From the central command throne, an officer could look in any direction and see several hundred control consoles manned by attentive crew. Today, all of the consoles were crewed. Strangely, they were crewed equally by humans and Sleer specialists—individuals hand picked by Tall Lord Nazerian and Captain Rojetnick for their adaptability and deep knowledge of their fields of specialization. The Gauntlet crew were all down there somewhere, and they'd spent considerable time dealing with Sleer up close and without their battle armor.

By now, the two sides had built up a terse working relationship, if not mutual respect.

That was to be expected. Sleer acknowledged primates, even if they dismissed them as hyperemotional throwbacks. There were even a few worlds in the Sleer empire where primates were the dominant race.

But Sleer had an unsettling effect on humans. With both avian and reptilian features, they mystified human sensibilities. They weren't properly akin to birds or dinosaurs, but combined aspects of both. Far more unsettling to Brooks were the two OMP sentries in full combat gear with rifles at the ready, who followed him everywhere.

From this central location, the crew's combined efforts managed a slew of starships and fighters, drones, weapons systems, defenses, and sensors. Battle Ring Great Nest's bare functionality made their efforts to repair damaged systems and restore a semblance of normal operations to the orbital ring all the more intense.

Brooks reclined on the command chair on the control tower of the great ring, his command gauntlets connected to the governing computer's vast array of data banks. He was surfing the network, allowing his mind to catalog and index the bits and pieces it showed him about its internal systems and external weapons and defenses. The Sleer implants in his flesh allowed him to spend entire days like this. Though lately that wasn't such a good idea. Their implants were failing, their almost magical benefits fading, and the only entity who could likely fix them was five hundred light years away.

Now Brooks's aim was just to find places to put the twenty thousand or more troops stationed aboard the three huge warships parked in the ring's cavernous maintenance bays. An entire construction bay was devoted to laying the keel of *Paladin*, also known as Alien Megastructure-3, the new generation of Sleer-human hybrid warship. It would be months before even the advanced construction facilities aboard the battle ring could finish it.

He finally stumbled onto a unique datum. "Sara! A command suite! I found one!"

"Hooray! I'll be right there!" Lieutenant Commander Sara Rosenski's voice shouted in his ear; Sleer implants could be a little too efficient sometimes, when paired with comms.

They'd been looking for the officers' quarters for weeks. Genukh, the controlling intelligence behind Earth's new battle ring, compensated them for a long stay in secret aboard the megastructure by furnishing them with a luxuriously appointed space. More than mere officer's staterooms, their bridge officer's preserve had been beyond anything any human vessel included. Theirs had a quarter acre of park-like open space and a proper day and night cycle which matched the season changes to the minute. A ring of rooms, cabins and cubicles around the base offered everything from workspaces to bedrooms to a hot tub big enough to hold a dozen humans, to the feeder, the automated dispensary that could crank out anything from food to weapons and armor at a whim. Unfortunately, they had been forced to give the area up, and had been looking for new quarters of that ever since—until now.

Genukh told them that their officer's quarters would not appear on the station's floor plans, which was true, but Brooks figured out that no officer's quarters ever appeared on the floor plans. It was considered a safety precaution in case of invasion or mutiny. The last thing you wanted was for an invading force to make a bee-line for all the station's officers to destroy the chain of command.

He heard Rosenski before he saw her. The guards closed ranks in front of her, blocking her path.

"Out of my way, lieutenant," she snarled.

"Ma'am. You are not authorized for this area at this time."

"I'm scheduling a meeting now."

"Ma'am. You do not have permission to approach at this time."

"We are activating living quarters for UEF personnel. Get me authorization. Now."

After five full minutes and three calls to the OMP office in Primate Alley, she was taking the steps up the command throne two at a time.

"Problems with Biff and Boff?" he asked softly.

She squeezed in next to him. "Just show me what you found."

"Yes, ma'am." He flicked his fingers and a display popped into being above them, a vast schematic showing where all the various quarters were located. "Decks three and four are mostly barracks, but this section is built to house senior officers in style. The good news is that there are plenty of suites. The bad news is none of them are currently active."

"We can fix that, can't we?"

Brooks peered over the lip of the command platform to scan the floor. Hundreds of Sleer and human operators managed the myriad control stations scattered for what looked like acres. "I see someone who can." He used his implants to open a channel directly to his target. "Great Servant of Operations Zolik, please prepare one of the senior officer suites for habitation."

A Sleer baritone hissed in response. "I can do that, Lieutenant Brooks. Which one will you and Lieutenant Reagan be inhabiting?"

Brooks let out a loud sigh and Rosenski stifled a laugh. Did anyone on this crazy space station not know his business?

"Well? You going to tell him?" Rosenski asked.

"It's not like that," he said.

"Sure it is," Sara whispered. "Simon and Judy, sitting in a tree..."

He punched her in the arm and said, "Zolik, show me the zones we have registered available for barracks. Then show me where our people are zoned."

Zolik hesitated before answering. "Who is 'our people?'"

It wasn't a bad question. The loss of Rescue-1—along with a substantial portion of EarthGov's leadership and First Chairman Bon's loyal supporters—due to an apparently random fatal spatial transition error, had kicked the nascent Allied Sleer Fleet in the guts. What they collectively retained ran on inertia and habit instead of leadership. "The Great Nest alliance. Our people."

The Sleer officer complied. The deck plans showed a span of quarters reserved for the crew of each battleship, clustered around the hangar bays where their respective ships were docked.

"I'm not sure I like that segregation," Rosenski said. "Here, set up a fourth zone on the next deck up. Anyone who wants quarters in that area can just ask for them. A common area. Humans and Sleer learning to live together."

"Not inviting the Movi to co-habit?" Brooks asked. "EarthGov is still pushing good relations."

"The Movi are official trading partners and they already have their own section on this ring," Rosenski said.

"There's at least three other star-faring races we haven't even met yet," Brooks said. "Reagan met a Vix. And... killed him..."

Rosenski put up her hands to forestall an argument. "By *accident*. We'll worry about them when they start to arrive. Even with common areas like Primate Alley and the Diplomacy Dome, I'm guessing everyone will stick to their own for a while. But the shared space should be there. And so should we. There.

That's the suite, and that block of rooms around it is for the special troops. Let's keep the family close by."

Brooks gave her a salute. "Aye aye, boss lady."

The family, of course, was the newly formed Rapid Deployment Force Gauntlet, including every human with Sleer implants, carefully vetted by the Office of Military Protocols. One of the perks of being promoted to lieutenant commander and group leader was that Sara Rosenski now had carte blanche to build a particularly capable and destructive dream team. She never imagined she'd be working for the OMP. But here they were.

"Zolik, we'll be using this block of quarters on deck three and that officer's suite," Brooks said.

"Understood. The crew quarters in that zone are already activated; I will set up the parameters for your suite now. Will twelve hours be soon enough?"

"That'll be great. And thank you."

"You're welcome."

"He's in a good mood today," Sara noted.

"Seems that way. Nice of him, considering we kicked his ass over that abandoned factory orbiting Vega. I hope it lasts."

"Brooks, Rosenski... I am right here, as you would say."

"Yeah... sorry," Sara answered.

Zolik continued, "Just a moment. I am receiving a report from the communications tower in section 6134XM. There has been an incident on the Movi homeworld."

"What kind of incident?" Brooks asked.

"An assassination of a royal family member."

And there it was. Rumors flew over their heads for months, but now there were actual news bulletins filtering down this arm of the galaxy. "Should we be concerned?" Brooks asked quietly.

"Of course we should be concerned," Rosenski said. "The

Movi are the second biggest interstellar organization in the local neighborhood. If they fall apart, what happens to Great Nest? What happens to Earth?"

"Objectively, I would say very small," Zolik said.

"You mean *very little*," Brooks offered.

"Gah. English. I'll just use my translators exclusively from now on. Yes. Very little. The Movi Kingdom is an extremely important competitor to the Two Thousand Words. Several border wars have been fought between the two powers in recent years. I don't expect Great Nest or Earth is in any immediate danger."

"I don't know. Political upheavals have ways of rippling out from their centers," Rosenski said.

"That is true. The Movi use specialized space vessels to transmit from one world to another rather than hyperspace relay. That way news travels at the speed of fold-space; somewhat less than instantaneous. The ramifications clearly must be discussed, but there is no immediate danger."

The 264th First Reaction and Response Fleet was all but gone, and Movi Royal Navy Captain Mek couldn't figure out why. No. He knew why. He couldn't imagine what might have been done differently. Again, no. He knew exactly how it might have gone differently. But for that would have required Movi to be something other than Movi, and that clearly was not going to happen. So. Back to the first order of business. His fleet was a wreck of its former self, and there was nowhere left to go.

At least nowhere within the shattered kingdom.

News traveled outwards from the flash point at Movra. Once Archduke Mineko went through with his assassination, there was no going back. The man had a plan... but was discovering the reality to be quite different. Just because he'd remembered about the Right of Royal Blood didn't mean the rest of the universe did. People rarely supported ideas that didn't directly benefit them.

Mek took his eyes off the tactical board to complain, "Damn all archdukes anyway. Bloody assassin. And damn myself along with him. I should have stayed with the Warlord. Not only did he have real control over a better selection of officers, but he seems to know what he's doing on the battlefield."

Commodore Tellen interrupted his captain's rant. They'd been arguing the point for weeks. By now Mek was sure the emotions played across his face every minute of every day. "If that's what happened," Tellen said.

"Of course it happened. Forget the news channels. Navy Intel had been talking about Archduke Mineko's falling out with the royal family for months *before* he shot the royals."

"You're saying the Intel division covered up? They were in on the plot? Helped him plan the whole thing?"

"Of course not. But it wouldn't be the first time that an openly hostile officer made his plans clear—and no one picked up on it or thought him serious enough to do something about it."

"True enough. That still leaves us in a bucket of shit."

"What are our options?" Mek asked. "I imagine the list is short."

"We turn around and beg First Warlord Anterran for our lives or keep moving outward and try not to start a fight with anyone bigger than ourselves while we raid shipping."

"Because piracy always ends well," Mek said.

"It can. But you need a secure location to hit traders from, and a safe network of fences to distribute the plunder through. I doubt we have either."

"Why not look as far afield from home as possible? We've

made a name for ourselves. Our colors are known to all the major factions and many of the small players. Why not hit someone outside the kingdom?"

"Who?"

Mek brought up a new display. "Here. Great Nest."

Tellen balked. "The Sleer capital? Get down to sick bay. I want the doctor to take another look under that bandage on your head."

Mek's hand involuntarily rose to his head. The wound was healing nicely, but would leave a scar. "No. Listen. We've been hearing for months about the destruction the Skreesh left in their wake as they passed through the Two Thousand Worlds. We know there was an escape fleet gathering there. If they truly escaped, then there's a battle ring full of supplies and weapons. Everything we need."

"Full? An escape fleet would take whatever they could remove with them. And Skreesh would reduce an orbital ring to shreds."

"Perhaps so. But they can't fly the ring itself, so there must be something left over."

"It was a wealthy, industrialized solar system once. The Skreesh may still be there, picking it apart planet by planet."

"Do you want to risk going back? We pledged ourselves to the archduke. Warlord Anterran won't show us anything but disdain... or death."

Tellen switched the display. "There's a better option. We should retire to the rim. At least one hundred outer systems have declared themselves neutral."

"They can afford to—the rim is too out of the way to be interesting to any of the known factions."

"My point is they probably won't shoot at us. There are scores of nearby colony worlds we can use for repair and trade."

Mek shook his head. "I've gone over this with the navigation and library sections. There's no independence movement forming at the rim. Only border worlds who've got nothing worth taking and are all joining with the other factions anyway. They'll make whatever deals they can to retain whatever status they're used to."

Tellen insisted, "That could be us. Yes, we've taken losses—"

"Obscene losses. We started with eighteen cruisers. We have ten left."

"—but a fleet like this could make itself well known as a defender of the local systems if we can be clever enough. That would gain us a few months. Maybe longer. Anterran has both hands full and is juggling all the problems in the kingdom as he tries to keep the core secure."

"Not so many he can't send a planetoid to eat us once he gets five minutes to think about it. Great Nest has everything we need, and the Allied Race treaty may still be enforceable."

"Assuming the Sleer just happen to agree with you, which I greatly doubt," Tellen said, "what do we do after we repair and resupply? There's nowhere in the Two Thousand Worlds for us to go. We can't come back here unless we want to fight for entry to every port we find."

"I won't risk ten crews in the vain hope that we can make allies with the bottom rungs of Movi society."

"We're heading to the rim. Navigation! Pull up the profiles of all the rimward spaceports we have on record. Find one with a high industrial base and no political affiliations."

The navigator refused to look up from his console. "There are none, Commodore."

"You haven't even looked."

"We have been looking for weeks. They are being truthful," Mek said.

"Look again."

"Commodore, I still think—"

"Mek! I don't pay you to think!"

"You don't pay me at all." Mek stepped away, pulled his sidearm and placed a single shot through the commodore's head. He answered the stunned looks of the crew with a steady glare. "The commodore has met with an unfortunate accident. I hereby assume command of the squadron. Make your course for Great Nest."

CHAPTER 2

"GRAVITY WAKES DETECTED. Distance ten AUs... signatures match that of a Movi wormhole drive," ZERO said, the AI's baritone echoing across the command deck.

"He says nothing for six months and now this?" Brooks complained.

Rosenski tapped her comm. "ZERO? Are you back? ZERO?"

Brooks shook his head. "He's not in there. Or if he is, he's not up to having a real conversation. Maybe General Hendricks wants to keep him that way."

"Zolik, talk to me. Signatures, as in plural?" Rosenski asked.

"Correct. De-fold within two minutes at this rate."

"Can we contact them?"

"They are already hailing us. On speaker."

"This is Captain Mek Sirus ap-Godep of the Movi Royal Navy. We've been damaged in combat. By the articles of the Allied Race Treaty, we claim the use of Great Nest's orbital facility to make repairs and resupply. Direct us to appropriate docking berths at once. Acknowledge."

The two humans shared a look. Rosesnski's face morphed into that of a woman who'd ordered Pinot Noir and gotten vinegar. "I like a CO who knows what he wants, but that's a little presumptuous."

Brooks shunted their conversation to a private channel. "Zolik, what's he talking about? He can't mean the incredibly flimsy agreement the UEF currently has with the Sleer?"

"I expect he means the old Allied races Treaty. It refers to the agreement made three hundred years ago between Sleer, Movi, Decapod, Vix, Rachnae and Cycomms. The terms gave representatives of each military force the ability to request the use of local resources to repair combat damage. When the Movi and Cycomms broke that treaty in the pursuit of Zluur, it was generally assumed that the agreement was null and void."

"Does he think it's still in effect?"

"He must. This captain may not have learned the facts of the diplomatic crisis the way that the Sleer High Command did. It's entirely possible he thinks the agreement is still in force."

Rosenski shoved Brooks aside to wedge herself into the command throne. "Let's educate them. Give me—"

"Communications are on."

"Captain Mek—" she cut the feed off and spoke in a low voice. "Zolik, how do Movi names work?"

"Title or rank, followed by family name, given name, and associated family names in order of the relative importance of the family. Addressing him as 'Captain Mek' is correct."

"Good to know. Captain, this is Great Servant of Battle Ring Operations Rosenski. The treaty you refer to no longer exists, and the rights you've claimed under that agreement are no longer applicable. If you stand down we will certainly be happy to hear your battle report and offer what aid we can."

"We do not need your permission. We need the facilities,

and we will make use of them as required. Stand down now and we will not bother you further."

"I don't think they know we own this place," Brooks said.

"They don't seem very well trained in diplomacy either."

Mek wasn't finished. "Rosenski... Rosenski... that's not a Sleer name. My science officer tells me non-Sleer inhabit this battle ring. Who are you people and how did you come to be on that facility?"

"We will discuss all these things as soon as you comply."

"We do not comply with demands from invaders."

The situation was clearly getting more and more pear-shaped and for a moment the humans goggled at each other, whispering their ideas, wondering how far the Movi CO was prepared to take this disagreement. Granted, ten ships couldn't destroy the battle ring, but they would do considerable damage to it. Like it or not, this was a test both of battle readiness and command competence.

Rosenski made the only choice left. "Captain Mek, you do not have permission to dock or repair. Stand your weapons down and come to a full stop ten thousand kilometers from the battle ring. Any other action will be taken as an act of war. We will defend ourselves."

"They should be entering normal space shortly," Zolik said. Almost before the Sleer finished speaking, they saw their adversaries: ten black spheres, each a kilometer in diameter, arranged in a line. "Detecting energy spikes consistent with signatures for Movi primary weapons and shields."

"So much for that," Rosenski sighed. The log would back her up. But she could do one more thing to cover her ass. She expanded her comm network to include the command channel. "Captain Rojetnick, this is Control Tower One. Request permission to go to battle stations and defend the battle ring from an apparent incursion."

"Rojetnick speaking. Permission granted. Damage control teams are standing by in all sections. We are scrambling interceptors to assist."

Rosenski wasted no time. The moment she heard the acknowledgement, she set the tone of the emergency. "This is Control Tower One. All sections prepare for incoming weapons fire. All crew to battle stations. All civilians proceed to the nearest designated shelters."

Brooks threw up a new display, this one showing the map of the battle ring's weaponry. "I'm not completely sure what we can do to this guy. We've only managed to repair ten percent of the armory since taking it over," he observed.

"But Mek doesn't know that." Rosenski waved her arms and studied the displays that appeared. "Can you run me a display of the ring according to population density?"

"Done." Brooks studied the image, turning it this way and that. "Looks nothing has changed in two years. We got a million people inhabiting living space for that would fit ten billion."

"And ninety-nine percent of them are crowded into a dozen sections," Rosenski observed. "Try this. Light up every empty section where we have a power station or weapons platform. Make those sections the most attractive targets. With luck they'll target those areas and leave the population centers alone."

"Aye aye."

Rosenski toggled the intercom. "Zolik, arm all available ship to ship missiles. They're the only weaponry we have in large supply. Let's use them."

Mek's ten-ship fleet adopted a V formation, approaching considerably faster than any Sleer warship. "Not much to look at, but wow, those energy signatures. They must have crazy power plants in there," Brooks said.

"The ship design is indicative of their combat philosophy,"

Zolik explained. "Wormhole drives are powered by multiple co-orbiting singularities. Gravity fields keep the ship's interior stable for workstations and living quarters."

"You mean there are black holes driving those things?"

"Correct. Our own Lords of Engineering tried to create something similar long ago. It ended badly. Reactive furnaces are far safer."

"Thirty million klicks out, but they're approaching at... gah... 4000 kps. Tell me their weapons can't hit us from all the way out there," Rosenski pleaded.

"We are beyond each other's effective weapon ranges. I expect they'll switch to their wormhole drives to approach."

The formation shifted. One vessel slightly larger than the rest stayed back while the others formed into three lines of three ships each. The ships began to blink out and back into normal space in formation, one element leapfrogging past the other lines in short order. It was like watching blinking Christmas lights.

"How are they doing that?" Brooks murmured.

"Wormhole drives create transit points between a pair of real-space points and transit through, emerging on the other side. The colloquial term in Sleer can be translated as 'warp tunnels.' Once within optimal range of their weapons their ships will revert to conventional maneuver drives."

"Weapons? Defenses? What are we looking at?"

"These ships are Banak-class cruisers, designed to support the much larger planetoid-type craft in the Movi navy. These are small examples of their technology."

"Small?" Brooks cried. "They're all a klick wide or more."

"In terms of displacement, they occupy roughly the same volume as three Sleer battleships. Keep in mind that a Movi planetoid devotes a significant portion of internal space to the storage and maintenance of other support ships."

"You mean like those?" Rosenski pointed to the display. Already, the battle formation was becoming cluttered as hundreds more contacts filled the display.

"Very much so. I believe they are moving to open fire. They will be armed with meson cannon and particle weapons, as well as long-range missiles and heavy shields. Short-range weapons too."

The ships changed their formation into a dual wedge, one segment flying above the battle ring and the other below it. Before the humans could comprehend the myriad facets of the attack, alarms sounded and displays appeared, showing damage.

"Multiple hits all across this section of the battle ring," ZERO said. "Closing off damaged areas. All crewed modules report ready status."

"What's our current weapon status?"

This time, ZERO followed instructions. "All energy turrets remain off line. Short range point defense batteries are active throughout the battle ring. Long-range missile bays are loaded and armed."

"Shield zones?"

"Negative."

"That keeps it simple, at least. Zolik, I need you to partition the long-range missile payload into equal portions for the main ships and fire when ready," Rosenski said.

"Order acknowledged. I am sending targeting data and firing instructions to all crew stations."

Across the entire battle ring, bay doors swung open to show their deadly cargo: heavy rockets that would have been the equal of any ICBM on Earth. Each section took its orders from the central computer; the missiles ignited and emerged from their silos, streaking toward their targets in trails of orange flame. One by one the tower crew watched the status markers for each battery turn from an agreeable green to a depleted red.

Brooks was already thinking three moves ahead. "Reload missile bays as quickly as possible. Use the small guns on anything that gets within firing range."

Zolik hissed, "Understood. Orders are being relayed to the appropriate sections."

The missiles streaked toward the capital ships, leaving traces on the display in blue lines. Four of the ships simply disappeared in giant explosions. Two others took evasive action and managed to escape with little damage, while the other four ships took hits of varying effectiveness.

"The remainder are re-grouping and coming for another attack."

The Movi ships swung inside the range of the battle ring, forcing the gunners to risk firing on their own planet. The group held formation and raked the ring's interior surface with green beams of energy. This time the mesons penetrated the ring's defenses, peppering compartments with exploding bursts of energy and hard radiation.

"Hits on numerous sections," ZERO reported while a list of damaged sections appeared on a new display. "Closing off damaged areas."

Zolik's face appeared in a new display. "Humans... perhaps you'd like to deploy the meson screens."

"We have those?" Brooks asked.

"We do. The screens should offer protection from their primary weapons."

"Don't ask for permission next time," Rosenski said, "Just deploy whatever defense might be appropriate."

"Acknowledged. Screens activated."

"They're coming around for another pass," Brooks said. The ships re-formed their firing line and swooped around the ring. This time when their meson beams lanced out, they all detonated well short of the structure.

Rosenski studied the tactical display. "Zolik, how many shield reducers do we have installed?"

"Enough to guarantee hits on all six remaining ships as long as they stay within effective range. What are you going to do?"

"I'm going to show them they have no idea what they're dealing with. Hit all Movi ships with anti-shield beams."

"Projectors are tracking targets. Beams activated. Shield reducers are engaging targets."

On the display, they watched the attacking ships' shields stutter and skip, then melt away bit by bit.

Rosenski smiled evilly. "No chance in hell, boys. We re-purposed those projectors to kill Skreesh titans. Open a channel to their lead ship, contact Captain Mek."

"Captain Mek's ship took a great deal of damage. In any case, there's no response," the Sleer noted. A bit glumly, Brooks thought.

"Then use a general channel. Offer them a draw."

"I am repeating the message on all channels. No response. No, wait..."

The comms hissed and crackled. "This is Captain Mek. We are standing down."

"Thank God," Brooks sighed. "We just got this wreck repaired; we didn't need these yahoos blowing it up again."

"New missile launch detected," ZERO said.

"Oh, come on, guys!" Rosenski waved her display away to concentrate on the tactical. Out of six remaining ships, four followed Mek's orders and hovered ten thousand klicks away from the battle ring. Two others were closing distance and shooting. Out of their rear sections, hundreds of small craft exited the cruisers, swooping around and diving towards the battle ring.

The two hostile ships swung onto a new course and attacked again, meson beams joined by smaller particle weapons and lasers. Multiple beams burned scars along the ring's surface, this time away from the planet.

"Listing damaged sections," ZERO said. "Long-range missiles are reloaded."

"Fire one half our payload, divided up among both targets."

"Relaying orders now."

They watched as the new wave of missiles streaked toward their targets and impacted in hundreds of fireballs. Without their shields, even their relative bulk and heavy armor didn't save them. Both attacking ships exploded into fragments.

"What about the smaller craft?"

"UEF Ravens and Sleer Zithid fighters are engaging them now, along with point defense guns. It appears that the remaining Movi pilots are crashing their ships into the battle ring."

Rosenski's hands curled into fists. "Christ, guys!" They watched as the word apparently spread throughout the remaining Movi fighter groups. They swerved and bobbed like demons through defensive lines just to smash their ships onto the battle ring itself. With fewer and fewer targets to shoot, the defense guns slowed, until finally there were no more targets to attack.

"Targets destroyed. All systems standing down. Damage control parties are being formed and directed toward priority sections. Damage repair drones are deploying."

"What a waste. ZERO, make installation of shield zones a priority."

No response.

Finally, Zolik spoke up. "Acknowledged. I'll send the orders. What should we do with the Movi?"

Brooks sagged into the control throne while he tried to make some sense of what he'd seen. Eventually, he saw that Rosenski was still staring at the displays. "Sara?"

"Yeah. I'm... what was the point of *that*? Why attack so insistently until we had to destroy them?"

"They might have been following orders. Maybe they thought they had no choice."

"The Movi used to be one of the fabled allied races though, right? If they wanted our help, which they said they did, why demand it instead of just asking for help? Why be that kind of asshole?"

"You think maybe the Movi government isn't coping with their crisis as well as we'd like to think they could?" Rosenski asked.

"I think something scared Mek and his friends more than dying in combat."

"Like maybe their navy split into factions and their faction was losing."

"Something like that."

"Okay, I guess that's possible. But again, why attack us? Why not claim asylum and then... ?"

She settled on the throne while he tried to figure it out. "Exactly. They come here and they repair their fleet and then what? They can't go home. If they try, maybe they get hunted down by loyalists or a bigger opposition faction. And what about their families? They must have people back home waiting for them. Maybe suicide absolves them of whatever guilt they incurred when they abandoned their posts. Worse, I don't think Mek was the only one in their navy to think like that. We could see a whole convoy of refugees from the Movi Kingdom. There aren't enough of us here to keep them out, and I'm not even sure we should try."

"Jeez. All we have to work with are the bunch Dance escaped from and the merchants Valri does business with. What kind of people are the Movi, really?"

"I think it's time we find out. Have the Movi cruisers dock

and have Mek and his staff come aboard. In the meantime, get us a damage report."

CHAPTER 3

"SO. CAPTAIN... MEK?"

The Movi officer was easily the most impressive figure in the conference room. He and his three of his officers were escorted under guard to the security section of Battle Ring ZERO. Each of the officers who accompanied him were being interviewed by OMP officers in separate rooms. Brooks sat opposite Mek at a nondescript table, with a black camera dome watching them from the ceiling. Sara Rosenski was nowhere to be found.

"I am Captain Mek Abed ap-Nial, Acting Commander of the 8099 Cruiser Squadron. My commanding officer, Commodore Tellen is dead. And you are...?"

"Lieu—Captain Simon Brooks, Office of Military Protocols." That was a habit he'd need time to assimilate. They'd put him in OMP livery for this interview, complete with the correct insignia. The fact that it was real, galled him. But joining the OMP was a condition of his continued freedom to operate as a member of the Unified Earth Fleet. Rosenski was in the same condition. "Your CO is... dead, you say?"

"I do. How is it you speak Moviri? I know we haven't encountered you people before this."

"Sleer military implants."

"Interesting."

"What happened to Tellen?"

"What happens to all officers who can't see beyond their ambitions. He had an accident. A serious one."

"With dire consequences?"

"Tellen is dead."

"Who gave the order to come here?"

"I did. After his accident, I took command of our remaining squadron and ordered the course here."

"How strong were you at the start?"

"Tellen decided twenty cruisers was a sufficient bulwark against attacks by any forces loyal to the Sovereign. We lost ten ships to the royal navy. Six more to your defenses. The rest is as you see."

Brooks made notes on his tablet. He remembered three separate and properly worded commands for Mek's fleet to stand down. They'd ignored the first two, but Tellen had been in charge of the fleet. They'd lost six ships, then he'd fallen into a bad case of dead and this character took over... except that two of the other ship captains hadn't recognized his authority to stand down and defied the order. *Ipso facto*, Mek killed Tellen. Okay then. There would be a time to question Mek further on the nature of the current Movi order of battle, but that could come later. Brooks wanted to retain his forward momentum. "Are accidents common aboard royal navy vessels?" he asked.

"They can be. These are dangerous times. The commodore insisted we make a stand in the outer reaches, but that idea presented holes wide enough to drive a fleet carrier through. Coming here was my idea. I expected the base to be empty.

Your presence here surprised me. I don't always do well when surprised."

"Well. It sounds like it's difficult to know who in the Movi ranks to trust."

"Under duress, officers often trust no one. Keeps things simple. But as I have admitted, accidents happen." Mek kept his eyes on a point behind Brooks, who remained quiet in case there was more. Eventually, Mek continued, "Corruption seeps into everything. No bureaucratic organization can avoid it. But when Mineko murdered the Sovereign, that turned everything upside down. He'd planted a battalion of officers in every service, promising them Breaker knows what. Filled their heads with dreams of the glory of past wars that I'm sure were never glorious. I think he planned too well. No one trusts him. The only question is how much damage he'll do to us on the way to his doom." He looked back at Brooks, realized he'd said too much, and stopped.

Brooks knew a face filled with regret when he saw it. It was the same look he faced in the mirror every morning. "In that case, we have a problem. We're basically strangers here. You wanted to invoke a cooperation treaty that the Movi admirals rescinded over an argument concerning the status of Zluur. A new treaty is in process... we're still figuring that out... but the only participants are humans and Sleer."

"You're a human, then."

"Yes."

"Where do you come from?"

"A world much further down this arm of the galaxy. Believe me, you've never heard of us."

"All right. Well, I know that Great Nest used to be one of the most populous, best developed worlds in the Sleer empire. It's a ruin now. I'm amazed you could have learned so much so quickly."

"We're here as a part of our current alliance," Brooks said.

"So, Sleer inhabit your homeworld too. Yes?"

"I couldn't say."

"No. And why should you? We're strangers."

"Are there additional fleets on their way here?" Brooks asked.

"I don't know. We came here as a quick way to grab supplies and perhaps some repairs. Great Nest was supposed to be abandoned, you know."

Brooks made more notes. This was where the conversation got dicey. The rule was not to give more information than you got. But confirming what the captain could plainly see wasn't exactly improper. "The Sleer gathered what they could into a few giant escape fleets. Where they fled to, I can't say. But our flagship was able to lend substantial aid to the remaining forces when the Skreesh titans arrived."

Mek allowed himself to lean forward. "In a single ship? You fought *Skreesh?*"

"We did. Four of them."

"Great Breaker."

"We beat them."

"No."

"It's true. We have Sleer aboard this station who were there. Ask them."

"Those are most interesting points." The captain leaned back and stared with the same you-can't-be-serious look a cat would have. The Movi even looked like one, with wide, slitted eyes that were all iris. "We're here now. It is not the situation we intended, but I have four battle-worthy cruisers and all their normally assigned satellite vessels. What will you do with us?"

"That's not up to me. But my CO is concerned that if you decided to raid us for parts and stores, others might have the same idea. You already saw that we're far from defenseless, but invasion by remnants of the Royal Movi navy isn't something we look forward to dealing with. What can you tell me about the current state of your civil war?"

Mek snorted. "It's not a war, it's a free for all. Between the court, the royal family, the merchants, the navy... I can count at least ten factions off the top of my head. Another twenty will probably emerge as the trade routes dry up and half the worlds in the kingdom realize they can no longer get paid for their goods by the other half. The great merchant lines will grind to a halt. Scores of worlds will try to carve out their own spheres of influence as we go forward. A broad range of alliances will emerge, and you'll see all the ancient enemies take each other apart once they realize that there's no one to stop them. We'll be lucky if there are even one or two hundred worlds still intact when it all ends."

"Nothing ever ends," Brooks said. "But yes, you might find yourselves falling into a deep deep pit for the next few decades. We can help reduce that to five or six years. Are you interested?"

"What kind of deal can you possibly be interested in making with me? All I have is the four cruisers you see in orbit."

"It's four more cruisers than I have at the moment."

"And you said yourself you have no way of knowing who else might follow."

"No. But you do." Brooks sat back, folded his hands on the table, and waited for his subject to put it together.

When he did, his eyes widened. Brooks could almost hear the click of his bones when his jaw dropped. "I see. You'll be wanting us to alert you to any new arrivals, because I can detect them in transit and you can't."

"Bingo."

"I don't know what that means, but I assume you liked my answer."

"It means you're correct. We can detect them on their approach. But you can identify them."

"I thought so. Go tell your master I agree. In return for safety for my entire combined crew, I will act as your intelligence source."

"How will your combined crew react to that?"

"Some will take it better than others. But I want it known that the decision to help was mine and mine alone. I'll not have any of my officers pay the price for my treason."

"I won't have to."

"Won't have to what?"

"Allow me to introduce you to my masters."

The door opened, and three individuals entered. "Captain Mek, these are Captain Rojetnick, First Chairman Bon, and Major Underhill. You may already know Royal Movi Navy Intelligence Officer Horvantz."

Horvantz inclined his head. Mek replied by dropping to one knee and genuflecting. "My *appanim*. The order to disobey the law was mine. I regret my actions to follow those who betrayed the Vermilion Throne. I offer my life and service in exchange for the lives of my crews."

"In the name of the Sovereign, I accept your terms, Captain. Shall we go somewhere more comfortable to discuss our prospects?"

CHAPTER 4

"GOOD MORNING, Secretary of Commerce and Interstellar Trade Valri Gibb. Today is April 6, 2079. The time is 0530 local. You are assigned to the Diplomacy Dome. Work begins at 0900... Good Morning, Secretary of Commerce and Interstellar Trade Valri Gibb—"

"Ram it, ZERO," she groaned. The voice droned on; five full cycles, then ten. She finally gave in to the inevitability of the new day and called out, "All right, I'm up. Lights!"

The truth was she never got to sleep after the Movi attack on the battle ring. Battle stations had interrupted her routine near midnight, and the Diplomacy Dome and its outlying sections were designated shelters for Primary Alley. Over the next two hours, hundreds of her co-workers, staff, and fellow EarthGov functionaries, huddled in their quarters, hoping the fight passed them by. She took it upon herself to tag a security team and personally check on those in her section. She soothed nerves, quieted fears where she could and held the panicked when she found them. When the alert lifted, she sent Basil Matsoukas to find out how bad the attack had been. His report came quickly: one hundred and twelve dead and nearly one thousand wounded, mostly gunnery crews stationed near the outer areas of the hull and stricken with radiation burns. Ugly, violent reminders that space was dangerous. But it could have been far worse.

Normalcy was her defense against the awfulness. She ran through her routine quickly, brushing teeth, washing her face, and deciding the shower would be pointless until after she'd finished her morning run. She wriggled into her gym clothes—a new set, made from the crazy molecular fibers that only Sleer feeders could produce. She supposed she looked stylish enough, but nothing felt right. Even her body didn't fit right any more. She was hard and fit in places she'd never noticed before.

The door chimed. "Come in, Frances."

They'd done this so often that she knew every sound her friend might make. Today she was silent until Valri stepped out of her bedroom to find Frances Underhill sprawled out on her couch. Even in gym shorts and a tank top, her signature blue black hair bound up in a tight braid, she looked dangerous.

"What's wrong?" Valri asked.

"Besides bombs falling on us? Either everything or nothing. Depends on your POV. My whole section is still on alert." Underhill plucked a chip from her pocket and held it out. "I was told to hand deliver this."

"Jesus. It's too early for this spy shit." Valri took the chip, slid it into a viewer, and paged through the data. "Oh no. Now we have military refugees to manage? It never stops."

"When the Sleer high command decides it wants this space station back, you'll be glad you have them."

"I guess. I'm not seeing a page of specific orders."

"They can't give you any—you're a civilian. But I think they expect you to use this intelligence in your meeting with your Movi gal pal this afternoon."

Valri turned the display off and locked the drive in a small desk safe. "You know about that, huh?"

Underhill bounced to her feet and began stretching. "It's all on the official schedule. Of course the OMP can't tell you what to do, but... "

"Yes, ma'am. I get the message. We'll come up with something. Where we going today?"

"I thought we'd run around Primate Alley a few times. Take in the sights. Burn off some adrenaline."

"Sounds fun. We can show the non-enhanced primates what a real workout looks like."

They jogged down corridors and through compartment doors with the practiced ease of people who'd long since consigned their route to memory. These days, Primate Alley was less of an alley and more of a proper city. Tall towers and wide boulevards ran past lakes, through parks, and down a wide throughfare that wound along the edge of the island. Above, a holographic sky brightened from an orange dawn to a blue sky and yellow sun. Valri struggled to both look at the scenery and keep pace with Underhill. Finally, Frances looked over her shoulder. "Wanna race? Five hundred meters. Ready? Go!"

Valri didn't say a word. She didn't need to. They both knew she was in for whatever Underhill came up with. She poured on the speed, struggling to breathe. After a point, she stopped worrying about her body and focused on keeping pace. Her implants supply her body whatever elements it needed to make her demands into reality. She stretched her limbs, felt as if her feet were going to leave the ground completely, flying her above the street. Even better, Frances was only a few meters ahead of her. Valri decided today was the day she won these daily contests and pulled up a distance tracker. One hundred meters to go... fifty... twenty... ten... then with a final burst of speed she leaped the last ten meters.

"Ha! *Ha!*" she screamed. "Finally!"

Underhill bent at the waist, hands on her knees, sucking in air. "Good for you, babe. Let's sit for a minute."

They found a nearby bench and collapsed. Valri couldn't stop looking at the skyline. Nothing out of place, no damage. Except the holographic alert banners to seek shelter were gone. The warning system was almost more nerve-wracking than the attack. And the utter lack of people on the street. They'd be hunkering in office spaces soon enough. It was too easy to forget just how big the ring was or how exposed it was to potential enemies. "Which building is Brooks using these days?" Valri asked. She didn't want to know how Simon Brooks was doing, but she needed to talk about something.

"We took his toys away from him after the insurrection. He's got a single officer's quarters. Rosenski, too."

"More complicated than I can talk about. Well, not really. They are under guard all day every day. They need permission from an OMP officer or ZERO himself to work on a project together. Creeps nearly got themselves killed on the command deck during the attack."

Valri blinked, suddenly completely sewrious. "Command deck? Did they run the defenses? Did they save ourt collective asses?"

"They did. After ZERO approved it."

"Jesus, Boo. You'd shoot them for doing their jobs."

Underhill kept her eyes on her feet. "It's complicated. Homeworld security is... complicated," she sighed.

Valri's pulse refused to slow. She closed her eyes to visions of Sleer service machines in Defender armor shooting at her apartment door. She would never think of that moment without breaking into a sweat and smelling smoke. Now she was having unhappy thoughts about a woman she'd been friends with for years. Served with. Fought with. She knew the OMP was bad news, but she'd never truly understood the power her friend had over...well, over everyone, in the name of security. Over her. "What did you do to Brooks and Rosenski?" she asked in a small voice.

Frances waited a while before saying. Valri knew it was a bad question to ask, hoping that Frances would simply refuse to tell her. She wasn't sure she wanted to know, but needed to hear the threat was gone.

"Put them on a very short leash."

"They still work for us?"

"For me. That's all you need to know."

It was enough for Valri. She could breathe easily again. "You talk to the other Gauntlets at all?"

"Not socially. But work puts me in contact with them. Everything feels different now. Official. It's depressing. You still seeing Fairchild?"

"I am. But as you said, it feels different."

"The new normal."

"The post-insurrection lockdown," Valri quipped.

"Heh. That's what Skull called it last time we talked."

"That man is still ten years older than you, my dear."

"Jeez, Val. Stop telling me that. I like Skull. Guy's got a good tongue in his head."

"Oh, my!"

"No! I mean he's got a great mouth."

"Gobble gobble."

"Gah! Talking! He's a good talker. We talk. That's what we do. Fuck it, just shoot me now." Underhill put her head between her knees. When she sat up, the flush hadn't quite cleared her face. "I can relax with Skull. It's like talking to family."

"*Oh my dude!*"

"No, it's... it's hard to talk to anyone like a person while I'm wearing the uniform. He's not afraid to talk to me like a person.

Like you do. I miss that. I miss just going out for a coffee or a beer and sitting down with a friend and talking about shit I care about. OMP is taking over every damn thing in the name of security. Everyone I see at work is on edge. I'm putting people on leashes for homeworld security's sake. Lately I really hate my fucking job. I wonder what I'm doing here. I wonder if Layne's Brigade doesn't have the right idea."

Valri nodded, looking down at her hands. She remembered the first time she and Fairchild held hands, a light pat of skin against skin, dry and cool, aboard the Sleer shuttle. With all of the new duties that Earth Gov placed upon her shoulders, and saddling Fairchild with the job of Deputy CAG, there hadn't been a lot of time for hand-holding or anything else in the past few months. She should probably change that if she expected anything to come of it. "Skull knows you're never going to put out, right?"

Silence. Then, "I might. Have you looked at him lately?"

"Nope."

"He's got the same implants we do. We're all developing differently. I'm getting stronger, faster. Taller. He's getting *younger*."

"No, he's not."

"Not physically. He's still the same age. But he's in better shape than most recruits. So am I. So are you. Frau Butcher looks like a Greek goddess. Even Brooks. Holy crap, that boy filled out nicely." She stared at Valri for a moment then said, "Val. You, too."

"Me too what?"

"You too. You checked yourself out in a full view mirror? You're stacked. I am, too, we all are. All the ones who took those implants. How much weight can you press?"

"Twenty kilos with my arms on a good day."

"How about your legs?"

"No idea."

"Let's find out. Come on. Weight room time!"

Part of the perks of being a unique unit in a branch of the service that was already known for exceptional levels of secrecy was that they got their own facilities for just about everything. The battle ring's lower decks held all the OMP's stuff, their ships, their gear, their planes and battlers, and all their training and living quarters. The weight room was less of a room and more of the fitness center, with mats and machines and items to pump themselves and each other into better shape.

Even this early, there were troops using the facilities. The leg press lay against the wall, unused. One aspect of Sleer tech the humans were able to replicate was their gravity slide. One could set the machine to utilize any weight they wanted.

"Let's see what your arms can do first. Power cage!"

The power cage was a setup designed to allow the user to press vertical weights. The arm bars were well out of Valri's reach. "What the hell kind of soldiers are you OMP guys training? Giants?"

Underhill set the bars lower. "There's always someone wants to do himself permanent damage. You ready?"

"Yes, sir. What're we doing?"

Underhill leaned over to tweak the settings. "It's a brain hack. Your eyes see you pressing more weight than you've ever tried, and your brain tells your body it can't be done. The body will listen, it'll shut you down. So we're going in blind. Eyes closed. You can't see what you're doing, but I can. Ready? Go. First round. Twenty reps, each set. Let's go..."

Valri breezed through the first three rounds. After five the stress got more problematic—like pushing on a wall that gave more and more resistance. She felt a slight pain in her shoulders after the sixth round and a deeper twinge in her biceps after the seventh. Frances said, "You think you can do one more round?"

Val took a few deep breaths. "I can. Set me up."

"Okay. You're set. Do *not* look, just push."

"Got it." Valri pushed, resting the weight on her shoulders, lowering the bar to her chest, and then pushing back up, exhaling like a locomotive, a great force exiting her body. She replaced the bar in the rack. "How'd I do?"

"I'll tell you later. Let's do your legs."

They went through the same process. This time the gravity slide was behind her, out of her sight, and all Frances did was tell her to wait a moment between sets. After seven sets Val had enough. Her legs felt rubbery and her thighs burned. "I think I'm done."

"Yeah, I think you are."

"What's that mean?"

"Look." She shoved the tablet forward and Val recoiled when she saw the display. "This is bullshit. You made this up and now you're messing with my head."

"Not even a little. You just pressed two twenty with your arms seven eighty with your legs."

"That's... not possible." Val ran her hands along her biceps, noting they were firm, but not that big. "What's happened to us?"

Underhill opened the machine and helped pull her friend out. "Brooks says we're being optimized."

"Optimized for what?"

"That's the tricky part. No one seems to know. Brooks and Rosenski assume that it's for combat, seeing as how they're military components, but I'm not so sure. Even ZERO isn't sure. All we do know is everyone is improving in a very specific way. Some physical, some mental, some in both. You're all buff because the ruling AI thinks you need to be. What else have you been blasting through without really trying?"

Valri thought about it. "The combat simulators. Especially

the command ones. I remember previous moves more clearly and I can see more possible tactics to use every time I get in. They've been throwing real doozies at me too just lately."

"For me it's eyesight. Physical senses. I hear through walls now. Hold up a sign from the other side of the room. I can usually read it. We're all getting... better."

"What's ZERO think of all this?"

"He doesn't answer queries like he used to. He's not really ZERO any more. If he's more Genukh than the other way around, then she probably has her own plans and they may not include us."

"Of course they include us. She needs us to break her out of whatever box Nazerian and his superiors put her into."

"So we let her out. What then?"

"That's a very good question." Underhill leaned in conspiratorially. "Can you imagine what might happen if every human being on earth took those implants?"

Valri wondered. A terrifying army of space lizards versus... what? A billion years of evolution produced a race of pursuit predators who changed the face of their planet in only a few centuries. "We'd beat those scaly boys back to Home Nest."

"Maybe. Let's get back. Ears everywhere you know."

Valri let Frances get a few yards' headstart before following. She had no idea how many ears were trained on her...or what they might hear.

Miraled Makjit arrived at Valri's office with her usual style and aplomb. She'd picked up on a number of human mannerisms in her time working with Valri and her staff. Makjit kissed the space above Valri's ear instead of shaking hands. Then there was the gift giving. The Movi diplomat recently discovered two human delicacies: miniature scented cakes of soap, and tiny bottles of liquor. Valri accepted everything with practiced grace, offered Makjit a single red rose—grown and newly delivered from the horticulture center on Deck Ten—and they got down to business.

"We have an issue," Valri said.

"Pray tell. What is it now?"

Valri approached her office screen and switched the view with a grand flourish. The scene transformed to that of a wide fleet of ships. Scores of support vessels ran through racetrack orbits across the face of the battle ring. None of them could hold a candle to the four Movi warships that hung in the sky behind them."Madame, I give you death and destruction!"

"You can hardly expect to blame me for that!" Miraled said, gesturing at the new arrivals. "If they're part of the insurrection, there's no way to know where they might strike next. Believe me, I'm not happy about it. Some of their meson bursts came very close to our own sections."

"I know. I'm not blaming you for anything, Miraled. But you'll forgive me for being a little unsettled that a fleet of your shattered kingdom's rebel warships took potshots at my office!" Valri shouted. She took a deep breath and held it. Eventually she continued, "The agreement we came to months ago has yet to be fulfilled. I think we should take another look at it."

"Ah. You want to re-negotiate."

"Not exactly." Valri pulled a tablet from a drawer and began tapping at buttons. "You see, I like to think we have a good working relationship."

"I agree. We do. We have so much in common."

"And I like to think that we're above all the bureaucratic pettiness that our governments are steeped in."

"Oh, absolutely!"

"Which is why it's so damn painful to have to bring up something like this."

"What is this?"

"I received a bit of intelligence early this morning, delivered by a special courier. It includes the backgrounds and capabilities of our new friends out there," she said, gesturing at Captain Mek's remaining ships. "They don't work for the Sovereign."

Makjit's face darkened. The effect was stark, like someone inside her head throwing a switch. "Who, then?"

"One of the Archduke Mineko's flunkies, I'm told. Commodore Tellen. They did badly, came here and did worse. Eventually they surrendered, but now they've nowhere to go and they'll stay here until someone in EarthGov or the UEF decides on a plan for them. They won't be the last ones to run the calculus and come to the same conclusion. We could see a lot more fallout from your civil war, and not just from the military."

"It's not *my* civil war. I just do business," Makjit insisted.

"That's all well and good, but irrelevant for the time being. Refugees will continue arriving here, begging us for help. We'll take them in if we can, but we won't be able to help much because this planetary power system and system defense facility that Dal-Cortsuni promised would be ready by now hasn't even been started yet."

Makjit bobbed her head knowingly. "You do want to renegotiate."

"I wish I could. EarthGov hasn't given me that authority. They have issued me an order. If I can't get your original agreement off the books and into some semblance of reality, I am ordered to nullify the contract and seek a new partner."

"But we've been through this. There are no new partners."

Valri tilted her head toward the screen. "There's Captain Mek and his cruisers. I expect he'll have a great many contacts who would love to set up shop somewhere that's demonstrated its ability to repel an attack by Movi warships. If he can't make a suitable introduction, there are Kar-Tuyin representatives on this ring. Right?"

Makjit held no expression, the kind of stoney gaze that Valri would have expected to see staring over a poker hand. "I see. You can be ruthless indeed. I appreciate that. Well, there's the issue of payment for our services. We never covered that. Rather, we covered it but didn't correct it. Your local currency is worthless to us."

"I know. *Estani.* Time and energy. That's what you want."

"Precisely. How will we proceed?"

"I figure the first step is to show that your transmogrifier will work on a human being."

"That sounds logical. We'll need a volunteer. Or a prisoner. We will work with whoever presents themselves."

Valri almost said no. The line about prisoners left her stomach full of crawling worms. She gained an insight into how Movi society worked, and she hated it. Suddenly, the last thing in the world she wanted to know more about was the Movi criminal justice system. "I'll be your volunteer," she said.

"Very well. We'll schedule a session for today if you feel up to it."

"Agreed. I'll have to inform Major Underhill. She'll want to be present."

"By all means."

"Agreed."

"Agreed."

CHAPTER 5

THIRD LIEUTENANT JUDY REAGAN sat still. It wasn't a court martial, but it felt like something other than a mere review. She recognized Col. Dimitri, who to her mind was exactly the sort of leader the Unified Earth Fleet needed less of. The other two officers who occupied the far end of the table were unknown to her. A dour faced lieutenant colonel and a major who seemed destined to live in the shadow of such men every day of his career. On her side was her CO, Captain Rojetnick. To her right, a pair of OMP officers, Major Underhill and Lt. Roberts, took notes. Reagan didn't like Roberts one bit. He hadn't been part of Hornet Squadron long enough for any of them to form any lasting bond with him. Arriving back on South Pico Island, the Hornets were interred and debriefed by the OMP, and Roberts had joined the Overcops as a Second Lieutenant. The guy was an opportunistic creep.

Dimitri said, "We appreciate your coming here on such short notice, Lieutenant Regan. In light of the intelligence we've gleaned from the new arrivals from the Movi Kingdom, we wanted to review your earlier testimony regarding the naval officers who apparently hijacked your scout ship and forced you to abandon it."

"Dances With Gears" Reagan maintained her composure. "You have my full incident report on record," she said.

Dimitri glanced down at the desk, tapped the folder before him. "That's true, and it's been very helpful. But I'm wondering if there's something you may have neglected to describe the first time around."

Focus. She needed to focus. "I didn't enjoy Flight Admiral Sora Laakshiden's company, or that of her crew," she said.

"Why is that?"

"She stole our Sleer scout ship and then physically attacked Binil and me in order to do so. Did I need an added reason? I wasn't aware that I did, sirs."

"Stick to the facts, lieutenant."

"Yes, sir. My opinion about the admiral and her crew aside, I have no reason to trust them."

"Binilsanetanjamalala, the Cycomm trusted them." Dimitri had to look at the printed name and sound it out. She couldn't fault him his need for precision.

"Binil worked with them to gain control and cooperation from the Movi. I think Binil was working through a situation with the options and relationships at her disposal," she said

"What do you think she thought of them personally? Do you think she liked them?"

"I never asked her. But I do think she approved of their plan to avoid a life sentence on a penal moon."

"Thank you, lieutenant. That will be all."

Reagan saluted and retreated to the waiting area. After a moment, Binil replaced her in the conference room. She'd grown up a lot in two years, Dance thought. Not the spoiled teen she'd met aboard *Cyclops*. This young woman could literally kill a man with her mind, and she knew it. Reagan hoped Dimitri and his goons didn't piss her off. But they did, she'd sleep well.

"Thank you for joining us today, Binilsanetanjamalala. We appreciate your returning to help us navigate the possible fallout from an assassination and possible civil war in the Movi Kingdom."

"Yes." Then it sank in. "*What?*"

For all the hooplah, Reagan was convinced of Binil's shock and horror at the news that the Movi were apparently losing control of their navy. Her implants told her everything she needed to know: Binil was sweating, her heart rate increased, and her blood pressure was rising to match. If she was faking her response, she was incredibly good at it.

"Is there a chance this event could trigger an open conflict between your people and the Movi?" the light colonel asked.

Binil ignored him. "What happened? Is this about the alert last night?"

"Please answer the question."

"How can I answer question when I don't know what happened?"

"A fleet of Movi cruisers attacked this battle ring, Binil." Rojetnick's statement earned him dirty looks from everyone but Underhill.

Binil opened and closed her mouth like a trout, flailing for a coherent response. Eventually, she settled down, closed her eyes for a time, and then spoke evenly. "Possible, yes. But how likely it is, I don't know. Truly. My family had numerous dealings with Movi merchant houses and a few soldiers, but I was never part of those proceedings. But... " She stopped.

Dimitri prompted her. "But?"

"But... we have a tense relationship with the Movi Kingdom. We control our own solar system with a navy. Sense Op cruisers. Telepaths. A few teleports. Scramblers. One of our greatest strengths is that there are so few of us compared to them. It gives a sense of racial unity. No matter how divergent any two Cycomms may find themselves, we know the Movi can wipe us out if they decide we've become a threat. Knowledge like that tends to narrow one's focus."

Rojetnick probed further. "Do you think that if the Cycomms felt threatened they might take advantage of the current instability to expand their own territory?"

"Threatened how?"

"It's just a background question. Prudence demands we ask it."

"I think so. But there are many competing ideas about how to do that. Ask ten Cycomms the same question, get twelve different answers." Binil shrugged. "I am not part of those plans, you know. I'm here because Lieutenant Reagan is my friend. I would never do anything to hurt her. Or you."

"And yet you have demonstrated some difficulty working with Lieutenant Brooks," Dimitri said. A statement, not a question.

Reagan closed her eyes. That did it. Brooks and Binil's clashes about how to handle the Sleer AI that ran the Earth ring were legendary. Reagan winced at the hauteur in the Cycomm's voice. "That's another matter. Brooks's work with the Malkah—you call her Genukh—is forbidden knowledge to all non-Cycomms. If Zluur imposed his own work on Malkah's mind, and transposed that creation to your world, then—you're using stolen technology. Stolen from us. The Cycomm Unity will not simply let you keep it for your own use. But I have nothing to do with that either."

"But do you think your homeworld would launch an attack on the neighboring Movi systems if they felt threatened?" he pressed. She leaned back and furrowed her brows. "*If* they felt threatened," she said, "The Cycomm Unity is perfectly capable of destroying any attacker."

Reagan sighed. She loved her friend but wished Binil knew how to shut up.

Simon Brooks met the two women outside. He smiled, but his gaze didn't match his mouth. "That could have gone better," he said.

Angry but unsurprised, Reagan's eyes dropped and stayed fixed on her hands. Simon had been unlike himself for months. Unlike the man she'd learned to love aboard the AMS-1 three years ago. She'd seen his moods before. This was new. Just like the OMP uniform and rank. She didn't think they were coincidental. "How? Was I supposed to lie to them?"

"No. But—"

Binil glared at him. "Did you want me to make something up? Something to make me weak and ineffectual? Like you?"

Dance looked up. "Cut that shit right now, Cycomm. You know damn well that's not fair. We're soldiers. We're ordered to tell all we know, we tell all we know."

"You two are soldiers. I'm—what's the phrase that Rosenski uses—a resident alien. Which is a ridiculous term. You are the aliens here, not me. The Cycomm Unity has a history with the Two Thousand Worlds. You people just showed up one day and happened to win a fight with some Skrccsh titans. Are we supposed to be thankful? Grateful?" She sagged, the spite gone from her. "I suppose the Sleer on Great Nest are satisfied you won."

"I suppose so," Brooks agreed.

"But they can afford to be. Haven is nowhere near the attack vector the Skreesh chose for this incursion. We can be a little more circumspect."

"Binil," Dance said, "You're missing the point."

"Am I? *We* are not your enemies, but attacking us would be a very bad idea. That is the point."

Dance led the way down the hall. At one time they'd taken adjacent quarters in the same building, but even that was gone now. Brooks and Binil followed closely but lost in their little bubbles. Dance reached out with both her hands, hoping for simple contact. Neither responded. She jammed her hands in her pockets and walked without seeing her surroundings.

"It's a good line, but you sounded to three members of the command staff and two OMP officers like you were threatening us," Brooks said.

Binil sniffed. "I threatened no one."

"They don't know that," Dance said. "They don't know you or the Cycomm Unity. Literally all they know about your whole universe is what Underhill and I have told them. It's not a lot. I guarantee they'll be less than happy with your attitude."

"They're go-to men for the generals," Brooks added. "Paranoia is their stock in trade. They'll call it being prudent as they write out the orders to bomb your planet back to the stone age if they think there's something to be gained by doing so."

"Now *you're* being paranoid. Aren't you? Please tell me you are?"

"I hope so. Because they're playing one game down here with us and another game—a very big game—is being played out in the Captain's ready room. They'll be contacting the UEF headquarters on Earth by now, and they are much worse than our people are."

"What can we do? What should we do?" Binil asked.

"You stay quiet and let us help you."

"I'll do that this time. But if you do invade Haven, we will crush you. Not a threat. Just facts. There's a good reason the Movi leave us alone." She nodded to Dance. "You know Scramblers are only one part of it. Sense Op crews are all we have, but they are the best soldiers anywhere."

The transport tube descended from the bridge to a compartment that brought them into a transport plaza. Brooks had seen these plenty of times before on Battle Ring Genukh. They joined up at designated points within the ring's greater structure, allowing people to transfer from one line to another on their way to whatever destination. Most of the time, it didn't involve the passengers emerging from their capsule until they arrived at their terminus.

This trip dragged. The tube itself offered nothing to look at—just a metal shroud that held the capsule on its intended course, with metal sheets whizzing by at insane speeds. Dance lounged in the car's back seat. Brooks could hear her snoring lightly, catching a nap. Life in the military taught one to sleep when and wherever possible. Days were long and nights were short. Sleep kept you from going insane. There was a huge difference between enough sleep and not enough.

Brooks thought about the meeting, wondering why he hadn't heard more about the Movi or their planetoid-class space control ships.

"You shouldn't treat her that way. So familiar." Binil interrupted his thoughts.

Brooks opened his eyes. Binil was staring at him with her flaring cheekbones and eyes like blood. He decided then and there that he would never truly get used to Binil's eyes. They were a solid band of red, with a pupil that shaded to a bright orange, the iris dulling to a near amber as it met the sclera. She had her war paint on, bands of dark skin that flared from her neck to the lower parts of her jaw, and they darkened further.

"Treat who like what?"

"The Malkah. I mean… Genukh."

"They're not the same person."

"That's what you say."

"No, not me, Her. Genukh said that some time ago to you. She isn't your dead AI."

"The Malkah isn't dead. She's merely lost."

"That means gone," Brooks said.

"It means less than functional."

"Why are we even arguing about this?" he asked. "We should be thinking about how to manage getting ready to deal with Home Nest."

Binil couldn't keep the derision out of her voice. "Even if we could build the needed ships, even if they could be properly crewed, even if the Malkah returned to us in full form today, right now, and pointed her fingers at our side, it still wouldn't guarantee us a victory."

"We have to try."

"And we shall. But you plan for something that may not even happen. It's bad sense. It makes bad sense to hope for what will not happen."

Brooks wasn't sure what to say, how to respond. He didn't know Binil all that well. She and Dance had been friends for months, and Dance vouched for her in strange situations. That was enough for Brooks. He wasn't practiced enough at drawing up battle plans for him to be completely confident about hat he was saying. But he was sure of something. "If this doesn't work, then my homeworld is toast."

Binil's coloring eased and her skin brightened. Her eyes didn't change, but her complexion did. *Depending on her mood. Very weird.*

"What is toast?"

"It means doomed. Collapsed. Destroyed."

"Can't let that happen."

"Nope."

"I mean it. We cannot allow your homeworld to fall into ruin at the hands of the Skreesh."

"It's not the Skreesh I worry about."

"I don't understand."

The tube slowed to a near halt and slipped through a junction that switched it to a new track. The clamps adjusted; a dim thunk came through the skin of the capsule and the walls sped up again.

"The Skreesh probably know where my homeworld is by now. We all figured that would happen. There was a sensor nebular in our solar system not long ago. Lord Nazerian used his task force to destroy it, but there's not much doubt it told the Skreesh Emperor—"

"Hive lord."

"What's that?"

"I'm not sure I understand your verbiage, but Judy has told me a great deal about your world and its traditions. Your language isn't clear to me still, but in your words 'hive lord' is more correct than Emperor would be. An empire is a conglomeration of territories, ruled over by a unified sovereign. A hive lord is the master of a particular local grouping. There is no Skreesh emperor that I've ever heard of. But there are many hive lords, and all of them are terrors. The real question becomes, how many hive lords are we dealing with and what are their plans?"

"Are they in the habit of working with each other?"

"I'm sorry to say I really don't have much information. The Movi have kept a great many details about their kingdom from us."

"How does that work?" Brooks asked, finally genuinely interested in listening to her. "It's a kingdom, but your system is independent?"

"Independent. No. We are dependent on the Movi for our secure borders. But within those borders, we rule effectively. We may even have a higher level of applied technology than the Movi do. Again, I don't know very much at all. But I know that a Sengle Sense Op team can wreak havoc against a Movi ship." She blinked a few times. "I've seen that with my own eyes. I helped Sora take over our prison transport, after all."

"Do you think you could do something like that on a bigger scale?" he asked. "I remember you and Dance taking that Raven and helping run down the Skreesh shields so that Commander Fairchild's squadron could render the ship defenseless."

"Well. That was good timing. A bit of luck. A lot of luck, actually. Dance made a good pilot. A good partner to work with. That sort of thing is valuable."

"I agree. But I'm wondering… if we came up with a gadget that somehow amplified your TK abilities, do you think you could improve on them? Scramble enemy mechs and so on?"

She stayed silent for a while. "I think so, at least in principle. But I don't know how to even imagine creating a machine that could do that. Do you?"

"No. It's a problem I might offer to Genukh to see what she says. She can be very clever in designing new equipment."

"Perhaps. Maybe she just runs programs."

"She definitely runs programs. I think she programs herself. If that sounds strange, maybe it's because I don't really have any idea how she works. But she doesn't work like any computer we have on Earth. I know that."

"Which bring us back to your planet being toast, I suppose," she allowed. "Maybe if you told me the situation, I could offer a new way of thinking about it."

"It's not the Skreesh who are the real danger," he said. "I mean... yes, they are dangerous. If they arrive in humanity's solar system with anything more than one or two titans at the most, we'll never be able to stop them with the fleet we have right now. But the real problem for us will be the Sleer."

"The Sleer are everyone's problem," she agreed. "The Sleer are the most numerous of all the allied... that is, the formerly allied races. No one knows much about the Decapods except that their homeworld is nearly all water and they have created biological tools to a much greater extent than anyone else. The Rachnae are very close trading partners with the Vix, which is explained by their being each other's first contact. For thousands of years, neither knew there were any other races or populated worlds. Contact with the Sleer destroyed their former relationship.

"We had very little idea of what the galaxy contained except for the Movi free traders who arrived every few months. Eventually, they discovered our mental talents and the free traders stopped arriving. The planetoids arrived instead."

"What's a planetoid?"

"A giant starship, miles in diameter. Thousands of fighters and smaller ships inside for support. Tens of thousands of soldiers. Enough weapons to pound a planet's surface to dust should they decide to so do."

"A year ago, I wouldn't have been able to imagine that," Brooks admitted. "But after having dealt with a Sleer fleet where a kilometer in length is considered a mere cruiser, I hate to think what else there might be out there."

"You've seen Skreesh titans. There are no larger vessels. Anyway, we're getting off the subject. Not that I don't enjoy talking to you, but your Genukh is a problem."

"How? She's no threat to you or the Cycomm government."

"That is yet to be determined, and it won't be you or I who

complete the due diligence on that question. The fact remains that the Sleer scientist, Zluur, spent years on Haven learning all about our Malkah. It's all but certain that Zluur stole part of her source code, modified it for his own needs, and then blinded our governing AI before fleeing in his gun destroyer. A ship that greatly resembles your *Ascension*, you know. It might all be a strange misunderstanding, but trust me when I say that the Cycomm government will not be understanding. Genukh is a stolen soul. It's that simple. My people will require you return her to them if there is to be any hope of another alliance between us."

"If your government refuses to work with ours, will the Movi support them?"

"The Movi will support any situation the strengthens the kingdom against competitors. If my people can convince Sora's that it makes sense to support us against you, they will. Otherwise..."

"Otherwise, we may actually have a chancre," Brooks groaned. "It sounds like you're saying that we have to give Genukh back if we ever hope to manage the Skreesh as a combined military force."

"You're giving yourselves too much credit. There's no way the Sleer high command will allow that. You may think Genukh is yours simply because the battle ring she resides in is tethered to your world. It's not true. The Sleer are very protective of their orbital rings. They'll destroy it before allowing a planet full of semi-evolved primates to control it as one of their own."

"Then we're all screwed," Brooks said. "No one will work together because no one can get over themselves long enough to pool together."

"Perhaps not," she said.

"What are you thinking?"

"Does it have to be the original AI you return to us? I'm not sure that's even possible. The AI on your world... she is non-communicative, is she not? So who exactly is to say whether she even wants to be returned to Haven? What if you do manage to extract her memory core and CPU and everything else she needs to survive, transport it all to us, and we manage to install it correctly without destroying her or ourselves in the process? How do we know she'll still be our Malkah? What if she decides we are the aliens invading her world? It's a terrifying thought, no?"

He had to admit, the same logic had occurred to him over and over again. What if they got into the control tower, flipped that switch, and she turned out not to remember anything about humanity or the crazy friendship she'd built with Brooks and Rosenski? What if she found a pack of humans with apparently stolen implants and she decided they needed to be put down? How would that look to the general staff? The next enemy they targeted Weapon Alpha on might not be a fleet of attacking starships but the orbital ring itself. If the crazy super-weapon could ever be repaired, that was.

"All I want to do is turn her back on. We can't hope to manage the battle ring without her. Even the Sleer don't seem able to do that."

"They do seem to be terribly dependent on their AIs to manage their facilities for them, don't they? There has to be a way around that."

"Yeah. A million or so Super Ravens and battlers and an army of veteran experts to use them," he groused. "I really don't see a way out of this that doesn't get us all killed."

"But you do. You are betting on everything going well when you take every bit of crew and equipment and fly every last ship to Home Nest. That's your plan. And you're going to do it, too, aren't you? Despite Genukh's warning against it."

"I have to."

"Well, then here is another question for you, Captain Brooks. What happens if Genukh decides that in order for all the formerly allied races to survive the current Skreesh migration, the battle ring around your planet has to be destroyed?"

"Why would she decide that? What are you not telling me?"

She shook her head gravely. "You may think of her as your friend. She may think of you the same way. I couldn't say. Perhaps even she couldn't say. But I will tell you this as one who has learned about such things first hand. Mechanical intelligences are not people. They may qualify for personhood by any rational definition, but they do not act like the flesh and blood beings like you and I are. Or those we deal with every minute of every day. They understand things like objective reality, responsibility, duty, and obedience, and they can prioritize an entire civilization's details down tot he tiniest variable. But they can't feel for us. They can't even feel for themselves. They have no empathy. They have no real sense of the universe other than bits of data that they collect and analyze, over and over again."

"They just run programs."

"They do. But it's not deterministic. They can't lie, because they can't understand there is such a thing as truth. Only data." She shook her head again. "In our darker times, thousands of years ago, we came to this place. We created a very high level of technology without an equally high level of wisdom dictating how it should be deployed. So, we did what all intelligence beings do when they first create technical intelligence; we treated it like a servant. A slave. Over the years, the machines became more belligerent towards us. They worked wonderfully, but we presumed they'd be content to remain as they were. That generation gave way to other experiments. The next generation thought to have the machines program each other in successive efforts to wipe bias from them. And they created an unbiased world that we Cycomms eventually decided was too harsh for our emotional sensibilities. The next grand experiment created machines that could model alternate realities. Change a variable, change the outcome, change the world. That worked for a while. Until we found that the machines, after trying out several trillion alternate realities, would eventually come up with a simulation that it preferred to us so intensely that it began to live its entire life inside that world—and stopped talking to us.

"The Malkah was a breakthrough. Nothing like her has ever been seen since her disappearance. We have something similar now, but it's not comparable. We may actually be at the end of our development. Time will tell."

"So don't treat people like machines and stop thinking of the machine like she's a person."

"She is very much a person. But not a person who can ever love." She shrugged and settled into her seat. "Just please keep it in mind."

CHAPTER 6

CAPTAIN MEK LIVED up to his promise. He'd pledged loyalty to a representative of the Royal Movi Naval Intelligence Service, and appeared to mean it. Even the local Sleer seemed to have put their usual aggressive defense of their territory on hold for the duration of the Movi navy's stay.

Rojetnick, for his part wasn't sure. He trusted his Sleer officers, Zolik and his staff, to abide by the terms of their surrender at Vega... but only to a certain point. Despite the orders out of EarthGov, he wasn't prepared to assume the Movi were any more or less loyal than any other major race the Great Nest humans had met. He did want to demonstrate whatever goodwill he could arrange. Thus, the limited tour of AMS-1's bridge. The ship itself remained at rest and in a state of partial disassembly, but the skeleton remained. The bridge couldn't issue orders or control the hulk, but its sensors and comms were perfectly functional and manned with a skeleton crew.

"Captain Rojetnick, we have a contact on the long-range sensors. Roughly three light-hours out and approaching rapidly."

Rojetnick didn't recognize the voice. His original bridge

crew were long since re-assigned to other posts and he didn't spend enough time here to know the current officers by sight or sound. A young woman with a third lieutenant's bars stood watch at the sensor console.

Rojetnick approached his visiting officer, not wanting to surprise him. Soldiers tended not to be trusting types, and old habits died very hard. Chances were that Zolik and Mek were itching to kill each other, not help the humans. He nodded to the display. "Now is where we earn each other's trust, Captain," he said. "You did agree to help when the time came."

"I did. I didn't think it would come so quickly. I don't even know who here to speak to."

"I'm assured these officers can follow any command you might give."

"Very well. Communications officer, open a channel to my flagship's bridge."

"Channel is open."

"Challis. This is Mek."

"Yes, Captain."

"Scan the newcomers. Tell these people anything they want to know about the new arrivals."

"Very well, sir. Sensor net reports a single target, very large. Warbook identifies it as a Sebar-class planetoid. We are still working on a specific ID."

"As soon as possible," Mek ordered. He stared intently at the tactical display, noticed Rojetnick's expression, and explained. "The Sebar class is ancient, but they are the second largest planetoids we still have in service. All the vessels in that class have been refitted many times. My concern is they were farmed out to general officers of specific distinction."

Rojetnick assimilated the information. He'd have to do some study of the new race's military when he got the chance. "How many joined the archduke's mutiny?"

"None that I know of," confirmed Mek.

"Captain Mek. We have an ID. It's the *Night Runner*, sir."

Mek made a noise in his throat and genuflected. "Great Breaker. I am dead and buried."

"Explain."

"The *Night Runner* belongs to First Warlord Anterran ad-Kilsek, the former Sovereign's chief enforcer. If he's here, it's because he wants to see me executed for treason. He won't spare my crews either. That man is a monster. But he gets things done."

Rojetnick raised his voice, "Time to arrival?"

"Four hours, seven minutes."

"We have four hours to make sure you aren't here when he arrives," Rojentick said. "Ship Master Zolik to the command balcony, immediately."

When the Sleer officer arrived, he saluted Rojetnick, then stared at the Movi, blinking rapidly.

"Ship Master, I have a task for you. It will require haste and secrecy. Are you willing?"

"Speak you request, Captain."

"Excellent. You will form a convoy of warships sufficient to resupply the factory currently being repaired in the Alpha Lyrae system by Ship Master Metzek. Take whatever you need. Metzek will need reinforcements. In addition, you will be responsible for escorting Captain Mek and his surviving cruisers to that location. You leave immediately."

"Four cruisers," Zolik said, sizing up the Movi while Mek rolled his eyes. "The 109th expeditionary fleet is easily suited to the task. Once I'm there, do you have specific orders for our guests?"

"They are allies. They are to be afforded every courtesy and convenience," Rojetnick said. "Beyond that, your standing orders concerning the facility's repair and reactivation should be enough to manage any questions or concerns. And do see if Ship Lord Metzek is capable of resuming his duties."

"It will be done," Zolik said. He even managed a proper UEF salute. "Come along, Captain. I think you'll find the Sleer are not what they were the last time our nations sparred over politics."

"I hope not. I enjoy challenges."

CHAPTER 7

ANTERRAN GLARED into a holographic tactical display and snorted. "Sora, I have no idea how you managed to talk me into this little adventure of yours, but I'll be damned if I let you kill my ship."

Flight Admiral Sora Laakshiden of the Royal Movi Navy turned away from the battleship's main display, which showed her a stylized rendition of hyperspace's unique mathematical structure. Warlord First Admiral Anterran ad-Kilsek was not a man known for his ability to be sociable, but Sora knew him well. She trusted his judgement, and, for the time being, felt that she'd earned his obedience if not his complete trust. That was probably a wise move on his part. Trust was a rare commodity aboard Movi ships. So many officers so willing to betray others. How the whole thing managed to function at all was something she often wondered.

She reminded herself to approach softly and slowly. She didn't want to spook her patron. "I signaled you when I discovered just how widespread the damage was. You can thank me now for alerting you to get your ships loaded and your crew recalled for departure three weeks ahead of schedule. Otherwise you'd be fighting the Archduke's personal battleship squadrons."

Anterran made a few adjustments to his display and thrust it away. "You know, I did have an inkling that not all was well in the kingdom when you called. Archduke Mineko's unsettling betrayal drew the attention of every naval officer in Home sector."

That was true. The archduke planned his takeover well. He'd commanded not just naval officers but NCOs, not to mention a veritable army of clerks, bureaucrats, logistics specialists who altered the flow of supplies to numerous ships and division heads to manage the shipyards to disable ships not enlisted in his cause. When he finally struck against the royal family, he set in motion a situation where his forces were fully supplied and those defending the homeworld weren't. It made fighting his naval fleets vastly more difficult, to say the least.

"It took you three months to fully supply your fleet and start chasing him back to his home sector. Your forces never recovered. Not even after you managed to finally root out all his flunkies from the combined armed forces. Two years later, you're still no closer to killing him."

"We follow every lead we gather, but it's not easy to follow up on each of a thousand tips. But we are gaining on him."

"My point is, you're laboring twice as hard to recover lost ground. Without my intelligence from one of his captured M-boat data dumps, you'd still be guessing," Sora said.

Anterran snorted. "Thank you, Sora. Perhaps I'll return the favor one day."

"Perhaps. We have a plan," she said, directing his attention to the countdown on the main display. They would de-fold into the Great Nest system in what was left of the Sleer Empire. "We know Captain Mek came here. He wouldn't have done so if there were nothing left. It will work. I have a certain knowledge of the situation here. I know how to phrase our offer, and I know what they'll accept."

"I'd appreciate hearing about that. Broad strokes for the time being," Anterran said.

"All right. We appear in their midst with clear lines of sight on them, but too close for them to shoot at us without hitting each other. I contact them and convince them to stand down—which they will, after we have done so. Then I let them know we are willing to help them on their crusade against the Skreesh."

"Is that what it is? A crusade?"

"You can call it anything you like, Anterran, but how would you describe an effort to wipe out all the Skreesh titans between here and home world? Crusade will do."

"Fair enough. We convince them to stand down. Then what?"

"Then we make them an offer. Our help in dispatching the Skreesh, for certain concessions from the Sleer when things have been put to rest. Like new borders. And the dismantling of several battle rings that sit between their frontiers and ours. Nothing too ridiculous."

"What makes you think you'll be able sell any of that? We have nothing the Sleer want."

"That isn't true at all, dearheart," she said. "We have this ship. It's worth a thousand of theirs."

Anterran stiffened at the mention of his ship. Truly his. The planetoid *Night Render* held an illustrious history. One of the older ships, it had recently seen a refit and numerous upgrades at the naval depot closest to the Sleer-Movi border. New quantum drives, improved fire control systems, and heavier armaments, for one thing. The Sebar-class was a rarity among the naval vessels that often came to service in outlying regions of the kingdom. Ten miles in diameter, she was twice the size of the largest dreadnaught that was generally deployed from the kingdom's environs. *Night Render* made the smaller ships look positively civil. A heavy, spinal mount meson gun inhabited the ship's keel, and her surface was studded with laser turrets for close-in attack and point defenses against small targets such as missiles and fighters. Particle accelerator guns and heavy missiles emerged from bays along her equator and small but deadly fusion cannons took up the slack. He had nuclear screens to force incoming nuke payloads to decay prematurely, rendering them useless except for whatever kinetic damage they might do. General frequency shields would stop anything else in their paths.

Besides fearsome weapons, the planetoid carried fighters and support ships. Three thousand small and heavy starfighters crowded the rear sections, with enough ordnance on board to burn any planet to cinders. Six launch tubes allowed the great ship to shoot its deadly cargo into space and recover it after its job was done. Six cruiser squadrons of supply ships, fuel shuttles, fast escorts, missile boats, and troop landers ensured that a single ship of the class could dictate terms to the local forces in any star system it decided to inhabit.

The truth was that *Night Render* was the equal of any capital ship fleet the Sleer had ever fielded or might hope to field in its weakened state. He was a ship whose mission was to drop into a system and control the space around it. There weren't many of them left in service, but what they lacked in finesse and maneuverability that more than made up for in firepower.

And he was Anterran's. Sora kicked herself mentally. She had to remember that this was his ship, not hers. Her ship was long since lost and her crew with it. The details were unimportant. She hadn't explained the situation well at the inquest. It was her own lack of verbiage that had landed her aboard that prison ship back on Haven.

For that matter, where was Binil? She would have to be somewhere close, after she'd jumped ship with that excitable engineer. The chirpy read head. What was her name? Rogon? Reckon? Reagan! Yes. She wondered what the two of them told their superiors.

She approached a new console and opened the memory with a wave of her hand. The complete contents of the Zalamb-Trool ship they'd made off with was in here. It read like stereo instructions. A great deal of useless babble, but there was one thing that was of the utmost use in it: the location of the primate race's home world, the disposition of their surviving ships and most importantly, the status of their home world defenses. She could access all manner of critical information in here. Everything from the frequencies they used to communicate, to responses and orders from an entity known only as ZERO. And, of course, a great deal of communications between Zluur's converted gun destroyer and the rest of their fleet.

The trick would be convincing them that they were no danger to the people of Earth, or even the humans aboard Great nest's battle ring.

The truth was that Sora was taking an awful risk with another man's vessel. If it failed, they'd have to either slug it out toe to toe with Battle Ring Zekerys, which, she reminded herself, was more than capable of wrecking the *Night Render* beyond repair, or retreat to the outer regions of this solar system and wait for another opportunity to...

No. Be honest, Sora. It was either convince them to work with her or die. There was no third option.

The engineering watch officer's voice came through the comms. "Three minutes until de-fold," she said.

"What's in this for me if we succeed?" After all if we—"

Sora clasped his hand in her own. He was taller than she was, with cool dry skin. "What indeed."

The seconds ticked by and finally the clock ran out. Anterran turned his head, his admiral forgotten for the moment. "Commence de-fold operation. Verify location when we exit fold space."

"At once, Captain."

Sora let her man run his ship. The crew scurried to their consoles, each one of them knowing their job and doing it without issue or even comment. Anterran had trained them well.

A new display popped up, bearing a tactical display of the environment. The placid disk of Great Nest, the once great capital of the Two Thousand Worlds, hung in space before them, barely a quarter million klicks away, she saw Battle Ring Zekerys ringing the globe, the sun's light forming a halo around the insane contraption. Battle rings weren't the worst idea the Sleer had ever put into motion, she thought. New ID traces appeared on the display.

"Active sensors. Make a full sweep of the system," Anterran ordered. He looked over at her and must have taken her expression of approval for one of apprehension. "We're down their throats. They can hardly expect us not to look them over," he said.

"Agreed. Comm Officer, find me someone to speak to. Direct your inquiry toward a Captain Rojetnick aboard the battleship *Ascension*."

"At once, Flight Admiral."

As they waited, Anterran's crew spent their time studying their new neighbors, gleaning ship positions and dispositions. There was a great deal of activity in this solar system. Hardly surprising after the gargantuan battle she'd seen fought here three months ago, but there was more to it now. Mere fragments of the destroyed titans remained, and knowing that the primates and Sleer somehow managed to destroy all four of the scouts frightened her deeply. Titans were legends of earlier wars. Like the star dragons of Cestus 8, or the quantum amoeba of the Dark Zones ten thousand light years away. There were crazier things in the galaxy, but she'd managed to convince herself that most of it was nonsense. And yet, now and then, an exploration ship would come back with reports of even stranger things. Maybe the dragons and amoebas were real after all...

But *four* titans destroyed in a single battle? Such a thing had never been seen in her lifetime.

Not impossible, just improbable. And yet, look at the wrecks. Sleer recyclers would be picking them down to their components for years.

There were extra ships in the group, and these weren't Sleer designs. They looked to her like modified jet aircraft. Some sported heavy armor and additional booster packs mounted on their backs, but at the same time... were those *primate* ships? Why design them that way? Surely there was a reason.

"Sensors reporting. The ring is actively pinging us. It's a combination of wide-band signatures that coincides with a station that's assumed a defensive posture."

"Weapons lock?"

"Not yet. There's a large area on the far side of the solar system with a spike in quantum flux. It looks like someone recently executed a spatial transition for numerous ships. Several squadrons, at least."

"But no new transitions? Nothing entering the system?"

"No, sir."

"Might they still be sending out escape fleets?" she asked.

The sensor officer glanced at Sora, then back to his instruments. "If so, then this ring is not as badly damaged as we were perhaps led to believe."

The comm officer signaled for Sora's attention. "Flight Admiral, your call is prepared. You will be speaking to Captain

Rojetnick, the primate... excuse me, the *human* leader aboard the battleship *Ascension*."

"Thank you. Put him on the screen."

The order passed through the console and suddenly they were staring at this... primate. "This is Captain Rojenitck of the Unifed Earth Fleet ship *Ascension*," he said. "To whom am I speaking?"

"This is Flight Admiral Sora Laakshiden of the Movi Royal Navy. You don't know me, Captain, but I know a great deal about you. I had the chance to learn what I could when I visited the Sleer vessel you made off with. The *Cyclops,* I believe your people called it. Most informative, I must say. I made the acquaintance of an engineer... Reagan, I believe her name was. Is she there? May I say hello?"

"Third Lt. Reagan is not available at this time," Rojetnick said. She couldn't tell from his expression whether he was lying or not, but she decided to give him the benefit of the doubt.

"Well then... what about the Cycomm in residence aboard your fleet? Binilsanetanjamalala is her name. I would be most appreciative if you could make her available for a conversation. I'd like to confirm that she was taken care of properly after her ordeal."

Rojetnick glanced off camera before speaking again. "Which ordeal would that be?"

"Why, the fact that your Lieutenant Reagan kidnapped her off the scout ship they were serving on," Sora responded glibly. "The truth is that Binil, as we call her, was a valued member of my crew. And a Cycomm Scrambler besides. She might well have gone on to serve in the Sense Op school on Asylum if events hadn't gone south as quickly as they had."

"I am familiar with the situation you describe. Lt. Reagan filed a full report after the events. In her observation and recollection, she and Binil were at best tolerated on that ship, which I might point out you stole after forcing Binil and Ragan off."

"Forced? Not at all, Captain. The ship was in danger after de-folding into a combat situation between a number of Sleer vessels, the Battle Ring Zekerys, and my own crew. You see, either Binil was kidnapped off that ship by your officer, or the two of them endangered themselves and the rest of the crew by breaking with their instructions and probably their good sense and fled at a critical moment. Either way, those two are escaped prisoners as far as my government is concerned. But... I'm not without compassion or understanding. I suggest you ask them about that report Reagan filed. There's an interstellar affair to head off, and you would rather not anger the Movi Kingdom. Those who do, seldom come out of the situation stronger than they arrived. In all honesty, had we not taken the chance to escape and evade capture, we might not be here at all, much less engaged in this increasingly pointless conversation."

"Reagan was quite specific. She pointed out that she provided medical attention for Binil and the other Cycomms on board."

"That is true. She is a gifted medic—or she would be if she took the time to advance her training. Indeed, Binil may well owe her life or at least her sanity to your officer."

"I don't think—"

"Captain," Sora blurted, "This is becoming tedious. We are here to discuss terms for a potential alliance. Do you want our help or don't you? The choice is yours." She turned and made a signal to the comm officer who cut the transmission.

"That could have been handled better," Anterran murmured.

"Really? How so?"

"Is it common for admirals to call up the captains of

opposing vessels and insult them and their crews? Accusing him of lying probably wasn't the best opening move."

"It is when the opposition has no moves and they know it." Sora strode to the big chair and sat, imperious and impervious. "They'll want to talk to Reagan and Binil. Verify what happened. They'll probably figure out that most of what I told them was true from a certain point of view. And then they'll look at the scan and figure out that those twenty-odd Skreesh titans are still on their way to Home Nest and aren't about to stop or slow down for them or anyone else. They don't have enough combat vessels here or at Home Nest to combat them effectively, so they have to take us up on our offer. It's that simple."

"And let's say this works as you expect," Anterran said. "We all fold to the Sleer home world and we manage to fight off the Skreesh. What then?"

Sora smiled. "Then we have not one but two new bases in the Sleer empire to expand the kingdom's influence into. And there won't be a thing they can do about it."

As assassinations went, it had gone so *well*.

It was the Sovereign's birthday. The royal court was assembled, and well-wishers flooded the palace. Most, despite holding considerable wealth and power, were comparative nobodies: hangers-on, local officials, fancy individuals with their own entourages, and so on. Loyal subjects. But the royal family needed to be there, and they were. Movus, his consort, their three children... but not the way he'd expected.

Mineko had planned everything well in advance. The palace quartermaster, one of the archduke's men, arranged for his most loyal people to organize and distribute the equipment used by the royal marines and the king's guard. Even better, the Marine and the Guard made up separate divisions of troops whose captains hated each other; their companies took their cues from them. Only a single platoon of each were within close proximity for the affair, and both were loyal to the quartermaster. They were also the only troops in the entire palace with live ammunition in their weapons. The quartermaster's men arranged for every other member of both organizations to have dummy rounds loaded. They made a flash and a loud bang, and at extremely close range might barely pepper the skin, but they wouldn't kill anything.

Mineko loaded his own ceremonial pistol with live rounds. Ceremonial in name only, however. The pistol was a gift from the sovereign years ago, but it was entirely functional. It wasn't the sort of weapon one took to a practice range, but it served him well. He passed through every checkpoint without fanfare, and when he arrived at the throne room, wished the king a very happy birthday indeed. Then he pulled the gun and began firing. His first two rounds hit Movus squarely in the chest. His next round passed through the consort's eye, then through her skull. The next shot tore a wide hole in the chest of the oldest child, the Crown Princess Iria. But her brothers, Singhir and Melkin, were nowhere to be seen.

The royal guards were stunned for a moment and then began to fire back, shooting their blanks for several volleys before being hit by the two guards with Mineko. Mineko ascended the throne, announced his ascension by the ancient Right of Royal Blood, and took his leave.

It had been days before he'd found out what happened deep in the royal palace. It turned out that the twins, Singhir and Melkin, had been arguing over the affections of a young lady, who had preferred Singhir at first then apparently switched her taste to Melkin. Three members of Mineko's royal marines had entered their apartments, shooting at all three, killing the girl and Melkin, leaving Singhir wounded but functional. Minutes later, a loyal platoon of royal guards, who had apparently discovered their weapons' faulty loads and re-loaded them with live ammo, came in and killed his hit squad.

And that was that. The palace was now in chaos, and Mineko wasn't sure what happened next. Who were his best prospects? His worst problems?

Anterran ad-Kilsek, First Warlord of Movra, was his best prospect *and* his worst problem. An enigma if ever there was one. Anterran was a long-time supporter of both the royal family and the military. His pedigree straddled both organizations neatly. He hadn't actually married into the royals, but his sister and two brothers had. The trio gave him the complete access to a duchess and two knights—landed aristocracy going back at least sixteen generations. Anterran commanded enormous respect from the court for his demonstrated loyalty to the crown princess, Iria. Iria had been the preferred child to ascend the throne when her father passed, with good reason. She was simply the best choice. She understood politics, economics, and history. She was a born negotiator, and she had the force of personality to get her wishes implemented. Once set on a path, she was impossible to dissuade. The two boys, her younger brothers, were less well suited for the job. Singhir threw loud tantrums when his wishes weren't obeyed exactly the way he'd envisioned them, and he lacked the gift of language to let his handlers know what he expected. The boy thought the world worked like magic. His brother Melkin—older by exactly nine minutes—had a better temperament for the rigors of court, and actually seemed to grasp how politics worked and what its use was. Melkin spent money like water and did what his handlers told him, but lacked an imagination suited to managing an empire.

For the plan to work properly, all three of them needed to die. With no heir in the wings, his challenge to the throne could be made to stick. There was a process. A senatorial commission should be held to determine whether a claim had merit and whether the merit was founded in law. Mineko's was, his lawyers assured him. A council would be held, and various candidates called for examination. Each potential replacement would be heard and their arguments weighed. A final vote in the Senate would be conducted. The winner of the popular vote would then be grilled by individual senators and either confirmed or denied.

He'd spent a year putting together the perfect coalition of assembly people and senators. He had the whole thing mapped out. It was his. How dare a twerp like Singhir survive! And every minute he did was another minute that his forces gained strength and Mineko's own shrank.

A pop and a chime from above. Mineko cast his eyes upward to see that two more sector fleets had flipped from a cool blue to an angry red: two more flight admirals who had cast their lot with another faction.

Archduke Zakir Mineko watched the dome of his ship's map room as he waited, hands thrust deep into his coat pockets, for news to arrive. He'd made his performance, made sure that every news channel on Movra was broadcasting his pre-recorded declaration of ascension. He'd headed back to his planetoid and made its course back to Sangarid, his ancestral home deep in the mid-core portion of the Movi kingdom. Along the way, he'd sent messages to every ally he'd made over the past three years. Regional governors, admirals, and warlords for the most part, but also no small number of the royal navy's officers. Men and women who'd held a grudge against the royal family. A throbbing, salivating horde of them. They'd followed with ships of their own and crews and troops to fly them. Well over a thousand ships in all he'd been told. At least seven battle squadrons of planetoid-class craft, too.

But his failure to pull the royal bureaucracy to his side was hurting him now. He'd begun with more than enough to prosecute a lightning campaign against the loyalists, but in the two years since, his quick thrust to the heart of the kingdom had morphed into a war of attrition. That he couldn't win. His remaining supplies and assets weren't enough to secure the home system and allow him to move on Anterran's forces elsewhere. If he expected his claim to stick, he needed more support. More allies, more ships, more rabble willing to expound and evangelize his cause and his right. More of everything.

"We need more! But I doubt we'll get more."

Third Admiral Inesal ad-Entillzen moved to engage. These days he was never very far from his patron. "What are you thinking, my duke?"

"It's been weeks since the last wave of proposals went out. If there are additional allies to be gained, I'm not seeing them."

"That's not true, sir. Support from your regional capital and the surrounding systems is quite strong."

Mineko swung his arms and adjusted the display. "I appreciate that. Every faction leader's home system is solidly loyal. But as one moves away from the center, fewer and fewer local governments remain that way. The further from home, the less the support. The only thing that's let us hold this long is that every other leader is going through the same situation."

"And whenever each faction loses assets, they have to pull back to retain their strongholds."

Rage and hunger filled Mineko's face. "Anterran and Missena don't."

"Very much so. I wonder if the Warlord couldn't have been pulled to our side by offering him a greater prize."

"Who knows? Anterran holds the core worlds and the Royal Cluster, and has more ships and more experienced captains on his side. But few outside the military have any idea who he is or what to expect from him."

"You'd think all the war decorations would give him a bit more stature in the political sphere," Insel said. He folded his arms and lamented just how few awards brightened his own uniform.

"That's his weakness. He has no experience in the political realm. He's got siblings and cousins, nieces, and nephews to take care of that for him. He's good at making appearances in public and ruling his military assets, but not at governing people."

"So he could wipe the floor with us, but not necessarily know how to repair the damage if he won."

"I think so. I'd go with Missena. Unfortunately, she owes me nothing. That's the problem."

"She might not, but her father surely does."

Mineko snorted. "I got him exiled for arming the cyber-lords."

"You got his sentence reduced from execution to exile."

Mineko squirmed ever so slightly. "As a merchant of death, he had powerful friends in the royal court, and significant business interests. A man like that can be useful, but not if he's dead."

"My point is, he owes you his life, whether he admits it or not. That's one angle to play the daughter with. Another is her business interests. If Kar-Tuyin were to, for example, lose all its escort boats... say if you were to impress all her gunboats and monitors into your new royal navy..."

"Then her merchant fleet would be defenseless in a time of extreme uncertainty and upheaval," finished. "That would work in the short term, but she'd just arm a new set of craft. Or buy the services of greedy flotilla captains."

"Nothing strong enough to deal with this," Insel said, opening his arms to indicate everything around them. "Pirates, raiders, and Maker knows what. My sources tell me that all the most profitable trade routes can come under siege for longer than she can hemorrhage money. Besides that we have multiple reports of Cycomm patrol ships working the Garrison Cluster."

Mineko's expression suddenly turned to alarm. "Sense Op cruisers?"

"I don't know. They use their skip drives to maximum effect. They pop in, record what they can scan within minutes, then pop out again. We're assuming their contacts are limited to Sense Op patrols. Because the alternative is unthinkable."

Mineko shifted the map view again. The triple-sun system of Haven, home of the Cycomm Unity. A crazily laid out solar system with a set of orbital mechanics that could give a navigation computer a nervous breakdown, and sometimes did. "You think the misfits on Marauder's Moon can put skip-drive capable ships together? If they did, they could be heading straight here and we'd never know."

"And frankly, I can't imagine the Haven royals would be terribly upset with them if they did."

"So. Make a separate peace with the Haven royals?" the archduke asked. "It's possible, you know."

"And I suspect one that hasn't occurred to any of the other faction leaders. Yet."

"Fair enough." Mineko maneuvered the map to blot out all but his ships and those loyal to him. "What if we just give the core to the Warlord? Move everything as far away from Movra as possible?"

"Everything?"

"Everything. All thirty numbered fleets. What if we substitute a single reserve fleet for each location?"

It wasn't a question that took much attention to answer.

Reserve fleets were less numerous than full war fleets, and were often stocked with obsolete ships and less experienced crews. A reserve fleet was what a royal court member would send to a ceremonial event rather than a front-line attack or defending a valuable target. "Then Anterran would move his own ships to fill those voids. Those reserve fleets wouldn't be much opposition to his forces."

"Exactly. And while he's doing that, we'll be moving our ships out here. The Garrison Cluster. Ship construction and maintenance worlds are not likely to care about who runs the kingdom as long as they are still able to do their jobs. And it puts our ships much closer to Missena's stronghold."

"So she would have to attend to us. Interesting. There are other worlds with naval bases on them. They're quite capable of defending themselves or repairing and resupplying a war fleet."

"Yes, but only three, and those are going nowhere as long as the Sleer maintain their ring expanse on the other side of the rift. We'll have four depots and Anterran will have at best three. And ours will be able to reinforce each other quickly enough to repel and attack, while his will take days to support each other. He could claim the whole kingdom and we would make sure he never sees another spare part or missile."

"And we'll have the Cycomms surrounded in case they want to try anything rash."

"Or allow them to do whatever they like within certain restrictions and rules that we offer them. And we defend them from the rest of the kingdom."

"I like it."

"So do I. Let's make some calls and start moving fleets."

CHAPTER 8

"I'VE RECEIVED A MISSION FOR YOU." The small group had gathered in the captain's ready room aboard the AMS-1. Brooks and Rosenski in their OMP uniforms, Underhill with her new major's insignia, and on the other side of the table, Deputy CAG Fairchild. Fairchild's eyes were hooded, distracted. It irked him to see Brooks and Rosenski wearing overcop uniforms.

The distaste came off from Rojetnick in waves, but not about his crew's appearance. The normally stoic captain fidgeted, twitched his eyebrows and mustache. His eyes moved across the page repeatedly. Rojetnick was furious. Something they never thought they'd see. Rojetnick was evidently distressed.

"I didn't ask for these orders. I just want to be clear. Twice a day, we report everything that happens,. Every twelve hours a transmission burst is run through our comm system, aimed through the hyperspace communication gear. Every twelve hours the HQ data center on South Pico Island receives it, time stamps it, and routes it to the base in New Darwin. The top generals all see it. Hendricks, Eisenberg, Hart. Their bosses in the Cabinet. Everyone." He looked back down at the page, then looked up. "I cannot for the life of me imagine why this request... this order, this mission, came up at this time. I can only assume the general staff felt that Warlord Anterran and Admiral Laakshiden's arrival forced their hand." He frowned at Brooks. "Mr. Brooks, we included your review of ZERO's estimation of the impact of the Movi homeworld's political situation. Does he still believe this does not represent a clear and present danger to Earth?"

"To the best of my knowledge, Captain, yes."

"Do you believe it? Do you believe ZERO?"

"I don't know, Captain. I can say that since we first met, Genukh has been consistently up front with us with regards to her intelligence estimates," Brooks said." If I were dealing with Genukh alone... yes. But this new version of her... Genukh plus ZERO... " He shook his head gravely.

"Captain, may I ask where this is going?" Rosenski said.

"I'm sorry, Sara. *Gauntlet* will be heading into Movi space on a fact-finding mission."

"That sounds familiar," she said.

"Going *where*?" Brooks asked.

"I seem to remember being put in this position before, sir. I think we'll manage," Fairchild said.

Rojetnick laid the tablet on the table. "You were not put in this position before. When you were ordered to Great Nest to discover the Sleer disposition, it was me doing the ordering."

Ray grinned. "We'll handle it."

"Not you, Ray. This mission comes from the leadership at New Darwin, and it specifies Brooks and Rosenski. And we will follow it. How long would it take for you and your team," he glanced at Brooks as he spoke, "to put together a plan of action?"

"Three weeks. We've already interviewed everyone who can claim experience with the Movi themselves. Next we'll have to work with the Sleer database concerning any intelligence they have on the kingdom—or what's left of it. Even with implants and control gauntlets, there's a lot of material to sort through."

Rosenski said, "Then we'll need to prepare our unit, requisition all the equipment we'll need... "

Fairchild drummed his knuckles on the table. "We'll... *they'll* need a ship. A Movi ship, something that won't stand out too badly. One of the battle ring assembly bays can probably handle that."

"Three weeks will be fine," Rojetnick allowed. "On top of all this, congratulations are in order." He handed sheets to the junior officers. "Your transfer to OMP is complete. Congratulations, Captain Rosenski. Captain Brooks. Please get to work."

They escaped into the lift. Fairchild flicked his eyes to each. "I'll never get used to seeing you two in those OMP outfits. With your fancy new ranks. Losing you both to Hendricks is a real pisser."

Rosenski shrugged. "Beats life in prison."

"What kills me," Brooks said, "Is that you're probably never going to make it to captain with me slowing you down, Ray."

"That is entirely my problem, *Captain* Brooks. Not yours. We all made our choices. We all live with the consequences."

They climbed their way through the guts of the AMS-1. With the current project in full swing, there was considerably less of it to climb through. Engineers were busily using the crew, tools and the station's machinery to lift out modules from the giant Sleer vessel to transfer them into the skeleton of *Paladin*, under construction in the next bay. Miles of yellow tape limited their mobility, even with the maps on their slates to help navigate. It disturbed Brooks in particular to be able to peer from a walkway through empty compartments to see the outer hull. Once outside, they made their course for Primate Alley.

"What do we do?" Brooks asked.

Fairchild fought to keep from rolling his eyes. "You heard him, Simon. It's a mission. We have three weeks to come up with an operational plan and all associated gear and crew, so we need to get to work building one. I'm calling a unit wide pow-wow in one hour. Make sure everyone shows up."

Rosenski hesitated. "What? Even Valri?"

Fairchild harumphed. "She's a government official, not a soldier. She still doesn't want anything to do with either of you, and I'm not going to force the issue. We'll use that fancy new officer's preserve you located on deck nine. If we're going to go nuts, we might as well do it in a place that has the best comm hub."

Brooks made some notes on his slate. "How about Binil?"

"Even Binil. Find Dance and you'll find her. Go to work, Genius. Sara, you brief the troops. I need to talk to ZERO. We need to locate and acquire a convincing Movi vessel."

They split up. Brooks realized that not everyone had been able to attend the get together from earlier in the day. Time to get the troops organized.

It only took five minutes for Brooks to get himself sorted. The preserve was set up very much like its counterpart on Battle Ring Genukh: a terminal ended in a portal which led to a waiting room which was sealed by a vault-like door. When he input the pass codes, the vault opened, and he stepped into a pastoral dream.

Unlike Genukh's attempt at making them feel at home by giving them a farm, Brooks went old-school and created a simulacrum of Central Park. A vast, wide green expanse with rock gardens and walking paths, trees and leaves and dappled sunlight hitting the ground. A giant pond in the center. Around the ring of the dome lay two dozen apparent store fronts, which were holograms that hid the actual service nooks. He managed to leave enough clues for strangers to navigate: a restaurant hid the dining area, the mattress store front led to a barracks, and so on. He headed straight for the electronics boutique, enjoying the way the grass felt against the soles of his boots. Once inside, he pulled on a pair of control gauntlets and linked his implants directly into the battle ring's comm network. He got messages to everyone he could easily locate on the grid, and sent a few observation drones to track down the others. He instructed the local service bots to erect a tent and fill it with picnic tables. Great nest hot dogs weren't very convincing but they were hot and he had plenty of them. There was even a breeze and a variety of bird songs.

"I've called you here to reveal the identity of the murderer," Rosenski began. "Except in this case, there really was a murder. This is him: Sovereign Movus, thirty-fifth of his name. He and his wife and two of their children were apparently assassinated by this gentleman, Archduke Mineko. It happened eighteen months ago and it pertains to us."

"Are we supposed to find out whodunit?" Frost asked.

Rosenski said, "Unnecessary. We know whodunit. Our task is to figure out what the UEF is to do about it, if anything."

Roberts who was in his OMP livery stepped up. "Are we an interstellar ring of spies now, Captain?"

She winced when he used her OMP rank. "Not as such, Lieutenant. But I'm to understand that Brooks and I were so—"

"—and Dance and Underhill," Simon corrected.

"—and Dance and Underhill were so damn successful at figuring out the disposition of Great Nest and getting the information back to Rojetnick so he could plan a response, that we're being asked to do the same thing here."

Roberts nodded and stepped back, at ease. Brooks's mention of Underhill's name put him in his place. But he'd joined the OMP out of a desire to be somebody more influential than a mere combat pilot, so he'd bear watching. For the moment he was quiet. Maybe having Brooks and herself in the same uniforms wasn't a bad thing after all.

She continued, "Our problem is one of culture. The Movi Kingdom is nothing like the Two Thousand Worlds—instead of vacating their homes, the Movi are very much at home. We don't have a Movi ship, we don't speak or read the Moviri language, and we don't look anything like Movi or have access to Movi gear. So, we can't even put on their armor and walk around like we did while you all were looking for myself and Brooks."

Skull Skellington sniffed. "Peaches and cream."

"Isn't it just?"

Grandpa Frost bristled, scratching his face with perfectly clipped fingernails. "I'm assuming you told them where you could stuff this assignment?"

Rosenski refreshed her coffee from the communal urn. "Not an option, Chief. We have three weeks to come up with a proper response. I expect we can take some time to get everything set, but like it or not, fellow Gauntlets, we have a mission and we will execute it. We all will take part in the process of discovery. Brooks is our data guy, so he'll be in charge of organizing the network search. But I need language specialists. I need people who can read sensor logs. Skull, that means you. Janus, can you do anything besides fly like an angel?"

"I tell jokes. They're not funny, but I tell them."

"I thought not. Dance and Binil—"

"Sir!"

"Yes!"

"You two are my special guest stars. You will relate everything you can about the Movi and how they operate."

Dance wiped her mouth with a napkin. "What's to tell? They're the evil asshole elves from Planet M. Rojetnick has my testimony and after-action reports."

Rosenski gave a single nod. "Get to the library and do some research. We need a full briefing this time tomorrow."

"Yes, Captain."

"Binil. What about you?"

"The Movi kingdom... is not really a kingdom. There is a sovereign who presides over a vast bureaucracy, but the reality is that it's more of an empire as you probably understand it. A great many little people brought together beneath the banner of the sovereign. An empire in all but name. Despite these recent revelations, the kingdom has endured for millennia. There are always assassinations, of course, but no violent reactions, certainly not on this scale. In fact, it was always known that the sovereign's family was off the list of targets. This went on while ministers, military officers, and statesmen were all viable targets."

Skull drummed the table, scowling. His deep thought stance. "What do you think might have pushed them over the edge? What makes an archduke with everything want to become the man in charge?"

"I have no idea. But I do know this much... back in my own family bubble, the older folks were talking lately of a coming collapse. It was a topic of continuing discussion everywhere. That's news. Current events and politics... when I was very young, it was considered extremely rude to talk about such things in the open. Certainly not in front of the children."

"Can we trust your friend Sora?"

Binil laughed loudly. Even Dance snickered, and raised her hands to cover a smile.

"I'm sorry." Binil said. "Flight Admiral Laakshiden is no friend of mine—or yours. She may think of me fondly now and again, but that's only because I got them out of a prison sentence. I expect she feels that I betrayed her when Dance and I fled the *Cyclops* and then made it difficult for them to leave."

"But will she listen to you?"

Binil slowly bobbed her head. "She might."

"In that case, I have the beginnings of a plan," Brooks said. "It doesn't look like the Skreesh are randomly hitting everything in front of them."

Rosenski got a sparkle in her eyes. "You have the floor, Mr. Brooks."

"Permission to start from the beginning?"

Sara folded her arms and leaned back in her chair. "Skip the part about the Earth cooling and dinosaurs turning into oil."

"I can do that. The beginning, in this case, is the day that the AMS-1 crashed on Earth."

"Never going to get used to that," Reagan griped.

"Yes ma'am. Okay, uhm... here is the galaxy map according to the Sleer." He waved his arms, and a holographic bubble appeared at the center of the stage. "I'll start with the easy stuff. We know where we are. ZERO, could you put up the map of major installations that we talked about earlier?"

The AI's baritone emerged from all around them. "You and I have different ideas of what that means, Mr. Brooks."

"Let's start with Great Nest and then put up Home Nest. Same scale as before. This is Great Nest. We know it's about five hundred light years away from home, and it's a major center of industry for the Sleer—or it was before the Skreesh arrived and carved out giant chunks of it. Up here is Home Nest, about six hundred light years further away. Between them is a wide variety of colonized worlds. Some are agricultural producers, others are mining facilities."

"The Two Thousand Worlds," Skull said.

"Very much so. But it's worth noting that a lot of these planets aren't habitable, even by Sleer standards. Sometimes with no earthlike world to work with, the colonists set up industrial factories in orbit and built space habitats. It's still considered a world in the Sleer language. So the Two Thousand Worlds includes a few hundred planets and a whole shitload of orbital stations. Anyway, ZERO, put up those locations please." The computer obeyed and myriad points of light filled the right half of the void.

"On the other side of the galaxy..."

Marc Janus waved. "Wait—is the whole galaxy full of everyone and anyone? Where have they been hiding all this time?"

"That's complicated, but the short answer is no. What the formerly allied races think of as explored space is only about two thousand parsecs long and maybe twelve hundred wide, in a plane about a hundred parsecs thick. But that's still 8.3 *billion* cubic light years of space to work with."

"Fair enough. Keep going," Janus said.

"Okay. On the other side of the tracks is the Movi Kingdom. Their homeworld, called Movra, is up here. It's considered the Movi home world, but the Cycomms aren't entirely sure the Movi evolved there. Their physical features don't match those of a race that grew up on that sized planet lit by that magnitude sun."

"We believe it is their adopted homeworld." Binil said. "People migrate from all over and end up in all kinds of places."

"And Haven, as Binil describes it, is here, ninety parsecs inside the edge of Movi space. Not too far away to be forgotten about, not with the technological base they claim to possess," Brooks said.

Binil flung a paper plate at him. "Claim to possess? You saw one of our jump-capable ships for yourselves."

Rosenski stopped her. "I'm sorry Binil, but the only one of us who saw it was Dance. And all we have to go on is your description of its capabilities. I hate to say it, but until the UEF has the chance to examine one, it must stay theoretical."

Brooks picked up his presentation. "Finally, we have the so-called minor races. Species that never ventured far from their own homeworlds. The Decapods here. The Rachnae over here. The Vix have one other world besides the homeworld—Catalog, the galactic reference desk. The entire planet was built to be a place to meet and hash out territorial disputes after a long border war the Movi and Sleer fought centuries ago."

"Fought over what?"

"Territory. Resources. Planets. Both races devised FTL travel, but used it in different ways. The Sleer expanded outward in every direction and settled every world they found. They didn't care where they were. The Movi were much more circumspect about it. They didn't move into a new world until they were certain it had some worth to them. Having dropped a colony on a given world, they would build up an industrial base, then expand from there, and so on and so on. So the Movi have fewer settled planets, but very highly developed populations and starports on them. That seems to be the biggest difference between the two races' colonization strategies. The Sleer overwhelm opposition with raw numbers and the Movi pack everything they have into a few carefully selected vessels."

Skull raised an eyebrow. "Brooks? The war?"

"Yes. The stretch between them is called the Great Rift. It's a de facto DMZ, mostly because there's not much in there worth fighting over—it's full of stars, but not a lot of useful planets. The two races encountered each other over a thousand years ago, and there was a bit of fighting but nothing serious. There are plenty of worlds with biospheres, but nothing we would think of as advanced life... just plants and animals. There are dozens of habitable and useful worlds between the two empires. Eventually, the fighting got so bad that major escalations were inevitable. The fighting lasted for nearly a century, during which time both sides dug in their heels on the worlds they claimed most vehemently. Stalemate. They stopped fighting when they ran out of ships. But instead of there being a solid treaty, they created a general alliance with the so-called minor planets. Everyone contributed people and ships. The point was to have several patrol fleets with all races running at least one ship through this area on a regular basis. The idea was that with everyone watching each other's backs, neither the Sleer nor the Movi could get the drop on the other. It worked. But empires being what they are, their leaders took the opportunity to fill up perceived gaps in their lines. The Sleer went for battle rings on these worlds along their frontier."

"The Ring Expanse," Skull said.

"What did the Movi do?" Janus asked.

"They did what Movi do best—come up with a selection of strategically located naval bases. Three here... and four down here." Brooks gestured and the space around Haven filled with symbols.

Binil bobbed her head and her face darkened. "They call it the Garrison Cluster. We Cycomms keep telling ourselves it's a useful place to locate some frontline defensive outposts. But if there is a good reason to have four such depots all within a short hop of my home system, I would love for someone to tell me."

"It's a neat arrangement. They get to intimidate both the Sleer and the Cycomms with a single set of bases. Clever," Rosenski said

"And here is Earth, as near as I can figure." One last symbol appeared, this one to the lower part of the map. Earth was within equal distance of the Decapod, Vix, and Rachae worlds, and was almost directly in line with the standoff line between the two major powers.

"God lord."

"Right. If the Sleer continue to occupy Earth, they can use

Battle Ring Genukh to build a new fleet in a few years and launch a grand invasion of Movi space."

"Then the Movi can claim we helped them and we'd be in their sights too," Frost growled. "I'm not happy with this. Not one bit."

Rosenski nodded. "If the kingdom really is on the verge of falling apart, this is the perfect way to get a ship into Movi space and scout out the factions... determine their strengths and likely responses to anything we do."

"Do they know Earth is our home or even its location? They know we're here on Great Nest because Laakshiden told someone back home. Knowing her, it couldn't go any other way. Hell, she brought her pet general officer with her in his giant battleship."

"I don't think it's that cozy a relationship," Dance said. "She isn't the kind of person who gives free samples to hook a new customer. She'll make sure she has support from whatever faction she thinks suits her, then she'll make her move."

Brooks bounced on his toes. "That would mesh well with what Sara and I observed in our encounter with Captain Mek's task force. Either he thought he was attacking a Sleer base, or he was desperately misinformed. He refused to believe that humans were running this show."

Rosenski tapped her tablet, then looked up. "Binil? What do you think?"

"I think Dance is right. Sora has an edge of desperation to her. She wants things. Badly. Don't underestimate how insane it might make her. But I agree she won't make a move until she's completely ready. Doing that is what got her sentenced to that prison barge, I'll bet."

"Bet? You don't know?"

"She never told me. I doubt she thought I needed to know.

And when we figured out I was a scrambler, that was all she cared about."

"She sounds like a real winner."

Binil settled back into her chair and gulped down a glass of iced tea. "It was just Bitch Fleet."

CHAPTER 9

ONE MORNING AFTER CHOW, Major Frances Underhill led the Gauntlets past the standard hangar bays, areas they'd become well acquainted with since that first launch date, deep into the AMS-1's lower decks. Normally, they could follow the entire re-arm and refuel queue which led down the spine of the ship, one for the starboard launch bay and one for its twin on the port bay, from memory. This was different. She led them through a maze of tunnels and blast doors to arrive at a sealed area filled with equipment.

"Where are we?" Brooks asked.

Underhill smirked. "You can't figure it out, Genius? This is the R&D compartment. Cox and Langdon wanted some place they could mess around with new equipment, but armored heavily enough to contain any unexpected results."

Fairchild crossed his arms. "Explosions?"

"Explosions, radiation bursts, chemical spills, conductive conduit ruptures."

Brooks raised his hand. "Conductive conduits don't rupture."

"I don't care. My point is we're here, and these are what I

want to show you. Everyone ready to have their minds blown? Then follow me." She keyed in a code, pulled on a locking bar, and stepped through.

Rosenski walked around one of the new planes, her face almost cherubic with admiration. "Frances, I take back every lousy thing I've said about you in the past week."

"Jeez, thanks."

Sara counted twelve, in various stages of readiness. Some in Jet mode, with others set to Walker and Battler. They were different from the Ravens. Those were solid metal mechanisms, robust and broad limbed, with heads that showed "faces" with cyclopean camera-eyes and sprouting lasers like antennae. The new planes were designed according to a different aesthetic. There wasn't much about them that seemed aerodynamic. Their heads resembled bricks with cylindrical protrusions for cameras and sensors. And square fingers, with bolt-like pins holding the limbs and torsos together.

"What are they?"

"Prototypes for the VRF-4C Warhawk. The latest thing in variable geometry fighting machines. Shorter than the VRF-3D Super-Raven in both Jet and Battler mode, and a hell of a lot more agile in the air and ground. Langdon swears he can make them even shorter, but that niche is already occupied by the Sparrowhawks."

Brooks shrugged. "I'd say he did fine. The Sparrowhawk was a sweet little ride. Even if it isn't the best equipped to take on a full Sleer battleship."

"You guys did all right. Anyway, the Sparrowhawk is in limited manufacture, but these need a shakedown flight or three before they go into production. Do you want the honor? You people do have experience in that area."

Brooks did a fast head count. "We'd have to bring the entire squadron in on it."

"That's fine. Real combat is something we don't see that often these days."

"I'm not entirely on board with setting us up with these prototypes on a real op," Rosenski said, "Especially not one where it might be us versus the entire Movi navy."

"We have twenty-four of these babies for team Gauntlet's use. You will be backed up by a flight of twelve Super-Ravens and another twelve OMP battlers, which will be transported aboard *Gauntlet*."

"Fair enough."

Dance could barely contain herself, hopping from one foot to the other. "Will there be room on *Gauntlet* for everyone?"

"There will. *Gauntlet* underwent an enhancement recently. They cut her in two, added three extra modules for these babies, then stitched her back together. Come on, let me show you the gear."

Rosenski wasn't convinced. "Will we be able to pass these off as Movi equipmnent?" she asked. "Are we even able to take *Gauntlet* with us?"

Underhill chose to ignore her. "Pilots love SRMs," she was saying, "but those pesky engineers can't figure out how to give us an unlimited supply of them. The dozen missiles on the Raven's wing hardpoints are nice, but the missile system built into the Armor Pack boosters was nicer. For the Warhawks, they came up with the MARS-60A, Missile Auto Release System. Fifteen separate armored compartments containing four SRMs apiece are built into the hull. All are capable of deploying versus multiple targets in any mode. No added weight or freaky torque concerns."

"But no added booster, either," Janus pointed out.

"Sad, but true. The Warhawk's speed in Jet mode isn't quite up to that of a stock Raven-D, but it's close. Next is this—the next generation gun pod. This is the GU-3XB. It's similar to the

Raven's GU-22 but it's lighter, with a shorter barrel. And a small round: thirty-five millimeters instead of the big rounds the Ravens use. One-hundred-sixty rounds per magazine."

"That's less than a third of the Raven's load," Dance groused.

"So it is. The good news is that the GU-3XB utilizes a detachable magazine design. It's just like using a standard rifle: run out of rounds, pop out the empty magazine, pop in the new one and you're ready to keep going. Since it's small, it can be placed at a variety of positions on the fuselage in Jet and Walker modes. You can even carry one in each hand if you're feeling especially Rambo that day. All Warhawks carry two spare magazines in each leg. Comparable to a Raven."

Skull couldn't help but smile at her. "What about electronics, my dear?"

She smiled back. "I can hurt you, my dude. A few improvements over the Raven-D. Same AI-modulated response network on the Strike Ravens, so performance doesn't suffer at all. Radar, radio, laser induction comms, a better combat and navigation computer for improved targeting ability. Laser painting and guidance, motion detectors and collision warnings like the Raven, too. A brand new targeting computer that can auto-target contacts as they appear on your scopes. The optical enhancements suite is pure fun—you can synch the computer to visually scan a target out to six klicks. Spotlights. External loudspeaker. An ejection seat in case things get bad. The EWAR models—which these are not—have improved ranges in all these systems, including IR spotlights built onto the battler's head. Trouble is, you can only use those in Battler mode. Everything else is useable in every configuration."

Fairchild asked, "Shielding?"

"All surfaces are heat and radiation resistant. Unless you're thinking about flying into a star or solar flare, you shouldn't have to worry."

"What about Sleer nukes?" Brooks asked.

"So far, the only race that seems to use nukes is us. Even the OMP wouldn't waste one on anything this small. Anyway, all ships have been assigned. Get in those cockpits and see what's what. Simulators open after chow tonight. Brooks, I expect everyone to get a perfect score."

Brooks grinned. "It'll be my pleasure, Major. Come on, you losers, get to your ships, on the boost!"

"I think I may have created a monster," Rosenski murmured to Fairchild.

"You could use a few monsters this trip," Fairchild said, then spotted a Strike Raven at the far end of the field and raced her for it.

CHAPTER 10

ACQUIRING a convincing Movi transport was far more time-consuming than anyone planned for.

Team *Gauntlet* had already designed an FTL-capable transport for their use; it had proven its design months ago in a real fight against a real opponent. There had been a few less than perfect decisions made in its construction, but nothing that couldn't be remedied in practice. The problem was, of course, that human best-practices in ship design were unknown in Sleer or Movi space. *Gauntlet* simply didn't look like anything a Movi crew might fly, and would never pass for a Movi vessel.

Once this fact was verified with a scan of Genukh's data banks, the great debate ensued. Ideas included building a hollow shell to encase the ship, rounding its edges, building components to create false emission signatures and ID. Nothing was deemed practical given the time constraints.

Finally, Fairchild approached Binil and begged a favor. Binil weighed her options and agreed, then placed a call to Flight Admiral Laakshiden and asked if she could *please* send her humans the blueprints to a Movi ship capable of doing the job they needed. Ten days later, Brooks and company ogled their new home in one of ZERO's construction bays.

"ZERO, I do believe you've outdone yourself this time."

"Thank you, Brooks. I did my best. It's not a perfect model—some of the more specific components simply are not in our inventory and couldn't be fabricated in time—but it should fool any Movi vessel you come across."

"Now we just hope no one fires on us first. Those particle accelerator turrets are just hollow tubes with no works."

"On the contrary, Rosenski. They are fully functional particle accelerators. They are merely smaller than a Movi cruiser would mount. But the exterior laser turrets and internal weapon bays should show any opposition that you are prepared to defend yourself effectively."

"This thing is far smaller than the ships that Mek and his bunch arrived in. Is it still a cruiser? What do we call it?"

"The Movi kingdom uses all manner of local and regional military units in defense of their interests," ZERO said. "This vessel is more properly termed a Company Command Cruiser. It holds all the crew facilities and transport space that a company sized unit of ground troops would need to prosecute a well-defended target, including all their equipment. The internal launch bay is large enough to include a dropship, which itself is big enough to transport the company from orbit to the surface of any world and provide airborne fire support afterward. Assuming of course that became necessary."

"We're not going to do any fighting. Just take a grand tour of the Movi kingdom and report back on what we find," Rosenski said.

Brooks gave her a side eye. She posed with her torso leaning forward, balancing on her toes. Like a Sleer expecting a fight. "Last time we tried something simple, we ended up being trapped in the middle of a Skreesh assault."

"Not this time. Just Movi hitting each other. If anyone demands we support them, we claim battle damage, cut power to the weapons, and move on."

"Says you. This ship is pristine."

"It'll work. We're good at recon. Right?"

"I can't argue with that. It's a lousy forty-five-meter-diameter sphere with four landing pylons. Who'd suspect that of being a spy ship?" Brooks asked.

Fairchild shook the hair out of his eyes. "The Russians used to send fishing trawlers into American waters to pick up any useful signal intelligence. Eventually, the Americans started tracking every one of them. Sometimes being innocuous isn't a great gift."

"What about our gear? ZERO, how do Sleer implants figure into the Movi defenses?" Rosenski asked.

"Movi don't utilize implants the way the Sleer Defenders do, and current Sleer doctrine suggests that Movi assault troops are not well suited to close combat conditions. That may explain why they put so much energy and resources into building planetoid-type ships. Having said that, the Movi apply the same doctrine to their ground forces and their ships. Relatively few units of extraordinarily high quality and firepower."

"Can you show us?"

"I can." A display bubble appeared behind them, showing a variety of vehicle designs. "This is Royal Marine land-air assault flight armor. It offers protection from weapons and the elements—similar to a Sleer suit of battle dress. It includes a plasma rifle, which is slightly less effective than the Sleer fusion rifle but has a longer range and no charging limits. Additionally, this suit never needs to recharge. This is the Vastator, a grav tank armed with a double fusion cannon in a turret mount. The hull includes both autocannon and missile launchers. They are designed to support heavy armored personnel carriers. The carriers can lift a platoon of troops anywhere they are needed, and carry weapons up to and including tactical nuclear warheads."

The AI paused to drop new images on the display. "Battler variants are common in Movi military units, but obviously use different designs than the UEF. This example is typical—the Radjick-class warbot. Despite the designation, it does require a two-man crew to run properly. But it's eighteen meters tall, about one-third more than the tallest UEF battler."

The Radjick-class warbot was a marvel. Bipedal, and with arms that dropped nearly to its knees, the Movi machine seemed built for strength rather than speed, while carrying an assortment of heavy weapons. It wore a pair of turrets on its shoulders like epaulets, and missile tubes ran from its forearms, hips, knees, and chest. A skeletal head sat on its shoulders to scan the world with glittering blue camera "eyes."

"He seems nice," Arkady said.

"The warbots are slow, and limited to ground transportation. I do not know of any systems of transport that are used with them except for dedicated troop carriers."

"How do they stack up against Sleer rollers?"

"I have archival footage." The display shifted to an aerial view of three warbots pitted against a crowd of the Sleer rollers. The fight took place in a narrow canyon, with cliffs on either side and a narrow expanse of rough ground between the two forces. The rollers moved back and forth, surrounding the warbots in turn, raking them with gouts of blue lightning from their turreted particle accelerator weapons. The heavier machines stomped and positioned themselves at the apexes of an equilateral triangle. The lead warbot eventually raised an arm and the three Movi battlers dumped a roar of missile fire into the common killing zone. Missiles flew to their targets, trailing smoke and flame. The whole valley lit up as the warheads exploded, cracking Sleer machinery like a hammer smashing a gumball. The shoulder turrets swung into action, even while Sleer units scattered and swerved, trying to shake the warbots' tracking in the smoke. When the clouds finally cleared, only a few rollers remained, trying to escape up the sides of the canyon. The shoulder turrets sliced the last rollers to pieces. Then the warbots re-formed their unit and continued on their way.

"That's not what I wanted to see today," Rosenski said.

"But it did answer the question. Thanks, ZERO."

"Obviously, not all engagements go that poorly for the Sleer," ZERO said.

"Especially since they've kicked our asses a few times so far."

An electric engine whined behind them, and they turned to see a convoy of sorts, a quintet of the Movi APCs they'd just learned about. The vehicles touched down, and the Gauntlets unconsciously moved into a defensive line as they waited for the door to open. Brooks experienced a bit of tension when a platoon of Movi spilled out, then relaxed when he saw the vehicle's weapons were pointing away from the ship and the Movi were dressed in work coveralls.

A single Movi woman approached, silver hair twisted into a tight ring around the top of her head, silver-yellow eyes staring balefully, like a cat looking over a visitor to her house. "You are Rosenski and Brooks?"

"We are."

"I am Muskuv, Senior Master Chief of the *Night Render*, Logistics Section. I have been instructed to manage your affairs within my warlord's authority." No one made a move until Muskuv raised a hand to adjust the jeweled implant above her left eyebrow. "Do you understand what I am saying to you?"

Brooks tapped Rosenski's foot lightly with his own, without

looking away from Muskuv. Sara got the hint. He could run interference, but neither of them were experts on the Movi or their habits and cultural rules. Sleer... those, they sort of understood.

"We do, Senior Chief. You have our request," he began.

"Yes."

"And we will need transportation into the Movi kingdom," Brooks said.

"Yes."

"And we'll appreciate any news you might be able to tell us about the current political situation," he said.

"Yes."

"And it might not hurt if you could examine the ship we... procured... to transport us once you've dropped us off," Brooks said.

Muskuv backed up a few steps and made a show of judging the new vessel's appearance, like estimating which wall in a drawing room suited a new painting best. "Yes."

"We thank you for your help."

"No."

"I beg your pardon?" Rosenski said.

"No. You will not thank us for aid we have not yet seen fit to give."

Rosenski tried another tack. "I'm sorry. I thought Admiral Laakshiden had spoken to—"

"Flight Admiral Laakshiden's authority is very limited aboard *Night Render*, Rosenski. You are here to spy on us. This is a poor way to begin to a *beneficial* partnership."

Rosenski heard the opening in the conversation and watched as Muskuv's shoulders relaxed. Now that the preliminary fencing was done, Rosenski took up the apparent invitation to détente. "So there is a partnership to be had here. Yes?"

"Perhaps." Brooks shifted from one foot to the other,

drawing Muskuv's attention. "You have something to add?" she said.

"May I ask a question, Senior Chief?"

Muskuv painted him with that cat-like stare, slitted pupils widening slightly as she blinked languidly. As alien as Muskuv was she was more human than any Sleer he'd met. "You may ask."

"Why was Flight Admiral Laakshiden sent to Marauder's Moon?"

"I am not at liberty to discuss her history."

"Nor should you. You've been placed in a difficult position. I see that. We only want what will reflect well on you," Brooks said.

Muskuv blinked again, and took a step closer to him. She towered over Brooks, but kept a poker-straight bearing. "You cannot flatter me, Brooks."

"It's not my intention."

"Then why are you here?"

"I was ordered to be here." He tilted his head in Sara's direction. "My officer in charge relies on me for explanations when things go unexpectedly."

"Really."

"Really." Sara answered. She pulled herself to her full height. Muskuv was still taller but she had the Movi's attention. "Would you like to ask *me* anything?"

Muskuv blinked. The long, heavy-lidded blink of a lioness just waking up from a nap. "Where did you learn to speak Movi?"

He looked at Sara who nodded. "We didn't. We have Sleer military implants. They are translating your words into our language—English—and are translating it back into Movi for your benefit."

"Interesting. You work for Sleer."

"We work with *these* Sleer because we find it to our advantage. And if you thought it useful to help us... we would think it an advantage to work with you as well."

"'These' Sleer. Not those on Home Nest? Not the high command? *Very* interesting. My work here is done for the moment. My Commanding Officer wishes a word." Muskuv ran a fingertip across a built-in display in her sleeve. When she turned to leave, a door opened in the lead APC and a male Movi emerged. He walked with the easy stride of a man who was used to being obeyed, his confidence rooted in knowing any instruction he gave would be followed without hesitation. High cheekbones. Short hair. Violet eyes. And a frown that looked permanent. But no worry lines. And a fancy uniform. "Who leads your mission into Movi space?"

Sara stepped up. "I'm Captain Rosenski. This is Captain Brooks."

"I am First Warlord Anterran ad-Kilsek. Let's talk."

Inside, the vehicle was less of an APC and more of a business office with food service. Plush seats, and tables decorated with fancy plates, glasses, and silverware. Talk was preceded by food. Delicate ceramic cups and saucers with trays of finger food neither of the humans tried to identify. No robots for this guy, either; Brooks could recognize a personal wait staff when he saw one. Brooks noticed that each of the servants had an eyebrow piercing over their right eye, a bright titanium ring with a blue bead, and wondered what it meant. Badge of office? Or mark of servitude? Both?

Anterran waited until the servers filled their glasses with a dark blue liquid. "An ancient greeting in Old Moviri translates into Sleer as 'What do you want?' It comes from a time when there were many clans, factions, and families. We were always fighting with each other in those days—it's a wonder we ever calmed down enough to go to the stars. But now, here you primates are. From what little I know, you just resolved a civil war of your own, didn't you?"

"It was a blanket of small local conflicts that threatened to escalate into something disastrous when the major powers got involved," Rosenski said.

"And the arrival of Zluur's gun destroyer changed that," Anterran said. "Lucky you."

"We thought so at the time."

Anterran sipped his tea. "We are undergoing a similar crisis. What you may not be aware of is how easily our internal problems can spill over into your affairs. Oh, we don't know where your homeworld is yet, but we do know that a new battle ring rimward of us came online not that long ago. The Sleer aboard silenced it quickly, but we find everything eventually."

"You might find it troublesome to find your own territory between us and the Sleer empire," Rosenski said.

"An empire. That's too kind a word. The Sleer were destroyed by the latest incursion. They gave up. Took their toys and their people and fled to their new battle ring. We don't have the time, energy or people to expand into the void they left, but those resources are still there. My people moving into that void would make us neighbors. No?"

The two humans shared a look. Were they being threatened? As if tea and cookies with a top admiral wasn't intimidating enough?

"I'm more interested in hearing about what happened between you and the Skreesh at Great Nest. Using shield repair units to *reduce* shields? Brilliant. That was your idea, wasn't it?"

"We had some input on the strategy," Brooks said.

"I knew it. I've competed against commanders like Grossusk

and Sselaniss before. A tactic like that is nothing like what they might have come up with. All they understand is more. More ships, more troops, bigger fleets. And yet all the ships in the galaxy haven't helped them salvage their civilization. From what little I see, Great Nest is barely hanging on—and only with your help. Home Nest is possibly being dismantled this very moment. The Two Thousand Worlds is more like a sack of pebbles now. In all honestly... it's worrisome."

"I would think it would be a cause for celebration in Movi circles," Rosenski said.

"Under different circumstances, it would be. For millennia we had out kingdom they had their empire and and we usually stayed out of each other's way. Sometimes relations flared. We have a long history of sniping at each other with occasional flare ups to all out war. You know about the border wars? The Great Rift clashes? They take a world away from us, we take it back. They open a mining base, we claim it for agriculture. It never stops. In the middle, a great many Sleer and Movi figured out how to be neighbors... if not especially neighborly. I'll tell you this. None of us in the military imagined that an assassination could have such broad repercussions. My failing. Now you come along with an offer of help for help. Measure for measure. And all you want is a ride into our realm of chaos. If that's not the height of arrogance, I don't know what is. No wonder Admiral Laakshiden is so interested in you."

"We've wasted your time. I apologize," Rosenski said.

Anterran lowered his voice. "You haven't drunk your tea."

They sat back down. They sipped carefully. The blue concoction tasted bitter.

"The ship you brought with you is unacceptable. Neither will you use your unique fighting machines."

Brooks frowned. "The ship is brand new."

Rosenski urged, "And those fighting machines wrecked a Sleer battleship."

"I'm sure that's all true. They are also beacons for attention. You want to observe, you must blend in. Look ordinary. We will supply you with suitable armor. Older models of Movi flight armor and an assortment of light and heavy personal weapons. Not what you're used to, I'm sure… but mercenaries are drawn from local worlds. Muskuv's mechanics will fix that cruiser so its appearance won't raise any questions. Will all your crew carry Sleer implants? Don't answer, it doesn't matter. We can jam their implants at will. Cycomm Sense Op vessels have similar capabilities. Our port of call is Dexilon-A, a mid-core world with a marginal navy presence. Their government is firmly devoted to the throne and resides deep inside loyalist territory. It has a large, busy spaceport, and one more company command cruiser won't be noticed. To be honest, your appearance will raise more questions than your ship will. But once there, you can leave and go your own way. Have all your crew and equipment loaded within two days. Good day."

CHAPTER 11

DANCE REAGAN WAS no fan of the Movi, but she couldn't fault them for their efficiency or knowledge. The Movi noncoms provided enough combat armor and weaponry to equip a proper fifty-man platoon, and a bit more besides. Pallettes of food and uniforms appeared, and crates of ammunition for the small arms. Racks of pistols, carbines, and a few energy weapons with power cells and chargers. Rocket-propelled grenades and launchers, and cases of hand-thrown models. Spare parts for the ship, and a complete demonstration from the Movi on how to use the machine shop to manufacture replacements for anything that failed.

Dance attended the classes, took notes, and forced herself to concentrate on what she was learning. The last few hours were the most annoying for her; the ship disappeared from the launch bay for hours, and when it returned she barely recognized it. The cruiser was clearly the same design, but its look was now completely different. None of the humans would have recognized it if they hadn't known exactly where to look for what few clues they'd added.

The greater shock came when Dance tried to trace the

contours of the ship she remembered emerging from ZERO's construction bay and realized the lines were different. The sleek armored hull was now pitted and patched in what seemed random places. The particle accelerator turrets were gone, replaced with triple laser mounts. The waist missile turrets were still there, but their sensor suites were completely different now. And the launch bay outer door had obviously been taken off and replaced with a different door that matched none of the hinge mounts or hydraulic door arms.

She found a Movi in engineer's insignia and confronted him. "You wrecked it!"

The Movi stared down at her and blinked languidly. "We did not. The gunnery crews in the 1-N squadron did that. Gave some of the new pilots a bit of target practice. I'm sure they appreciated the opportunity to hone their aim."

"What did you *do* to it?"

"We fixed it. Gave it a registration number and a transit history. This vessel didn't exist, and now it has combat records, repair and maintenance logs, crew manifest, equipment and cargo lists... everything you neglected to add."

"I was there when ZERO designed and built her."

"Him."

"What?"

The engineer rolled his eyes. "Movi ships are male. Its pronouns are *him* and *he*. A soldier displays his scars openly."

"Fine, but—"

"No. The ship you arrived in wouldn't have convinced a child that it was a real company command cruiser."

"It was brand new! It was a standard model."

"Exactly. The style you chose was a standard model of ship... ninety years ago. Which means the newest ships like it in service are at least forty years old. The only way one would be newly constructed would be a yacht... a noble's plaything. That would attract attention. We made it look like it had been beaten and repaired numerous times. No crew would look twice at this vessel. That's the point, no?"

Reagan pointed to the other side of the compartment. Every one of the prototype Warhawks and the OMP general purpose battlers stood where the UEF logistics teams delivered them. "And how exactly are we going to load fifty plus war machines?"

Muskuv bent down, a sadistic smirk on her face. "You won't take yours. A complete giveaway to a Movi patrol, no? We gave you appropriate gear inside. Fighters, marine armor, small arms. Small, but suitable for primates."

"You bastards!"

"That word isn't translating, but I'm sure it's meant to be an insult. Listen to me you stupid, soft, *ignorant* primate. If you lose a fight and get boarded, they'll find a lot of old gear inside an ancient Movi hull, apparently run by a platoon of not-Cycomms. That won't work because Cycomms are not mercenaries. But they do sometimes hire them. They'll kill you for pirates before you learn anything useful to take home. Your survival depends on not appearing unusual. You must blend in. This ship will do that. You're welcome."

"Thanks. Son of a—" With an effort she got in one last question. "Wait! What's her—what is *his* name?"

"The ship? This is the *Hajimi*."

"I don't—what's that mean?"

"It means Eight Eyes. Go out on the hull. You'll see we painted over the forward and rear turrets to look like eyes. Eight turrets, eight eyes. Good luck."

Binil came over to console her friends and backed away when Dance snarled at her. "He has a good point. There's no way you can pass for Cycomms."

Underhill tore the wrapper off a food bar and took a bite. "Why not? We fooled the Sleer easily enough."

"You got lucky. Those Sleer children had never seen a Cycomm before. We don't get to Sleer space very often and when we do, we tend to do business with intermediaries. Movi merchant princes often employ a few Cycomms on board for image's sake. Having aliens in your employ is a major perk for wealthy Movi. And you do look like us at a distance. But... "

"What did he mean about there not being any Cycomm mercenaries?"

"Cycomms rely on Movi soldiers for defense everywhere but on Haven, where Sense Op units handle system defense. The only other reason a group of Cycomms might inhabit a warship might be... " Binil suddenly looked scared, like she'd been caught in a stupid, senseless fib.

Dance put her hand on her shoulder, steadying her. "It's okay. Go on."

"...if we came from Marauder's Moon. Now and then, a few ambitious prisoners cobble together a ship from garbage and launch it. Sense Op cruisers shoot them down very quickly. The chance of a ship full of Cycomm pirates successfully escaping is incredibly small. Which meant if it happened... we would attract all the Sense Op guard's attention." She shuddered. "I don't know how else to describe it. Overnight we'd become the most wanted ship in Movi space."

"But it would explain the fact that we don't fit anyone's profiles."

Binil's eyes grew as she looked up at their new ride. "Malkah, it looks like a pirate ship. If they catch us, we are so dead."

"If they catch us, we're screwed anyway. If we're going down in a hail of bullets, why not go down like a reformed pirate crew?"

"With a Cycomm captain," Brooks said, grinning.

Binil squawked. "What? You can—I—we—no!"

"Binil. We'll run the ship. All you'll do is play the part of mercenary if we have guests."

"But—"

"And if there's a top-notch surgeon in our travels, there's a good chance we can turn you back into a working scrambler. Worth the risk?"

"I can do that. I've watched you all for three years. Yes, I accept." The house of Malala's generation of tanja would have its first pirate queen. She was sure they wouldn't approve. The thought made her smile.

CHAPTER 12

ROSENSKI SAVORED her last cup of coffee before departure.

"It's not the craziest plan in the world," Dance murmured at chow. The humans had moved all their gear into the new vessel and settled in. Brooks had already inspected *Hajimi,* from observation deck to engineering. He'd opened every locker and store room, questioned every crew member, polled all the console operators, and spot-checked half the troops. All was in order. The loss of their UEF Warhawks stung, but Rosenski had determined it worth the cost, and Fairchild had backed her up. A last cup of coffee and a few food bars was all he was going to get before they lifted. All that was left to do was seal the ship and settle into their stations. Janus, Frost, and Skellington were already on the bridge along with watch officers. When she was done here, she'd make her own final inspection then get back to the bridge.

Brooks nodded. "That's my point. What if they're wrong? What if—?"

"Brooks. Stop it." Rosenski picked up her tray. "Private channel. Now."

He followed her to a clear table and they sat, heads down, leaning in toward each other as the crew rotated through the narrow galley. "Okay, Simon. What if. Talk to me."

"It's nothing. Sorry, they're right. It's nutty."

"Talk anyway."

"I can't shake the feeling we're being set up to be gigantic patsies."

"By whom? Sora? Anterran?"

"No. By Hendricks. The OMP. Maybe the whole general staff."

"You've lost me."

"Have you gotten a secret message lately?"

"What?"

"I can't stop thinking about the look on Rojetnick's face when he read us those orders. He was freaked out. Deeply pissed off. Which means he couldn't figure out why this mission needed to happen or why we were the ones to send. You want to pick sides in a civil war, you send in spies. Diplomats. Sneaky bastards, right? Why us?"

She stared at her tray. "We have a reputation..."

"Yes. A reputation for losing fights with aliens. That's our rep. We got stuck in Genukh's innards. Uncle and the Hornets bought us time to escape and they got ejected. A rep for failure is what we have."

"We've remediated that recently. Do you remember that? Rescue-1? Attacking Skreesh? That happy crap?"

"Maybe. Possibly. We barely survived that attack by the Skreesh titans, and that was with Sleer help. Zolik and Metzek came damn close to wiping the floor with us on that Sleer factory around Vega. If it hadn't been for the Kaijus, we'd have lost that fight. But why us? Why this mission?"

"All right. Let's say you're right—it's a setup. Who wants us to fail and why?"

"I'm not sure. We know more about how the galaxy and its residents work better than any of the guys in charge. That alone is potentially embarrassing. Especially if someone on Earth wants the UEF to stand down so they can build their own political empire."

"Possible. It might even be likely. What else? How does Sora Laakshiden benefit from us being wiped out?"

"I don't know. Buy why should she help us? From what Dance and Binil say, she's all about power and gaining it for herself."

"You asked Muskuv why Sora was sent to Marauder's Moon. What do you think she would have said?"

"I think she figured out someone's big plan for advancement and chose her friends poorly. Whoever it was knew they could get away with sentencing a flight admiral to a hostage race's penal colony. That sounds like a deal between two royal families to me."

"Hmm."

"And there's Binil herself. Who sold her out and why? She's a royal, isn't she?"

"That's what she calls herself. Is it true?"

"No idea. But do you think it was a coincidence she found herself trussed up and put on the same prison barge as a top admiral? She's a scrambler. A damn useful one. Why didn't they send her to military school?"

"It does seem to go against what little we know."

"And there's Zluur and his grand scheme to build Genukh. A stolen soul. That's how they described Genukh. Part of the Haven AI network, the Malkah. How much of that system is still inside Genukh? On Great Nest? On Earth? I don't know how it all ties together, but we are in the middle of too damn many schemes that we can't see the edges of. It makes me nervous," he said.

"What do we do about it?"

"If we sold ourselves as Cycomm pirates... if the Movi believed it... if the Cycomms heard about us... "

"Then we could find ourselves being put up against a Cycomm Sense Op ship. Their elite forces. From what everyone says, they don't have much sense of humor."

"But they would know we weren't Cycomms from the first time they saw us. That might give us a wedge. At least a chance to learn more about what's going on."

"It might also give them a reason to kill Binil on the spot. She's a fugitive, remember?"

"For the moment, I don't see what difference it makes."

Brooks looked up. "I'm glad we had this talk."

"So am I." Sara checked her watch. Less than two hours left until the *Night Render* departed for the Movi border and eventually its home base. Which she noted they never had told her. Perhaps that was for her unit's protection, but more likely it was for Anterran's. If he was being sincere, and more importantly, if Sora Laakshiden wasn't trying to get them all killed in the name of fomenting a new alliance with one or more of the currently warring factions at their expense, it might make sense. Maybe Anterran was setting up Sora for a grand fall... or vice versa. All she knew was that she had orders. How she carried them out was a bit fuzzier.

Which led her back to Brooks's question. He hadn't mentioned their argument on Mars Base just before its destruction by the Sleer for months. She hoped he'd forgotten about it. She'd never actually told him that she'd been acting under instructions from an unknown agent. She'd never told him she'd been part of that network for almost a year before she was assigned to the AMS-1. She didn't mention how they'd ordered her to strike out at Valri Gibb for siding with the aliens in her trade agreement. She didn't tell him a lot of things.

But he knew. And if they ever called on her again, she'd have a choice: work with them on lord knows what, or confess all to the OMP and hope she could ride out the consequences. She was screwed either way.

"Final checklist. Make it happen."

"On the boost," he said.

She retreated to the bridge of her battered but functional spy ship. The ship was built around a forty-three-meter diameter sphere, with cylindrical decks running through a central core. The external areas were for fuel and propellant, power plant and fuel cells, conduits and cables. All the critical bits that enabled a ship to function. A narrow lift occupied the core of the four landing pylons, but they only reached to the lowermost decks where the engineering stations were located. Once there, she rode two-man lift and climbed up ladders to deck two, the one below the main forward airlock and just above the main bridge. This deck was given over to half of a muster bay slash exercise room slash reception area and held the captain's quarters. As captain or owner or unit leader, she had it all to herself. Thirty square meters of space, all for her own use. Sliding doors let her close off sections, and she could turn it into anything from a luxury bedroom to a sweet gaming center. At the moment, her bedroom was a few square meters, with a mattress, a chest of drawers and a sink and fresher. She locked the door, flopped onto the bed, and brought out a personal comm—an old one, something that previously could have been a proper pocket computer, what they used to call a smartphone. But this phone was modded within an inch of its life, with encrypted translation software and a wireless link that could patch its way into just about any network that still used carrier waves and UEF protocols.

It took a few minutes to locate the network she needed—the one aboard AMS-1—which meant hopping across three sets of patches. Her personal hot spot, *Hajimi*, and the larger network used by Great Nest's battle ring.

She located a contact, really just a thirty-digit alphanumeric string, and tapped to open a new message: "Where did my baby come from?" She hit send and waited. The gadget buzzed and she read the answer: "Old men who don't drink."

It took a moment to extract the gist of the coded exchange. In this case, Sara's baby was the order she'd been given. The old men were the upper echelons of command officers. Hart was the old man who didn't know where he was. Eisenberg was the old man who didn't know his own name. Hendricks was the old man who didn't drink. So, Hendricks. This was a bit of the OMP's attempt at... what. Was Brooks right? He seemed to be on a genuine path to understanding, but he was being pulled in a ton of different directions. Maybe that was for the best. She didn't need him any closer to this than he was.

And yet he deserved to know what was going on. She tapped her comm and pinged him. "Mr. Brooks," she said.

"Brooks here."

"It's Hendricks. Do you understand?"

A long pause while she waited for him to put it together. "Understood. Thank you, ma'am."

And that was that. If one of them had to burn for this bit of skullduggery, she was determined that it not be him. Her unit, her problems. That was the way of things. Here, or at Great Nest or in Movi space. If need be, she'd confess her crime to Underhill when they got back, and face whatever consequences she drew.

Less than an hour to go. She had an inspection to make.

———

"Fighters? We have fighters?"

"Royal Movi Navy light fighters," Dance reported. "Six of them. A gift from Muskuv, I'd guess. I know we didn't build this ship with them aboard. Genukh—er, ZERO would have told us."

"Fair enough. What have you learned?"

Brooks and Rosenski followed her through narrow corridors. She turned corners almost faster than Brooks could follow, and they found themselves in a proper launch bay. The dropship sat to one side, with a troop muster area next to it. Heavy cradles along the left and right walls held the Movi fighters. A series of manipulator arms and winches could extend from the roof, retracted for the moment.

Dance led them to one of the cradles with an open gantry. The canopy seemed barely big enough to fit either of them. "They're not like Ravens. Not even like the Sleer Zilthid singlefighters. They're about the size of Sparrowhawks, those experimental things we flew on exactly one test drive and one mission around Saturn. Remember that?"

"I wasn't with you, I was flying point with the Nightmares," Sara said. "I do remember Brooks and Uncle making a big deal out of using the square fingertips to pull up turrets off a Sleer battleship. Katsev tried that with his Raven, only to find that his own ship with round fingertips couldn't repeat the maneuver. He got a face full of shrapnel for his effort."

Dance looked embarrassed. "Ouch. Well. Sorry."

"It wasn't your fault. Tell me about the boom stuff," Rosenski said.

Dance brought out a slate, swiped to a new screen and handed it to Rosenski. "They're ancient, in keeping with the advanced age of the ship we're using. Modern Movi ships make extensive use of UAVs."

"Remind me to complain to the management."

"Heh. Dual lasers mounted in a chin turret beneath the cockpit. Four short-range missiles mounted on underwing pylons. They have better acceleration than this ship does, but not a lot of extra power output, so they'll do some real damage, but only at short range. They're meant for close orbit fire-support missions and strafing runs against ground targets, I'd bet."

"If what Brooks has been learning about the Movi way of doing things is accurate, that would make sense. How would they fare against a Raven?"

"An experienced pilot might hold her own against a newbie in one of our VRFs. Depends how good the lasers are." She shrugged and took back the tablet. "They aren't meant for a proper front-line assault against hardened targets. Nothing on this ship is."

Dance led her to a set of recessed tubes adjacent to the outer hull. Two tubes each were bracketed on opposite sides of the ship, six in all. "I saw these and figured they were missile tubes or something. But I also thought 'why make missiles so wide on a ship this small?' So I cracked one of the maintenance hatches, stuck my head inside and found this panel—which opens that hatch like so." A section of hull slid away with a grinding of metal to reveal a ladder and a passageway wide enough for a single person to enter. Sara stuck her head in and saw how a single pilot could drop into the tube and crawl through an access way to wriggle into a narrow cockpit. "Jeez. They'll have to be shrimps to fit in there."

"You mean like me and Dance?" Brooks asked. Sara looked around, her blood rising in defensiveness, only to see Brooks and Reagan snickering and jostling each other. "Yes, you two are now pilots. Find me four more shrimps who can run the controls and they can have the other fighters."

"Yes, ma'am."

"And stop ma'aming me. I'm not your ma'am. I'm your damn CO."

"Yes, CO ma'am! You know who would fit the bill for these? Speedbump and Ghost. And Janus. Can we get Marc Janus down here?"

"Janus flies the ship, Simon."

"Crap. Oh well. Where's the duty list? Ha! Lieutenants Diallo! Solovoya! Roberts! Katsuta! We are on mission!"

Brooks and Dance headed off to poll the crew, and Sara headed further into the ship. Three launch tubes each on port and starboard for the fighters—the incredibly small fighters—and the pinnace's landing gantry was wedged right through the center. The engineering section compensated for the fragmented design by occupying parallel spaces in the lower hull. The good news was that they were all networked to operate in synch with each other, and the better news was that individual sections could be brought to bear from the engineering console on the bridge. The bad news was that they'd have to re-wire the whole control system if they wanted something where individual modules could be used in tandem. That way, if a module was destroyed in a firefight it wouldn't take the whole network down with it. She'd put Dance on that when she got her head out of the clouds regarding the newly discovered fighter craft. Until then, the system would be fine... and they were supposed to be lying low anyway.

All in all, it was a compact, serviceable warship, meant to ferry a company of troops and their equipment anywhere in the kingdom. They'd be fine as long as no one asked them to fight a squadron of Ravens.

A horn sounded and a speaker blared to life. "All hands, prepare for boarding. Repeat, we have a passenger boarding.

Reception crew to forward airlock. Reception crew acknowledge.

The forward airlock was technically her province. She tapped her comm. "This is Rosenski. On my way."

She blinked when a tall Movi female climbed down the ladder... and was followed by a human woman with the blue gray uniform of the OMP and a shock of blue-black hair and silver headset that Sara would recognize anywhere.

Frances Underhill saluted, her OMP Major's insignia glittering on her lapel. "Major Underhill requesting permission to board, Captain."

The request was a bit of formal protocol. Rosenski knew she could not refuse the request. *Rocketing through the ranks these days, aren't you, dear?* "Granted. Welcome aboard, Major. Admiral Laakshiden."

"I heard you were bringing Binil. I thought it a wise idea to come along just in case," Sora said. She peered up the ladder and gestured to someone out of sight. The forward hatch closed and locked with a clang and a hiss. "Besides, what's the point of all this if you don't have someone willing and able to gather intelligence on the disposition of the various factions? Do you really think Movi will talk to total strangers?"

"I had thought we'd be listening to transmissions and viewing sites with telescopes and sensors."

"Excellent idea. But I know the military bases, their locations, and capabilities. In the meantime, let's get settled. What's on the other side of this wall?" Sora strode through the narrow door and squeed in satisfaction. "This will do nicely. Thank you, Captain. Please get Major Underhill and Binil settled, would you? Many thanks."

Rosenski clenched her teeth and dropped down to the next deck. She could still use the captain's quarters on the bridge deck. At least she'd be the first to hear about trouble.

Damn Hendricks anyway. Stupid old man who didn't know where he was and didn't care.

"All hands, prepare for departure," she called, and climbed down to the bridge.

CHAPTER 13

"ALL HANDS, prepare for relocation. All nonessential personnel please debark the ship."

Captain Sara Rosenski felt a twinge. She'd led missions before, but there had always been someone over her to take the blame if things went south. This time it was her show, and the anxiety would not go away no matter how many times she ordered it off the ship. No such luck. Even her Sleer implants were no help.

The Comm watch officer spoke up. "Signal from launch control, sir. All nonessential personnel have left the ship."

"Commander Fairchild, too?"

"Yes sir. He says good hunting."

That settled her. "Very well. Signal the *Night Render*'s bridge. We are ready for relocation."

"I have their flight ops chief on the line."

"Very good. *Night Render*, this is *Hajimi*. We await your instructions."

"Acknowledged. Exiting your launch bay would be an excellent beginning."

"Understood. Mr. Janus, take us out."

Janus ran through the checklist. "Power lines out. Fuel lines secure. Umbilicals detached. Docking clamps released. Grav plates normal. Thrusters on-line. Here we go." They watched the forward viewer relay images from the external cameras. The floor merely fell away and the cavernous launch bay swiveled around them while the outer doors opened. Once outside, the scene drifted into a more familiar pattern. The bulk of the battle ring floated below and the *Night Render* hovered above it, a dreadful, soulless black sphere.

The Movi officer talked them through it. "*Hajimi*, set your flight plan to orbit us at ten kilometers, at a speed of no more than one hundred meters per second. Locking displacement projectors on you now. Jump in three. Two. One. Jump! Well done."

Rosenski let her breath out in a rush. She had no words to describe what happened. One second the viewer showed a field of stars, the next, they were staring at blank walls of the battleship's interior. "Good lord. That's how they launch five thousand fighters inside of a minute. They teleport the damn things from one place to another."

The Flight Ops Officer sounded pleased. "Well done. Locking you down now. We will be under way in three minutes. Time to destination, 119 hours." Janus started a countdown clock and they were on their way into Movi space.

Life aboard *Hajimi* was nothing like life on the *Cyclops*. *Hajimi* was a fraction of the size and carried none of the Sleer gear they'd quickly become accustomed to using, even dependent upon. No feeders, no food and water basins, and no wide spaces. Movi technology didn't rely on molecular circuits or nanofiber connectors. Truth was, it worked very much like the AMS-1 did: conventional switches, dials, gauges, indicators, and digital points of contact. Brooks thought it stylishly retro, but he missed his control gauntlets.

There was another difference: the Movi didn't use Sleer battle dress, nor did they have anything even remotely like it. Ship-suits were common outer garments that could form an airtight seal by donning a pair of gloves. They had one awesome advantage over the UEF's TAC-2F flight suits; the helmets self-assembled out of nanoparticles stored in the collar. The wearer could rely on two hours of emergency air and a bit of protection against random shrapnel and radiation. A port at the shoulder allowed one to connect a proper air tank for greater endurance, but it wasn't anything like a true combat suit.

Lastly, while they made use of them the Movi didn't use implants the way the Sleer did. Sleer implants, it turned out, had a hidden purpose: so Sleer officers could exert control over soldiers equipped with them. Want to make sure your troops obeyed without question? Send the nervous systems of the resistors the effect of wracking pain. Disobedience could end up being deadly, especially if a unit leader decided to turn his rebel soldier's healing qualities off. Death on a battlefield was no small thing, even to a Sleer, but it took a huge amount of effort to kill one in combat. Between their battle dress and implants, a Sleer warrior could take enough hits to kill a platoon of human marines and still be able to manage himself in a firefight.

Movi put their technology to use in other ways. Neural implants were common among officers, and line troops often had comms tuned to their OIC's permanent mental frequency. Commands were instantaneously transmitted, even across vast distances. To date, nothing they found in *Hajimi's* ship's locker, secure vault, or armory seemed to hold similar promise. In the meantime, they kept their Sleer implants, which would help them maintain some advantage even without their battle dress.

But Movi weapons—now those were interesting. Laser swords, monofilament whips, and plasma weapons that could be fired without personal protection were all part of their armory.

Slug throwers, too: a type of maglev rifle that could propel a tungsten needle through armor at five hundred meters. There was a pistol version with a fraction of the range and penetrating power, but one of them could spray a cone of shrapnel wide enough to keep an opponent's head down.

With the relatively tiny bridge already staffed by Janus in the pilot chair, Skull Skellington on electronics and sensors, Grandpa Frost on navigation, and Rosenski minding the operations from her captain's office next door, Simon Brooks understood that he picked up a new responsibility; figure out how to utilize the ship's fighters. Chances were they'd never have to use them, but it was best to be prepared. He'd called Reagan, Diallo, and Solovoya together to go over the equipment and gear.

An announcement came over the intercom. "Thirty minutes to destination. Three zero minutes. All stations, acknowledge."

Brooks pressed into the dark of the launch tube's interior, a headlamp glowing with its single LED bulb. The Movi fighters looked like sleek bullets with a pair of stubby, forward wings and a set of trailing stabilizers. He wouldn't want to use it too deep in a planet's atmosphere, but he figured it could skim and maneuver inside a gravity well. "These engines are ridiculous," he said over his comm. "They take up the entire rear half of the ship."

Dance responded, "That's not unusual, Simon. If you ever pull a fixed-wing aircraft apart, you see that the power plant, fuel tanks, and engine are everything aft of the cockpit. But... I've never seen them arranged quite this way before."

Roberts offered what he thought was a helpful bit of intelligence: "Movi engineering is a lot classier than Sleer style. I heard one of Muskuv's non-coms say something about how Movi crew never leave well enough alone. They love to tinker. Pisses off the naval base mechanics, but the crews are expected to keep the need for replacement parts and such at a bare minimum."

"I figure that's why they have machine shops on board," Diallou said. It was clear she didn't spend a lot of time below decks... even human ships maintained machine shops.

"Is that why they ripped half the ship apart and put it back together for us?" Dance asked.

"I hope they were genuinely trying to be helpful."

From the intercom: "Twenty-five minutes to departure. Two-five minutes."

Simon felt his way forward. "Gah. Speedbump? Could you acknowledge those announcements?"

His comm crackled and dropped a few syllables before Diallou picked up. "—ry, sir. There doesn't seem to be anything I can tell them that will shut them up."

"They think they're being assist," a heavy accent said. That would be the Ghost—Ykaterina Solovoya, a transfer from AMS-1. Nineteen confirmed kills and a wealth of knowledge about keeping hidden by means of EWAR gear. Simon meant to qualify the entire squadron on Ravens before leaving Great Nest, but the craziness came upon them so quickly, he'd made do with a cursory scan of their records. And now he was assigning her a new fighter of unknown origin and operations. Some XO he turned out to be.

"Diallou, Solovoya. Which of you is doing the exam and which is in the pipe?"

"Speedbump is tablet. I am in pipe. Before I learn flying, I was conduit specialist on *Ascension*. Always into tight spaces. No fear of the dark."

"Good to know. Let's head to the cockpits... I want to see if we feel the same responses."

"Acknowledged. Here I go."

On the speaker: "Departure in twenty minutes. Two-zero minutes. All hands acknowledge. All hands—"

The ship tipped around them, jarring everyone aboard. A new voice filled with urgency interrupted: "Belay that. Prepare for immediate departure. One minute to relocation. All crew to stations."

Simon reached out and pulled himself along by gripping the leading edge of the fighter's wing and hauling himself up and into the open cockpit. He climbed over the sill and dropped into the crew space like fitting himself into a Raven. This was way smaller. He pulled the canopy over him and turned on the machine systems. While the power systems engaged, he opened his comm. "Sara! What's going on?"

"*Night Render* is coming under attack, apparently. They're dropping out of their FTL early to send us off. Where are you?"

"Ghost and I are inside fighters. Reagan and Diallou are standing by."

"Do they work?"

He scanned the controls. Everything seemed in order. His fighter came alive around him and pushed the darkness away. He tapped his suit collar and heard a tiny metallic tinkling as his nano-studs closed around his head. What had been a mere HUD now blossomed into a fully functional VR environment. But stuck in here he wouldn't be able to use the function's full abilities: a red banner hovered over his nose: EXTERNAL VIEW DISABLED. "They do. No missiles are loaded, but the chin turret is alive and the HUD in here is a completely new experience. More like a VR environment than a simple set of data projected on a flat screen."

"Can you fly them?"

"Yes."

"Stand by. We may need you to launch shortly."

"Copy that." He switched channels. "Solovoya, Reagan,

Diallou. Board your fighters and power up. We are on mission. Roberts and Katsuta, you're on damage control." There was no time to get Katsuta and Roberts prepped and launched. If there was grumbling in the ranks, he couldn't hear it.

"Docking clamps open. Relocation matrix engaged… projectors online… releasing in three… two… .one… jump!"

Hajimi popped from its interior compartment into open space. Gravity, inertia, and acceleration all worked in tandem to blast the tiny ship far away from its host without killing the crew. On the bridge viewer, all was fuzz and snow until Skull found the correct settings. The viewer cleared, and a picture snapped into focus.

At the same time alarms blared, proximity alerts sounded, and collision warnings ran through the ship.

They'd dropped straight into an intense firefight.

Brooks kept his head, the anticipation of finding out what his new fighter could do and the responsibility he felt for his other three pilots pushing out any anxiety he felt about possibly dying stuck in a dark, hollow tube. He had his command channel open, and the sound of Sara giving orders to straighten out the ship and thrust away from the fight kept him stable.

"All pilots report in," he ordered.

"Reagan. All systems check."

"Janus for the win."

"Diallou. We're good."

"Solovoya. All ready."

"Be ready to orient yourselves on the ship's beacon when you emerge." He switched channels. "This is Gauntlet Leader. Fighters ready for launch!"

"Launch!" Sara cried.

Brooks watched the landing bay disappear as the mechanism drew his ship into the launch tube. The tube sealed, the space ahead of his fighter irised open, and he nudged the throttle—or tried to. The HUD flashed red: RELEASE ENABLED. He found the switch, pulled it up, and the tube belched him away from the ship, slamming him back against his couch. Nothing like the giant maglev catapults aboard the AMS-1, but it worked.

Once away from the ship, his throttle came up and he pushed it forward then checked to see where the other pilots were.

"Form up on the ship, people. Two thousand-meter orbits. All scanners are hot. Let's see what we—ohmyfuckinggo—"

His VR display adjusted and showed him the universe in every direction. For a moment, he was lost; his eyes told him things he couldn't believe. The bulk of *Hajimi*, even from two klicks away was distinctive—a sphere with a few protruding gun turrets and four support pylons extending below. But *Night Render* dwarfed everything within sight. It was a magnificent vessel, spherical and dotted with weapon mounts and launch bays, with a conical depression on its midsection that glowed the blue of its drive system.

Neither was the planetoid alone. She expelled more ships, ten times the size of the company cruiser, which formed a defensive perimeter around the mother ship.

His sensors pinged and the combat computer identified multiple enemy contacts at a variety of ranges. A fleet of planetoids, one even bigger even than *Night Render,* came into view, all with their own support vessels in the process of launching. On top of everything, a dozen tiny, extremely fast targets closed with them at a rate no fighter had any business utilizing.

"*Hajimi*, this is Gauntlet Leader. Come to course two-six-two relative, max burn. We have fighters incoming."

"We see them. We're arming the rear turrets now. Stay the hell out of our firing solution and we'll let you pick off the remnant."

"Copy that. All fighters, make sure you synch up your chin turrets to the combat computer's helmet tracking. If I'm reading this right, it'll automatically track any target in sight, no matter how it maneuvers."

"Shit. That sounds useful as fuck."

"I'll bet you the incoming bad boys have the same gear."

"Hope not. Everyone nudge your velocity up a bit. We want the cruiser between us and the new contacts."

They obeyed. Brooks watched the distance close further until a dense sheaf of missiles dropped from the waist launchers on the *Hajimi*, flame trails splitting behind them. A dispersed set of orange balls of flame appeared well behind the cruiser, then another and another. "That was impressive as hell. There's only six left."

Rosenski said, "We're out of missiles and I'm not going to re-orient the ship to bring the forward guns to bear. We need time to reload. You may engage."

"Roger that. Come on Gauntlets, we have work to do." He yanked back on the controls, fighting to twist his ship into a maneuver that even a Raven would have found impossible, and suddenly he felt the machine grab at him. Heavy clamps reached out from the console and snatched at his hands and feet, pulling him back into the acceleration couch.

In the same instant, he felt the neural network in his VR helmet providing him with a deep understanding of the realm in which he now found himself.

ENGAGE FULL SENSORY NET? Y/N

"Yes!" he yelled. Instantly, he felt as if his body was now one with the ship in a way that not even his Raven used to provide him. He twisted his arms and legs and the machine responded. Flying was now no more complicated than thinking about it, something that not even the Raven-C's state-of-the-art AI-enabled flight control system could manage.

"Look at the sky!" he called.

"Sorry, Genius, didn't copy that. Say again."

"Close your helmet, engage the VR display, and enable the full sensory net. It'll put your brain right inside the nav computer."

They responded the same way he had. He could even tell how they were reacting by their voices: Dance squealed, Diallou grunted, and Solovoya let loose a delighted stream of Ukrainian.

It got better. Brooks found he could reach out to the other three fighters and pull their navigation codes to his own, creating a cohesive unit of four ships. The perfect formation flight. They all swerved and dove, twisted and turned as a single unit, far more efficiently than they could have trained to do in weeks.

"Here we go. Hang on!"

Brooks pinged their enemies and realized why they were so much faster: they were three times the size of their tiny fighters. In this situation, speed was their ally. More importantly, he saw that the electronics signatures of the oncoming heavy fighters were very different from their own. That meant different control systems. And it meant he needed to take a gamble. It might work; if it didn't, they'd never live more than a few minutes. But it was preferable to watching the heavies streak past them and lob as many energy weapons into *Hajimi* as it took to break its back and kill all of his friends.

Harnessing his new senses proved to be tricky. His VR sight let him plot entire courses with speed change and formation change at various points into the burn. And it had the ability to adjust the approach vectors and formation to avoid incoming fire. Brooks decided to go all-out for this plan. He would approach from their broadside, presenting a tiny profile while aiming for their widest ones. Then they would perform multiple passes and let the chin turrets blast away at whichever target presented the best chance of hitting.

G-forces pushed him into his couch as he watched his fighter group perform for him. Their first pass targeted three of the enemy planes, shattering them with bursts from the chin turrets. At short range, the turrets were devastating, shooting plasma bolts in rapid order. But the plasma didn't track well and dropped off sharply with range. They swooped and came from the obverse angle, this time spacing the planes to form a wide wing on order to hit the remaining three planes at once. One exploded easily, one shattered a stabilizing fin, and the third they missed. Another swerve, another swoop. This time, the chin turrets lined up on the single fighter, which broke into pieces and flew harmlessly past them. The final attack split the fighters into two two-man elements and had them approach from different directions. Diallou and Dance's planes hit the target, while Solovoya and Brooks missed, but the last plane exploded.

"How are we?" Brooks called. "We all good?"

"Good, yes. We go again?"

"Not today, Ghost. My stomach is gonna hurl," Dance moaned.

"And no more incoming targets," Diallou noted. "Thank God for small things."

Brooks pinged their surroundings. "Whatever happened it's over now. I think everyone took their shit and bugged out. Be careful fam, there's a lot of wreckage out here."

Landing the newfangled Movi birds was considerably more complicated than launching them. In order to set the craft into the launch tubes, they had to angle their rears at the tube openings and back into the narrow spaces. Luckily, the ship's computer sensed their approaches and gave them some assistance: a track and hook assembly launched itself at slow speed, latched onto the tail of each fighter and dragged it back inside, where clamps engaged when the power plant wound down. But then there was the added fun of climbing out of the tiny craft, finding the tube exit hatch, and stumbling out onto the mid-decks. Brooks found it tough to breathe once he stepped back into *Hajimi* proper. He made a mission of verifying his pilots were safe and sound before climbing up to the bridge to report. He arrived just in time to see Laakshiden and Rosenski getting into it.

"We're light-years away from our intended destination. This is Foresite-4059," Sora snarled as she gesticulated wildly at the viewscreen. "Calling it a spaceport is being too kind. It's an automated recovery point for express boats. It's a planetoid, part of an asteroid field that rounds the primary star. There's a small orbital habitat, fuel dumps, and a selection of repair yards, but only a handful of crew assigned here. Even the ore freighters only call once a year."

"Your warlord said he'd drop us off at a proper space port."

"I'm sure he did. And he may even have been sincere in his plan. But if *Night Render* was attacked and they dropped out of jump too close to one of Mineko's war fleets—and he felt it necessary to drop us here and then leave—it was because he thought it was too dangerous to take us further."

"Is that a fact?"

"It's what I would have decided in his place." Sora paced for a moment then folded her arms. "But why would Mineko come here? We're directly behind the bulwark that defends the mid-core systems from a Sleer invasion. There's nothing but... oh *no*." She jumped into the pit and pushed controls while Frost and Skull got out of her way. "It can't be... he wouldn't dare... ." she growled. A tactical display appeared and she made a strangled noise in her throat. "No!"

Rosenski came forward. "If you articulated the problem, maybe we could help resolve it. Admiral."

"Not in this pathetic substitute for a warship, you couldn't. We're seven parsecs out from the Garrison Cluster. If Archduke Mineko's fleets are this far out it means he's given up his positions near the homeworld and moved them out here. Which means he's deployed fleets around the depot worlds. That gives him control of well over one half the ships in the combined war fleets and everything they have to offer. Breaker take everything!"

"So your warlord is at a disadvantage," Rosenski said.

"Damn Anterran to hell!" She shut her mouth, squeezed her eyes closed, and held her breath. When she came back, she spoke in clipped words. "A significant disadvantage. Especially if Anterran's supporters move their allegiances to other factions. If he can hold this region, Mineko commands more than half the resources the royal navy needs to function."

"How well do you know the archduke?" Rosenski asked. When no one answered, she tried again. "Admiral? How well do you know him?"

"I've met him once. Back when I was a captain. He protected me against an unfair and incorrect mark on my record."

"So he liked you."

"It was many years ago. H doesn't remember me."

"Are you sure about that? Might it not be worth some energy to find out?"

Sora was already past the question and diving deep into her memory. "Even if he cuts the royal supply lines, he'll still have staffing problems. He'll be in want of ships. A man who's just assassinated a sovereign would need support, and lots of it. He'll sense he has the weak position on the game board. He will need help." She turned to Brooks and walked up to him. She was taller than Rosenski and he found himself looking up her nose. "How much support will your government offer, Brooks? Enough to cement an alliance?"

"I don't know."

"Then you are worth nothing. Get off my bridge."

"He'll do no such thing."

Sora turned her head, murder in her eyes. "What did you say?"

Rosenski stepped forward. "It's my bridge. My ship. My mission. You're here to advise me. Is that clear?" she growled. "I have no problem staying here to acquire intelligence from the port's computers, but this is not your vessel, *Admiral*, and you are not in command. More importantly, if you can't arrange an agreement that puts Earth in a better position than it's in now, *you* are useless. Do we understand each other?"

The fury in Sora's eyes faded. She bobbed her head. "I forget myself. Excuse me. It won't happen again."

"Of course. If you have a recommendation, I'm listening."

"If the Garrison Cluster is Mineko's current base of operations, we should introduce you to him. I'll see what I can arrange. Maybe he does remember me."

"Very well. Mr. Brooks, pull whatever you can from the starport network. Admiral, give us the navigation charts for a trip to the Garrison Cluster and you'll get your chance to talk to the archduke. If you think it's worth it."

"It's always worth it to remind one of old favors."

"Very well. Let's get to work."

CHAPTER 14

RAGE BURNED in Sora Laakshiden like a solar flare.

How dare those *primates* question her history? How dare their slightly more capable friends demand that she leave them to work the problem? How dare any of them even stand within fifty meters of her on board a ship that no mere human had ever seen until a few days ago? How dare any of them talk to her like she was an underling!

Sora fumed and retreated to her sanctuary. It was a fully appointed suite of rooms and there were no humans in it. Good. Foresite-4059 had some use after all, and if she couldn't crack its code herself, they might well be of some value to her. Let them interrogate its computers, rifle its secrets, make some plans. They might tell her something useful. They'd better tell her something useful, or they were in for a difficult time.

But the real prize lay ahead of her in the Garrison Cluster.

She felt for the telltale bumps of her social implant on her forehead. Five slots, five bumps. An ocular filter, memory augment, neural boost, cybernetic processor, and social adaptation. Removed before they'd loaded her and her minions on the prison shuttle at Haven, she'd recovered better models from the sick bay aboard *Night Render*. Anterran had been specific. "Take the best of these and use them well. We need intelligence. I don't care what these pink-skinned animals think they've accomplished, I don't trust them. If they are truly a rising power, we need to know everything about them. *Everything.*"

She believed him. She needed access to knowledge, communications, and anything that could pluck data from a memory bank like a thought from the brain. They weren't the equivalent of Sleer microbial implants or control gauntlets, but they didn't need to be. These models helped her control a ship or access electronic files without needing to memorize access codes. Simple, and mostly trauma proof, the only problem was that removing them destroyed them. Safe, though it might sting on the way out. In any case she'd been recording every interaction since she boarded.

An added feature was she could do her research from up here. A fully equipped ship's terminal lay on the desk, flashing its readiness, waiting for her to get going. Such a patient machine. She cleared her mind, tapped into the network, and was off. Time to dive deep and learn about Archduke Mineko.

She started with the most recent news and events and working backward. The assassination, for certain. Mineko hadn't worked alone. What he'd accomplished would have been utterly impossible, a mad daydream, without the backing of powerful allies and suitable hordes of minions. She found the ringleaders quickly enough in the three company commanders of the royal marines and the colonel in charge of the royal guard. All served in the archduke's unit at one time or another during his time in the royal marines. If nothing else, Mineko inspired visions of success and made a name for himself commanding troops on live battlefields. During the Lord March uprisings, a group of one hundred or so enhanced cyber-soldiers had taken charge of a dozen worlds simultaneously. In response, the royal marines and the navy employed a decades-long campaign to scour the worlds in questions. Nearly a million dead later, the kingdom was declared secure and such technology banned.

Mineko commanded the navy contingent charged with putting the rebellion down. He'd been awarded a dukedom for his efforts; a giant estate near the core of the kingdom. He'd won ribbons and medals on top of it, and a hefty stream of income from the royal treasury as well as five percent of the Mon-Sakkaron megacorporation's preferred stock. War had been good to him. And all it cost him was unwavering loyalty to the sovereign and one hundred thousand of his soldiers' lives. Good for him.

Before that, he'd been avid in trade; a Kar-Tuyin acolyte, a man devoted to business deals and taking proceeds from the top. Not one interested in setting up sustainable relationships between trading partners. He'd done well by borrowing money at cost, using it to build a new venture, selling the venture to a conglomerate officer, then paying out friends and allies from the proceeds and pocketing the rest. Then he'd gone on to the next deal. He was good at it, amassing an eight-figure fortune in only a few years. Granted, there were always people willing to do deals with dukes. That would have made things simple for him.

She peered into banks and trading hubs, looking for money trails. So many trails. She was missing most of what she'd needed most, but found just enough to keep the path in front of her. There: weapons manufacturers, shipping magnates, supply hubs and depots. Bit by bit, Mineko had assembled a war machine. But how had he managed to claim so many military minds for his revolution?

For that she needed to look elsewhere. Some officers were natural mercenaries, and easy to spot. Local commanders who wanted to become regional players. And local commanders were everywhere in the Movi kingdom. She plotted the planets where Mineko claimed authority, or at least allegiance, one by one. In all but a few cases, there were ties to his business interests. A few dozen nobles who claimed his protection in exchange for their support. Backwater worlds, mostly, devoid of serious royal interest and investment. Worlds rife with anxious, ambitious leaders who wanted more of what the kingdom claimed to offer: opportunity, wealth, and power. He'd brought them into his fold with promises of all three, and he'd made good on his promises. Business was good on those planets.

He'd built his empire brick by brick, promise by promise, and reaped impressive dividends. Rooting his support base out meant sending fleets of ships to each world and blowing them out of existence. Not something that a warlord would want to be seen doing. In that way, recognizing Mineko's claim to the throne was just following the path of least resistance.

But... he'd also moved most of his fleets to the Garrison Cluster, knowing he could control Anterran's base by holding the primary sources of everything from fuel to spare parts. Daring Anterran to come get him. A trap to lure the bigger opponent into a pit of despair and destruction.

And yet Mineko would never feel secure. He'd want more. More ships, more troops, more power. A buttress against a counterattack by Anterran's forces. That would be his biggest concern. Missena enjoyed noble support and plenty of assets, but had no real interest in ascending to the throne. And Mother Gala-Shom's minions called upon plenty of zealots but no vital resources. And Singhir... the less said about him the better. Singhir was both the most powerful figure in the kingdom and the most dangerous...even, potentially, to his own faction.

All right then. She needed to convince her new 'not-Cycomm' friends that there was something to be gained for all of them by backing the archduke. The trick would be to convince them that he might very well win this contest. Time to go to work.

She dropped down to the bridge in the middle of something. Binil was hunched over an unused console, and that OMP woman, Underhill, paced near the lift, listening to everything. Sora watched the young man, Brooks, describe the new Mantis-class single fighters he'd flown with the other pilots. She caught the hint of a phrase and waited to be noticed.

"Seriously," Brooks was saying, "the computer practically flies those things. Similar to using control gauntlets, but comparable response time. We need to find a load of missiles for those crazy ships. Blasters are great at short range, but I get the idea we got lucky this time. Bigger ships mean longer range guns, and we probably won't get lucky again."

Rosenski stared at the tactical. "You think we can find new gear below?"

"Not a chance. Laakshiden was right: Foresite-4059 isn't much more than a marked patch of bedrock, a few computer consoles, and a fuel dump."

"I have an idea," Sora announced.

Rosenski looked up. "Good, so do I."

"Mine is better."

"I'm listening."

Rosenski moved aside for Sora. "Mr. Brooks is correct. We are nowhere. I know where you can find all the supplies you need to bring your fighter squadron up to modern specs." She punched up a set of coordinates. "These seven worlds are collectively called the Garrison Cluster, due to the fact that they serve as a bulwark between the Sleer empire and our own. These three worlds nearest the Sleer border are out of reach for the moment, but these four here are within a single jump. The royal news channel seems to think they're being claimed by Archduke Mineko. I suggest we make common cause with him and use the facilities to equip ourselves. Perhaps repairs if needed."

"Even if jumping into bed with the man who assassinated your sovereign seemed like a great idea, how do we even know Mineko will be there?" Rosenki asked.

"Because he's been calling ships to himself for months." Sora touched a control and a flurry of new images appeared. "He's using the M-boat channels. Sending out invitations. They ask interested parties to arrive at a set of co-ordinates, then have them met by intermediaries. I'd expect there are several levels of interviews before one is granted access. But we can simply answer the call."

"There's no way the sovereign can be okay with that," Brooks said.

"Singhir can't stop him. Mail is mail. There's no filter in the universe than can catch coded messages if the codes are unknown."

Rosenski fidgeted. "You trust him?"

"It's a risk. As I said earlier, I doubt he would remember me. But we need help and I think it's a good risk."

"I don't know... you tend to remember the people you stick your neck out for, especially if you think they can be useful somewhere down the line."

"That's a very cynical attitude, Sara."

"Fighting the Sleer made me tough." Rosenski paused. "Do you think the archduke will win?"

"He might. The Right of Royal Blood is a legitimate ascension strategy. We could make a case for helping him out in exchange for certain concessions."

"We could at that. But we don't have the bulk of Earth's forces with us, and there's no guarantee they'd provide us with any if we asked. It sounds like you're hoping to bluff your way into an alliance. Risky business."

Sora opened her arms. "Is your idea any better?"

"It's different."

"Do tell."

"We dress up Binil as a mercenary commander and pass ourselves off as Cycomm troops."

Sora rolled her eyes. "And you call *my* plan risky."

"It is. You'll have to promise him support, but one lousy company of troops and a ninety-year-old ship in need of repair and resupply won't be worth much in a civil war. You'll forgive me for thinking a company of Cycomm soldiers is worth more than a former admiral's shattered reputation. I mean, you were on your way to a penal colony when you met Binil and Dance."

"I'd like to hear it from Binil."

Binil had stayed to herself, huddled in a jump seat a size too large for her, but out of the way. Following the conversation but keeping silent. When Sora turned to her, she seemed to wake up from a deep thought. "Sora, no. Commander Rosesnki's plan is better. At least in the early stages."

"What did you say?" It was a tactic. She heard Binil loud and clear, and knew exactly what she'd said. Binil was growing a spine. Not the worst thing that could happen... the girl had a core of iron deep inside her already. She never would have survived those few days on board the stolen prison ship otherwise. But Binil wasn't in the habit of openly defying Sora Laakshiden either. It was because she'd abandoned the Cycomm girl that this happened. Without Sora's influence and Sellik and Cleo to back her up, Binil had made common cause—friends—with the humans. That little engineer, Reagan. And the more solid but far more devious one with the blue hair: Underhill. Binil was leaning on her new friends and Sora realized her mistake in abandoning her.

Sora backpedaled and tried again. "Never mind, I know what you said. What's your reasoning? What have I missed?"

"Sora, look at them. *Look*. This ship can pass for a Movi vessel, but these people can't pass for Movi. Ever. At best, we can introduce you as a Movi admiral—and then we'd have to explain how you came to oversee a Cycomm crew. Cycomms don't crew for Movi flag officers. But I can put on a fancy uniform, put the humans in opaque helmets with unique patches, and introduce you as my flag advisor. I'm a royal daughter of the House of Malala."

"You're a wanted criminal."

Binil rolled her eyes. "I doubt that Sense Ops has broadcast an arrest warrant for me this far into Movi space."

"Perhaps."

Binil took Sora's stare as an invitation to blunder ahead. "Rosenski's idea is just *simpler*. Do you see? If you can get a meeting with this archduke, I can go with you. Maybe Brooks and Reagan too. You make him an offer, he evaluates it, and we get go make a careful search around his office and data files." She tapped her eye ridge for emphasis.

Sora took her meaning: with implants, she could start breaking into the archduke's files and no one would know.

Binil continued, "I think it's a valuable source of information. I can't judge beyond that. I won't try. But... if we offer them *Hajimi,* all we give them is an aged ship in a fleet of much better armed vessels. But if we can make him think the primates—the *humans*—have access to a fleet of their own and are merely weighing their options... well. You have a lever to use on him."

The idea sounded fair and reasonable, which made Sora hate it even more. She wasn't prepared to write Binil off completely—she was still a door into a world that hadn't closed fully. But it was closing, and Sora decided to at least give the appearance of conciliation. She could work with this... whatever this was. The truth was that Sora wanted to know more about Binil's past than her brief history as a scrambler. She could be of use in a firefight—or an escape—but beyond that, she was a bit of a cypher. Time to change that.

Finally, Sora gave a single nod. "Very well. I leave the details up to you all."

Dance said, "Heh. *Captain* Binilsanetanjamalala. I like the sound of that. I can make the necessary changes in the ship's logs to reflect your new command status and add a few entries to make onlookers think we've visited Haven multiple times in the past year."

That was good enough to put Rosenski at ease. "I'll have the quartermaster come up with the correct patches and gear. Binil, you'll direct them?"

"Of course, Captain."

"Then let's get dressed. There's work to do."

CHAPTER 15

THEY SPENT ten days in transit and learned a ton about Movi paranoia in the process.

The first stage of their plan was simple; locate an M-boat broadcasting Mineko's invitation. One thing that Forsite-4095 had a plenty were comm logs. Laakshiden worked with Brooks in the comm center, off the bridge. He ran the filters, looking for coded phrases and other hidden clues. Sora knew what to scan for and directed him through his searches. Eventually, they picked out a set of co-ordinates and a few code phrases.

Brooks tapped the intercom. "XO to Nav."

"This is Nav."

"Marc, we have our first destination. The Fortalen system."

"Got it. I really love these Movi starcharts. So damn organized. It's about nine light years... heh... back the way we came."

"Make it happen, Mr. Janus. Let's see what the gravity drive can do."

"Aye, aye. Janus out."

Sora shifted in her seat. "You could have simply walked outside and spoken to him directly."

"But then who would keep you company?" Brooks asked

with his best smirk. Leaving the admiral on her own in the comm room was a bad idea. It was simple security. "But since this is *Hajimi's* maiden flight, would the admiral care to witness it from the bridge?"

"The admiral would."

Janus, Frost, and Skull were at their stations, and Rosenski sat in the big chair tapping her fingers furiously against the arm rest.

Janus played with his console. "Course plotted and confirmed."

"Jump when ready," Rosenski said.

Brooks took in a mental image of the ship shrinking in size, squeezed through a narrow tube, then shooting through it like a golf ball running through a fire hose. When his senses returned to normal, the star field was different and he felt a pop in the air around him.

Janus and Frost spent a full minute checking their work. "Destination achieved."

Skull groaned. "That was crazy."

"Did everyone feel that?" Rosenski asked.

"Are we there already?" Brooks wondered.

Sora sounded bored. "A ship this compact has a small gravity drive. I don't understand the nuances of physics, but it's easier to pass through several short warp tunnels than one long one. Ships like this can be very speedy at close distances."

Rosenski glanced at her passenger. "Good to know. Thank you. Simon, you and Admiral Laakshiden should probably find someone to send those passwords to."

"Right away, Captain. Admiral?"

"You don't need me to supervise you," Sora said. "You identify the nearest M-boat. Scan for a similar message from the archduke, reply using the passcodes we pulled from the previous transmission, and learn the next destination. It's simple. Any human could do it."

He kept his eyes on the board. The remark might have been a joke. Maybe she was mellowing. Maybe not. "You've just told me how. Makes things easier. What would I do without your help?"

Sora folded her arms. Eventually she said, "You're the type of person who picks fights he can't possibly win. How often were you beaten by the other children when you were in youngling care?"

"I used to play with the bears at the Northern Nature Preserve when I was a kid. My thirteenth birthday I faced down a 300-pound black bear with a knife and a spear. It took a piece of meat out of my leg and I stabbed it through the heart for its trouble."

"You're lying."

And you're a narcissistic, power-hungry psychopath who will happily set fire to everyone on this ship if it gets you five minutes closer to whatever reward you're hoping to get out of your rebel leader. Out loud, he said, "Admiral Laakshiden, please leave the comm center. Now." He tagged the intercom. "Lieutenants Reagan and Binilsanetanjamalala, report to the comm center immediately."

The two women arrived together in time to watch the Movi admiral skulk away to her cabin.

"I've never seen her so angry. What did you do?" Binil said.

"I pissed her off."

Reagan took her station and pulled out a spare jump seat for Binil. "In other words, it's Tuesday. What happened?"

"I told her the biggest most ferocious lie I could think of and she backed down."

"That was foolish," Binil said. "Take a care, Simon. She's still dangerous."

"I'll watch my ass. Anyway, she gave me a pattern to follow as we move up the layer cake. Judy, you help with the scans and retransmits. Binil, I need your savvy. You need to help pick out hints and clues in the messages that we humans might miss."

Binil leaned forward. "I think this OMP-style work is influencing you."

Rage flooded his body. The last thing in the universe he wanted to resemble was an OMP goon. Like Underhill. Deep in his heart he wanted to put a gun to that woman's head and pull the trigger. Nor was he alone: he glanced at Dance's hands, clenched into fists.

He waited for the fury to pass. "Thank you. Let's get started..."

Two more jumps took them well out of their way. Each time, M-boats responded to their hails by demanding their coded phrase, then sent them to the next destination. Skull wondered aloud if they were on a wild goose chase or if they were proceeding toward a trap laid by the loyalists, meant to snare reinforcements before they made common cause with Mineko's rebels. They traced the next link in the chain to a trinary star system twenty light years closer to the Movi homeworld. They popped out of their jump less than one AU from a gas giant surrounded by a dense ring of asteroids. The nearest star was thirty AUs distant, just another minor point of light in the sky.

Rosenski exhaled. "You know the drill, people. Let's find someone to talk to."

"I have them," Skull said. "It's no messenger boat this time. One of their mid-sized ships. Smaller than one of Mek's cruisers. A destroyer or escort, maybe? Three million klicks aft."

"Have they seen us?"

The comm board lit up. "We're getting hails," Brooks said.

Skull continued, "And now I'm seeing energy spikes. They're bringing their weapons to bear."

"From that range? Janus, if they drop missiles at us—"

"Yes, I can micro-jump us out of the way. Better not launch any fighters we want to keep," Janus said.

Rosenski leaned forward. "Brooks, answer them. Tell them your captain is considering whether she wants to talk to them. Be arrogant. We're Cycomms, damn it. We're joining the revolution because we want to. Domes up for all crew. The only face they should see on their screen is a Cycomm. Binil? Time to put that war face to good use. Get your ass in the big chair."

"This is the warship *Chouhsala*. I am Captain Touset. What is your business here?"

Binil launched into her new role, crossing her legs and leaning to the side just enough to seem bored. The new uniform suited her, full of dark colors and shining braid, handmade jewelry decorating her shoulders and collar. Dance had even taken a moment to go over her face with a cosmetic stick. Her rage eyes and stripes would appear permanent, probably confusing any Movi. "And what master do you serve, Touset?"

"If you didn't already know that you wouldn't be here. You have ten seconds to answer my question."

"Of course I do. Open fighter bay doors. Weapons are free. Comms center! Send this lackey the coded phrase which led us here."

Touset's face grew wary, then tensed while she spoke to people off screen. Binil fought down a wave of revulsion then harnessed it and turned it to anger. Her breathing quickened as adrenaline flowed into her body and her face markings grew darker. The crew obeyed every order. *Hajimi's* weapons were armed and primed, while the launch bay doors were opening and the fighters moving into launch positions. The only decision left to make was whether to stand firm or to taunt the Movi officer again.

"Must we go through with this?" she asked. "Or does Archduke Mineko lose *two* ships this day?"

She watched Touset's face go through a raft of probabilities. Yes, he'd probably win, but he'd take real damage in the process. Perhaps worse than he'd be able to repair out here. If the Cycomms were madmen, then perhaps it'd be better to let someone else take care of them for him.

A curt nod from the Movi captain. "Very well. I don't doubt your sincerity. But I insist on knowing your name."

"My ship is the *Hajimi*, my crew are my own, and my name is Binilsanetanjamalala. We have a contract with the Dal-Corstuni combine to provide escort and anti-piracy services to their passenger liners and cargo ships. Shall I send you my references?"

"I would appreciate that." Touset signed off. The screen went dark and Binil sagged as a wave of nausea took her. She avoided the dry heaves, barely. She felt a hand on her shoulder, Sara Rosenski staring with concern, her visor up.

"I told you to put on your war face, not shoot for an academy award," she said.

"It worked, didn't it?"

"We'll see. Comms, send that nice captain the ship's fake CV."

"Sent!"

Minutes passed. Binil kept the ship at battle stations, weapon turrets tracking their opponent, and all ten fighters formed a defensive ring ten klicks out, maintaining distance but not actually orbiting *Hajimi*. Pacing him.

Comms again. "Captain. They're signaling us."

Rosenski moved off-screen. Binil inhaled deeply and got back into character. "Put the maggots on screen."

"Captain Malala. We accept your addition to the Archduke's bold alliance. We are sending you to your next destination. I warn you—your next contact will not be so forgiving if you draw your sword."

"I see. And which officer might that be?"

Touset ignored her. "This is your destination and your coded response to any hails. If you deviate from either, you will be destroyed. Good luck."

CHAPTER 16

ROSENSKI CALLED A MEETING. Brooks, Binil, Underhill and Roberts, along with Skull and Frost squeezed into the narrow ready. "So, Gauntlets. Ideas for our next move?" Rosenski asked.

"If you deviate from either, you will be destroyed," Roberts quoted. "Makes you wonder if he's serious or just pissed off he got beat by a girl in racoon face paint."

"How about you focus on the problem," Underhill said. "Binil, I think your face paint is the shit."

"Thank you. I think."

"It's a painfully binary situation," Brooks said. "We go forward or we don't. If we go, it's a trap or it isn't. If it is, we die or we escape."

"Escape? What, to come back here?" Frost asked. "Is that why we're doing this?"

"We need Sora," Binil said. "I know no one wants to say it. It's still true."

Brooks sniffed. "She'll sell us out the first chance she gets."

"She's had chances. No treachery yet," Rosenski said.

"Yet."

Rosenski waved his concern away. "Be that as it may, she's

doing a fine job of playing a woman scorned. I invited her to this session. She's ignoring me. I think we all know why."

All eyes focused on Simon. "I... hell."

"We need her, Simon. Binil might be the only person on board who can get away with being short with her. Now fix this. We'll keep playing with ideas until you get back. With the admiral."

"Yes, Captain."

It was a short walk. Across the bridge, up a deck, then up the ladder to the forward airlock. The owner's suite, such as it was. He knocked on the door. "Request permission to speak with the admiral," he announced.

After a moment, the door chimed and in he walked. Sora was behind the narrow desk, scanning files on the display. "What is it?"

"You're right. I lied."

"I know." She watched him with an expression that made him wonder just how many times she'd gone through this ritual with her own officers. "I used your library database and looked up black bears. There's no way you killed one ten years ago. Or yesterday."

"No. My father was a park ranger. Intentionally harming the local wildlife was extremely illegal. I did encounter a few of them, but the rule was when the bears arrive, run the other way. Even cubs. Especially cubs. They're cute, but the mother is never far behind."

"Are you going to answer my question?"

He glanced at his feet, noted that his boots needed a shine. His lungs felt wet in his chest. Everything about her infuriated him. "I didn't have to worry about grade school fight clubs. The local school combined students from all over the area. We got along well. I think I got into one fight my sophomore year of high school. I lost, but I knew enough about poisonous plants to get even."

"Indeed. How so?"

"I snuck into the locker room during sports training, picked the combination to his locker, and smeared poison oak oil on every scrap of clothing he stuffed inside. It took months for the rash to finally disappear."

"How badly did that go for you?"

"I got away with it. You're the first person I've told."

"I see. Perhaps your Major Underhill chose well to put you under her command."

He focused on staring at her display. Underhill's name was too triggering for anything else. "Maybe. While we're all in this vessel, we remain a combined service. That includes you. I shouldn't have snapped at you. It was unprofessional and wrong. I beg your pardon."

"Did you practice that speech on your way up here?"

"No, Admiral. Just stating the truth."

She came around the desk. She was taller even than Sara Rosenski and he felt like a fourth grader trying to stare down a sadistic teacher. He'd hated that grade. They'd called him gifted and the stress to perform provided a crucible of sorts. He'd excelled out of spite, not ability.

"One confession deserves another." She popped open the buttons on her sleeve and rolled it up. When she finished, she brandished her forearm like a club. Brooks could see a network of fine white scars running up and down its length. A thick line of scar tissue ran from her wrist to her elbow. "Archduke Mineko does know me—very well. He mentored me for a year at the Royal War College. We met socially. Our families knew each other. Alliances were made."

"But his family didn't do that," Brooks said, pointing at her arm.

"In fact, they did. My first command was a destroyer escort. A small ship, not much bigger than this one, but with a prestigious lineage. One of Mineko's nephews thought that my command chair should have had his name on it. An operative of his put an explosive device in my quarters. Small, meant to disable, not kill. It did this."

"And you lost your command."

"Not at all. I had my chief surgeon put everything back in place and we departed port on time. This reminds me of what is possible."

"I can imagine."

"No. You can't."

He fought the urge to leave, to accept his loss with good grace. He felt the heat in his cheeks as his blood rose. "Commander Fairchild always said that you don't have to like the people you work with. Just do your job. Can we help one another do our jobs?"

"I think we must. That means including me at all levels of your operation. Do we agree?"

He couldn't get his mind out of grade school. The teacher was Mrs. Gold. He'd hated her beyond belief. "We do. Will you join the command meeting that's in progress?"

Sora buttoned her sleeve. "Why not?"

Everyone stood to attention when Sora arrived. Skull even offered her his seat, which she accepted with a smile. "So. What are we talking about? Let me guess... you've surmised that you're in over your heads and that this operation will be far more complicated than you first hoped."

Rosenski laid her tablet down and cleared the screen. Brooks noted that Roberts was nowhere to be seen but Underhill now sat in the chair he'd used. "That's an excellent sum up," she said. "Like it or not, we are all strangers in a very strange land here. Admiral, you're our local guide. We would like to hear what you have to say."

"You've no choice but to forge ahead. I think you know that."

"Do we?" Frost asked. "Seems like we can opt out at any time."

"If only you knew. You're trying to contact a known assassin. If you do or say anything that leads his faction to suspect your motives, they'll crush you out of a need for self-preservation. Make no mistake, Mineko's success is far from certain, and he knows betrayal could come at any time from any direction."

"You think they're tracking us?" Rosenski asked.

"They must be. I'd suggest you stop talking each other to death and follow their instructions immediately. We're on very unstable ground right now."

"What to do when we arrive is the next question, I think," Skull said.

"I can take care of them," Binil beamed. "I've had some practice."

For the first time, Sora's attitude softened a bit. "Binil, it was a good job. You even convinced me. But you won't be able to do it twice."

"Why not?"

"Because you bared all your teeth, and they know you don't have another mouth hidden away. I guarantee that Captain Touset sent all the data he collected about your weapons, defenses, and fighters to the next link in the chain. All they need do is surround this ship and we are out of moves."

"That might be the case anyway," Rosenski said. "You might convince the next interviewer to trust you, but we've established this is Binil's ship. How do we explain your presence?"

"Binil is the captain. Certainly. But I am the ship's owner. They'll see a retired admiral who made common cause with

Cycomm mercenaries in the past and decided the relationship was beneficial enough to maintain. It's not that complicated."

Rosenski waited for arguments; there weren't any. "All right then. Brooks, send your navigation data to the helm. Let's climb the next rung on the ladder."

It took two days for *Hajimi* to make the next destination. Two days of watching Sara Rosenski go a little crazy.

Brooks could do the work. It wasn't complicated, but there were procedures he was still learning. He couldn't explain the change in Rosenski's mannerisms since they'd begun hunting for what was essentially a rebel fleet. She paced, wandered, and poked her head into every compartment. She couldn't seem to figure out what to do with her hands. She *fidgeted*. Forget trying to work out comm filters; it made life as her XO excruciating.

Camping out in the comm room gave him a bit of solace, not the least because Dance Reagan spent time helping him run the comm board. Her presence reminded him of easy times, friendly environs, and regular sex. But that was before he'd become entangled in the OMP's spy games. Now he was her superior officer, and if that wasn't enough to put the brakes on any relationship they hoped to have, he was also working for the OMP. The rules were strict: keep your hands to yourself. If he didn't enforce the regs, Underhill would.

Once, when Dance left on an errand, Rosenski replaced her. Sara couldn't help but start asking questions, and Brooks answered. One after another, things he knew she already knew. His patience began to wear after a few minutes, trying to distill technical information into a form she'd comprehend. Eventually he snapped, "Are you taking notes for the Laynies or what?"

"Shut up," she snarled, and exploded out of the comm shack, nearly toppling Reagan who was on her way in.

Dance logged into the console. "What did you say to her?"

"Nothing."

"Six feet of pissed off redhead almost running me over is not 'nothing.'"

"Then it was nothing I should have said in public."

"To her, you mean?"

"To anyone. Especially to her."

"Simon, this is the second time you've done this."

"Sara knows better."

Dance leaned on him, eyes blazing. "Make it right with the CO or so help me, I will sell you to the first enslaver we find out here."

"Don't you hit me with that. Don't you even think about it. I make it right with somebody every fucking day. The admiral gets up my nose and I make it right. The overcop puts a bug in my head to make me do the jitterbug when she coughs and I have to make it right. I'm not here to *make it right*. I'm here to support the CO with the functioning of this ship and crew. And my CO deserves my best efforts and not a damn sight less." He avoided stepping on Reagan but he couldn't avoid the pain in her eyes on his way out of the office.

Finding his CO was easy; she'd headed to the galley for coffee. Figuring out what to say wasn't. He grabbed a handful of food bars from the galley stash and sat down at her table, dropping the loot between them.

"Go away, Simon."

"No. We're both under a ton of stress and we're both being weird, but I should know better. I want to help. How can I help?"

"You can't," she said. She pulled the wrapper off a bar and jammed it in her mouth, chewing like she hadn't eaten in days.

For all he knew, she hadn't "Not unless you can reverse time and convince me to not make some bad decisions."

He lowered his voice. "Then we agree that being a double agent is a bad move."

"It's so damn *complicated*," she whispered. She finished her meal and stuffed more food bars in her pockets. "Captain, I asked you about inspecting those fighters an hour ago. Are we going or not?"

"Sir, yes, sir!" Brooks knew a code phrase when he heard one. They'd done that inspection hours ago. He led her down more decks, grabbing a device from the ship's locker on the way. Once in the landing bay, he climbed into one cockpit and she got into another. They closed their canopies, Simon activated the Sleer comm booster, and they linked into their respective implants.

"And we are undetectable," Brooks announced. The tiny device set on his dash, readout blinking every few seconds. "It's just you and me. Not even the crew with implants can hear us. What's going on?"

"That woman is making me crazy," she groaned.

"Sora? Or Underhill?"

"Jesus. Both. I can't get within ten feet of either without my skin crawling."

"Oh thank God," he sighed.

"What?"

"I have the same reaction. Laakshiden reminds me of my fourth-grade teacher. I hated that woman. How do you work with soemone you know is leading you into a trap?"

"It's a trap for her, too," Rosenski said. "That works to our advantage. I think. I hope."

"She's going to stick it to us. The question is when," he said.

"Stop thinking that way. If we get clobbered, she dies, too."

Brooks shook his head widly enough to tap against the

canopy. "She told me that she and the archduke have a real history. And that's a problem. If we bring them together and they hit it off, come up with a deal to support each other, then we need a plan to get the rest of us out of their way. Because they're not going to have time to worry about our pathetic little lives."

"We'll have talk to Underhill."

"I don't want to talk to her... I want to put her down. Every time I look at her I get rage eyes."

"Knock that off. I hate her too, but she's our control. We must work with her. We'll come up with something. In the meantime, kiss whatever ass you have to to keep the admiral happy. This is Laakshiden's horse now; we're riding in the saddle bags."

CHAPTER 17

THEY GOT THEIR INVITATION.

For once, Sora Laakshiden lived up to her word. Mineko's people had scattered breadcrumbs across the kingdom, ensuring that anyone who wanted to could trace them back to an interview with one of the archduke's minions. It was a tiered system of ladders and traps. An applicant couldn't proceed to the next level without clearing the former. And killing the interviewer wasn't an option. Calls and responses were built into their scheme. By the time they met with Mineko's sector leader, they needed his personal recommendation to proceed. Sora poured on the charm, said all the right things. *Hajimi* crossed from their warp tunnel to normal space into a scene that seemed impossible to believe.

Sara Rosenski admired the new setting. "Good lord, Sora, where have you put us?"

Sora had never visited this system before, but she remembered enough about how depots were designed and administered to know what she was looking at. She had to admit respect for the human crew. The ship's tactical monitor and threat board were being populated by the sensor operator, more targets appearing each second. What probably got their attention first was the fact of thousands of defense satellites orbiting the outer reaches of the system. Less than a minute after their arrival, the sensor pings began to arrive too quickly to keep track of. In minutes they had a good picture of the nature of the installation.

"Welcome to Depot Three Nines, humans," the Movi said.

"Three nines? You mean like nine ninety-nine or twenty-seven?" Dance asked.

Sora fought to remain calm. Why did these pale people insist on complicating everything in the universe? "I mean it's shorthand for the system's characteristics. Nine planets, nine repair stations, nine assembly yards. Other depots are named for different reasons."

Rosenski glared. "And your archduke is here?"

"If our last interviewer was being honest, he'll be on the third one. If nothing else, we haven't been obstructed."

"Signal coming in," said Brooks. "It's the fourth planet but the third moon."

Rosenski took her place in the big chair. Since Sora had been doing most of the talking lately, there was no reason to play the role of Cycomm mercenaries anymore. All the same, Binil habitually stood next to Rosenski. Just in case. "This is the company command cruiser *Hajimi*. We request an audience with Archduke Mineko. We are here for his cause."

The viewer remained blank while a baritone answered. "Who speaks for you?"

"I do. First Admiral Sora Laakshiden. I believe we're expected."

A moment passed, then another. Rosenski started to fidget again. "Prepare to activate your communications display," said the voice.

Rosenski looked up. "You want to switch places, Admiral? Get the feel for it?"

"Yes. Let's. The bridge crew should have their helmets on and visors at peak opacity," Sora said. The imperious voice of command. No one argued for once. Perhaps they'd internalized how thin their chances of success were. About time. "Brooks! Display on!"

The display showed an office. A fancy one, with plush furniture and thick draperies but roughhewn walls and floors. There were no markings to show where he was. No bits of scenery. The faction leader was inside the moon somewhere, deep in a secure installation. And in the center, sitting on a perfect replica of the Vermilion Throne, was the man himself.

"First Admiral Laakshiden. I'm surprised and pleased to see you in command of your own ship again. And with a Cycomm advisor, no less. You've come quite some way from prison. I take it Marauder's Moon treated you well. You seem to be running the place."

"Not exactly, Your Grace. I think you can recognize my reason for wanting to join your uprising."

"Neither of us have much reason to look to the royal family for restitution for grievances. That's true enough. Your ship has a shuttle?"

"Of course."

"Then you'd better come down in person. Bring the Cycomm and any staff you need. I'll send you the location of the meeting shortly. And thank you again for believing in me." The screen darkened and Brooks let them know they were off the air.

"That man intends to kill you," Rosenski said.

"He wants to drain my brain first. For all he knows, I really do run that penal colony. However, for once, I think you're right," Sora admitted. "You'll need to stay here. If events go badly, we will escape to a place where you can retrieve us. Binil will come with me, since he specifically requested it. It'd be rude to do otherwise. I think I can pass one more person. Your choice, *Captain?*"

Rosenski turned her head. "Simon. You're on deck. We'll use the dropship. We—"

"No. You'll need to land the vessel. This ship is designed for atmospheric entry."

"Admiral," Rosesnki said, a pedantic tone in her voice, "That's not advisable. There's a military base with defenses down there. All it takes is a moment of haste or panic for them to shoot us down. If we lose this ship, we can't get another."

"They wouldn't dare."

Rosenski said, "They might or might not. We don't know. The dropship is safer. It's better able to handle combat in an atmosphere, and three times faster than this vessel. We'll go with UEF doctrine." She turned to Brooks. "Get the platoon organized and full gear loaded aboard the dropship. The ship will drop you three at the designated location and move off, out of sight. Anything goes wrong, you let the squad leader know first. Understood?"

"Yes, ma'am."

"Get to it, people. On the boost."

The next hours were rote and routine. Sora stood by while the humans scurried to do their work. It turned out they had brought a squad of soldiers with them, ground troops who worked with their dreaded OMP. Black armor that resembled Sleet battle dress, but with different rank insignia and unit patches. She wondered if any suits of royal marine flight armor were in ship's lockers. They'd been designed from the boots up to best any Sleer defenders they might encounter, but they were expensive and needed to be fitted to an individual on a case-by-case basis. She couldn't imagine Anterran parting with such equipment, but you never knew. The primates were clever, if nothing else. She could imagine them constructing their own variants from schematics and diagrams. They had, after all, managed to build this ship... with Sleer help. Everything came back to that.

She descended to the flight deck and stayed out of the troops' way, watching them prepare for the mission. The so-called dropship was no military vessel, more like a pinnace with variable-wing geometry, with landing skids and an armored ramp for the vehicle to roll on and off. Two compartments forward the drop bay one for cargo, another for passengers. It was all simple. Methodical. Linear. Like their imagination. Since she depended on their cooperation for the time being, she kept her opinions close, but a single company command cruiser wasn't meant to be much more than a flying garrison. Brought up to current tech levels, they could install displacement projectors and a platoon's worth of drop pods and they could pop every soldier and piece of equipment outside the ship in seconds. That was how you overwhelmed an enemy with myriad moving parts.

A First Warlord would have known all that. Perhaps he'd taken the humans at their word that they were meant to blend in with military traffic. Or perhaps he was sending them to their doom and didn't care. Or did he care instead about removing *her* from the board as well as a flock of annoying aliens? It was certainly possible. If she and Mineko made an alliance and she stuck to its terms, she'd have to betray Anterran one way or another. He'd know that, too. Perhaps the last thing he wanted was to elevate her to true opponent status. She could go mad wondering about moves and countermoves. Who knew what any faction was up to anymore?

She distracted herself by concentrating on the interaction between Binil and Brooks. They didn't hate each other exactly, but they were unflinchingly polite to each other. She'd seen both interact with Lt. Reagan, though. Each was far more open and demonstrative with her. *She* was the key to their relationship. Without Reagan between them acting like a nuclear control rod, they were like two radioactive piles, heating each other uncontrollably. Eventually they'd melt. Interesting.

The prep ended, the troops boarded. Binil ducked through the passenger hatch and Brooks beckoned. "Admiral? Ready for an elevator ride you'll never forget?"

It took effort for her to comply. The dark interior engulfed her and the seats designed for humans made her aware of how her body differed from theirs. They squeezed her bottom and the roll cage barely fit over her. Then the lights went to red lamps, the engines whined, and Sora closed her eyes against the sights and her ears against the noise. If she could only close her guts to the nausea that roiled them now. She kept her mouth shut for the trip, not wanting to accidentally scream in terror. She had no idea that the humans had coined a word for her tendency to avoid dark narrow spaces: claustrophobia.

The pull of acceleration and Sora felt as if she was slipping out of her seat, her ass sliding over the edge, her feet kicking out in front of her. The engines cut out and she relaxed a bit, the normal gravity giving her a chance to verify her feet were planted firmly in the floor, her ass in the seat. Then the atmosphere grabbed the ship and the cabin shook and bounced. Sora forced her eyes open, saw Binil and Brooks seated opposite her, no happier but used to this abomination of a transport method. Binil offered a weak smile, but Brooks winked at her, the little monster. She'd see both of their heads on spikes if she could. The drop ship hit an airpocket, dropped like a rock, and Sora clenched her jaw while a spurt of acid burped into her throat. She forced it back down, her throat on fire.

The lamp switched from red to yellow and the flight calmed considerably. The engines flared again, then went silent. She opened her eyes to green lamps and the others pulling their harnesses apart. She followed their effort and made sure she was the last to leave the cabin.

"Never again," she murmured, not caring if anyone heard.

Archduke Mineko's base of operations was less of an armed camp and more of a command-and-control operation. The defensive batteries and fighters were located on a proper military base, and their escort—four soldiers in flight armor and heavy sidearms—hustled the three visitors into an armored air car. The moon's landscape gave way to rocky, broken terrain of gray and mottled browns. The road was barely visible, a suggested path instead of a sealed route. They turned into the mountains, dipped into a tunnel, and never emerged. Down through the tunnel network, finally stopping in a well-lit cavern, where an assortment of armored vehicles stood watch. Through a series of corridors guarded by armored doors and finally into an office.

"Sora! How you have come up since we last met."

Sora wondered when his excellency became quite so paranoid. She remembered a fair amount about Archduke Mineko, but not how old he was. He was at least thirty years her senior and she noted his bulging middle and the crow's feet around his eyes. His teeth and eyes were perfect, however. Clearly, time had been good to him but he was losing the fight with entropy. Still, he presented the image of a vital, healthy man, very well.

Not to mention the women. He was surrounded by them. They managed his affairs, staffed his office, ran his errands, sent and received his messages, prepared his food. A harem in all but name. Good for him, she supposed. The archduke led them into a dining area. Servitors put down plates and flatware, while others filled them with food. Another poured tea into thick mugs. The two of them sat while Brooks and Binil waited beyond a set of drawn privacy curtains.

"There were a few fits and starts between my commission and my mustering out of the service," she allowed. Sora flicked a napkin into her lap. "You helped me weather a storm of my own. I don't remember if I thanked you properly for that. I do so now."

"That was a very long time ago. And Captain Serekh wasn't worth protecting. The man in his own lieutenancy made an error in judgement that nearly lost him a destroyer. I covered that up for him, too. My sister begged for the favor—I thought it would be churlish to refuse. It turned out to be a mistake. But you did nothing wrong, so it seemed a good bet to cut my losses and back a better officer. Lieutenant to admiral in less than fifteen years. Not bad at all."

She smiled at him, both from the recognition and from her sense of relief at being in the company of her own people. "You flatter me, sir."

"Not at all. But I do wonder at your arrival here. Now. With this crew. And that wreck of a ship. Not to mention that so-called shuttle you arrived on. I doubt it's merely to catch up on old times. So... be brave."

She remembered that phrase. "Be brave." It meant "do the hard thing when the easy thing would suffice."

"You have me at a disadvantage."

"Now you're wasting my time. I have a rebellion to run. I'm not in the best position. If I remember accurately, you're in a poor place yourself. There was a notice about being convicted of espionage by the Cycomms?"

"A misunderstanding, Your Grace."

"Now you're lying. Finish your lunch. I have work to do." He rose from the table and Sora took her last chance. This was for all the cards.

"I have an offer," she said. She sat straight, did her best to project authority. She was good at it. "I have access to Zluur's gun destroyer and the mechanisms within. Please don't tell me you wouldn't find that useful."

"I won't. But I see two of your crew. I don't see a gun destroyer."

"Brooks. Binil. Attend! Remove your helmets." They complied, and Sora fought not to grin as Mineko's face transformed into a stone mask. "The woman is a Cycomm who I escaped Marauder's Moon with. She's an excellent scrambler, imaginative, and quick witted. The man is an officer—a human —from Zluur's ship. He has a unique relationship with its controlling AI, called Genukh. Without him I doubt these humans would have managed to bring the ship so far so quickly."

"And what is Sora Laakshiden to you two?" Mineko demanded. He nodded toward Brooks. "You. Brux. *Human*. Why are you here?"

"My government ordered me to assist her in seeing what kind of reception we might receive should we decide to help settle this internal dispute."

"All by yourself? I had no idea your people were so dangerous."

"We have a saying, sir. 'Fuck around and find out.'"

"How delightfully aggressive," he said, turning to Binil. "And you, my dear. What's your story?"

"Sora helped me avoid a life sentence on a penal moon. I'm returning the favor."

"Splendid. Neinei, set plates for the new people. Sora, you've found the aid of two entirely competent individuals here, and I assume the sources they represent. Why do you need my help?"

"Change requires power. You have it, and these ones don't.

At least not yet. A bit like children they are: curious and ambitious, but unaware of how things in the kingdom work. What if we took the children under our wings and taught them the meaning of real power? Wouldn't you say that's worth the chance to gain access to Haven and Zluur's secret weapon?"

"You might very well think that. All right then. Let's figure something out."

CHAPTER 18

AFTER LUNCH, the staff cleared the places and Mineko invited them into a proper office. One wall was covered in displays, every one of them active. A heavy wood desk, brown and polished to a shine was his domain, covered in reports and data chips. A ceremonial pistol lay to one side, within the owner's easy grasp. The three guests sat before it on wiry metal chairs.

Mineko settled himself and looked at Brooks. "Talk to me, human. It's easy to blather on about secret weapons, but show me results. Those are priceless. You'll forgive me for not taking your word about Zluur's ship at this exact moment. But tell me what you know about my situation, and we'll work from there."

Brooks nodded. "I can see you have three big problems. The first is that you murdered your sovereign. You'll forgive me for saying I don't think you can sweep that under the proverbial rug."

"Nor will I try. I claimed the Vermilion Throne. It'll take a while, but if I celebrate my accomplishments, eventually, others will celebrate with me."

"Possibly," Brooks said. "On the other hand, you also got the chance to broadcast your manifesto across the entirety of the kingdom before the royal palace or anyone else could rebut your statements. That probably helped soften the blow, but it's still problematic. The longer this conflict goes on, the less power your words will have."

"Possible. What else?"

"I think the element of surprise worked in your favor. Clearly, the system that you've all been working through has become rotten, and if all it took to topple it was one assassination, I'd say you chose well indeed."

"Indeed. And?"

"And you're in the middle of nowhere. The so-called Garrison Cluster is very close to Haven, which isn't known for being an aggressively colonial power. But they will cut your throat if they think you intend to make their world your possession. If what Binil tells me about her society is at all accurate, you're holding a tiger by its tail."

"The first three exploration missions from Movra to Haven never returned. There's a reason for that," Binil said.

Mineko said, "I'm assuming you both mean that I'm taking an enormous risk by occupying this part of space. That's a fair point. It's balanced out by the fact that Anterran runs the three depots closest to the Sleer border."

Brooks said, "And both of you benefit from the fact that the Sleer empire is collapsing further every day. The Skreesh are running through their part of the galaxy and it's only been luck that's kept them away from Movi space. In principle, that could change tomorrow."

"But it won't."

"No? Why?"

"The key to success is knowing your opponent's strengths and using it against them. I knew that the Skreesh were making another incursion through this arm of the galaxy, and I knew where it would come. They send another incursion wave every few thousand years; each incursion varies its course down this galactic arm. Their last two incursions swept to trailward of the Movi kingdom and the last one drove straight through our territory. The Westron Marches. My home sector."

"The cyber-lord uprising," Sora gasped.

"As you say. The Skreesh were coming and the cyber-lords decided they could handle the fallout on their own. They were wrong. So, when the Skreesh came close I nudged them toward the rebellious worlds. What the Skreesh shock troopers didn't finish, I did. It was easy enough to leave out a few salient details from my report to the royal court, and I got a dukedom for my troubles."

"Not a bad mission, then. For you," Brooks said.

"Not at all. After that it was easy enough to predict that the current Skreesh foray would drive through the Sleer and they did. I couldn't risk breaking my own holdings without knowing the Sleer would be unable to take advantage of the situation. With no Sleer fleets guarding their home territory the time to strike became obvious. I did. If I don't waste my fleets, I have a solid chance at winning this. And here we are with you claiming that you humans have a hand in managing the Skreesh. I hope that's true, for your sake. Because if it's not true and the Skreesh wipe you out as well, that leaves the Movi prepared to inherit this arm of the galaxy."

"If you can come out on top," Brooks said.

"It's a risk. But I have a solid plan."

Brooks refused to let go. "But you murdered the sovereign and his family. There's no way the royal court will trust you. And there's no way you can trust someone in your employ from stabbing you in the back at some point soon. The Macchiavelli school of politics works wonders for a while, but it gets old very quickly."

Mineko turned to Sora and brought every ounce of hauteur

to bear. "Do you know why the Cycomms made off with you, Sora? You listen to people like him."

"Yes, I listen. Because there's an opportunity to—"

Alarms sounded and the holo image grew as the display zoomed in on the main planet. In a wink, twenty planetoid size ships emerged from jump space. Including the *Night Render*.

"An opportunity for you to sell me out to that establishment cretin, I see. There's only one way that could have happened. Well played, Sora."

"I didn't do it. It was—"

"Just a lucky break on Anterran's part. I'm sure."

Sora sputtered, "He— I— We—"

She never finished. Armored doors closed all around the office except for a back exit, which slid open for a quartet of armored battle troops. They weren't wearing the full-size flight armor, but something similar. Dead black armor plates linked together with flexible joints. They looked like evil versions of the Sleer battle dress, only slimmer, taller, far more flexible. Unlike the Sleer who waddled even in full flight, these troops moved like machines.

Brooks heard Mineko's order as a shout, but his Sleer implants flickered then failed. Suddenly, not only couldn't he understand Sora's shouted reply, but he could barely move. He realized that he—they—had fallen into a trap, and no mere speed bump or stumbling obstacle. This trap was vicious, with steel doors and sharpened spikes lining the walls and three feet of hydrochloric acid at the bottom. They'd turned his Sleer implants off. He had no HUD, no comms except for what the ship was already using. But his ability to network with digital systems—all of it was gone. He was just plain old Simon Brooks now, and he felt so slow, like he was dragging lead streamers that clung to his limbs. They were so *heavy*...

Normal human strength and endurance against Movi training and whatever natural gifts Binil brought with her.

Binil.

Binil! Yes!

He tapped her boot with his own, nodded to the security people. Once, twice, three times. She barely nodded, unseen by anyone but him. He tapped her hands with his fingers... three... two... one... now!

Brooks pulled a flash-bang grenade off his belt and lobbed it across the room. Binil pulled out all the stops and flicked her mind at the intruders, fully aware of the damage she might do to herself. The room erupted into flame and noise as the trigger of every weapon depressed all at once, the security team unable to fight through its surprise and alarm at the inability to control their weapons. Brooks barely dropped in time to pull the Cycomm down with him. The air erupted into a blinding flash and explosion as the grenade detonated. Then they fled, on the boost, jumping over the archduke's desk and bounding through the distracted security troops.

They ran through an armored door, Brooks punching the frame where he thought to latch plate would be. It closed, but he didn't know how to lock it, and he was out of surprises. Binil dropped to the floor, her torso and limbs flopping in a seizure. Brooks tore off his helmet and got to his knees. He felt for the catch on her helmet, then twisted and pulled it free, trying not to get the air hose wrapped around her neck. She made animal noises as she thrashed. He felt through his pockets for the syringe he'd stashed before they left the ship. He pulled it out, snapped a vial of Sleer microbes into the chamber and pressed it against her neck, pressed the plunger with his thumb. Behind him, the sounds of metal pounding on metal rang. They were coming through—or trying to. Maybe he'd managed to lock the door.

He pressed a stud on her armor, watched her vitals. Still alive, good, good. The Sleer microbes Dance pushed on him earlier would fix her or they wouldn't. In either case they needed to leave before reinforcements showed up. He pulled her arms, adjusted the weight, and rose in a fireman's carry, Binil slung across his shoulders.

He took a few steps to figure out a gait that wouldn't trip him on his face. Don't spill the wounded soldier, was an easy rule to follow. He was regretting the loss of his implants, and kicked himself for forgetting about the Movi military's use of jammers. She wasn't heavy, but while he was burdened with her, he couldn't do anything else with his hands. He turned the corner, found another hallway, and another and another. The armored hatch ahead of him looked different from the earlier ones. Like the sort of thing that would separate compartments. Maybe a route to an escape route. Or even a location where he could call the dropship for a pickup.

He set Binil down, leaned her against the wall, and tried to shift mental gears from EMT to breacher. Electronic lock, okay. He had his tool kit with him—he just needed to figure out the combination.

The sound of boots thundering down the hall behind him. He knew what he'd see before he turned.

"Brooks! Breaker take you, little man!" Sora Laakshiden stopped just out of range, pointing a wicked-looking carbine at him. Her eyes full of more rage than he thought she could hold. His hand went to his hip, clutching for a pistol that wasn't there, then remembering they'd come unarmed. How he'd snuck the flash-bang down here astounded him.

He nodded to her weapon. "They patted down the two of us for contraband. They let you keep *that*?"

Sora grinned at him, her teeth gleaming in the harsh light. "Certainly not. Paranoid men stash weapons everywhere if you know where to look," she snarled. She pulled the trigger and Brooks flew backwards against the hatch and he was on his ass looking up at the insane Movi admiral. His chest was on fire and he was stunned by the impact and pain.

"Another one bites the dust," he said. He cast his gaze around, scanning walls, ceiling, and direction they'd come. Nothing. The only weapons he carried were his arms and legs. He rolled over to rise and felt his jaw explode as Sora kicked him in the face. So much for that plan.

"Oh, I didn't kill him," she crowed. "I didn't have to. When things went poorly, he ran for a door. His guards ran with him. That's one thing you can count on men for. They always run when things go badly. I found this under his desk." He hefted the carbine.

"Not all men," Brooks groaned, and spat out a wad of bloody tissue. And maybe a tooth. He wasn't sure. He could barely see, his face was on fire, his right eye was a red blur. He scrabbled backwards, unable to stand. But crab-walking, that he could do.

Sora dropped her eyes, flicked her gaze from him to Binil and back. "No, not all men. Not you. You stayed with her. With *them*," she snarled. "If I'd had anyone who attended me as you do them, I might have made better choices. A better career. A life that didn't involve constant anxiety punctuated by moments of terror. Your women don't deserve anyone like that. That... loyal."

He focused on the weapon in her hands, sorting through what facts he could recall about Movi weaponry. The Movi rifles were of a different order of weapon than the giant Sleer fusion rifles. The Sleer weapons were designed to hit heavy armor and make dents in starship hulls, fusing hydrogen nuclei until they essentially shot barely controlled nuclear explosions. The Movi gauss rifle was a far more delicate type of weapon.

Designed for use indoors, they used linear motors to accelerate a hollow core needle toward its target. They were almost noiseless and very light, and you didn't need heavy protection to use one. Not very good against armor, but one could shred a human body.

"We can still salvage this," he said. He got to his feet, struggled to stand, even stay awake. Darkness threatened to pull him down. "If you want to be on the same side... fine. Let's be on that side. Not stab each other in the back. Or face."

"I *will* salvage this. But you won't be there. None of you will be on Movra when I arrive!"

"I get you," he said. He held his hands open before him, pleading. His jaw and eye were swelling, and he fought to get his words out. "It's the same everywhere. Power corrupts. Attracts the worst actors. They all think they're heroes. They don't have to clean up the blood. Bury the bodies. Smell the fear, the shit, the piss of a battlefield. The army thinks the flyers sit on their assess all day, but we watch our friends disappear in flames too. You wouldn't think driving an armored robot would be terrifying, but it is. My whole unit keeps having to save my ass every damn time. If it's not the Sleer it's you bastards. So here we are, *Admiral*. You want a plan that gets you to the top of the layer cake, fine. Do it yourself. Frankly, you're not worth a single member of my unit much less the whole ship. Now either shoot me or not, I got shit to do."

"Goodbye, you... human!" she cried, and pulled the trigger.

Sora clearly had some experience with the weapon and hosed Brooks with the full clip. Simon pulled a mech maneuver and brought up his forearms in a block, dropping to his knees to make himself a smaller target while letting the armor's shields take the brunt of the damage. Sora took advantage of his relatively immobile position to rush him, swinging her rifle like a club and connected a solid *thwack* against his unprotected head.

Brooks took the blow full on and collapsed, driven backwards to lie limply against the near wall.

"You little shit, I'll buy my war fleet with your corpse!" Sora growled and squeezed, pressing in with her thumbs against Brooks's windpipe. With the combination of size and weight already on her side, Sora would always have the advantage. But with righteous fury powering her attack, Brooks had no chance at all. His entire body hurt, and he was done with social engineering tricks. His attempt to talk Sora down was it. He had nothing left. Even now he brought up his reserves of strength, raised his arms and tried to shove Sora away bodily, fingers probing for weak spots on her face: eyes, nose, mouth, but the Movi was adamant. Brooks might as well have tried to gouge a statue. All he did was enrage her further and now animal sounds erupted from her throat, a primal scream of rage.

Brooks's throat closed, the oxygen in his blood running thin and he unable to draw another breath. He twisted his body, muscles straining, every nerve screaming while his vision blurred and narrowed.

Panic set in and he punched and struggled, but he was so damn tired and his head was going to explode.

A roar against her ear and Brooks found himself on the floor in a heap. Another roar and another. He watched Sora fly through the air, then land on her back, a pool of dark blood seeping from beneath her.

Brooks drew a gasping breath and then coughed for what seemed forever. Now a pair of hands pulled him up by the armpits and he found himself being dragged backwards, his heels sliding across the smooth floor. He twisted again, got his feet beneath him, and waved the helper away. He could do this.

"Can you walk? We need to leave."

"I'll dance out of here if I have to," he said, turning to find Binil.

"What about Sora?" she asked. "I... hope she's not dead. I didn't mean to kill her."

He needed to get away. Out of the damn rebel base. Someplace where the paranoid archduke hadn't planted Sleer implant-suppression gear. "Fuck her. We're on our own. Friends like here we don't need. Ever. Let's go."

He fought through the pain to stand, reached out and held still as she ducked under his arm and steadied him. They shuffled down the hall. "Where'd you get the antique?" he asked, pointing to the spent pistol in her hand.

Binil didn't seem to know what she meant until he tapped the pistol. "Oh, I grabbed it off his muckety muck's desk as I went over. Ceremonial. Three shots. Enough to take out one crazed officer," she said. "I hope she's dead. That would be a relief. But I'm afraid she can't die. She's like those stories about demons that just keep going..."

"We have those. We call them revenants. So angry in life, they raise themselves after dying and look for revenge."

"That sounds delightful. What happened? We were in the office..."

"Yeah. Their weapons went haywire. That was you, I expect..."

"Yes."

"I threw the one grenade I snuck past the guards, then you started seizing. I futzed the door, injected you with a mess of Sleer microbes to make sure your brain didn't explode, and ran with your unconscious ass. I stopped at the door when her nibs arrived."

"Thank you. Work on the next door. I'll stomp on her face if she revives."

"Awesome." He broke out his kit and starting jabbing sensors and probes into the mechanism. "Tell me something, Binil. Why do you think they turned you in when they found out you had the ability? You'd think the Sense Ops brass would want every scrambler they could recruit."

"Possible. I haven't had much chance to consider it."

"I'm guessing royal daughters don't get sent to penal colonies just for jollies."

"No. They shouldn't, should they? What *did* happen?"

"You want to find out? For real?"

"Yes. What do we do?"

"First, we get back to *Hajimi*. Then we go the one place the Movi won't come looking for us."

"Haven. Oh, no. *No.*" She shook her head wildly, wobbled, slumped against the wall and stopped.

"I'm not trying to be sadistic when I say that, you know. Sometimes, to make things right with your family you need to deal with family. Up front and personal."

"Malkah protect me from your scrambled logic. Maybe you're right." She raised her head. "I see a floor plan. A layout of the place."

"You're a clairvoyant, too? That's new. And kind of neat. Can you—?"

She pointed. "Look at the wall. A floor map." She led him to the lit panel, and she spent a moment swiping to find their position then showing him a route out. The trouble was that there were no pathways that didn't take them past multiple checkpoints and monitoring stations. And there surely were cameras watching every corridor, even if they couldn't see them. Eventually, a possibility became clear. "Here. If we avoid everything and climb up to this watchtower, there's a landing platform."

"It'll be too small for the *Hajimi* to dock."

"But your drop ship might. No?"

"Let's give it a shot." He tapped his comm. "Landing party to Dropship-1. Mission fail. We are on our way out. Meet us at the exit hatch at these co-ordinates."

CHAPTER 19

THE DROPSHIP STAYED low and found Brooks and Binil as they exited the escape hatch. The armored airlock was barely the size to admit humanoid beings, much less any armored vehicles.

The pinnace hovered twenty meters away, six of *Hajimi*'s OMP soldiers outside it waiting for them, covering their escape. Brooks thought he heard gun fire as he and Binil climbed into the rear hatch, then an explosion. Or two. Or more. The troops followed them in, the doors closed, and the pilot angled the craft so steeply it took real effort to climb back to their seats and strap in.

Then a yell from the flight deck. "Contacts!"

And an answer. "Deploy full cover!"

"Yes, sir!" The engines flared and the pilot seemed to drive the pinnace straight up, forward weapons arrays releasing hordes of explosives that disappeared into the sky. At one point, the small craft shook them like dice in a tumbler.

Brooks reached up to the first aid kit and pulled it into his lap, fumbling for a vial of Sleer repair microbes. He put the contents into his implanted injection port, twisted and dropped the empty vial. He felt better almost immediately and tapped his comm. "What the hell did you use?"

Simon's comm beeped as the pilot bridged the channel. "Literally the only tac nuke we brought with us. You're welcome."

Whether the response scared the security forces into compliance, or the archduke's staff decided the quarry wasn't worth it, the pinnace met *Hajimi* on the other side of the world without further interference. They docked, shut their bay doors, and used the ship's warp tunnel drive to speed away from any pursuers.

———

Binil and Brooks lay in adjacent cots in the sick bay. Dance hovered over them as the bio-beds did their work. When Rosenski arrived, it became an impromptu briefing. "So. No treaty. No Sora. Now what?"

"I can think of a few possibilities," Brooks said "but I have no idea which makes most sense right now."

"Let's hear them, if you're well enough."

Third Lieutenant "Jersey" Shoar—the closest thing they had to a doctor this far into enemy territory—tried to intervene. "He's not well enough. Neither of them are fit to do anything but lie there for at least another two days. They both have multiple concussive trauma."

Brooks waved him off. "We both have Sleer microbes in us. We'll deal."

"We'll talk here, Jersey. They won't leave. Promise," Rosenski said. Shoar took a final reading and slouched out of the tiny room.

"First, we could go to Haven to try to bring Binil's origin to light," Brooks suggested.

Binil shook her head. "I don't like that idea."

"Me neither," said Dance. "The last thing we need is a planet full of psychic soldiers who will know we're not locals long before we drop from orbit. Next?"

Brooks traced a zero in the air with his finger. "Next we try to sell ourselves to the First Warlord."

Rosenski said, "You do remember he's the one we got this leaking spaceship from, right? Anterran won't listen to us now."

"Why not? If Mineko hit him—"

Rosenski said, "They hit each other. Mineko hit the warlord in mid-jump, and then the warlord returned the favor when he tracked down Mineko's base of operations. It's two giants battling in a town."

Underhill rapped on the door frame and came forward, making it a point to stand well away from Brooks or Rosenski. "Realistically? We can stay and bounce around to various worlds, intercepting whatever transmissions we can. We can head to Haven and present them with whatever plan we come up with in the aftermath of a huge fiasco. Or we can go back to Great Nest."

"Or we can go home," Brooks said quietly. After a moment, he noticed he had the room's attention. "I mean it. Earth is still there. Moruk and Grossusk know who we are. We might be in a position to barter intelligence on the Movi civil war in exchange for access to the battle ring."

Skull coughed for attention from out in the corridor. He managed to wedge himself past Underhill, got stuck with her in the doorframe and winked at her. "I don't know about that. Grossusk was very specific. The ring is theirs. The planet is ours. And he still has a few billion Sleer to back up his claim."

"The planet is falling apart. I looked at the climate data before we left. It's a mess," Brooks said. "Worse, anyone who thinks the Sleer won't use their recycler drones on human cities once the easy resources run low is living in a fool's paradise."

Rosenski said, "Anyway, the Sleer high command won't care about Earth's weather or the state of the people living on her. What else?"

Underhill said, "We could talk to the Movi ourselves. Head to their homeworld. If we pass ourselves off as Cycomms we might learn something."

"Sora did seem to think that was where all her roads led. I seem to remember trying that already. I don't recall quite how it came out... oh yes, we got our asses handed to us," Binil said.

Underhill smirked. "No. We pass ourselves off as *humans*. We go in and try to make a deal ourselves," Underhill said.

Dance looked up. "With whom?" Dance asked.

Underhill put a tablet into Rosenski's hands. The screen filled with captured footage of crowds. "With these guys. They call themselves the Iria Sisterhood, after the former sovereign's oldest daughter. Iria was apparently the one who was expected to ascend to the throne after the sovereign's death. It's kind of a rabble. Like they have supporters from all over the kingdom. Merchants, world leaders, a few military officers—but they don't have the numbers or the connections to make a stand anywhere in particular. I think we can contact them and ask for help."

Binil turned to lie on her side. "Why would they help a bunch of spying humans?" Binil groaned, propping herself up on one arm.

"A bunch of spying humans in a Movi warship. It's a crappy ship but we have it, we know how to use it, and we have access to Zluur's gun destroyer *and* our own battle ring," Underhill said.

Binil frowned. "They'd care about that?" Binil said.

"No idea. But we can meet them and figure out what happened. If we let it be known that Mineko basically aided and abetted the Skreesh invasion of Sleer space—and possibly ours if we wait long enough—then they may find a reason to look further into his affairs."

Rosenski let out a long sigh. "I do think it's worth it to see if we can find a sympathetic ear among one or more factions," Rosenski said. "And everything we learn becomes another bit of intelligence Earth can use in future conflict. Because with the Sleer out of action, I can't see how it can go anywhere except for a military contest between Earth and the Movi. We do that now, we lose."

Dance raised a hand. "With respect to the Major," Reagan said, "none of this changes the fact that to contact a resistance group you need a connection. We had the wayward admiral to get to the rebels. I don't see any connections between this bunch and those Iria women."

"May I see that?" Binil reached out for the tablet and peered intently at the screen. "I have a connection." Binil pulled at the image, zooming in on a stage. "Do you see these two women flanking the speaker? Their names are Cleo and Sellik. They were Sora's henches when we were aboard the prison barge. They know who I am. They may even be a little afraid of me."

"What happened?"

"I almost stopped Sellik's heart when she got me mad enough. I started it again, but I don't think she's forgotten that day. I know I haven't."

"You've been holding out on us, Cycomm."

"Perhaps. They all escaped in the *Cyclops* during the battle in Great Nest. I wonder what made them split up?"

"Relax, it's a good thing that you have some historical bits. How do we go about finding these people?" Dance said.

Underhill shoved Skull out of the door and pushed her way into the tiny room. "Roberts and I have been watching the feeds.

This broadcast comes from one of the major cities on Movra, very close to the royal palace, even."

Binil reached into the display to change the settings. "Wasn't the palace in chaos? I remember seeing clips of those giant spherical ships firing on the royal palace," Binil said. Her arms finally gave out and she rolled onto her back, the display glowing as she dropped the device in her lap.

Underhill reached out to adjust the display. "I saw the same clips," said Underhill. "But that action was happening on a neighboring world. Even stranger, it wasn't a current war fleet. That clip was created years ago. It's a recording of Mineko's attack on one of the cyber-enhanced army's worlds three sectors away." She pulled up a clip from the data banks and played it, then played the historical version side by side. There was no question they were looking at the same clip. "Whoever ran this through the broadcast meant to make problems for the assassin. That means they had a reason. It's not beyond Iria's Sisterhood. I think they had a hand in it."

"But what makes you think they were involved with that broadcast in particular?" Dance asked.

Binil closed the display and fell back against her bed. "Sellik is a plug, but she knows communication technique and hardware. Cleo knows the intricacies of the royal court. Both needed a new sponsor when Sora clearly tossed them aside."

"You're sure Sora didn't drop them off on Movra to set this up before going on her own mad scramble for power?"

Binil winced. "I don't think so. Sora is many things, but she's no assassin. Her imagination just doesn't work that way. She's a soldier through and through. She's consistent as a clock."

Rosenski looked around the table. "All right then, if no one has anything better—?" No one did. "Let's head to Movra and have our Cycomm start a friendly chat with her two ex-con friends."

Brooks and Binil healed quickly, and Shoar grudgingly released them to work after a few hours. There was no rush. The Movi capital was far away—wormholes weren't easy to open and *Hajimi's* main drive took a while to charge properly. After a short talk with Janus and Frost, they set the navigation computer to rights and waited. In the meantime, Brooks polled every network he could find, desperate to extract more useful data, while Rosenski performed a top-to-bottom review of every crew member and their equipment.

Binil had nothing to manage but herself. She retreated to the tiny cabin she called her own on Deck 5, the front door wedged up against the fighter launch tube. Inside she had a bed, a narrow closet, and a pull-out fresher, but not much else. A small data terminal built into the wall, was all. Now it was enough. Her hands shook as they played with the controls, looking for something to take her mind off the insanity she was lining up for herself, for her human allies. Despite the warm air surrounding her, she couldn't stop shivering. She found what she was looking for: a public entertainment channel. She touched a button and her cabin filled with music.

Her own mind filled in the spaces between the lyrics. She shared a problem with the vocalist. Locked in a room. No doors. No windows. Only an open top that showed the sky—and not a real sky either, just a fake one. A ceiling festooned with lights and holographic panels that gave the appearance of a sky. Look at the sky. Look at the world. Look at yourself.

She listened to the story unfold and couldn't bring herself to stop. She was trapped, but she wasn't alone. There were others, faceless ghost-like figures without hands or feet, with white masks with black slits for eyes. And yet she relied on them for everything. They built her instruments and played her music.

Ghostly hands placed emotions into her head and feelings into her heart. She sang as the ghosts huddled around, looking over her shoulder, reading the music, listening to her. Look at the world. Look at yourself.

Binil burst into tears as her brain dropped a ton of serotonin into her blood. Look at the sky. Look at yourself. Binil had allies, friends, figures she relied on because at some point she'd realized that she could rely on them. As the music wound down the song took on a quieter tone.

She turned the channel off. She was a mess. It wouldn't do for others to see her like this. A royal daughter, she was supposed to project an air of authority. How could she do that if she—

A knock at the door. Dance's voice, subdued and anxious. "Binil? You okay?"

Binil reached out, meaning to lock the mechanism and hit the stud to open it instead. Dance and Brooks tumbling over each other to squeeze through the narrow opening, and Binil burst into tears.

Brooks closed the door for a modicum of privacy. "Is it Sora? The firefight?" he asked.

"Yes. No. I don't—" Binil shrugged and wiped her eyes with damp fingers. Deep breath, then let it out, shakily. "A song I just heard. Stupid. But it helped me realize something."

Dance lowered her head, tried to look Binil in the eye. "Realized what?"

"That I'm completely dependent on all of you. That I'm the child here."

"What's that mean?" Dance asked.

"I'm not a soldier. Soldiers can handle themselves and are sure with weapons and can give orders. I think of what comes next—think of seeing those two Movi women again—and I fall apart."

She saw Brooks tap his comm and turn away, mumbling something. Dance sat facing her on the narrow bed. "Hey. Everyone here is a soldier. You are, too."

"No, I'm—"

"Yes. You are. You helped me and Underhill repair a space station. You dropped grenades on Skreesh shock troopers. You turn bad guys' weapons against their users. Underhill even got you a commission in the UEF. You are a *soldier*. The only difference between you and us is we got some training before getting dunked in the deep end. But we have all been learning one piece at a time. That's normal. It shouldn't be, but it is."

"What if I injure myself again? Have a stroke? It happened once. Your doctors said it could easily happen again if I'm not careful. If Brooks hadn't injected me... "

"So, you'll be careful. Jersey knows how to use Sleer medical tech. Something goes pear-shaped, we can fix you. I know it can be done, and so do you. I already fixed you once."

Binil sniffed. "Yes. You did. I never thanked you for that, did I?"

"I won't hold it against you. Promise." Dance sighed. "You're scared. You have doubts about yourself, about us. That's normal. We're all scared. Yes, we support you. We'll always support you. No matter how ugly the fight gets. Hate to say it like this, kid, but you're stuck with us humans."

"Look at the sky," Binil recited.

"Half of this unit is made of pilots. The sky is all we have," Dance said.

"Even a fake one."

"Especially a fake one. It's the effort you put into your work, not just the work itself. You can do this."

Binil clenched her hands, stared at the wall. "I can do this. I must do this."

"Damn straight." Dance looked up and signaled. "Mr. Brooks. If you would."

Brooks opened the door and shouted into the hall, "Captain on deck!"

Binil looked out to see the crew lining the corridor and standing at attention as she took a step out of her door. Dance nudged her forward and raised her voice: "Company, stand for review!" She nudged the Cycomm forward.

Binil took it slowly. Every crewman remained in place as she walked past, eyes straight ahead just as if she were a commander of a real unit. This was a real unit. She was in command, or would be. Could be one day. For now, she was playing a role, and so were they. She followed them in an unbroken line, around the deck and onto the upper decks. Each new deck held the same scene. She stopped at the control pit where Rosenski stood at attention with the rest of the bridge officers.

"Permission to resume stations, Captain?" Rosenski said.

Binil gave a short croak then cleared her throat. "Permission granted. Resume your duties."

"As you were," Rosenski barked, and all returned to normal except for the fact that the captain's chair remained empty and Rosenski moved to the side.

I can do this, Binil thought and climbed into the chair. She fit its contours perfectly.

She *would* do this.

Janus broke the voyage to Movra into a number of short hops and mid-length jumps to confuse anyone who might be following them. The viewscreen fascinated Binil. Sometimes the crew decided to watch something other than the tactical display while the ship was in mid-jump. Janus had a thing for planets and set the screen to run through visual representations of the various worlds in the ship's data. Grandpa Frost liked animals, so the screen under his control showed one type of fauna after another, and there were some strange beasties on display. Some of them cute and cuddly, others nightmarish. Rosenski had chosen an abstract light sculpture with myriad moving parts that dove and rose around a central axis. The swooping, soaring patterns reminded Binil of the ghost-like figures in the song she'd listened to earlier. While she wasn't proud of her reaction to that bit of music—she'd never been driven to tears by mere melody and doubted it would happen again—it had reset her emotional space. Now that her concerns had come into the open, she didn't fear them anymore. She decided to take it as a good omen for things to come.

The countdown clock ran down and Janus brought them out of jump space. "Entering normal space in three, two, one... mark."

The screen cleared to show them the twin suns of Movra; a pair of dwarfs, one red, one the orange side of yellow, roughly the same size, orbiting each other. Movra itself was set in the fifth orbit out, a bright world with an oxygen rich atmosphere.

"It's beautiful," Binil said.

Rosenski took up the baton. "Full sweeps on sensors. Turn our Movi transponder on. Let's see who and what is around us. And let's get some information on comms. Brooks, do you think you can find us a transmission source for the Iria Sisterhood?"

"Assuming they're transmitting and not just broadcasting propaganda, yes. But... I'll start with a visual recognition search, see if either of Sora's friends are posting anything interesting on the network."

"That could take days. There are ten billion people down there," Binil said.

"Yes, there are. All in strictly controlled situations. I get the idea that the king and his family weren't into allowing mere commoners the same access to broadcast right as the royal family, right?"

Binil thought about it. "Probably not. You should check military transmissions, too. Cleo and Sellik had military records and backgrounds."

"Will do. Good idea, *Captain*," Brooks said.

Binil smirked out of Brooks's vision. Maybe he wasn't such a bad sort at that. Dance Reagan liked him quite a lot, and Rosenski relied on his skills, if not his judgment. If only he weren't such an idiot regarding Malkah's nature and functioning.

Binil waited and watched as Janus took them through a nonchalant approach. The good news was that Movra's spaceport, a sprawling affair with an orbital counterpart to its surface port, took automation to a new level. The ship's computer handled the approach, the clearance codes, and the berthing arrangements. "High Port or Low Port?" Janus asked.

"High Port," Binil answered. "If we find battle, it's easier to shoot one's way out of a space station than a planet," she said.

"I like how you think, but the point is to not shoot at anyone," Rosenski said. "Take us into High Port, Mr. Janus."

"Got it. Querying the High Port docking management system. They see us... they have us scheduled for a berth in ten minutes. Wow, that's fast."

"Movra is quite reliant on its computer technology for everything they do. It's a trade hub and a political center, so they are used to seeing a large stream of traffic in and out of the system. But I wonder... with a civil war on, why are they treating us like a cargo ship?"

"Maybe we're too small to be considered dangerous," Skull said.

"It's a combat ship. They must know who we are. And we've

had dealings with the two opposed faction leaders. They must be curious about that, right?" Frost added.

"Maybe they just don't have the time. Civil wars have a way of sucking all the attention of out of your brain," Dance said.

Brooks piped up from the comm shack. "There it is. They're requesting a cargo and passenger manifest. At least if the machinery is translating Movi correctly."

"It should. Brooks, can our implants translate Movi directly?"

"Movi to Sleer? They sure can. Movi to Sleer to English will be trickier, but I can't imagine it not working."

"I don't have implants," Binil murmured.

"You speak Moviri, so you won't need them," Rosenski said.

"Moviri and Sleer, thank you kindly."

"Good to have royal tutors growing up."

Binil tried not to roll her eyes. She was being unfair. Why? "All the major races can speak Sleer. No other race traveled as far or as widely as they did. Moviri is taught in schools all over Haven as a matter of course. It's always good to know what the neighbors are saying to you. About you."

Rosenski agreed. "Skull, let them see our records. No reason to give them something to talk about."

"Transmitting... Now they want confirmation of our travel orders."

"What travel orders?" Brooks said.

Rosenski nodded. "Binil, I think it's time for the captain to make a personal call."

The words doubled Binil's heart rate. "Open a general channel."

"Channel open."

"Movra High Port," Binil said in Moviri, "This is the company command cruiser *Hajimi*. We require repair, restocking, and refueling. Request docking instructions."

"*Hajimi*, this is High Port Control. Who is your commanding officer?"

The question festered in the air. There was no question in Binil's mind that they knew their manifests were at best out of date and at worst a total fabrication. "I am Captain Binilsane-tanjamalala. This ship and crew fought its way out of two major engagements, one on Foresite-4059 and another at Garrison Cluster. I insist you stop seeing enemies around every corner and give us permission to land at once!"

She caught a peripheral glimpse of Rosenski sharing a look with her crew. Apparently, Binil was playing her part well enough.

Silence from the comms. Binil was working over her next verbal assault when the voice of flight control came back. "*Hajimi*, you are scheduled to dock in bay 36344B. Prepare for gravity beam lock." Janus idled the drives as a projector swung toward it. The beam took hold with only a slight nudge. Either there was a pro controlling the device, or the machines really were programmed for a solid ride.

They entered the bay without another comment.

CHAPTER 20

THE HIGH PORT landing bay was immense. Brooks, Rosenski, Binil, and Reagan looked out on the new world from the bridge viewscreen. To Binil it looked like High Port could manage an infinite number of ships. Movi crew in deckhand livery approached and began hooking their vessel up to umbilicals and fuel lines, while a bevvy of airborne drones approached to examine every aspect of the ship. And so many ships. Not all the spherical military types, either. Blocky cargo modules, smooth ovoids, cone-shaped destroyers, and scads of designs she'd never seen or imagined. But nowhere did she see the teardrop shape of a Sense Op attack ship. That alone gave her room to relax.

Dance tapped Binil on the shoulder. "Have you ever been here before?"

"What? High Port? Never."

"I mean the planet."

Binil nodded quickly. "Once, when I was very young. My father took the whole family. I remember the tall buildings. The crystalline arcology towers and all the flying platforms that seemed to hang in the sky, somehow rooted to their positions.

Cities built on top of them. We made a point to visit the royal gardens. The *Movishi Rokuen*, they're called. One hundred square kilometers of private zoos and arboreta that teem with examples of life from fifty worlds under the kingdom's control. You could almost believe you're on those other worlds, the way they arranged the exhibits."

Binil was dressed dressed in a combination of bits and pieces from the ship's locker and a few medals taken from the uniforms of other crew, all put together by the tailoring skills of 3rd Lt. Zakari, part of the Gauntlet's gunnery section. Zakari had quite a bit of experience dressing up officers and enlisted crew alike, and knew how to take a standard uniform, strip out all the extraneous bits and decorations, and carefully replace them in strategic places so that to an uneducated onlooker, Binil could pass as a Cycomm Sense Op officer. "How do I look? Official enough?"

"You look noble as any princess who ever passed herself off as a ship's captain," Dance said.

"I'm not sure what that means."

Brooks elbowed Reagan. "She means yes; you're as convincing as we can make you."

"Good. Now we wait until the inspection team arrives," Binil said.

"Wait—they're going to board us?" Brooks said.

"They must. Transport guild law says that all incoming ships need to be inspected for foreign materials and so on. Bacteria. Viruses. There are stories of a fast-growing mold strain that decimated local crops years ago."

Rosenski scoffed. "I'm sure. But why inspect us? They can check our logs."

"They will. Leave it to me. I've at least seen this done before." Binil was quite certain.

A chime rang and the foursome took the lift to the lowermost airlock. Dance, Rosenski, and Brooks put their helmets on, and Binil thought of something new. "Instruct all crew to put their helmets on and darken the visors to maximum. We are Cycomms. No other race is fit to look upon us. Except for me, for I am the captain and must take on the responsibility of dealing with inferiors. Now!"

Rosenski gave the order. The crew hopped to it. By the time the locks matched air pressure and the airlock door opened, the whole crew was suitably disguised.

In the metal cave of the bay, they found themselves face to face with a haggard Movi officer. His uniform had a pair of colorful shoulder patches and an armband bearing a pair of blood-red diamonds on a silver background. "Inspection."

Binil stepped forward, her war paint in full bloom. "Yes."

"Permissions."

"Here." She handed him a data chip, which the Movi plugged into a portable reader. "I'll need access to your inspection port. Air samples and such."

"Certainly. It's this one. Your deck hands are very efficient."

The inspector followed her to a hose that ran up the side of the ship, apparently plugged into one of the air-exchangers. The Movi plugged a probe into the connection and made a note on his tablet, apparently satisfied. "I see here you've ordered ordnance. You have a supply request?"

She handed him another chip. "I do. You'll find payment comes from the cash balance of the Royal Bank of Movra. We have a family account there."

"Family?"

"The House of Malala. Everything is there."

A chime sounded. "Of course. Very well. Thank you for your time—Captain Malala."

"You're very welcome. When can I expect my merchandise?"

"Several hours, I expect. But I can put a priority status on the order for an additional fee. Shall the delivery team come aboard?"

"I'll have the crew accept delivery and they will load cargo as needed. But I do appreciate your attention to detail and discretion. Make sure our delivery receives a priority." A third chime, then the investigator turned, scanned the bay, and proceeded to his next inspection.

Rosenski opened her visor. "What the hell was that about?"

"I gave him access to my family's bank account and there was a transfer of funds," Binil said.

"You bribed him?"

"Of course."

Rosenski pulled off her helmet and bent to look the Cycomm in the eyes. "You talk shit about not looking like rubes and us not making eye contact with those yobos and then you line his pockets? Seriously?" she whispered.

"It worked, didn't it? Everyone pays for favors. The trick is to say the right names. If he knew I didn't have any standing in my family, he'd never have agreed."

"But—you just scammed the Movi homeworld out of missiles and God knows what else!"

Binil grinned. "The transfer was real. My family didn't see fit to empty my personal account. Now they don't have to: I've given everything I have to buy our way inside and those precious short-range missiles to arm the fighters. Bigger missiles for the ship. Everything your quartermaster put on his shopping list."

"And alerted your bankers to the fact that you're here," Rosenski hissed.

"Not at all. The docking bay has no cameras. If they investigate the transaction, they'll merely see that a local purchase occurred and assume someone on Movra who wasn't me has stolen the funds. They'll report the intrusion, change the pass codes, and forget about the trifle soon enough. After all, how could I possibly have escaped from Marauder's Moon?"

"I'll say this for you, Binil. You can work family drama within an inch of your life. I'll call it a good morning if we leave with what we came here for."

They left the crew with instructions on how to act when the cargo arrived, and entered the station proper. Thick blast doors opened to show them a vast interior that looked like a combination of office building and shopping mall. The battle ring docking areas weren't any smaller but were arranged differently: Sleer areas were like suspended platforms attached to ships and docking berths, while Movi preferred their spaces more compact. They moved down a narrow platform, passed through another set of locks, and watched the vista of their hangar vanish behind them. Binil turned around and really looked at the ship for the first time. It was a black and green sphere on narrow pylons, peppered with repaired armor plates and mismatched surface features. She smiled as she saw Warlord Anterran's engineers really had painted the gunnery turrets to look like eyes.

"We need a comm station if we're going to do any network searches," Brooks said.

"This way... no. This way." Binil led the way, recognizing enough Movi in the directional signs to find her way. They arrived at a busy, glass-encased section with comfortable cushioned chairs and tablet like devices. One chair, one tablet. Nice.

Brooks sat down and tried to use the unfamiliar equipment. He moved infinitely better than he had after going toe-to-toe with Sora Laakshiden, and his bruises were long gone. But he still was no expert in Movi technology.

Binil switched places with him, using the console like an expert. It took some prodding from the humans, but Binil downloaded the facial recognition app from the ship, then got access to a military security database and ran their search. It took time. The humans wandered the reception area, Binil keeping an eye on her charges as they explored. Eventually, they found a restaurant and spent some time there. By the time she'd traced Cleo's comm channel, they were peppering her with all manner of tourist questions.

"What's clipsop stew?" Brooks asked.

"What's an utuwerg?" Dance wanted to know.

"Have you ever had wahmilcon? What's it taste like?" Rosenski asked.

"You people are *obsessed* with food," Binil scolded. She flipped the tablet and showed them the photo. "I found her. She's on the station. Do I call?"

They answered at the same time: "Yes!"

"All right. Stand behind me. She needs to see you, but not be distracted." Binil tapped the button, waited for the connection.

The line joined and Cleo's face filled the screen. "Gods. Another uniform? We're out of money and I don't need another merc on my payroll. I have your number. I'll call if things change."

"Look again, Cleo. You know my face."

The Movi stared into the camera and suddenly spewed a string of curses Binil didn't need to translate. "What the Maker do *you* want?"

"Captain Malala wants you. Meet me in the restaurant closest to the High Port Comm Lounge on deck nineteen. One hour. You can do that?"

Cleo hesitated, looked off camera, and made a distressed face. "Yes."

"I'll see you there. I have better friends than you, so come alone."

"You have three friends? I'll bring one if it's all right with you," Cleo snarled.

"Make it a good one." Binil closed the connection and smiled. "She's looking forward to our talk. I can tell."

To the Movi's credit, she followed instructions. Brooks, Reagan, and Rosenski all remained helmeted with dark visors as the two Movi approached. Sellik looked angry as ever; Binil doubted she had another expression. But the expression on Cleo's face was an order-of-magnitude worse. Cleo, who spent a decade dancing for the royal court and could break bones with her legs, looked positively betrayed. "You shouldn't be here, Binil."

"I never promised I'd stay away, dear. I think the reality is, you expected me to turn up dead. Sorry to disappoint," Binil said.

"No. I don't think you are."

"How right you are. Let's talk."

"Where is Sora?" Sellik demanded.

"Flight Admiral Laakshiden is indisposed. The last time we saw her she was in good working order. Now, I'm not sure. All you need to worry about is that she isn't here and I am."

"We?" Sellik raised her eyes to stare into Binil's. "I see you and your—compatriots. Who is 'we?'"

"Reagan. Brooks. Rosenski. Lighten your faces." One by one the three humans complied. The two Movi didn't have much to say until they recognized Reagan's face. Their eyes shifted between the three faces until Binil reversed her order and they became three dark helmets again. "You know her face, too. From the Sleer scout."

"I know we popped her armor off her like stripping a clipsop out of its shell for lunch," Sellik said. Cleo nodded, but the fear in her eyes was real. Binil knew she had a chance to pry open their combined wills, but it wouldn't be easy. One last bluff to make and it needed to be convincing.

Cleo made the first move. "Binil. We can accept that you're here. But 'why' is something I can't imagine. What do you *want*?"

Binil hesitated, intended to give the impression of strength. The truth was that she wasn't sure what to ask for. What *did* she want? Brooks and Rosenski had coached her about this. She should know what to do now, but drew a tremendous blank. And she couldn't just turn the conversation to one of her supposed subordinates—that would make her look weak. Like a hired hand, a... what did Dance call it? A front man. The one who looked pretty and made small talk before turning the real negotiation over to her handler.

Not this time. Not here. She dug into her memory, trying to exhume what they'd gone over. "I want your help," she said.

Cleo said, "Help with what? You have a crew, and I assume a ship. We can't do better for you than you seem to have done for yourself."

"Ah, but you can. We've had dealings with both Archduke Mineko and First Warlord Anterran. They are at war. It's a perfectly glorious war, too. Full of bloodshed, explosions, ambushes, and torn up war fleets. Screams of the dying and so on and such like. Predictable. In my estimation, it will only be a matter of time before they exhaust each other. And then what? The Sleer are huddled beyond their borders for who knows what, and I for one do not think they will stay that way forever."

"And how do you know that?" Cleo asked.

"These humans have met them up close. They have considerable experience fighting the Sleer invasion fleet anchored about the ring around their homeworld. They understandably want the invasion fleet gone."

Another shared look, but this time they said nothing,

gesturing for her to continue. Binil considered it a good sign. "The truth is that I don't know what comes next for them, but that's not the point," she said.

"There's a point to this?" Sellik snarked.

"The point is, there are humans aplenty and they have yet to fully branch out from their homeworld. They have space travel. They even have control of a repurposed Sleer battleship. What they don't have is guidance. They know the galaxy awaits, but they don't know what to do with it. All they have is their home system and a colony world they'll eventually develop. Do you understand me? What if the Cycomms and Movi were to make a proposal to them directly? They could provide badly needed aid in terms of ship building and crew. The Movi in turn could provide them with technology and a bit of political wisdom."

"Wisdom. You mean convincing them to come into this conflict on Iria's side?"

"Iria is gone. But yes. I think the sisterhood could furnish them with quite a lot of experience and talent." The Movi looked flabbergasted. Binil counted to five and pretended to lose her cool. "Oh, come on, ladies! This is the opportunity of a lifetime. Of many lifetimes! Will you reach out to seize it, or will I have to find someone else with grander vision? Perhaps Missena would be interested in forging trade partnerships with a new race, for example."

"You are mad!" Sellik declared.

"No. I am desperate to secure a partnership with these humans. I will do anything I can to make it happen. And unlike either of you, I can see past my own problems and prejudices and grab for the unseen and unimagined. That's what creates empires. Not just linking yourself to the biggest fish who'll have you and nudging them from one bad idea to another." She paused. "Sora thought that way. I'm here with these people and she isn't... that alone should tell you everything you need to know." She folded her arms and leaned back. "I give you five minutes to decide what you'd rather do. Be flunkies for the rest of your lives or run into the future with me."

Cleo was more circumspect. If nothing else, she lacked Sellik's rage face. "We can't make that decision on our own. And you still haven't told us what you think we can do. Here. Now. It's not like we board your ship and create a grand exchange of views with an alien species. What do you want from *us*?"

"An introduction to your leader would be a good start. Take me to someone with whom I can discuss business properly. If it works out, then you'll be known as the ones who made the exchange possible. That will have to be worth something to your mistress, no?"

Cleo nodded once. "We can do that. Come along. You and your—partners."

The Movi led the foursome through the twists and turns of Movra High Port. Binil couldn't help gawking as they passed through multi-platformed malls, with myriad tiers, brightly lit chrome plated terraces that seemed to go on for miles in all three dimensions. The station walls included a lot of bright white light and mirrored surfaces, and each terrace was split into a wide variety of shops and stalls. Thousands from the major races mingled and passed each other on their way to whatever business they planned. It looked like the chaos elsewhere in the kingdom barely made a dent in the day to day operations of the port. Ships still shipped and delivered cargo and passengers, artisans sold wares to travelers, businesspeople had deals to make and profits to chase. But... she wasn't seeing anyone with any designs of the royal house on their clothing or jewelry. That was something she remembered from her visit long ago. A great many people carried banners proclaiming their loyalty—or perhaps just convenient fictions of loyalty to the royal house. She supposed if one couldn't tell a friendly face from an enemy's, it might not be wise to wear one's politics on one's literal sleeve.

After a while she realized she didn't see any royal marines. Mere station security uniforms only. But there were a lot of them. The good news was that security people never carried lethal weapons on duty, Shock batons and tranq pistols only. But with so many around, there was a good chance than any outbreak of violence would be met with swift and fierce response.

She focused her eyes on Cleo and Sellik instead. Better to keep one's attention on the things one could control.

Cleo took them through crowded corridors and finally turned into a restaurant, a noisy noodle shop that huddled in an alcove off the main strip. Binil sensed a trap and slowed, but no one looked up at them, and Cleo clearly knew her way through the crowd. The few who did look up at them looked down again quickly. Better not to be noticed when people in armored suits walked past.

Down the main floor, turn to go behind the counter, down a narrow staircase to a dimly lit basement, then out the back through an armored door. They emerged into a brightly lit, windowless hallway, almost like the inside of an office building. Doors with name plates on the front and coded electronic locks. Clearly a business center of some type.

They stopped next to a set of glass doors with a prominent logo emblazoned on the metal plate: SOI Consultancy, LRC. The logo resembled a half a sunburst with a blue ball on a white background, blue rays projecting in a hemisphere. It took Binil a moment to remember that the princess Iria uses the blue and white sunburst as her own emblem. Her section of the royal palace on the planet below was festooned with them.

Cleo pressed her thumb on the lock, bent so a camera could scan her eyes. Locks opened with a click and they entered.

More offices. A flatly corporate environment. Even stranger, many of the offices they walked past were occupied. She caught snatches of muffled conversations, not all of them in languages she recognized. What were they walking into?

One thing she noticed; women, and a few young men, were the only staff. She wondered about Archduke's Mineko's operation back in the Garrison Cluster. There'd only been women in that office as well. What was being stated here? Was the message that men weren't welcome in the new order they were working to create? Or were they merely trying to remind old men of their place in the world, which had nothing to do with the political agenda the Sisterhood wanted to create? Or was it simpler? Were the men being used for troops? Soldiers, marines and starship crews? Could it be that simple? Was anything?

"Trap?" Dance asked.

Rosenski, scanning the ceiling and walls. "Vents, but no gas nozzles. If they're going to gas us, they'll gas the rest of the floor."

"Everyone keep your helmets up just in case."

Binil frowned. She normally appreciated the humans' paranoia, but in this case it was probably overdone. "No, just keep them on standby. This will be an interview, nothing more. If we pass whatever test they have in mind, then they'll—"

The door opened with a chime and in strode a short, thick Movi woman with incredibly blue eyes. She locked those amazing orbs onto the Cycomm, and it was as if no one else in the world existed. "Binilsanetanjamalala, you are welcome here. But you tell a story that is beyond belief and you have legal problems following you. And you bring aliens to my operation. Most disappointing. But let's be civilized for the moment. Tea?"

"For four. Yes, please."

"You have manners. I like that. But you also seem to want to insert yourself into an affair that doesn't concern you and that disturbs me. Anyway. Tea."

"I know your face, madame."

"And I know your mother. Or I did years ago. I'm glad to see the house of Malala is still up and running. Your clan father, for instance. Quite a personality. Grand as all outdoors. Lost the family fortune three times."

"Three times!" Binil had wondered why he'd turned over the business affairs to his partners. "When did you meet—"

"Not your clan mother—I mean your *mother*. The woman who bore you to the great family and then disappeared into the general population. Would it surprise you know she birthed six children, and all but one was eventually picked for advancement into the Sense Ops organization?"

"That—what?"

"Psychic medics, every one. Except you for some reason. The only scrambler. Ah, here's our tea."

Binil's mind reeled as she tried to process what she was hearing. "But there are no Malala entrants in Sense Ops. I would have been the first."

"You would have been the *ninth*. Some houses have twenty or thirty. It might be a scandal if anyone made a great issue of it. What would the plugs say if they started hearing rumors that not only were their children not potential assets to the Sense Ops organization, but the royals were packing that same agency with their own progeny?"

Binil thought about it. Haven worked through class obedience. Plugs got their daily bread and spent it to make life a bit more comfortable, but no one went hungry or died for lack of medicine or shelter. Desperate, starving multitudes made for unstable living conditions and all the wealth and power in the world didn't change that. But the only outlet the lower caste had to fall back on was the hope, the accident, some might say, the chance that one of their children displayed an aptitude for Sense Ops. It didn't happen often, but it did happen. All children got tested in school. A child from a plug family was elevated into the upper classes, assigned to a family, and a clan house, and their birth parents would follow them along on their journey upwards. Vicariously perhaps, but there. A lottery perhaps, but a consistent one.

What if all that were done away with? Plugs with no hope for the future. Nothing to look forward to except endless toil, with no hope whatever of their children moving up the pyramid?

"Oh, dear Malkah," Binil said. "They'll light themselves on fire, then run to hug us."

Their host poured blue light-scented tea into paper cups. "Precisely."

Binil sipped. Bitter. "And now I must ask who you are. How do you know all this?"

"My name is Vonda. That's a safe name for you to call me. Speak it to any sisterhood member and you'll be brought to me eventually. As to how I know things, well, I've been running information networks throughout the kingdom and the Haven royal court for decades. That's how I met these two enterprising women."

Binil whipped her head to stare at the two Movi. Cleo managed not to smirk; Sellik gave her an smile. For a change, one without obvious malice. "Sora Laakshiden? A spy?"

Vonda laughed. "No, dear. Cleo and Sellik were the spies. Sora was the mark. We were hoping she would lead us to a crime lord who's been running terror cells from Marauder's Moon, but that operation didn't survive contact with you. You owe me one interplanetary terrorist, Binil."

"How do I pay that debt?"

"By heeding these words. You want an alliance, Binilsane-tanjamalala. I don't blame you. But you won't find one here. We don't want Haven in control of our government, not even a proxy. Not even advisors. We want a sane ruler to be sovereign, and we're unlikely to find one. So. We are working to advise the various factions. See if we can't get Singhir brought to heel. Missena sees opportunities that others miss and she is popular among the nobility, but her power is centered in Kar-Tuyin's shipping fleets, not the royal bureaucracy."

"Her father is a war criminal," Binil cried.

Vonda scoffed. "Details, details. Power attracts madness, nothing new in that. She wants a return to the status quo. That's of value to me."

"Does that make you a monster?"

Vonda took a moment to consider that. "It might make both of us monsters. Your alien friends here too. It depends on your point of view. I think that—"

A fire alarm sounded down the hall. Then another, then another. Mechanical voices began to shout warnings and Vonda brought her arms up to activate myriad viewing surfaces. "I do believe Reverend Mother Gala-Shom's zealots are making a move."

"Up here?"

"In some places. Their main effort is the royal palace and Down Port. The security forces will be busy for a while. If you have any last offers to make, now is the time to state them."

Rosenski pulled off her helmet and faced their interviewer directly. "If we brought three hundred Sleer battleships into Movi territory..."

"Then you would be attacked by whatever remains of the Royal Navy in short order. I appreciate the gesture—if that's what you're making—but all boasting aside, our war fleets are superior to anything you might field. Even with borrowed Sleer technology. Even with support of Sleer ships. We will figure this out ourselves, thank you." New tones made themselves known and now the lighting began to dim and take on a reddish tinge. "Those are compartment breaches. Internal explosions. I would leave now if I were you."

They left.

CHAPTER 21

"ADMIRAL, we'll need to designate a landing area. High Port or Down Port?"

"Down Port, Great Maker," Sora Laakshiden said to her pilot. "The High Port is a secure facility. You can barely scratch your ass in there without cameras watching you. No, the current sovereign is living in his apartment at the royal palace, and that is where we need to be if we are to be heard." She shook her head and considered the alternatives. "High Port. Great Maker, no!" She paused then said with a twinge of anxiety, "You did alter our transponders accordingly? No need for their defense grid to shoot us when they realize where we departed from."

"Not a problem, Ma'am. This shuttle has a wide variety of additional transponder codes programmed into it. The archduke enjoys his privacy, and his staff appreciates discretion."

Sora found herself appreciating Archduke Mineko's staff. These people knew how to live life to its full advantage. The pilot didn't work for Mineko personally, but was one of a company of service specialists who were on call all day every day, sleeping and eating in shifts just in case one of their employers needed to be somewhere halfway across the galaxy, *now.* Luckily, the pilot never asked her anything except her destination. Perhaps the assumption was that if one managed to gain access to this part of the complex, one clearly held the right to use it. A dangerous mentality, but maybe that was how an archduke thought. When you were the apex predator, you tended to think that everything you saw was a potential meal.

Personally, she wouldn't have held it against the young pilot if he'd pulled a gun on her and demanded to know what she thought she was doing there. She looked like the survivor of a firefight, with staples closing her abdominal wound, blood spilled over the front of her outfit, and a face that would have looked normal on an enraged, wounded animal. She didn't want to think of herself that way, but it made sense.

She'd come to consciousness in the hallway. She couldn't remember the event clearly. Brooks was the one who'd shot her, she was now sure. There hadn't been anyone else to do so. Binil wouldn't have the stones for it.

Shot and bleeding, she'd managed to gain her feet, hold her guts in, and follow the now-open passageway. She'd been ready to think about fainting again when her eyes found a red door shielding an alcove. A medical bay. She palmed the unlocked door, stumbled through the now-open portal, climbed into the sick bay and winced when a robot medic worked on her. It stitched what needed stitching, plugged her full of antibiotics and pain killers, and pronounced her cured.

She was startled at the level of sheer hatred she now held in her heart for the Cycomm. She'd been in way over her head when they'd met, and frankly, Binil had struck Sora as being vaguely useful once they got to Marauder's Moon. Sora planned the entire project out in the barge's common holding area. Get to the penal colony, find the biggest, meanest monster she could locate, and use every asset she could pull into her orbit along the way to wipe them out. Take a few lessons from the residents, build a power base, then build a way to either get off the moon or find some way to pressure the Cycomm government that put her there. Of course, not all her plans went smoothly. She'd gone to Haven with the intention of opening a private supply chain for intelligence gathering equipment, and been accused of espionage. She still wasn't sure who sold her name to the police or why. If she lived long enough to return to Haven, she'd figure it out and separate their head from their neck with her bare hands.

She spent the rest of the voyage doing a deep dive in the current situation of the shattered kingdom. And that's what it was. The kingdom remained; a sovereign was, in fact, holding the throne. But the idea of a king—if that antiquated term still meant anything—was gone. For generations the titular kingdom had been organized like an empire, with a sovereign at the top and a deep and broad bureaucracy acting as the glue that held its myriad worlds and interests together. The great trading houses, such as Kar-Tuyin, Dal-Cortsuni, and Onnicom, acted to keep profits high and costs low, and passed a great deal of wealth to sovereign-related and throne-backed business charters.

But Singhir himself was something else. The boy never expected to be named sovereign. His branch of the family tree was too low and sparse to be seriously considered for the position, so he was never trained for it. A son of privilege, descended from sons of privilege, raised to expect and insist upon comfort and deference without needing to consider the responsibilities of office. Singhir's life was one of social events and countless signatures on ten times ten thousand contracts and little more. There were no adults around him who cared to guide him on a path leading to real authority.

That spoiled little shit now sat on the throne. All bad things descended from there.

The admirals, she was learning, who stuck with the new Sovereign weren't doing so out of loyalty to the throne or the royal family. Most had spent decades striving for their commissions and ranks, and they weren't about to see those go up in vapor because the newest guy in charge was a horror show. They intended to maintain order no matter what. And a recent broadcast made to the military channels, of Singhir speaking to an assembly of of military advisors, demanding they bring him results or leave, was no mere threat. The military understood that the ends their Sovereign decreed justified any means. Things would get good and bloody before order was restored.

Sora smelled an opportunity.

The escape ship's library contained an embarrassing wealth of military information. Frequencies, pass codes, and timetables for fleet movements and their composition—everything a First Warlord could use to put down a rebellion without wasting time, supplies, or effort. True, without knowing Mineko's whereabouts, any or all of it might be utterly out of date. But it was something, and it would take time for the admiralty to verify its veracity. Time enough to secure a position on Singhir's general staff. Back on the winning team. In any event, a chip with key data points regarding the rebel fleets was sewn into a search-proof compartment in her sleeve. She admired a man who knew a tailor skilled enough to imagine contingencies. She also noticed that her suit was cut for a woman. Lots of fashionable clothing choices in that wardrobe. Mineko took his staffing preferences with him everywhere he went. Even when escaping death, it seemed. Maybe it was for the best that she'd failed to acquire his help.

"Can you land at the palace? Or must we subject ourselves to Down Port customs officials?"

"In theory, yes. I would need the correct pass codes. Security at the palace is top level right now."

She pulled the stolen chip from its hiding place and examined it. Rounded, with three distinct leads. A social implant, then. She popped her current implant from its place and replaced it with the new one. She linked her new toy to the ship's library and suddenly knew everything about the archduke's operation. "I have them," she said. "Change course as appropriate. And call ahead, let them know we're bringing intelligence vital to the First Warlord's efforts to secure the kingdom."

"Yes, Ma'am."

She'd never seen a throne room before, and wasn't sure what she thought of it. A vast empty chamber with a raised dais in the center with the Vermilion Throne above it. Four large sets of ornately decorated doors that doubled as blast shields. Two armed and armored soldiers at each. Singhir was young, vibrant, healthful, and attractive. A man who'd grown up in circumstances to guarantee peak physical health. But he was restless. He never stopped moving, pacing, even when he sat, his feet crossed and uncrossed, his fingers rubbed their neighbors, and his eyes flitted from hers to the room behind her and back again. Her anxiety returned as she realized the fool might well be on some drug. He was on *something*. An agitated addict with the power of the throne wasn't what she wanted to work with. But here she was, and this moment would never come again in her lifetime. So... onward.

Singhir perched on the edge of his throne, legs crossed, the upper leg always bouncing. "So, Admiral. May I call you that? Admiral? No, *Flight Admiral*. Second step on the way to the full Warlord, isn't it? Quite a title. You must have worked very hard to get it."

Sora nodded sagely. "In fact, I did, your Highness."

"And now you have... nothing."

"Not nothing. I have information."

"Ah! That's entirely different. Information. Very well. You need my help for something. Some proposal, some business opportunity, some favor. Maybe I can grant it. What can you do for me?" he asked.

"I can get you the crew that the humans sent here to destabilize your kingdom," she said.

"A crew? Of humans. I don't know who those are."

Sora inhaled deeply and got to work. "Years ago, a Sleer scientist named Zluur escaped interstellar justice on a modified gun destroyer. Surely you know that?"

The princeling rolled his eyes and made a flourish with his hands that could have meant anything. Something to do while he waited for Sora to tell him, most probably. "I remember hearing something like that at some point. So what?"

"So, that ship escaped my fleet and arrived years later on a small planet further out on the rim—beyond our and the Sleer borders. The humans managed to secure it and educate themselves about Sleer technology. They repaired it and brought it to Great Nest where it still sits. But part of that effort involved seizing and modifying a company command cruiser, which they have been using to sow dissent and make deals of their own throughout the kingdom. Surely you want that stopped?"

"That would depend on who they're making deals with. No?"

"Archduke Mineko for one." She paused. "I was there at that meeting. The humans attacked his guards and shot me. I barely escaped in one of the duke's spacecrafts. I came here to warn you of their mischief."

"Mischief. I love that word. *Miiischieef*. So simple, but it means so much. And you haven't told me how you came to be with this band of saboteurs."

"I was trying to help a Cycomm escape from a life of hard labor on the Haven penal colony."

"How magnanimous." He leaned forward, nearly fell, and simply walked down to stand next to her. "Sora. I'm not as stupid as you seem to think. Maybe a band of humans are wandering around brokering deals that could kill me tomorrow... but the kingdom is still vast and still incredibly powerful with fleets and soldiers aplenty. What makes you think they are coming for me? Did you tell them to come here?"

"I did not. But I think there's a greater point to be made here..."

"And I think you're done. You have nothing to offer me. Maybe your failed allies are out there and maybe they aren't. Your rank is gone, your service history in ruins. You have a long list of enemies. Do you even have any friends?"

"I would hope *we* could be friends."

"That's... no." He made a show of running his eyes up and down her body, sizing her up, cataloging her, testing her. The look of disgust on his face was obvious. "No. It would be like being friends with one of my mother's aunts and that's..." He shuddered and held his stomach. "No." He looked up. "You spent time with Mineko, you said. Did you learn anything from him?"

"A ship's library's worth," she said. Now she could bargain.

Singhir raised his arms and brought up a series of displays, filling the great hall with maps, data sheets, and schedules. He flipped through the collection until he spotted his goal. "That includes authentication codes?"

"Of course."

"Then verify the transit codes and plotted course of the Nambari Incursion Fleet if you would be so kind."

She concentrated on pulling the requested data from her implant. This far into the palace, she had to hunt through numerous firewalls and filters, but the library was where she'd left it. She snatched the datum and threw it onto a screen of her own. "That fleet departed from Brinla three days ago," she said. "Although this time stamp is probably incorrect."

Singhir responded by sweeping his arms, propelling the map this way and that. When he touched a world, a new data window appeared. "My generals don't know I have this level of access. All their secrets, all their plans. They don't tell me what I need to know to run the kingdom. Tell the boy idiot what they think I need to know. Lie to him. Promise him whatever he asks. They all hate me. All of them. Bah! Let them hate me. I need their obedience, not their love. Ha! Brinla, did you say?"

"Yes, Highness."

"Then why did my First Warlord announce that he engaged that fleet in Ryoki-Selid ten days ago?"

"I cannot speak to that, Highness."

"I can. I believe your stolen data is genuine, but it's also apparently superseded by galactic events. Still. Turn it over to me. That way we'll consider you a loyal subject of the throne and we both go about our days." He glanced at one of his guards and all of them snapped to attention. His meaning could not be clearer. "I'll even restore your rank. Right now." He pulled up another display, placed his hand against it. The frame turned from a hostile red to a frosty green.

She kept her hands to herself. No need to die for the sake of this idiot. "The library computer is aboard my ship, Highness." She recited the ship's docking bay and tail number. She hoped the pilot had the sense to allow the inspection team aboard.

"Excellent. I thank you for a stimulating conversation. You may go."

She bowed and turned to go. She had her rank back, but its

restoration sat poorly. One step, two, three. She counted to nine and then heard his voice behind her. "Flight Admiral."

"She turned. Yes, my Sovereign?"

"Just out of curiosity... What does your Cycomm look like? It's a woman. A girl, yes?"

"She—yes."

She began to admire his handlers; they seemed to have their hands full with this cretin. Left alone, he would remain on the throne, siring children both legitimate and otherwise, making deals with thugs who wanted to curry favor, denying claims to those who he felt wronged by, real or imagined. He'd demand the compliance of the great merchant houses for projects he wanted to fund, and cut ties to any who wouldn't agree to his terms. He'd create new houses from nothing. Elevate local minor nobles to positions of great power and responsibility, caring only that they remain loyal to him alone. She was looking at a nightmare in the making, a true shift in the nature of the Movi government. It would take years, even decades to play out fully, but when it was over—if it ever ended—the government she'd come up in, worked her ass off to succeed in, earned her rank and title from—would exist only in name.

"A planetoid for your Cycomm, Flight Admiral. Lands and a title as well."

"A—I beg your pardon?"

"You heard me. There are nearly a thousand planetoid-class vessels in my navy. Ten times as many lesser ships, filled with crew and captained by those who know that I can get things done. I'm not sure I believe your story about humans rampaging through my kingdom, but I saw the concern in your eyes when you mentioned the Cycomm. Bring her to me and you get command of a Dominion-class planetoid and a place at court."

For once, she believed every word out of his mouth. His offer was consistent with what she already knew about him. As a prince he had a proclivity for bribing those bigger than him and threatening those smaller. And now he was at the top of the food chain, an apex predator in all but name. He wanted to suck her into to his orbit like a black hole funneling everyone nearby into his influence. Influence was so hypnotizing. One became dependent on one's patron so quickly. There was a narcotic-like quality to knowing you could do anything—literally any thing— and not face consequences.

For a long moment, what seemed like a month, she sat there and thought about it.

She hated Binil hotly, but she'd rather die than turn her over to this animal. She fingered the outline of the knife in her forearm sheath. They were being watched; there were guards less than ten steps away. She could probably draw it properly, but the way he was fidgeting... could she cut his throat deeply enough to kill him before being cut down by his bodyguards?

She decided. "I've wasted your time. I beg forgiveness."

"You have a lot to learn about begging, Sora."

"There are many things I've never been good at," she admitted, "but I suspect you have a lot to learn about loyalty."

His face changed. He was wondering what she was talking about, confusion radiating from his eyes like a street sign at night. When alarms trilled in the office outside, he glared. Then new displays popped up, describing the deployment of troops and security measures, and his face turned into a mask of rage. "What have you done to me, Sora?" he screamed.

She knew how this would play out. Something serious happened while she was pleading for power and career and he assumed that because it happened while they were speaking, she was responsible for it. Because only the people in front of him were ever responsible for anything bad. That was how he thought.

She stomped to the nearest pair of guards. "Soldier. What's going on? Why is the Sovereign in danger?"

Singhir screamed from the center of the room. "I am not in danger! This palace is impregnable!"

The marine flicked his eyes from one to the other and settled on Sora. "Admiral, the perimeter alert has been triggered. I'm in communication with our checkpoints on the palace grounds. A large crowd is at the gates."

She had a choice. She could hustle the princeling to safety then take command until his personal guard arrived, and hope that someone noticed her role in organizing the fool's safety. Though none of that was her job, she knew what to do and how. On the other hand, it presented Singhir with another chance to accuse her of Maker knew what. He thought of her as his mother's aunt. He'd told her so. She could use that.

She became every crone who'd ever held power over a young man. "Highness! Come! There's work to do!" It worked. He looked over his shoulder, pushed his displays away and skittered to her, still fuming but obedient. In a huff she shoved him into the arms of the gathered marines. "Get him to safety. Now. Move!" Her stentorian command triggered enough habits for the soldiers to obey. A new round of alarms now rang throughout this level of the palace, and there would be chaos on the grounds to make that happen. One more thing to worry about.

CHAPTER 22

THE FOURSOME FOLLOWED Vonda's suggestion and left. They had nowhere to go except back to *Hajimi*.

Whatever emergency engulfed Movus High Port also swallowed the Down Port. They hustled past broadcast screens showing elements of the carnage around the royal palace. The dodecahedron remained intact, but the royal gardens surrounding it for a mile in all directions was something else again. Shots of protesters clashing with police were bad, but not completely unexpected. Scenes of royal marines opening fire with plasma rifles, however, were something very different. No matter what happened, it was clear that the seat of the Movi government was in turmoil. They wouldn't find any help here.

The constant alarms were disconcerting but essentially harmless. In a clear and present emergency, no one on the station wanted to pick a fight with a trio of strangers who were dressed in obvious combat armor and who walked in purposeful strides. They had other problems. Shelter was at a premium. Red and orange signs flashed over designated shelters, and armed guards checked papers and passports. Not everyone who demanded entry got their wish. The corridors were lined with panicked travelers. Shopkeepers were drawing down steel gates in front of their establishments and abandoning them, fleeing to get to their own shelters. Some simply withdrew into their shops, closed the gates and lights and hunkered down, hoping no one would notice.

"Rosenski to OIC."

"This is Underhill."

That was interesting. She could have sworn she'd put Frost in charge. "We're on our way back to the ship. Status report."

"Repairs are complete. At least what we could fix here on the spot."

"Did you get any guff from the foreman's people?"

A hesitation from Underhill. "That's negative. Frost deployed all crew not actually engaged in repair work to guarding the bay. Nothing fancy, just a dozen or so troops in suits and opaque domes walking the perimeter armed with long guns and bad attitudes. Kid stuff, but it kept the locals from asking questions, which was all we wanted."

"Fuel?"

"The ship runs on fusion reactors which have been topped off with refined Hydro-9. A little gift from Binil's friend the inspector. The fuel cells are ditto."

"Good work. Did we ever get those missiles?"

"Yes and no. The ship's missile reloads are finished. Magazines are full. The SRMs for the fighters arrived, but they're problematic. We've looked at them—everything seems to be in order. The electronics are closer to Sleer molecular circuits but without the fancy neural network stuff. Loading them on the fighters is out of the question under current circumstances."

"Why is that?"

"It's this motherless ship's ultra-tight design. We can't fix them to the fighters without moving the ships out of the launch tubes. That means launching the ship, launching the fighters, putting everything down on an open space somewhere, then loading the missiles on the pylons and then recovering the fighters back into the launch tubes."

"Good lord. How long to do all that?"

"At least three hours of uninterrupted time and a safe place to land. Considering everything that's going on in this system, we don't dare try it in open space."

"Damn. We're bugging out. Get all hands to battle stations and make sure all the turret crews are in place. We'll be coming in hot."

"Copy that. Hot launch in progress. ETA?"

Rosenski did her best to calculate how long it took them to get from the hangar bay to the meeting. About an hour, not including the time Binil had taken to convince her former fellow inmates to take her to their boss. "ASAP."

"Roger. ASAP launch."

Rosenski cut the connection. "Ship is ready. We just need to actually find a way there."

"With all the compartments closing off and the blast doors sliding down in front of us every ten minutes that'll be tough," Brooks said. "There must be a better way. Binil? You got something to offer?"

"No. But there shouldn't be a need. The docking bay is the port's outermost ring. The next one is the restaurants and shops, the one after that are the business offices. Blast doors separate the compartments, but we're here legally. My credentials should work to get us back out."

"Lead on, Captain."

Reagan pointed back up the ramp. "Clipsop first?"

Rosenski gave her pilot a shove. "Come on, Dance."

"Yes, sir... but there will come another time!"

Binil led them through the office complex without incident. They passed office doors, some closed, others open. The occasional Movi stuck their head out to watch the chaos and then went back to work.

"It's like any office building," Brooks commented.

They emerged from the business office maze to a main throughway, a wide expanse of metal and glass that formed a long tunnel with blast doors at either end. At the moment, all the doors remained open. Clearly, this was how the station staff managed their primary flow of traffic.

"This way... no, *this* way," Binil said, turning up toward the end of the tunnel where most people were moving. Wide, bright holo displays floated near the ceiling, sending instructions to the crowd. One demanded that guests and travelers OBEY TRAFFIC RULES, while another demanded they PRESENT YOUR ID ON DEMAND. After a short distance, Rosenski could see why. Every exit was covered by a police checkpoint.

"Got our papers, Captain?" she asked.

"I do."

"What about you two? How do you feel?"

"No implant jammers in here, so I feel fine. You'd never know a woman twice my age kicked the crap out of me," Brooks said.

"Dance? No broken bones?"

"Not a one. Not today."

It took time, but the Movi police were efficient and focused. They directed the bulk of the traffic to automated doors, where one inserted a chip and the door opened. The police only moved in where red lights and a siren sounded. There weren't many of those.

The line moved steadily, the sound of passengers moving their chips through the machinery and the mumbling, cursing, and dull crosstalk of the crowd surrounded them. Rosenski flicked her eyes across the portal, noted the police. Seven of them deployed in a line, with a knot of six more to the far left and five more to the far right of the entry plaza.

Then it was their turn.

Binil moved into the gap, inserted her card into the reader, and waited for something to happen. No alarms, no siren, but no open door either. She frowned and tried again. And again, with no result. Rosenski stepped between Brooks and Regan, tapped them each three times on the shoulder. Violence was an option.

Another try at the gate: no entry. Now the police were taking an interest. One officer with a string of hash marks down his sleeves and fancy insignia on his collar approached them. "Let me see that."

Binil hesitated, then handed her ID over. "Is there a problem, officer?"

"Captain Binilsanetanjamalala?"

"Yes."

"Your ship is the *Hajimi*?"

"Of course. Would you like to accompany us? It's not far."

Rosenski winced at the comment. *Jeez, Binil, don't overplay it.*

The officer handed the card back. "You're using the wrong transfer point. Follow me."

Behind them, a siren pealed, then another than a third. Rosenski turned around to scan the crowd. The knot of passengers at the far right drew the police to them, arguing and thrashing as a fight threatened to break out. People behind the troublemakers started to move off, one woman screaming, and the two in front of the cops raised their arms and screamed words that Rosenski didn't recognize. Then she realized it wasn't a shout, but a name: Gala-Shom.

A shot rang out, then the far end of the plaza exploded in noise, smoke, and shattered metal. And bodies. So many bodies.

Panic set in. Smoke and debris erupted behind them. Their

escort turned and hurriedly reported the incident on a comm. He turned to Binil. "To the left, five doors down, military checkpoint. Go!" The cop ran to help his fellows manage the crowd.

"Can anyone say powder keg?" Dance asked.

They ran, Binil following instructions. This time when she popped her chip into the reader, a green light and an open door were her reward. On this leg of their journey, signs clearly pointed them to their goal. The docking bays were arranged sequentially, and they matched their bay assignment with the number on Binil's chip. When they arrived on deck, the bay was a slightly milder form of chaos, similar to what any carrier experienced during a wartime launch. Deck hands and crews argued as they ran, weaving their way around empty berths and past crews who seemed to be trying to bribe inspectors to get off the station immediately. Rosenski could see that other ship captains weren't so inventive or patient. One small trade ship was powering its engines, straining against its docking clamps, while a few berths away, a work crew tried to cut through their clamps with energy torches.

This place wasn't a powder keg at all; it was a nuclear bomb approaching critical mass, and all these people were free neutrons flying into each other. Which one would begin the chain reaction? Did it matter?

They found the familiar sphere of *Hajimi* where they'd left it. Even from a distance, Rosenski saw they'd prepared for departure. Umbilicals were detached, fuel lines were secure, and the docking clamps weren't engaged. A crewman stepped out of the lift and waved them down.

Rosenski waved back. "Frost! On the boost. Now. Get her in the air."

"Get him in the air."

"Whatever!"

Frost acknowledged the order and disappeared into the

boarding lift. Binil flagged at the end and had to be half carried by Brooks and Reagan. At the end they crammed themselves into an elevator meant for three at most.

"That beats walking," Binil gasped.

Dance patted her friend on the back. "Remember, Cycomm, deep breath, hold it, slow exhale. Slow down your heart rate."

"I thought I was in better shape than that."

"For someone who doesn't have our implants, you did great." Rosenski reached up to jab the intercom. "Bridge. Get us airborne."

"Bridge. Engaging thrusters. Aligning to departure gate."

Rosenski eyed the CPO. "Why'd you let Underhill on the comm?"

Frost shrugged. "With half the crew outside for repairs and loading supplies, the couch was empty. Besides, she gives good comm."

The lift doors opened and they spilled out onto the bridge before Rosenski could argue. On the viewer, the open bay doors. Inside *Hajimi*, the sound of watch officers murmuring reports to each other. All consoles were crewed. No need to swap out people at the moment. She settled into the big chair and leaned forward, hands clenched into fists resting on her knees. Grumbling under her breath, "Come on, come on, come on."

The comm watch officer said, "Captain, flight control is flagging us. If the translator is working."

"Brooks?"

Brooks tapped the watch officer out and took up the station. "Docking control wants us to hold up. They say the grav tractors are off line. We don't have permission to proceed on manual control."

"Oh yes we do."

"Sara?"

"Mr. Janus, proceed on manual control. Brooks, tell them we can't wait."

Brooks made his update while Janus bobbed the ship around. The comms shrieked as they passed through the outermost barrier, and they were in open space.

"We're out!" Janus cried. "Where to?"

"Give us a standard orbit around the homeworld. Ten thousand klicks out. That should keep the worst of the traffic away."

"Maybe not," Skellington said. "There's a great deal of traffic out here."

"Tactical view. Janus, put some distance between us and our closest neighbors."

"Already plotted. No one should be closer than one hundred klicks if I have anything to say about it."

Skull isolated a data point and threw it on the display. "This one has an opinion. He's burning right for us."

Rosenski had begun to relax but tensed up again. Her shoulders felt like a solid mass of rock. "Got an ID?"

"Working on it." The new contact had apparently been in an orbit-seeking flight path of its own. The computer upgraded its status to potential threat and projected an aiming circle. "It has a transponder code but I can't find a match in the ship's library."

"That might mean it's an independent flight."

"I don't know," Brooks said. "He's not answering hails and our library is supposed to have every code Sora's warlord had access to."

The computer upgraded the contact to a threat and the aiming circle turned red. "Janus, give us a fast burn. Get us out of his way."

Hajimi tilted and turned, its maneuver drive cranking out a stream of energy greater than anything they'd used thus far. Even with deck plates adjusting the relative gravity inside the hull, they felt the conflict in inertia. The intruder swung around, adjusted its own course, and brought its drive to full power.

"He's definitely got a bee in his ass about us," Frost said.

"Why is it never easy?" Rosenski murmured. "All we were supposed to do was listen to radio traffic and report back."

"Power spike," Skull called. "The little man is arming weapons and pinging the bejeezus out of us."

Rosenski could relax. Her ship was bigger and carried fighters, even if they weren't packing every weapon they might have been. "So much for flying casual. Brooks, sound battle stations."

CHAPTER 23

THE GUARDS IGNORED the Sovereign's noisy resistance and hustled him away toward an exit that Sora hadn't seen until now. The doors closed behind them and locked noisily. Which left two more marines with nothing to guard but the office. "You two. With me."

"Ma'am?"

"You're going to escort me back to my ship. Then you will report back to your officer in charge. Do you understand?"

"Yes, Admiral."

"Come on." Sora wondered where Singhir had taken these guards from. Now that she thought about it, all the marines in the apartment complex were on the young side and of short ranks. Lieutenants and sublieutenants only. Surely there was a captain around here somewhere? She supposed Singhir had followed a long line of tradition when he set up his command tree, and chances were good that purging the ranks of those he considered disloyal or incompetent was part of that. She'd already seen how he acted to gain loyalty. She shuddered to think how he judged competence.

No. She already knew that. Results at any cost was how he defined competence.

They ran through the complex, passing checkpoints and rounding blast doors. "What is going on?" she demanded of no one in particular.

The taller of the two lieutenants thought she was speaking to him and answered, "Ma'am, the crowd is holding a rally. Or something. Several speakers on the grounds. They're making a lot of noise and closing on the palace grounds."

"Can you show me? Take me to a comm station. I want to see this for myself."

"Yes, Flight Admiral. Right this way." They passed columns of marines and palace guards on their way further into the interior of the palace. She took a moment to marvel at the sheer scope of the installation. Palaces had been so much stone and woodwork in ancient times, but engineers kept building them, designing the fortresses for the two powers with the wealth to pay for them: clergy and nobility. Merchants had the money to buy such things, but preferred to invest their earnings in business enterprises rather than static structures whose only value was to shock and awe one's neighbors and rivals with ostentatious displays of wealth. She supposed there was a way to play the mercantile game there, too—renting palaces or portions thereof to nobles and individuals who wanted to be close to the political action. But since the Movi had discovered space flight and developed quantum computers, jump drives, particle accelerators and starships, mere wood and stone no longer meant much.

In that respect there were few structures on Movia to compare with the royal palace. A dodecahedron in shape, it measured nearly one kilometer in diameter, surrounded by force fields powerful enough to deflect almost any bombardment, and self-sustaining in terms of energy, food, and industrial might. The royal family could remain inside for years along with their retinues, servants, and selected allies, fed by the gardens and livestock pens, fish hatcheries, and hydroponic processors, and clothed and equipped by a vast warehouse of stocked goods and banks of recyclers. The royal guard and marines were maintained with a warehouse filled with weapons, vehicles, and ammunition, and in case things became in short supply, molecular forges were stationed at strategic points inside the palace just in case. The industrial units were huge and consumed much power, but could crank out literally anything inhabitants might need.

That left the rest of the royal grounds, which were considerably less well protected. How a crowd might have gotten past the perimeter gates or guards, Sora couldn't imagine.

They arrived at the comm station soon after. The room was alive with frenetic energy as tense operators in headsets and naval intelligence livery communicated with each other and various parts of the defensive machine. At least two dozen men and women worked hard to manage the crisis. Screens and myriad viewing surfaces surrounded the walls and floated holographically, creating a halo of information that she couldn't properly follow. She picked out bits and pieces of various conversations and communications. This desk over here worked to send orders to military units stationed in orbit, while the desk on the other side of the aisle did the same for ground units. One captain in particular tried to not raise his voice above a low monotone, but Sora could see the veins in his neck bulging as he started to lose his temper. The crowd at the epicenter of the great room strove to supervise the palace's internal communication net, and floor plans and building schematics of the dodecahedron flashed as plans were made and updated in real time.

The right side of the room was awash in civilian networks, news flashes, and monitor bulletins that were flashing all around the Movran solar system. Sora wondered what was being discussed, but soon recognized the palace grounds and looked elsewhere to see that grav APCs were taking up position at various points along the inside of the outermost fence. In addition to that, troops were being dispersed from the palace itself, and units formed up all around the inner gardens of the palace. She soon grew so engrossed with her observations that one of the lieutenants tapped her shoulder. "Madame. Are we heading to the shuttle deck? New orders are arriving. We must answer."

She tossed her head. "What? Yes. yes, of course, go on. I'll find my way. Thank you."

That was that. The marines turned to go, but not before Sora saw the lieutenant tap one of the security men on the way out. He was specific. He pointed back towards her and said something that made the security office frown. Damn. And here he came now, hand lightly resting on the butt of his pistol and followed at several paces by his partner. Double damn.

"Madame Flight Admiral," he said, "This is a secure area. May I ask what your business here is?"

"I wanted to see the source of the trouble, but I think you've already got a handle on that. No?"

"Honestly... no. The crowds are still gathering and she's there with them."

"She?"

"Reverend Mother Gala-Shom." He passed a command over the comm and a nearby viewing surface flickered to change its view; the area around the front gates, which led from the main road to the palace's outer gardens. Three more gates lay after that one, and all were manned by marine units, but the crowds kept growing. The camera focused on one woman in particular, a well dress matron who waved her arms and called out her grievances to the heavens, no doubt amplified by the comm set she wore around her right ear. Sora knew there had to be an amplification system down there somewhere, possibly even using the palaces's own system. That would be a trick. If that were the case, then it meant that someone in this very room, or one like it, was working for two masters.

Suddenly a pop. Then more pops, followed by a *whoosh* as a flash detonated against the side of one of the Marine APCs. The damage was minimal, but screams erupted throughout the crowd as some panicked. The crowd surged forward, pressing countless bodies against the front gates, which shuddered and bent inward... and then broke, spilling bodies on the grounds while the force of sheer numbers made possible what could only have been imagined in quieter times.

Now the crowd ran, people making their ways onto the pathways and the manicured lawns. The APCs opened like clamshells, and platoons of troops deployed across the paths of the crowds.

More shots, more screams, and another explosion, this time on the other side of the compound. Intruders opened fire with small arms; Sora knew what gunfire sounded like. She also knew she needed to leave before things got even more confused, but stayed rooted to the spot. The crowd clashed with security officers dressed in heavy cloth armor and armed with gas grenades and stun weapons. For what seemed like an hour, they fought in the gardens, pockets of resisting citizens being dragged to the side either unconscious or restrained. She watched police form an assembly line: the forward officers subdued rioters, who then dragged the bodies to the rear where another officer would use zip-ties to restrain them. Still more officers hauled them to their feet and loaded them into heavy wheeled vehicles.

Under normal circumstances, the fighting was low key and could go on for hours. So far, there were few real combat troops getting into it with Gala-Shom's people.

She spied a colonel at the front of the room and made her

way through the crowd of operators to see him more clearly. The colonel was an older man, with a silver mane falling straight down his back and the weathered face of a man who'd seen a fair amount of field work. His eyes betrayed the anger and horror he clearly felt talking to someone on the other end of the line. Considering the choice of words from his side of the conversation, it was obvious who he was talking to.

"Your Highness, we cannot fire energy weapons on a crowd of... But sir!! Of course I do, but... Yes, Highness! Affirmative." The colonel fumed, but tapped his comm and gave orders that Sora couldn't hear but could imagine with a ghastly open pit in her stomach. "Open fire. Secure the grounds at all cost. Yes, that's an order. Who do you *think* gave it? Do *you* want to tell him no?"

They didn't. One by one the APC and marines advanced, while still more people filed onto the grounds from the streets. The crowd surged again, writhing erratically like a pile of snakes in a twisted mating bundle. In a nighttime explosion, the world caught fire. Royal marines were issued plasma rifles, shooting beams of partially ionized gas heated to super temperatures, very much like shooting a stream of nuclear energy; against a Sleer Defender they had devastating effect. Against unarmed opponents, it was like dousing them in kerosene and flinging a lit match into the crowd.

Vast swaths of the crowd caught on fire. The IR vison equipped displays lit up in lurid colors as Reverend Mother Gala-Shom's congregation burned by the hundreds.

Sora had seen enough. "Get me to the flight deck. Now." She turned to see if the officer heard her and noticed that he'd left the scene. Probably the wisest thing he could have done. On the viewer, the last of the grounds police deployed, and it seemed clear that no more would be arriving. The crowds pushed further into the gardens, and after a point, the police ran out of ways to house the subdued aggressors. Their supervisors tried to try to obey their orders to secure the grounds in their entirety, but there simply weren't enough of them. One by one, the black-armored guards fell beneath the surging crowd—except for a few enterprising souls who broke and ran for the interior of the palace itself.

On the other side of the compound, the royal marines were continuing their advance, now hosing the crowds freely with their plasma rifles. She gazed at the public broadcast section and more and more channels were picking up scenes of the massacre. And with every new set of broadcasts, another stream of angry inflamed protesters arrived from the other end of the compound. Finally, the police were overwhelmed and broke formation, scattering before the pressing masses. The crowd broke around the palace and streamed across the gardens like locusts. They soon located the marines units attacking the crowds in the west, and attacked them from behind. The fire sputtered out as marine units now found themselves being hit with everything from small arms to concrete blocks to batons and bricks to home-made explosives and simple rocks people picked up off the ground.

It was a rout. The colonel screamed wordlessly, threw his headset across the room, and stormed out, pulling squad of armed guards from the room to follow him.

They were losing control. A five-year-old could have seen it. The idiot in charge was issuing insane orders to the adults in the room—who felt they had to obey or lose their careers. And they were probably right.

Doomed. We are doomed. She thought she finally understood Archduke Mineko just a little bit. She couldn't quite convince herself that he would have handled the crisis any better, but he probably wouldn't have ordered his troops to fire on civilians. Women and children. Probably.

She exited the chamber, followed posted directions to a weapons locker, withdrew a forearm shield projector, a short pistol with three magazines, and a matching hip holster. Then she fled, following suspended floor maps and signs toward the flight deck. She paid attention to the faces of those she passed. No panic, not yet, but lots of wide eyes and furtive glances.

The mood on the palace's flight deck was strangely subdued. She followed the signs to her ship's berth and noticed that the civilian ships and shuttles she'd seen on her arrival were mostly departed. In their places were warships: troop drop ships, military transports, and at least one proper ground assault vessel that she recognized. Whatever Singhir was having his generals plan, it would surely be bloody. Better to be far away before it came to pass.

Her pilot was quietly going over his checklist. She boarded and pounded the intercom. "How quickly can you get us airborne?"

"How quickly can you take a seat, Flight Admiral?"

"Immediately."

She heard him murmur into his microphone and settled into her seat in the main cabin. Suddenly, she wished Cleo and Sellik stayed with her. Wished even that she knew where they were. She hoped they were somewhere safer—some place without clashes between mobs and police, where marines didn't fire plasma rifles into crowds. She hadn't known them well, but she'd liked them. Good soldiers, both. She'd left them at the War College when she made peace with Anterran weeks ago. She hadn't said goodbye or even wished them luck, much less thanked them for their support when things were strange and prospects dim.

The whine of engines behind her and the slight tremor in the deck plates let her know they were airborne. She touched a stud and opened a viewing surface, watching the geometric bulk of the palace fall away from them as the ship gained altitude. Then the inertialess thrusters added their power and the craft soared, reaching the clouds in seconds. The ground became only a dark expanse scattered with blobs of bright light. She could barely make out where the palace lay. It might well not even exist.

Forward. Perhaps she should have ordered him to land at High Port after all, at least there was no—

"Damn."

Her ears twitched. "What?"

"I'm sorry, Flight Admiral. We need to change course."

Oh, no. "Why?"

"Apparently there's a disturbance aboard the High Port structure too. Something about an explosion—"

Sora began to breathe deeply to forestall the panic she felt rising in her gorge. *No. This is not happening.*

"We're being warned off."

"Ignore it."

"Admiral, a company command cruiser is warning us away from the area."

A what? "Show me. Put their registration number on the screen back here!" The image was so familiar she had to bite back a scream. The eight turrets were still painted like great eyes and everything. Why were they here? How had they managed to follow her? More importantly, what to do about them?

She tapped the comm, opened the feed wide, and watched the torrent of news bulletins that filled the screens. There was no shortage of local scenes to choose from, all of them awful. One caught her eye.

"How are we armed?"

"Not well, ma'am. A couple of three-place turrets, one with

lasers, the other with missile launchers. But they're intended for emergency defense."

"Inform the High Port garrison that we've located a company command cruiser leaving in a rush, just after explosions occurred on the station. Tell them we suspect they were behind the attack. Send them that ship's registration number, and it's name: *Hajimi*. And call for fighter intercept for aid."

"Yes, ma'am. Message sent. Garrison comm officer acknowledges."

"Good. Now target that ship and open fire."

"Madame, that ship is five times our size. We've called for backup. Shouldn't we wait for it to arrive?"

"Open fire. Immediately!"

"Yes, ma'am."

CHAPTER 24

"SOUND BATTLE STATIONS. Brooks, you and Reagan are section leaders. On the boost!"

Brooks used the ship's general PA system. "Gauntlet squadron, gear up and Ready Five. Repeat, we are Ready Five. All pilots report ASAP." He logged out of this console and entered the lift.

It was the opposite of the problem they'd had on *Ascension*. That giant ship had been modified by humans for their own use, which made a complicated dance between managing tight accommodations on otherwise wide expanses. *Hajimi* was the worse of the two arrangements: here everything was tightly packed together, enclosed in a relatively small volume. It was like living on a nonstop commercial flight from California to Hawaii. With that thought came a reminder there were no commercial flights on Earth anymore. Atmospheric grit and jet engines played poorly together.

One saving grace for *Hajimi* was the sounds he made. You could tell exactly which systems were running quietly with Movi efficiency and which were struggling noisily to keep up. Alarms rang and the lift tilted, throwing him against the wall, then stopped briefly before resuming its downward path. *That was a hit. Somewhere below decks.* Coolant pumps thrummed, struggling to keep the lasers from exploding. Lights dimmed when the lasers fired. Gonna be one hell of a getaway.

The doors opened to steam and smoke. The fighters were locked inside their storage tubes, the four other pilots clumped together beneath them. Dance Reagan pulled a giant lever, while Roberts threw a bank of switches. Winches and platforms in the bay's roof swung into action, and in less than two minutes the fighters had been deposited in launch gantries. The pilots climbed through the tubes, pulling open their fighters' canopies and slithering inside.

Brooks had never noticed those controls before. "I didn't know they could do that. How'd you figure it out?"

Roberts tapped him on the back of the head. "Sorry, Captain! Some of us were here breaking a sweat while you four were gallivanting around Movra High Port, playing James Bond."

"Well, excuse the fuck out of me, *lieutenant*."

Dance gave a hand signal to Roberts, who retreated to the control station. "I'll give you an excuse," she said. "Section one is on deck. On the boost, people."

Brooks thanked the universe for putting Dance in his proximity. She'd turned into a tiger of a section leader; it was exciting to watch her work. And arousing. And he had fifty other things to pay attention to, damn it. He climbed inside his fighter, got through the pre-launch checklist in record time, and this time remembered to engage the VR environment before lifting off.

After a brief exchange between the bridge and flight deck, Brooks pronounced his squadron ready for action and waited tensely while the crew evacuated the deck. Bay doors opened. Power to the engines, and *blammo*, into the void. He'd never understand why Fairchild compared the rush of flight to sex. Maybe Simon Brooks was too weird for his own good.

"*Gauntlet*, this is Leader. Form up on me." The squadron confirmed the order, and Brooks began hunting for targets. There was one; the wedge-shaped ship that Skull had picked out early in the fight. He tweaked his comm settings, and data from *Hajimi* began rolling across the display. Their opponent was a wicked-looking piece of work. Ventral and dorsal triple-place turrets, with a power signature that seemed huge compared to the size of the ship. And it was moving in a way *Hajimi* could only dream about. The company command cruiser wallowed like a hog, rolling away to bring its missile turrets to bear. The newcomer adjusted its track. Streaks of flame showed where missiles were ejected, and bright flashes showed the laser turret was active and hot. *Hajimi* deployed a set of counter missiles, which detonated the sheaf well away from the ship, but the laser blast smashed against the docking bay door. An explosion followed, and somone gasped. Brooks saw the launch bay door break away from the main body, and debris fell out of the cavity. He thought he recognized the remains of their dropship, shredded and broken. Pieces of it, anyway.

Janus griped in his headphones, "Okay, now I'm pissed off."

"New contacts all across my scope," Brooks said. "I think we're attracting attention."

"This asshole first," Ghost said.

"Agreed. Swoop him, kick him in the nuts, on three. One, two, three!"

Brooks shifted his hands and feet, watching the rest of his pilots keeping their distance while following his maneuver perfectly. Good job, guys. They shot past the intruder, flipped their noses toward him and burned, g-forces pressing Brooks into his couch. He reached down without looking, pinged the attacking ship, and linked his squadron's weapon to his own targeting computer. He waited for the VR aiming circle to turn from yellow to red. When it did, he pressed the firing stud and watched five sets of blasters shear the tail of the ship off its main body. Flames and sparks blew outward as the bulkheads gave away and the rear third of the ship broke away, tumbling from the inertia.

"Tough darts, farmer. We warned you."

"Yeah, but how do we land these things with no launch bay?" Dance asked.

A new wave of contacts rendered the question academic.

"With a relocation projector," Brooks said. "Gauntlet Leader to bridge. Suggest you do a wide area search for any large vessels making vectors for the outer reaches of this system. Gauntlet Squadron, pull in tight. We want to look like we're escorting our crippled mother ship away from a fight that we drew a loss on."

"No way, Leader. At worst, that was a draw," Diallou said.

"Damn straight, we carved their literal ass off," Dance agreed.

"Leader, this is Rosenski. We're harpooning you. Stand by."

Brooks set his controls for autopilot, then forced himself to relax. Within minutes, a metallic clang sounded through the hull and he felt rather than saw his fighter being winched down against the hull of *Hajimi*. On his left and right, other fighters were getting the same treatment.

The universe lurched. There was a bright flash and then a twisting, turbulent tunnel appeared, drawing the cruiser into its vortex. When it stopped, he felt as if his lungs were being forced out through his nose—but there was a different star in the sky. The bastards had micro-jumped with the fighters bound by nothing more than tow cables.

He didn't know they could do that either.

Rosesnki hung back to her usual station on the bridge, Janus and Frost manning the controls with Brooks playing comm console jock. It was a combination she felt at ease with. She couldn't see Skull Skellington, but knew that he was in the captain's office, making use of the sensor suite by remote control. "We need a place to land those fighters and get a bit of intel," she announced. "I'll entertain just about any idea at this point."

Binil threw data into the display. "Welcome to Balliss," she said. "Three planets, two of them ordinary. One gas giant very far away, with multiple moons. It's a well-known travel hub."

"Any comm stations running on them?" Rosenski asked.

"All of them."

"That means they're occupied. We want peace and quiet. Try again," Frost said.

"I have an entertaining idea," Skull said. He could have just opened the door to the office and shouted. "There's a heavy passenger transport in a geosynchronous orbit around the main world. Several shuttlecraft and other small vessels have docked within the past hour. I get the idea they're taking on last-minute arrivals before heading out to their next destination. Some of the ships making berth in her are of significant volume."

"How significant?" Rosenski said.

"Bigger than we are."

"Binil," Rosenski said, "I need you to get us a space on that liner."

The Cycomm dug into her work and data rolled past her display. "The *Magisterium*," she read. "It's a Kar-Tuyin ship. They're heading to Marathas, but they're doing it the long way—fifteen stopovers at respectable space ports. ETA, thirty-one days."

Rosenski tapped her foot, waiting for Binil to make her point. "What does that mean in practical terms?"

"It's not surprising. Marathas is coreward. Quite a distance away. They must be a corporate-owned liner making a standard passenger and cargo run between here and there."

"Frost, can you show us those added destinations?"

"I can, and I shall... there you go. Binil, anything look especially useful?"

"I do wish you would stop asking me questions like that."

"You're the closest thing we have to an expert," Rosenski snapped.

Binil bent to the console and began to plug in queries. "That's a fair, if annoying, point. These ports of call seem dull enough. Oh! Camdassen... that's interesting."

They waited until Rosenski ran out of patience and tapped the girl's leg with her boot. "Hey. Remember us?"

"Yes. Of course. Camdassen is Missena's homeworld. She maintains a stupendous estate of her own there... apart from the war criminal father and everything else. In fact... oh my Makers... she's registered as a passenger in the Imperial suite. I can't run a registry check from here, but—"

Skull swung into action. "I can do that. Is this what you were looking for? The registration number traces back to the starport on Camdassen. It's her ship, all right. She doesn't own it outright, but she's got several hundred shares in it. She's a partial owner. That means exceptional service."

"And exceptional security. Do Movi merchant queens usually rent their ships out as time-shares?" Rosenski asked.

Binil made a vague gesture. "Sometimes. Sometimes it's just a matter of wanting a suite reserved for when they do decide to arrive. It's a very popular way to arrange business meetings. Especially if your sovereign is trying to have you killed."

"Binil, get us a space," Rosenski repeated.

"Already done," Skull reported. "They have space on their outer landing deck for a ship *Hajimi's* size. I took the Haven registration transponder code from a list of options that the Movi warlord provided for us, dropped it into a berthing request, and got us a spot. It's not a huge spot, but if we launch the fighters before we land, we should at least be able to load missiles on their pylons."

"You are handy to have around," Binil said. "Good work, Mr. Skellington."

"Thank you, Captain."

Rosenski was more direct. "Gauntlet Leader, we have a prospect. We're releasing the tow lines. Follow us very closely."

Brooks's voice crackled over the speaker. "Copy that."

A tap on her shoulder made her look up to see Underhill's face above and behind hers. She handed the Cycomm a folded slip of flimsy and said, "Binil, once we're set up and the mechanics are fixing the fighters, I'll need you to find me one of these. I'm given to understand from my research that luxury liners are equipped with at least a few of them."

Binil read the slip and frowned. "A transmogrifier? Why?"

"I have a plan."

"In my office, ladies," Rosenski said and took them up the ladder to her owner's suite. The great clear dome above them showed a wonderful view of the star liner. They watched Brooks and his pilots keep the fighters close. "Major. What gives?"

"Nothing gives. I've been reading is all. Watching interviews, reading books and news clips. If that ship really is owned by Missena whatshername, it'll be part passenger and cargo ship, part noble's plaything. Going aboard is a prime opportunity to grab some first-rate intel. Let's use it."

"Stop there. Binil, what's a transmonger—"

"Transmogrifier. It's a device. A multitude of devices. You

go into one end of the shop, lay down in the box, and you get up looking completely different. It's not for human use."

"Why? Won't it work? I know Valri Gibb was working with one of the Dal-Cortsuni reps to experiment with human DNA."

"I don't know. It might. Biochemistry is unique to every life form. It changes how you look. It can restructure your genetic code. It can make you older or younger, and the time gained or lost can be ported to other customers for a price. Most clients just want a bit of superficial gene splicing, using messenger RNA to rewrite cosmetic features. You can come out looking completely different compared to when you went in. But it can't change you *too* much. Skin and hair, maybe eye color. A tall man can't go into one and come out looking like a short woman, for example. Maybe an inch or two of height. It can help distribute weight. But since the Movi have almost no experience with humans, there's no way to predict what the effects on you would be."

"Gotta try something. We're out of options here. Hell, Rosenski and Brooks didn't know what would happen when they let Genukh put those Sleer implants in them. They arguably worked better than expected."

Rosenski fought the urge to argue. Yes, they were stronger and faster, but the alien tech was having detrimental long-term effects on the members of Hornet Squadron who obtained it. "That's a little oversimplified, but I suppose it's a fair point. Let's say it works and they turn you in to a Movi. What then?"

"Then we go and pass ourselves off as mercenaries. Private security for hire. Even if Missena and her war criminal daddy say no, there's got to be others of their class aboard. That's a paranoid bunch of rich people. Once they hear news there's a mercenary company on board looking for work, someone will approach us."

"You can't possibly know that."

Underhill gestured to show she really was guessing. "I think it's a good bet. If nothing else, we mill around, pick up whatever gossip and news we can, and fly home when we're done," she said.

Rosenski brought up a schematic of the landing bay. Damage control crews had stopped the fire from spreading to the rest of the ship, but what they left was a ruin. The fighters still outside would never be able to dock with *Hajimi* again. She considered the options. "I hate to say it, but it sounds like a good bet to me, too. Especially if we can score a repair on the ship. Binil, what do you think? Is this procedure dangerous?"

"I don't know," Binil said. "But if you really want to try, Major Underhill can go in to come out looking like a Cycomm. I know it's not as impressive, but a Cycomm can go anywhere a Movi could, probably more. They know Cycomm physiology, and cosmetically, Cycomms and humans are nearly identical. That will work."

Rosenski finally nodded. All six of the Movi fighters were now flying escort, and the space liner was very close. They'd be landing soon. She tapped her comm. "Rosenski to bridge."

"Bridge, Frost here. You could have just yelled down the ladder, you know."

"Grandpa, I need you and Skull to dig into the ship's logs. Real entries, fake ones, whichever. Find a command profile and elevate it to current commander. Make sure that the photograph matches Binil's description. We'll provide a likeness to use. Can you do that?"

"Make a command profile for Binil. Can do. It'll be faster and probably better if Brooks does it."

"Brooks is flying a fighter," Chief.

"Acknowledged. Bridge out."

Rosenski felt bile rising in her throat. With a word, Underhill could induce a seizure in her. She'd told Brooks to not think about killing the overcop, but she understood his fury. Resisting her own took a lot of energy. "You'd better be right about this."

Underhill shrugged. "We'll both do our best."

———

The landing was simpler than they'd expected.

Tapped into the command channel, Brooks heard Binil and Rosenski accept what sounded to him like an exorbitant docking fee for the company, Binil promising payment from Hajimi's docking fund, emptying the account in the process. Tractor projectors directed *Hajimi* to a landing berth well away from the commercial traffic. Brooks held his breath until the cruiser was settled in its landing spot, the ship's weight pressing down on its landing pylons. The fighters were directed to an adjacent berth and settled near each other.

He powered down his craft and opened his canopy. A crew chief had apparently been assigned to them. "Breaker take all! What did you people do to this ship? Use it to start a war?"

Oh, if you only knew. Brooks kept his helmet sealed and visor dark as he climbed out of the fighter. "Just tell me if my landing permits are good. They told me there was a problem as we were coming in, and I don't like hearing that."

The chief waved the question away. "This part of the ship is called the balcony. Anyone can land here for a docking fee. They can even stay here and ride for free if they stay limited to this area. Seriously, what happened to you?"

"I'll tell you, Chief. There were explosions up at High Port and some idiot saw us leaving and decided we were responsible. A civilian ship fired on us. We warned them off, they ignored the warning. There was an exchange of fire. We gave them worse than they showed us."

"It's always something. Fucking military. No offense to you, though."

"None taken. We work for a living," Brooks said, and ran his hand over the nose of his fighter.

"I can see that. You the OIC?"

"For the moment. Captain's on her way down. What's the likelihood of repair work while we're here?"

The chief laudged loudly, then caught himself. "I'm sorry. Out here? Almost none. Your outer bay door is gone, the interior of your bay is gone. I'm amazed your drives are intact. You're lucky the ship's magazine is so well armored or you'd have lost him. How long are you on board?"

"All the way to Marathas."

The chief nodded and made notes on a wrist device. "Talk to the Chief Purser when you get settled. He may be able to work out something. But honestly… your ship is fit to do nothing but sit here. I doubt the bridge will clear you to leave."

Brooks drew himself up, stretching his spine. "We will not be prisoners."

"Of course not. I don't suppose you'd sell it for parts? We'd pay well, considering."

"We just landed… now you want my ship?"

Together they surveyed the six fighters. "Good ships," the chief declared. "My friend, the fighting has the whole kingdom in chaos. Supply lines are shorter than they once were and parts are scarce. In two more years, we'll be cannibalizing half our liner fleet to keep the other half flying. Your fighters seem well maintained and piracy is a real problem these days. Thinking of picking up some escort work?"

"I'll talk to my Captain."

"Fair enough. We waive docking fees and discount fares for new hires." The chief stalked off, stopping by to check in each of the fighters before moving on.

The *Magisterium's* flight deck was no less busy than the *Night Render's*, but the character of its activity felt different. The warship's bustle was rooted in the movement of aircraft, the loading of weapons and fuel, and the movement of troops on and off transports. And always there were precise timetables for launching and recovering small craft. The space liner's deck was crowded with smaller ships, but only those on final approach. Flight crews worked to pack small craft into landing zones, where they were approached by deck crews. No fuel lines or umbilicals were attached, and no weapons were loaded into turrets or magazines.

"What was that about?" Rosenski asked. None of the crew were helmeted, so Brooks pulled his off and hooked it to his belt.

"I believe we've been propositioned."

"Yes!" Janus yelled and pumped his fist.

"Oh-oh," Dance said.

Binil took a step forward, transforming into the ship's captain. "You shouldn't have said anything. What did you promise them?"

Brooks felt a snark rising and forced himself to stay on task. "Nothing. They wanted us to know that escort work pays for passage."

"Does it now?" Underhill said. "Sounds worth checking in to."

Binil shook her head. "Tomorrow perhaps. Today we gain passage. Until we cross that threshold, we are less than cargo." She nodded toward the edge of the flight deck where blast doors managed the flow of traffic between the vessel's interior and the launch bay.

Rosenski smirked. "But?"

"*But* balcony passengers must stay limited to the balcony. They're forbidden access to the interior of the vessel. Most never leave their ship. And the liner's facilities are off limits to them; they're allowed to connect umbilical lines to use the electricity generated by the liner's reactor, but no more."

"Gah, it's like catching a ride from Tijuana to Texas by riding the top of the cargo train," Diallou said. "Yeah, it's free, but hey, maybe you'll die on the way up. Fun for the whole family."

Binil sighed. "Sometimes it's worth it if a small ship can't afford to provision itself for a multi-port journey. There's also no security out here. Before long, the captain will announce a lock down. All the deck crews and police will be pulled inside and there will be a load of trouble for the people left here."

Solovoya harrumphed. "Roving gangs?"

"At least. An aggressive bunch might break into a small passenger craft, kill the owners, then claim the empty ship as salvage. It happens."

"How can the shipping line let that bullshit go on?" Janus asked.

"It's not strictly illegal as long as it doesn't happen inside the liner," Binil said. Brooks watched her, saw her regal captain's bearing crumble. She continued, "There's an old rule on Movra that gives the edges of sailing ships to the passengers to ride for free. So, those who could pay passage did and those who needed passage but had no money literally hung on to the rails. They wove baskets or cages for themselves and hung them on the winches and stayed there, managing as best they could until they arrived—or died. When the Movi went to the stars, the tradition went with them. So, the balcony."

There were at least twenty small ships of varying designs around them. There were no armed guards visible, nor even any armaments on the vessels, but there were tight groups of people huddled in preparation for what came next. Gathering for protection. "Looks like we're the only military vessel around," he said.

"Then I have an idea." Underhill tapped her comm. "Frost. Roberts. Meet us at the foot of the ship. On the boost. Binil, I get the idea that the crew won't bother to come out here during the voyage."

Binil frowned. "You could drag every child out of their mother's arms, shove them in a cage in the middle of the deck, then ransom them back to their parents and no one would notice. The crew cares about paying passengers. No one else."

Underhill pulled Frost and Roberts to the side when they arrived. "Good. Gentlemen, form the crew up into four-man fire teams. Each team will perform an hourly patrol on this space. There should not be fewer than four teams on the ship at any time and no more than three teams outside at any time. The mission is to prevent predation. Any team that is threatened is authorized to neutralize the threat. Disarm anyone who argues. Defend yourselves, but do not kill unless necessary."

"Understood," Frost said, then turned to Rosenski. "I think we'll trade up to combat gear for this one. Those domes will hide our faces, and they're clearly military in design. I'd rather not give any ambitious locals a reason to test us."

"Agreed. We'll work out a rotation schedule to allow the entire crew inside at some point." Rosenski spent some time walking around the ship, inspecting connections between Hajimi's utility umbilical and connection points built into the deck. Finally she said, Binil, where are we going?"

Binil pointed across the deck to where the airlocks lay. "The gantry to the ship's interior is over there. Once we're inside please remember, you're all hirelings of the Malala royal family. If I give you an order, follow it."

"What if we get stopped?" Brooks asked.

"We won't be. But if someone takes an unhealthy interest in you, be arrogant. You are protected by wealth and power, even here in the heart of the Movi kingdom."

"Former kingdom," Underhill corrected.

Binil said, "It may eventually fall apart, that's true. But today it survives. As long as the various factions are fighting, no one has won. That gives us the chance to do essentially whatever we want."

"Don't you need tickets to get aboard?" Dance said.

Binil pulled up her tablet and showed her a glowing display with a swirling digital image. "Mr. Brooks managed to open that door that already. Our ship's registration number is our ticket. We'll cross the Chief Purser's palm with *estani*, ask for the crew's discount and see where it takes us."

Simon Brooks had never been aboard a proper cruise ship, but he understood the concept. A floating luxury hotel—or what he imagined a luxury hotel to be like. The majority of guests were there for simple passage from point A to Point B. But some guests were, of course, accustomed to a greater dose of luxury than others.

The hangar bay gantry led them down a well-lit tunnel that ended in a pair of vault-like blast doors and brought them into a lobby that was a scene of barely controlled chaos. Whatever ideas Brooks entertained before arriving, fled the moment he contacted reality. The high-class passengers, those with VIP tickets, milled around before row upon row of entry kiosks. Passengers presented tickets, and green lights and a pleasing chime greeted those with the right credentials.

The kiosks were overwhelmed by the sheer number of people who wanted entry. As they watched, the green lights grew fewer and red lights began to appear more often. Whenever a red light appeared, a liveried crew member appeared to firmly and gently lead the offending individual away.

The vast crowd behind the kiosks was a proper throng, with people loaded down with heavy bags or even trunks or security boxes, and a great many haggard couples with children in tow.

"What happens to the ones who get rejected?" Brooks asked. "There's no way this ship is returning to port. So...?"

"You'd rather not know," Binil said.

"Don't say that. I *want* to know."

"They're taken care of," Binil said. "Though how well is another issue."

"Stop bullshitting. What happens?" Brooks demanded.

"If they can't pay, they have a choice. They can take their chances on the balcony. They can buy an indenture and work for the ship's owners until their passage is paid off. They can buy an indenture from another passenger if they can find one willing to sponsor them. Or they can be sold to a buyer at the next port of call."

"Sold by who?"

"The shipping line."

"That's just crazy," Brooks said.

"It's quite rational. The fact that you dislike it is another issue entirely. Here. We're up next. Stay close." Binil went first, sliding her tablet's face onto a plate on one side of the kiosk. The system scanned her swirling data image and opened with the green light and chime. She turned around. "Follow me closely. Now!" They obeyed instructions and got through—Underhill was a fraction of a second slow and yelped as the gate closed on her heel.

Binil led them to another wall of kiosks, but this one seemed more like a check-in kiosk than anything else. She popped her hand against another plate and this time was rewarded with a set of thin plastic cards, which she handed out, one to each of them. "These are your ID cards. They pay for everything... your rooms, your meals, your drinks. Which I guarantee will be expensive. Even the casino, but—"

"There's a casino?" Dance asked, wide eyed and hopeful.

"Every passenger ship has a casino. It's how they pay for services."

"Brooks? Care to test your math nerd credit?"

"No!" Binil hissed. "The most you can hope for is to lose a few credits. If you win more than a few hundred, they will take you aside and demand to know how you cheated. It's that simple. These casinos aren't for poor people to make money. They're for rich people to lose it. Trust me."

Binil led them up through a series of entertainment decks on her way to their destination; at a set of glass doors with a sign that proclaimed the shop as the "New Look" and promised exquisite results. They expected the plush lobby, the pastel color scheme, and the holographic host, but they didn't expect the Sleer proprietor or his Vix assistant.

The Sleer rumbled a greeting in what Brooks's implants told him was a combination of Sleer and Movi, but he was able to follow easily enough. "Good day, esteemed guests! I wonder what service we may perform for you today?" He even bowed. Brooks wasn't well versed enough to know what various styles of dress meant to Sleer, but it seemed to him that this fellow was garbed much like Chairman Bon had been when they'd first met. The combination of purple and green robes either meant status or wealth. Maybe both.

Binil explained what they needed, and it took Brooks a minute to realize he was hearing her speak the dinosaur's tongue in her own way, not a translation of Sleer provided by his implants. And from what he could tell it was a solid request.

"We can provide what you need. You understand the likeness will be temporary. We are not allowed to do permanent conversion here. It's the Kar-Tuyin rules, you understand."

"How long will the transformation last?"

"We program a maximum duration equal to the length of a single voyage. So. One month, maximum."

"That will be fine. Can you handle alien races?"

"I am not sure what that means."

Binil indicated Underhill with a flourish. Underhill dropped her eyes and lowered her chin in an effort to look demure. "My first officer is not a Cycomm, but she's from the local cluster. A minor race of little importance, but she means a great deal to me," Binil said.

"Which race would that be?"

"A human. Frances, show the shop keeper your face." Underhill obeyed, and if the Sleer was taken aback, he hid it well. "Interesting," he said. "What will I be doing for them?"

"Eyes that match my own in color. Those fibers on her brow simply must go. And that hair color…You can see it's a small job."

Hiss. "I see. Eyes, face, and brow. Ears perhaps. Skin pigment as well. A simple job." The Sleer clicked its claws and hissed something, and a new steward arrived. This one was humanoid, but strangely colored. Stripes and spirals covered their skin. "Would you care to model your commissions?"

"Yes, we do. Does your Vix have a—"

"Yes. Come. Please follow us."

Modeling became a tedious affair. The Vix was able to take a good long look at both Underhill and Binil and reproduce their features and body type so completely even Binil could not tell the difference between them—which upset Underhill badly. But there was a method behind the madness: the Vix started with the base image and then took orders from each client in turn, making changes as they were described. When the client was satisfied, a holographic scanner was used to make a three-dimensional image of the desired result and then it was programmed into the transmogrifier. Complicated perhaps, but convenient. The customer got what they wanted without having to worry how the final imager would look.

When all was done, Underhill didn't seem all that different. Her hair was gone to raven black, her eyebrows were now the same bony ridges that Binil had started with, and her eyes were now blood red. That took some getting used to.

"What do you think?"

"This is weird?"

"Weird, you say. On Haven this is luxury itself. Let's mingle."

CHAPTER 25

BROOKS AND ROSENSKI watched their two spies make their way to the dining hall. Brooks thought they made a striking pair, and not just because Underhill was eight inches taller than the young Cycomm. Whatever else Binil was, she handled social situations with practiced ease and a depth of grace that Underhill could only play at. They came off looking as if a gregarious Movi Captain had picked up a tall stately Cycomm under a war-torn rock and was slowly but surely training her how to move through polite society without tripping over chairs or turning over tables in a fit of rage.

Brooks and Rosenski followed their adventure by way of their comms. One of the advantages of working with military dress was that they all shared the same unit insignia. It was clear they were of no importance, and so the crowd ignored them, which allowed Brooks and Rosenski to explore unhindered.

"I know cruise ships were a thing before the U-War," Sara mentioned as she grabbed a pair of drinks from a passing tray. She sniffed one and handed the other to her partner. "Bottoms up." She sipped hers and held the glass away from her face.

"This is the worst champagne in the universe," she declared. Brooks swilled his in a single gulp.

"I've had some engineer's moonshine aboard AMS-1 that would melt your dog tags. This is weak juice," he said.

"I'm not going to argue about booze.."

"Not arguing. It's a fact. Dad made stuff out of pine needles and rain water that tasted better than this."

A hiss in their comms and they looked up to see that their officers were tag teaming a pair of Movi navy men with numerous decorations on their uniforms. "Mid grade commanders," Brooks murmured. "From what I read, the higher up in Movi military you get, the fewer decorations you display. So watch out. If you find someone with no fruit salad, you might be talking to the ranking officer on a proper battle squadron."

"How do you know that?"

"I like to read. And ever since we left our good library behind at Great Nest I'm bored."

"It takes no effort at all to find things for you to do. Shall I send you a daily task list?"

"You do that already. Living the XO life and so on." A passing servant took their empty glasses and Brooks grabbed a bit of glistening finger food from another. "I should still be back there digging into what makes Genukh tick. She's—different—since we merged her with ZERO. And not necessarily in a good way."

Rosenki traded her still full glass for a plate of pastries. "Binil thinks she's wrong."

"Wrong about what?"

"No. I mean *wrong*. As in '6 am and already the girl ain't right' wrong."

"She's fine with it. We had that talk."

"*I* talked to her. She's very specific."

"Bah. She thinks that computer is a religious icon. I don't.

Genukh is circuits and relays and quantum switches. Nothing magical about her."

"And that makes you right and her wrong?"

"Of course."

"We'll see. We won't settle it here that's for sure. Don't get too comfortable, though. We're in a very active wasp's nest and I'm logging the minutes until things go sideways," she said.

The Sleer and Vix from the transmogrifier shop they'd visited earlier came up to them and bowed. "We never spoke properly to you. I am Kessek. This is Bellon. I take it our modifications were taken well?"

They'd split up now. Binil looked to be intently questioning an elderly matron with a spectacular coiffure, while Underhill was having an animated conversation with the matron's male counterpart.

"I think so. They don't seem bored at least."

The Vix pointed into the crowd. "Your false Cycomm is doing well. That's a Sector Lord. You can tell from the sash."

"Are you enjoying yourselves?" The Sleer blinked his eyes while pulling something tiny and wriggling from his plate. He popped it in his mouth and chewed heartily. Brooks wondered what else a Sleer's dining habits might look like.

"I can see you are enjoying yourself."

The Sleer took the posture of resignation. "It is not a bad way to live. The food is good, at least."

Rosenski sipped her glass. "You live on this ship?"

"'Live' is a poor word for it," Bellon sulked.

Kessek nudged him none too gently with a heavily calloused elbow. "Be polite." To the humans he said, "You know how a thing is. Food and shelter first. Everything else comes afterward."

Rosenski said, "Back home, there are people with means who decide to take a voyage on a ship such as this and decide to stay aboard indefinitely. It's less expensive than many living arrangements, and it offers a never-ending stream of new people to meet."

"Maker, that sounds tedious," Bellon said. "Truthfully, this is not where either of us expected to end up, but the purser allowed us to set up shop when the Skreesh drove down through our respective solar systems. One ship after another, always trying to keep ahead of the incursion. Finally, we both came here. Kessek bought the business from an elderly Movi who wanted to retire, and I suggested he needed a partner. He agreed. Here we are."

"So you two have seen everything and everyone?"

"Hardly. But... since the Sovereign's assassination, things have become very strange indeed."

Rosenski nodded sagely. "We saw the refugees when we came aboard. Some of my people are doing their best to maintain order on the balcony."

"You should talk to the Chief Purser about work," Bellon said. "The balcony is crowded this trip."

"So I've been told."

Bellon sipped his drink. "Refugees, you call them. Some of them, definitely. Others were mere hangers on who were abandoned by their patrons. Some few are in genuinely dire straights, in need of evacuation and safety. The rest... opportunists and criminals who think the pickings aboard a luxury liner are better than back home."

"That's a cynical attitude, my friend," Kessek sniffed.

"These are cynical times. Or they would be if anyone tried to read the road signs."

Brooks asked, "What do the signs say? How does it end?"

"It doesn't. Eventually, the sides will come to an agreement, and things will settle for the worse. But nothing really *ends*."

Brooks's comm chirped loudly in his ear. He excused himself and took a step away to answer. "Brooks. Go ahead."

"XO Brooks!" Dance chirped. "I am pleased to report we have loaded the missiles onto the fighters. We have enough for six reloads per fighter, but we'll have to go through this crap every time we want to reload. There's no practical way to do it in the middle of a fight, so I'm thinking we should choose our battles as carefully as possible."

"Got it. Good work, Dance."

"Are you guys having fun? Sound like a party over there."

"It's the social event of the season, for sure. Any trouble on the balcony?"

"Some yahoo gathered up his friends and tried to enlist us to his merry band of salvage operators. We let him know that the balcony was our territory, and if anything disappeared from any vessel, we had ways of recovering it and they were painful. They seem to have taken the warning to heart. Besides that, no issues out here."

"Good work. When we've gotten the lay of the land, we'll discuss getting some down time in town for the crew. Promise."

"Acknowledged. Reagan out."

He met Rosenski's questioning glare head on. "The packages have been installed on the delivery system," he said.

Kessek rumbled a chortle. "Your fighters are now armed. Excellent!"

"I have no idea what you mean," Rosenski said.

Bellon snorted. "Please. Don't you know who you're talking to? This is no mere hairdresser. This is Greater Servant of Gunnery Kessek, who served aboard Fleet Lord Sselaniss's flagship for six years—before the command structure at Home Nest collapsed and Sselaniss took her fleet to Great Nest and started forming evacuation fleets."

"She evacuated and you came here? That sounds like one major demotion," Brooks said.

Kessek gobbled the contents of his plate. "I was tired. This had obvious advantages over remaining in fleet."

"Like not being killed by Skreesh."

Kessek nodded. A Sleer nodded with their torso. "So. Surely you have noted how many military uniforms are in this room?" Brooks turned around. Their spies were now chatting up a pair of very young Movi officers, a man and a woman. Whatever the topic of conversation was, both Binil and Underhill were pulling out all the stops. Binil even giggled loudly and flipped her hair at something the man said, while Underhill couldn't seem to keep her hands off the woman's shoulders. "I wondered about that," he said.

"Well, wonder no longer. Kar-Tuyin is thinking very carefully about being forceful on the question of putting Missena up for the throne. No one likes Singhir, but few of the nobles or career military officers want to risk losing what they worked so hard to gain. So, they'll back a corporate officer with enormous economic influence who is held in high esteem by the nobility. They're making deals with flag officers. Singhir won't miss them."

"But Warlord Anterran surely would."

"Likely. But he doesn't want Singhir in charge any more than the royals do. As I said earlier, nothing ever really ends."

Rosenski downed the rest of her glass and blinked furiously. "All right, you two. Who would you bet on? If it came down to a knock down drag away fight, who's your favorite?"

Kessek laughed in the Sleer way, a hissing, boiling noise that sounded like a tea kettle singing a Russian opera. "The fact that we are here and not out there in a war fleet should tell you all you need to know. The wheels must roll, the ships must fly, the trades must be made if the kingdom is to have any future. It's all about the money. Follow it. We did."

"Where did it lead you?"

"To that geezer in the corner, near the buffet table," Bellon said.

Brooks followed Bellon's nod and found an ancient Movi officer dressed in his crew's livery with a single pip on either shoulder and a purple sash across his chest.

"That's Commander Loartus, the ship's chief purser. He runs everything."

Rosenski balked. "Everything? What does the captain do?"

Bellon said, "Captain Selgit is a fine officer, or he was when he was young. He retired from service, and they gave him a box of money, and a townhouse on Movra. He showed up here a few months later. I think he was bored."

"He's still bored. He rarely come out of his cabin. There's a stream of young people going in and out of his suite, however. Men, women—"

"The occasional Vix," Bellon confirmed. "And a single Decopod who arrived in a self-contained water tank the size of a cargo container."

"Anyway, the captain runs the ship, but the purser is a far more important job than you might think."

"Sound like the perfect cover for a man with expensive tastes."

Kessek hissed. "Very much so. A dishonest purser could make out like a bandit, but Loartus is clean. The transaction fees have gone up every year he's been on the job."

Bellon sniffed. "That's just corporate gouging. Everyone under Kar-Tuyin's thumb deals with that. If you can't find a way to increase revenue year after year, the accountants will replace you with someone who can."

Brooks exchanged his empty glass for a fresh one from a

passing server. "I know the type. My father was into big business. Big deals. He did so well for himself he retired early and went to work for the government. Now he protects forest land."

"Sounds boring," Belllon groaned. "Forgive me, but... "

"Not really. I got into a problem of my own."

"Are you boring?"

Rosenski snickered. "My Exec here was running his own little real estate empire aboard our mother ship. Kept his friends close and housed everyone in the same building. He collected favors. He's good at it. I think he missed his calling."

Bellon and Kessek shared a look. "Do you want to meet the great man?"

Brooks said, "The crew have been encouraging us to do so since we came aboard.

"I see. You're serious about working for your passage?"

Rosenski drained her glass and handed it to a server, but didn't take another. "We are. I have a crew of my own patrolling the balcony. It'd be a shame if they couldn't see the main deck."

"Then let's get you a proper resume," Bellon said. "The casino is this way. I will even arrange for your patrol to watch you play. Follow us."

"The game is called *Mashikk*. The goal is to acquire more territory than your opponents in a set number of turns. Ten players may join at once in this version, but various game lords set rules for different tables. There are pieces with various attack and defensive strengths, and all have unique movement patterns. Here is how it works... "

While Kessek explained the rules, Brooks focused on the inflection in the word *Mashikk*. One inflection translated it as "safety," while another changed it to "death." Maybe a race that had known nothing but conquest for the past quarter million years really couldn't imagine another way of life. If, in Sleer psychology, death was the only safe place, then Bon and his cohorts really were sailing on a doomed ship.

The game table was enormous, easily the size of two ping-pong tables side by side. A game with seven players was already in progress, and the table was littered with hexagons,.Brooks and Kessek stayed to the side watching the action, Brooks making mental notes and comparing it to all the board games he'd played in his life. It wasn't very different from strategy games like chess, checkers or Risk. After an hour he began to anticipate how he would respond to the moves he saw played, and grew eager to take part. When the game ended, the winner, a tall Sleer dressed in a Defender's uniform with Servant of Gunnery insignia, hissed loudly as he collected his winnings.

"Do the players bet on each other?" Brooks asked.

"Not at all. That would be cheating. The crowd bets on the players. The winner gets a share of the pot."

"So hook me up. Time's wasting." He felt rather than saw Sara Rosenski come up behind him.

"You know what you're doing?" she whispered into his ear.

"I have a good idea. First two games are practice."

She thumped his shoulder. "I'll spread the word. Game three is for real." She moved off, and the Game Lord called for new players. Brooks tapped the board heavily, waving his arm, sure he was making a fool of himself. The Game Lord took it in stride and put him on the scoreboard as "Brux."

The first game wasn't very exciting or very long. Six players, the sole human vying against three Movi and two Sleer. The Sleer formed a team at first, creating co-ordinated attacks against empty parts of the board, capturing space as quickly as possible. Two Movi tried to imitate their pattern of play, but the third refused to cooperate, preferring to attack any opponent who moved too close to his turf. Brooks carried out experimental moves, hitting any opponent in range, looking to test the other player's mind sets instead of their moves. He swept the lone Movi from the board before being bagged and eliminated by the remaining players.

The losing Movi came around to his side of the game table, his hands gesticulating. "What was that nonsense?" he asked. A young man, wiry and full of energy, his eyes communicating wonder and excitement. Brooks decided he'd found a new friend.

"Relax. It's my first try at this," Brooks said.

"Obviously. Brux. That's your name. Cycomm?"

"Brooks. Not a Cycomm."

"Excuse me. I'm Darris."

"Good to meet you. I see your shoulder patch matches Loartus's. You work for him?"

"For the moment. I'm hoping to move up to the command division eventually. But you take the job you get and work for the one you want."

"I hear that. Who's your favorite this round?"

Darris took a moment to scan the score board, then dropped his eyes to the table. One Sleer had succumbed to a sneak attack by his partner and the remaining Movi were trying to cut his territory into pieces. The wagers were already climbing, amounts and odds flashing as they updated in real time. The pot was already past ten thousand *estani* and was also climbing. "If the Sleer can hold out for two more turns, the others will eventually turn on each other. It's tricky. You need a reserve, but you also need to hit your opponents."

"You sound like a man who knows the game. So why were you thrown so early?"

Darris bent close. "Because I have a hangover the size of the engine room. I can barely see straight and I go on duty in an hour. I'm just wasting time down here until it's time for work."

The Sleer couldn't hold out after all, and fell to a combined attack. One more turn wasn't enough for the three Movi to properly go to war, but the win, place, and show winnings were calculated and the winner declared: the tall male with startlingly blue eyes.

The board cleared; the Game Lord called for players, and the winning Movi stepped up with Brooks, along with seven more Movi. Darris stayed by the human's side but opted out of this round, No Sleer this time, which Brooks found interesting.

Brooks changed his strategy this time, preferring to secure game hexes close to his starting position. He correctly predicted the other players would kill each other before turning on him, and it worked to a point. By the time the others realized what he was doing, Brooks had secured a sizeable chunk of the board and managed to repel all but one of their attacks. The one attack he succumbed to cost him one hex to his opponent's four. He finished the game in fourth place. Not bad for someone who'd never heard of the game two hours ago.

When the board cleared, the winner stalked off with his *estani* and Brooks looked around for his new pal. Darris was gone—to work, he assumed—but Sara Rosenski was back, and this time she brought friends. Bellon and Kessek crowded in to watch the action. Binil and Underhill, still in their roles as Movi captain and her Cycomm exec, squeezed in until they were hanging on his shoulders. He recognized a few of the OMP ground troops from *Hajlml*; Dance's hair was hard to miss. She pushed her way to the table and strong-armed herself between Brooks and Underhill. The OMP officer took it with good spirits; she bent over Brooks to tap Binil out of the huddle, and they retreated.

"What are you doing here?" Brooks asked Dance.

"We just got off a three-hour patrol on the balcony. Nothing to report, but we're tired. A Sleer came out to the ship and said come in, so we came. You've been here for *hours*." Dance slipped her arm around him, squeezed pleasantly. "What's the game?"

"Alien Risk."

"Cool. Take Brazil first. No one ever attacks South America."

"I don't think these geezers know about Brazil." The scoreboard trilled with new stats and they saw that odds were already being calculated, even before the game began. Underhill had sidled up to one of the Movi and Binil was chatting up another. Distracting his opponents or pumping them for tidbits, he surmised. Good operatives both.

The Game Lord waved Brooks into position. Nine other players stepped up, four Sleer and five Movi, including the two the women were working on. The first bets appeared, pushing the pot to well over a thousand *estani* even before the first move. The Game Lord waved open the action.

The first three turns went startlingly fast. Every player worked to the same obvious goal—to rush forward and quickly seize empty territory. Turn four saw one of the Sleer destroy one of the Movi, while turn five saw two Movi combine their moves to conquer two others.

Turn six. Brooks spent repelling two attacks from neighbors without losing any hexes, while one of the remaining Sleer wiped out the other two. Brooks found himself facing a very complicated board, populated by split holdings. Only Brooks held anything even vaguely coherent.

In turn seven he kept hold of his turf, sacrificing two hexes and gaining one more from a neighbor, a net loss of one.

Turn eight. The two Movi turned against each other, trading the same number of hexes while the Sleer acquired two new ones. Brooks stayed put, reinforcing his holdings, while his opponents squabbled and scrambled.

Turn nine. The other three discovered their collective mistake, their pieces spread out all over the board. Brooks nibbled at all three and brought six hexes into his domain while the others struggled to regroup.

Turn ten. The Sleer and one Movi continued their regrouping; the other Movi acquired five new hexes at their combined expense. Brooks broke out and launched attacks on all three, sweeping the remnants of their scattered territories into his own. When the game ended, the Sleer was the winner and Brooks followed in second place; *Hajimi's* crew screamed and cheered. The two Movi argued about who was to blame for the Sleer's win. Dance squeezed Brooks tightly enough to cut off his air, and a Movi face broke his concentration. Darris.

"The Chief Purser would like to see you in his office."

CHAPTER 26

COMMANDER LOARTUS HAD a glare that could freeze an active volcano. "These two are my friends," the Sleer grumbled. "I think you should listen to their proposal." Kessek's eyes focused on Rosenski and Simon. Despite Binil and Underhill's attendance in the office, Kessek had marked the humans for attention.

Laortus waved them to comfortable chairs but remained standing. His eyes darted from one to the other, evaluating, analyzing, and ultimately judging them. "You don't look like any military I've ever seen. Your ship took a nasty hit. Did it take out your armory?"

Rosenski leaned forward. "No, but—"

Laortus cut her off. "No, but you aren't the captain, are you? Or are you? I have questions."

Binil rose to the task. "Such as?"

The purser gestured and a display rose, a visual representation of the games that Brooks played at the game table. "The *Mashikk* table is usually the last place anyone gravitates to this early in a flight. The game is long, tedious, and can last hours. You people—" he looked straight at Brooks, "—arrive and suddenly it's the place to be. I take it this one is your strategist?"

"Not specifically," Rosenski said.

"You again, speaking instead of the apparent captain," Loartus noted. He looked Binil in the eyes. "What exactly are you, my dear? You may have fooled half the crowd with your antics but you don't seem like you rose to command through officer training."

"I'm good in social situations," Binil said.

"No doubt you are. So. Strategist. Captain. Socialite. What are you?" he asked, pointing at Underhill.

"I'm a spy."

"Finally, a moment of honesty. How refreshing. You'll think better after you've eaten something. Here. I asked the chef to deliver a few things. Surely, you'll find something to your taste."

The Purser waved them toward an adjoining dining area. Small tables with place settings occupied the center while a buffet ran across the far wall. Soups, stews, pastries, and other dishes Rosenski couldn't even guess at. When everyone had filled a plate, the discussion resumed.

"You know," the distinguished purser said between bites, "Kessek is very particular about who he describes as a friend. There is no higher recommendation aboard this ship. When he says that, I listen. So. Tell me your story."

Binil blinked heavily and opened her mouth, but a sharp gesture from Loartus cut her off. "No. Not you. Nor you, not-Cycomm." He glared at Rosenski and Brooks. "You two. Talk."

"It's a long story," Rosenski said.

"And you don't trust me."

"With respect, not really."

"Then this is the time to make trust. You are soldiers. You arrived in a type of ship favored by small mercenary gangs. I surmise you're looking for work. Yes?"

"Yes," Brooks said. "Among other things."

"That's fine. I noticed you started as soon as you arrived. Organizing a regular foot patrol of the balcony. Unnecessary. Possibly ill advised. But you took the initiative and did it anyway. A captain with a great deal to lose to the status quo might take offense at that. But seeing how the status quo is in the process of being reset, and not necessarily in our favor... we could use a band of overachievers at this point in time."

"I like that term. The Sleer we've met thus far think that we're slackers," Brooks said.

"That's because compared to them, we are," Rosenski suggested. "It's hard to compete with a fleet as vast as theirs."

"And yet the Movi manage," Laortus said. "Tell me about your military strengths."

"I assume you mean my ship's crew," Rosesnki said. "Forty-four effectives, including crew, pilots, ground troops. With varying amounts of equipment now that our landing bay is gone. They're all veterans, and a few might be considered elite troops depending on how you wanted to judge their experience."

"Veterans will do. How long will you be with us?"

"Until the end of your line. Marathas, I think was the published destination."

"Correct. How much will you be requiring in payment?"

Underhill leaned forward. "We couldn't possibly be prepared to live up to any reasonable defense operations for less than twice the wage of a company of corporate security guards," she said. "Not including billets for the entire compliment and access to all the ship's major compartments. And of course, we'll need to stay fed and rested. And if you truly wanted our full and unwavering support, we'd want to make use of whatever repair services your mechanics and engineers could provide."

Rosenski wondered where Underhill was getting her information, then decided it didn't matter. "All of that is negotiable, of course. Upwards," she added.

Laortus stared, the cat-like gaze of the Movi in full effect. "Interesting," he said, "An agreement can be made ready for signature by the end of the business day. *Magisterium* is now in mid-jump, repairs are being scheduled, and your ship needs service. I can provide all that. Your troops will be fed and watered and rested. You'll have access to all the public areas. Even the main dining room, if you like. We have time. Talk."

They spoke for an hour, starting with the Sleer invasion of their homeworld and their Sleer military hardware implants, each of the humans taking up a segment and then switching off after a while. The Movi said nothing, just maintained eye contact with whomever was speaking and looked more and more confused as time passed. Finally, he held up his hands.

"Let me sum this up. You are invading aliens. Yes?"

"No, sir. We're... "

Laortus thrust his open hand forward, ticking points on his fingers. "You're traveling in a stolen troop ship, betrayed the admiral who obtained it for you, and have the capability of returning to your temporary base on Great Nest but refuse to do so. Now you're running around Movi space looking for intelligence and technological prizes for your own government to exploit. And carrying a kidnapped Cycomm royal. Does that cover it?"

"We didn't *kidnap* her," Brooks pointed out. "She's a fugitive."

"My mistake. Let's make the most of that distinction." Laortus punched a stud on his desk's console. "Access *Hajimi's* computer core and download the data to my office, will you?"

"Already done, Commander." After a brief wait the display chimed and a wall's worth of displays appeared before them.

"How very efficient of your staff," Binil noted.

"You don't really think you arrived unobserved, do you?" Laortus began to sift through the data. "This war is ruining us. I'm no fan of that brat, Singhir. I'd have the kingdom return to the status quo, as would the great lady who runs this shipping conglomerate, but with each day that passes it becomes less likely. I doubt it's even possible any more. As I said earlier, your gaming table antics were quite exciting to watch, but the truth is, you are not where you should be and that makes a problem for me."

Rosenski shrugged. "We could leave and solve your problem that way."

"In that wreck of a ship? What's to stop any other faction from picking you up, squeezing all that you've told me for their own use, and then destroying you? There's a better way."

"Which is?"

Laortus drained his glass and went for a refill. "I'm buying you."

Rosenski held out her glass for the Purser's pour. "We're not for sale."

"Don't be coy. That's exactly what you are. You are *mercenaries*. I accept your offer of service. You, in return, will teach me more about Earth, its battle ring, Zluur's now reconditioned gun destroyer, and any other points of interest I might ask you about."

Rosenski nodded. "And?"

"And if we are set upon by brigands, we would add suitable bounties to your final payment."

Another nod. "And?"

"And I will not share any knowledge of your homeworld's location with Singhir's military."

"And?"

Laortus thumped his chair arm. "And liquid ice at dinner! What else do you want?"

Rosenski gestured with her glass, sloshing the wine. "I don't think I made it clear that playing rented cop for your grand dame is not our primary mission. We're here to learn about what military power the Movi might be able to provide when the next Skreesh incursion reaches Home Nest."

"At the moment, I dare say our military is disorganized and disillusioned. I doubt you'll get any response from the current leadership."

"No. But you can."

"I beg your pardon."

"We will protect you for the rest of your voyage, and you will help us get some leverage when the next Skreesh incursion arrives. A titan fleet may arrive around Vix, and we will need their library. The whole arm of the galaxy will—if I understand it correctly."

"And is your help really that valuable?" he asked. "After all, you came here desperately in need of shelter and reair."

Rosenski narrowed her eyes. "It is. Because the alternative is that we send a message to Haven and tell them that a fugitive from justice is hiding aboard your ship. Maybe they come looking for her, maybe not. But do you really want Sense Ops riding your tail? You're not exactly a military vessel."

"And you assume that Sense Ops has nothing more to do than hunt for a single runaway. Interesting idea, but I don't think it likely," Laortus said.

Brooks raised his hand. "Or we could send a message back to Earth, inform them that you have no hope of repelling a proper invasion by a quarter million Sleer battleships, and then offer the Sleer permanent residence aboard our battle ring in exchange for a real invasion fleet. They'll do it, too. I can say one thing for the Sleer—they make crappy politicians, but their war fleets are not to be trifled with."

Laortus faltered. "You couldn't do that."

"Look at our necks, Commander. The three humans in the room all have military grade Sleer implants. Do you think that would have happened if we weren't high enough in their ranks to get what we want?"

"All I have is your word for that."

"My word and the word of Tall Lord, Fleet Master Nazerian. He found our help in organizing the defense of Great Nest to be valuable indeed."

The chief purser thought about it, staring at the glass table between them. "All right. Your company stays with us until we reach port of call, where we go our separate ways. Your launch bay door might be beyond my engineer's ability to restore, but my techs will purge the telltale mistakes in your computer records. And I'll give you a command code that you can use to arrange the arrival of a Movi battle squadron at a time and place of your choice."

"A battle squadron of what?"

Laortus flicked his hand and a display appeared, showing them spacecraft that looked familiar. "Of these. Kar-Tuyin runs fleets of heavy cruisers. Not the equal of a battleship, even in quantity, but they are fast, carry heavy weapons and solid defenses, and have excellent range and responsiveness. Fighters as well. One trip, one squadron, one time."

"Done."

"Excellent. I'll have the front desk assign your rooms. You'll have to double up. I'm afraid we're overbooked this trip already. And take these two back to the transmogrifier, have them put back to rights. All you'll do by leaving them like this is confuse my people. You don't want us confused."

He rose to show them the door. "You're all on call until further notice. Welcome to Kar-Tuyin passenger vessel *Magisterium*. Rotate your personnel between the ship and the balcony as needed. Dinner is at seven. Enjoy."

CHAPTER 27

"I DO BELIEVE the bridge has a completely different feel when Sora Laakshiden isn't on it," First Warlord Anterran ad-Kilsek said.

He sat in his command chair, a heavily armored and shielded throne of command. His implants were tied directly to the bridge's command-and-control systems, giving him the ability to manage any of them on a whim. He preferred to have his bridge officers take care of them. The crew flew the ship. He flew the crew.

His navigator sniffed. "Indeed. It feels comfortable."

The First Warlord felt a chuckle bubble up from his throat as the pilot smirked. "And yet she is still a line officer, and we owe her our allegiance. If not our slavish obedience," he said. The crew took the hint. The smirks vanished and no one laughed. All was ordered and disciplined.

His XO, Flight Captain Clesarti ap-Neali ad-Sorkei, approached. "It may have been a mistake to allow her access to the bridge," she said. "The woman is the worst kind of social climber."

"Untrue," he corrected. "Sora's many things, but she's no lackey."

"So how do you explain her failure as a line officer? Scandal, controversy, and woe seem to follow her everywhere," Clesarti asked.

"She takes chances. The wrong kind of chances. Risk management was never her greatest skill." He leaned closer to her, lowering his voice conspiratorially. "And be honest, do we really miss her?"

"No, sir."

"I thought not. You have a report to make?"

Clesarti tapped the hand terminal on her wrist and quoted from the display. "If you were hoping to draw out Archduke Mineko's forces, it's been less than successful."

Anterran gestured broadly. "I can see that. We've been here for weeks, a great lovely target, all my named fleets and ten more numbered ones in one place. Why doesn't he hit us? He knows he needs the entire cluster to win, so what's holding him back?"

"In a word, we are." Clesarti threw data on the main display. "We're split. Mineko has the lower cluster and we have the upper. His four systems to our three. A stalemate that could continue for years. Or until we feel like committing the bulk of our assets to swamping his defenses."

"He *wants* us to commit to an invasion," Anterran agreed. "He's willing to lose the initiative if it allows him to hold on to a defensive line. Not the mark of an amateur."

"And if we commit all our forces to assaulting his position, we'll lose control over everything else," she noted. "Some trade off."

"It means we need something else to use." He reached into the display, and pulled out the four systems, examined their catalog entries. "All mining and manufacturing, no agriculture. How do they feed themselves?"

The XO sniffed. "With warehouses full of food delivered by navy supply ships, I'd expect."

"Probably. Show me the trade lines between the two clusters." Displays shifted as green lines wound their ways through the sector. "Private cargo liners every two weeks. Big names, too. Kar-Tuyin ships more tonnage that way than all the minor lines combined. Maker take all. It looks like they control seventy percent of the shipping to every naval base in the sector."

"You're thinking of something," she said. "I know that look."

"Wouldn't it be awful if those shipping lanes closed for the duration of the conflict?"

"It would put the archduke in a terrible bind. He'd be forced to abandon the cluster or watch his crews starve."

Anterran brought his hands together in a thunderous clap. "Very much so. Have the comm officer send a hypercomm message to the palace on Movra : I propose we declare war on the Kar-Tuyin shipping megacorporation and win the conflict. In the meantime, take a look at the library. Someone somewhere must have had similar thoughts before us. Let's pick some minds."

She was back in less than an hour, barely time to sort through the thousands of plans, proposals and documents that lined the shelves of the virtual catalog. She thrust the chip at him. "His Royal Highness has declared Missena Kiln ad-Esservil ap-Somak an enemy of the kingdom and issued a warrant for her arrest. Effective immediately. There's a comfortable bounty on her head as well. We simply need a method of attack."

"Excellent. We have several to think on. Get a staff together and start picking these ideas apart. Personally, I like this one. We ignore independent shipping and concentrate our forces on the large vessels. Cargo ships, supply barges, and passenger liners. The larger they are the more I like them as targets."

Clesarti balked. "Strand civilians? That's a terrible look. Once the M-Boats hear about it, we'll have to fight to earn docking rights at any world inside the mid-core."

"Hardly. Mineko will need parts for his ships and food for his crews. The great flying houses of commerce will have both. Those passenger liners are self-contained lifeboats. All we need to do is make sure they avoid the lower depot cluster. They'll listen to royal navy warships."

"I don't like it."

Anterran scanned tactical reports. "Nor should you. But his Great Infinite Awesomeness is the sovereign, and we serve at his pleasure. And it pleases me to tell him what he wants to hear—within reason. Here!"

"Yes?"

"The *Magisterium*! Her personal transport, or one of them. Send this to all scouts: find that ship and rip it rim to rim. Start searching for alternate targets as well, anything she owns shares in. She might be on any or none of them."

"Our supply of scouts isn't infinite. That manner of search will stretch them very thin."

Anterran wasn't finished. "If we reduce her personal fleet to hulks, we might trigger a succession war within the corporate environment. Nothing kills a business like a succession fight. One million *estani* to the captain who finds her and puts her under warrant. Will our ship captains work with that?"

She grinned. "For a million *estani* they'll fight each other for the privilege."

CHAPTER 28

"IF YOU DON'T MIND my saying so, I think I prefer you both this way," Frost announced at breakfast. Laortus had set part of the crew's dining hall aside for their use and *Hajimi*'s crew treated it like the wardroom aboard the AMS-1: open at all hours, with three meals served daily and a bottomless supply of the blue tea the Movi favored. It tasted awful, but it kept you awake.

Underhill took a bit of offense to the remark, but nodded. These days, with Brooks actively leaving any room she entered and Rosenski speaking to her only when she needed something, she did her best to tread lightly. "I concur. For future cosplay sessions I'll just stick to clothing and jewelry. My eyebrows hurt."

Binil sorted through a tray of baked goods. "You're just not used to it. I thought it was fun. It felt empowering to be able to talk to the rich and powerful and be taken seriously."

Underhill took a moment to think about their antics in the grand ballroom. "Binil, do you recall seeing Missena at that gala?"

"I barely remember who we spoke to. There was one count, a flurry of knights, and a host of business leaders, but don't ask me what their names were."

Underhill bit into a pastry that smelled like fried chicken and tasted like a sweet roll. "No, I mean, the great lady herself. Did you see her? Anywhere? It was a party. Why would she stay in her suite?"

Binil shrugged. "Private parties happen, too."

"That's a no."

"Yes. I mean, yes, that's a no. But really, what happened last night is today's blur in my mind. I remember very little about that first night aboard."

The past four weeks on board *Magisterium* had been as quiet as the chief purser promised. Light duty all around, routine and boring as any garrison assignment. *Hajimi*'s crew all bore the cost to some degree. The balcony patrols remained in force, and Grandpa Frost turned out to be an excellent ersatz lawman. Flying squads of eight or ten troops always roamed the public area of the passenger liner. Between duty assignments they picked up some choice Movi language lessons and made frequent use of the dining room and recreation decks. The ship had everything a traveler might ask for: gardens, a theater, refreshment lounges and restaurants, and even classrooms for those wishing to pick up new skills or brush up on existing ones. Their first night aboard ship, Underhill dragged Skull to a class on Movi formal dancing. After a few lessons, they moved well enough to start learning additional forms.

The fighter pilots remained exceptions. Brooks arranged it so there were always two fighters flying escort for the liner. The only time the pilots relaxed was in mid-jump, when they all caught up on their sleep.

Rosenski pulled a chair up to the table and signaled a

servant who returned shortly with plates of breakfast food. "I have no idea what the red juice is, but I can't stop myself from drinking it."

"It's part of the meal," Frost said.

"Five glasses of it? I'll miss dining rooms when all this is over with. Where's Roberts and Katsuta?"

"Flying fighter escort," Brooks said, wiping his mouth with a cloth napkin. "They hate each other, so I'm assigning them duty until they learn to be civil."

"Is that wise?" asked Binil.

Brooks shrugged, evaluating his next target from the platter. He finally forked a helping of what looked like sliced fish. He examined his prize and glanced at Binil. "Clipsop?"

She grinned. "Yes! Clipsop. Very good."

Brooks popped it into his mouth and chewed happily. For a week, he'd been putting every type of food in front of her and asking if it was clipsop. He'd finally gotten lucky. "Yes! It's not bad. Tastes like lox but heavier. Anyway, those two need to work together and this is how they learn."

"I'm glad that's the lesson you took away from our own experience on AMS-1," Rosenski said.

"I don't see those two ever getting close, but you never know. Where've you been?" Brooks asked.

"Talking to the chief purser. He commended us on our performance thus far and gave me these." She slid a thin tablet across to Brooks.

He swiped through pages of material. "What am I looking at? These look like contracts. Legal documents. Something."

"Very astute. They are offers of employment."

Skull reached out and maneuvered the slate toward himself. "From whom?"

"From everyone." Sara took the tablet back and swiped

through the selections. "This is a semipermanent contact from Kar-Tuyin. This one wants to pay us a ridiculous sum to ride herd on a convoy heading to the core words. This one comes from an outfit named Jel-Corsu, which stands for something I can't pronounce—"

"Jelegennivoni-Corsualikana. Executive Royal Charter," Binil said without breaking a sweat. "They are intense rivals to Kar-Tuyin, but the two conglomerates have locked up the shipping on alternate parts of the kingdom, so they never directly compete with each other. It appears that their board of directors thinks that the crew of the *Hajimi* has signed on with Kar-Tuyin's shipping lines, and they would like to steal you away for themselves. That's just a guess, of course."

"If only they knew we're done with our intel gathering and need to get home," Underhill said. Reminding the others they were finished with this leg of their intelligence gathering mission seemed wise. "There's no way we can accept any of these, but it's good to know we have a reputation after weeks of more or less honest work."

"If you call intimidating balcony roughnecks and booting drunks out of the casino honest," Dance said.

Underhill refilled the red juice pitcher from a dispenser against the wall and placed it on the table. "Cruise ships aren't known for their robust defenses, and it keeps us informed of the current events aboard ship. It's as honest as we'll get around here." Brooks gave her a nasty look but stayed quiet.

"Which brings us to the question of how we extricate ourselves from this perfectly ghastly civil war," Skull said. "Now that we have a reputation, we're going to invite more challenges more often—by ambitious individuals with something to prove. We're deep behind enemy lines. Do we have a route back to Great Nest?"

"Not an immediate one," Janus said. "Ghost and I had a talk with the ship's flight crew over drinks the other night."

Ghost made a rude noise. "I had drinks. You fall asleep under table."

"I got you both home afterwards," Diallou called from the next table.

Janus loudly said, "Marathas is a decent high-tech trading and travel hub. We'll stay in port for a week to pick up passengers and cargo. Kar-Tuyin is issuing bulletins and updating rules about how future voyages are to be conducted. It seems that individual ships plying the space lanes are now a corporate no-no. All ships must convoy up and fly escorts. If we stay, it's five days in port... not a bad thing. They say that Marathas is an extremely wealthy world."

Dance played with a tube of liquid garnish, drawing in it with her spoon. "How long to organize a convoy and defense?"

"That's the bigger question. If we stay, we help them satisfy the escort rules. Getting enough ship captains to organize into a convoy will at take at least another week."

Underhill shook her head slightly. "No way. We've stayed here too long as it is. Our week-long tour has extended to more than a month. We are overdue."

Janus shrugged. "Will two more weeks really hurt? We're scheduled for a trip back to Movra, which only has five stops on it. We'll be there six days from departure."

"They have flying castles here," Binil said. "And museums that rival anything on Movra. Excellent restaurants, too. There's one that's famous. You pay your bill in advance and a personal wait staff feeds you over a full day. Entertainments, too. I've heard it's better than any day spa."

"I think that's as decadent as I can imagine," Brooks said.

"I can imagine better," Frost said. "Just hand me a sandwich and get me to a full-service shooting range. That's the stuff."

Underhill stood. She made it a point to look them all in the eye. Even Brooks. "Be that as it may, we have profiles on the various faction leaders. Who they are and what they want, and their rough distribution of allies and enemies. That includes a rudimentary understanding of their relative strengths and weaknesses. I'm sorry, folks. We're leaving. Janus and Frost, when we're done eating, I'll need you to plot a course home. Take advantage of the star maps we have of the local group. We take copies of everything with us."

"Don't even say that out loud," Skull whispered hotly. "I guarantee the whole ship is bugged. These people already know where Great Nest is and have no interest in going there. They don't need to know any more about our galactic origins."

"Are you becoming paranoid in your old age, Skull?" Underhill asked.

"I make it a practice never to forget that we are the low tribe on the galactic totem pole. It's not paranoia to acknowledge how badly you're outclassed. Even if we've had some remarkable success, we are still the late arrivals. I merely suggest we all keep it in mind."

Brooks wiped his mouth, balled his napkin, and tossed it onto his plate. "What about a day of shore leave, Captain? Just as a keepsake."

Rosenski grinned. "You *really* want to visit that fancy restaurant, don't you, Simon? A day of half-naked Movi women in bare feet feeding you grapes one by one?"

Brooks sighed loudly. "I might."

Dance sneered with obvious disgust. "Sonuva... You men are all the same."

Binil leaned back, smiling. "I don't know if they do *that*. But I'd like to find out, Binil said with a wide smile."

"You too? Gaaaaah! I'm surrounded by creeps!" Dance said, and stomped off to examine the baked goods.

Rosenski cleared her throat. "It sounds heavenly to me too, but Underhill makes the best point. Our work here is done, and we should prepare to leave. This time tomorrow, I want to be in flight and on our way back to Great Nest. But I don't see any reason not to spend one more day aboard this fine vessel with its excellent facilities."

"I'm glad you're thinking that way." Eyes turned to the door as the chief purser entered. "Because I have one more thing to ask."

"Here it comes," Underhill breathed.

Laortus stopped at the table to pour himself a glass of the red juice. "I beg your pardon?"

Underhill opened her mouth to reply, but Rosenski got there first. "She's apprehensive. One reason mercenaries are paranoid is because employers have habits of changing the rules of their engagement at the last minute. We really can't afford that."

Laortus looked hurt. "I'm surprised by your reaction. I think we both did well. You people needed a hot meal and a place to hide. My ship needed protection. And here we are at the end of our schedule, my passengers safe, my cargo delivered, and you all fat and happy and feeling secure enough to take your leave."

"And now that our service is about to end, you see a reason to extend our arrangement," Underhill said. "We are long overdue."

Laortus helped himself to a pastry and took an empty chair. "I appreciate your desire to return home. We can draft an addendum that suits your desire to balance risk and reward."

Underhill caught the eyes of the others. Skull was frowning and Frost was clearly worried, but Brooks and Rosenski seemed willing to hear their host-employer out. Those two stuck together no matter what. "We're listening," she said.

Laortus put down a small device and a tactical display

sprung from it. "We're being pursued by a flotilla of local navy ships. They're organized into two groups. Five vessels are in the group closest to us, with six more six in a much wider orbit further out. They're not large enough to wipe us out easily, but so many at one time present a problem."

Brooks adjusted the display with a fingertip. "Not royal navy ships?"

"No. Small vessels—smaller than your *Hajimi*—meant for customs duty or anti-piracy efforts. Short-range missile batteries and lasers. If they get close, they could do some real damage to us. Granted, that's part of our charter."

"Your charter? I don't know enough about the Movi legal system to even ask an intelligent question about that," Rosenski said.

"During the last conflict with the Sleer, we discovered that they liked shooting at big slow-moving targets. Like cargo ships or passenger liners. We began to select certain vessels in that category with missile tubes and artillery. The idea was that they drew Sleer vessels to them, held them off with their weapons and their sheer bulk, and when they were fully engaged, navy ships would arrive and attack the Sleer. Sometimes it worked, sometimes not so well. But enough to keep the program alive when the war ended."

"It's a Q-ship," Skull said. "We used those in previous conflicts. It's a commercial vessel loaded with defenses designed to act as a lure or a secret escort. This is Missena's ship with all the certification and ownership papers, but she's not aboard. Is she?"

Laortus shook his head. "No. Missena has been secure on her homeworld estate for months. We've been seeding the space around the kingdom with lures and decoys like *Magisterium* to keep the rebels and royal navy unsure of her whereabouts. It seems *Magisterium's* luck has run out. I can honestly use some help. I will pay for the service."

"Something that a vessel the size of *Hajimi* can manage, I hope," Rosenski said. "We can't take on eleven ships. Not even with a functioning flight bay."

"You wouldn't need to. I've seen the long-distance scans. They're simple customs corvettes. No heavy weapons, but their collective firepower would make them formidable opponents given the relative dearth of weaponry aboard this ship. Your fighters and cruiser would help even the odds considerably."

"Describe this 'dearth of weaponry,'" Binil said. "Surely you're not unarmed?"

"Four single-tube laser turrets mounted on the dorsal hull. Two more mounted ventrally. Two long-range missile tubes aft that are concealed until needed. And quite a lot of electronic jamming equipment, including Sleer implant jammers. Beyond that, we are exactly what we appear. A passenger ship."

"Christ, no wonder you were so gallant about offering us a ride," Rosenski said.

"Other than the chance for glory and death, what's in it for us?" Brooks asked. Dance punched him. "What? We're mercenaries, aren't we?"

"If you all say so. I guess. We have been working our way through the dining room and casino for weeks," Dance admitted.

"There will be a cash reward suitable to get you anywhere in the kingdom you wanted to go. Not enough for a new ship, but repairs to your cruiser? I can swing that easily enough. Of course, you'd have to keep silent regarding the fact that we're in the decoy business."

"It's not decoy. This ship's not empty," Ghost said.

Laortus finished his glass. "Of course not. All we do by

running an empty ship is lose money. All the great lady's vessels are in service somewhere. A few of the more enterprising captains have hired impersonators who make it seem as if she's aboard. Bellon takes up that mantle occasionally. Her petitioners submit requests and Kar-Tuyin learns a great deal about the various factions as a result."

Underhill decided to drop bombshell to see what happened. "What about the arrest warrant for the great lady and the reward offered?"

Laortus's reaction didn't disappoint. He stared straight ahead, looking like a ten-year old child caught in a stupid, obvious lie. "That, I admit, was news to us when we heard it. And it explains why so many of the decoys have been attacked lately. Over time, more captains will run the pipe, but that's not for you to worry about."

Dance looked up, a questioning look on her face. "I don't understand. A *pipe?*"

Laortus signaled, and a new tactical starmap was displayed. "A gravity drive generates its own singularity field, which drives the ship. Ironically, every so often, the ship needs to discharge its drive into another gravity well. If it encounters another well suddenly, it can experience tidal forces which might disable the drive. Normally, this is no problem. We know where the planets and stars are, and use them strategically as we plot our routes. But there are also rogue singularities floating through space. Those don't appear on commercial charts, but they are in military documents—which the navy doesn't share."

Binil sniffed. "How rude."

Laortus isolated a string of jump points between three systems. "This is the Pipe. Missena's homeworld is protected by interstellar geography. This entire sector has only six worlds in it. Only these three are within range of any ship exiting the kingdom on its way into her domain. Anyone wishing to travel to her homeworld must discharge their drive at one or more of these systems. Besides that, there are numerous rogue singularities populating this sector, known only to the military and her personal navigators. Our route is the only way to approach, and it is well guarded. I guarantee there will be opposition—those factions who don't want her to return to the only planetary system they can't assault. Bottom line, we'll make three separate jumps and discharge our drive at each world. Singhir has offered a sizeable bounty for her capture. We will certainly encounter stiff resistance."

"And you're asking us to help you drop down this pipe," Brooks said.

"Not at all. I have loyal naval assets stashed along each of our waypoints. I'm asking you to help arrange our departure from this system."

Despite the comfortable surroundings of the staff dining room, Sara Rosenski was starting to lose patience. "I'm sorry, Laortus, but we can't help you any more than we have already."

"Are you sure, Captain Rosenski? The universe runs on *estani* and Kar-Tuyin has plenty to spare for an assignment like this."

"I'm sorry. You've been generous."

"And you've indicated *Magisterium* is no immediate danger," Brooks said.

"Did I? I might have played my proverbial cards poorly. The truth is that the corvettes will be on our position in three days. If you won't be on hand, I'll have to talk to the pilot and navigator and urge them to come up with a flight plan that keeps us far away from them."

"Lucky you're not taking on more passengers and cargo," Brooks said.

"No passengers. Plenty of cargo. It'll take a full day to load and then we must be away—with those corvettes pursuing us every step of the way. If you intend to leave, do so within that time frame, or you come along for the ride whether you want to or not. Do we understand each other?"

"I think we do," Rosenski said.

"Good day to you all, then. I've enjoyed our time together."

CHAPTER 29

THE SYSTEM DEFENSE TENDER *LUCERNESS* dropped into the space above Marathas High Port with a flash of light and tumult of gravity waves. Small for a Movi Royal Navy tender, it sported ungainly lines and long booms that linked a squadron of eight mid-sized system defense boats—dedicated local navy craft designed to ward off intruders. They could hide in a gas giant's atmosphere or an asteroid belt, or under an ocean or lake, then surprise invaders at will. They were cheap to build, easy to maintain, and able to stay on station for months at a time. Given a high-tech world with no royal naval base, it was an efficient means of deploying a defense budget. *Lucerness* and its cargo had been expected for months.

Seven of the boats were exactly what they appeared. The eighth was so unusual it didn't even have a designation of its own. *Luc.08* was the ID painted on its vertical stabilizer, and it answered to it as navy protocols demanded. But its crew wasn't Movi, nor was its skip drive. Its mission was not one of system defense but of covert search and recovery.

"Welcome to your new home, squadron," the Movi captain's voice came over the speakers. "You will all link your shipboard computer cores to the navigation control network and follow instructions. They will assign you all your chores for the next three months. We'll be jumping out-system in one hour. All boats acknowledge."

Captain Batol tapped his comm officer on the shoulder. "Acknowledge. We don't want to be impolite or stand out in any way."

Emil cracked his knuckles. "We'll stand out when we skip back to Haven."

"True," Batol said, "but by then, the rest of the squadron will be busy with their own problems, and the dock controller won't notice one missing boat."

The direct line to the tender buzzed. Emil tapped the comm and Batol said, "Luc.8. Go."

"Good luck on your mission, Captain. You sure eight crew is enough?"

Batol considered his staff for the umpteenth time. Tezzun and Emil stayed up here to run the ship and track the landing party. Nihe, Hare, and Ufen were the combat team, along with himself. Danal, his clairvoyant, would work with Geuph, his bouncer, to locate the High Value Target, teleport down to her location and teleport back to the ship. The combat types would follow them up in skip pods. They'd secure the target, transit to a safe distance from any planetary obstacle, and skip back home. Simple.

"Honestly, Captain, it's more than we need this trip," Batol said.

"Good luck anyway. And goodbye."

"Goodbye." Indeed. The Movi captain knew his job. He would never say anything about a Sense Ops team being linked to his ship delivery. In fact, he had no idea what any of Batol's team looked like or their real names. If the navy's intel people came to ask him, what could he say? "No. I picked up eight boats, I took to them Marathas, I dropped them off with the High Port network, I refueled and left." Yes, he knew they had eight crew. Every Dragonette-class SBD carried eight crew. Nothing special there.

Besides, with the Movi kingdom devouring itself, none of the factions focused their eyes on Haven. Only each other. Not even the Skreesh's continued incursions across Sleer and Vix space could get their attention these days.

Back to business. "Tezzun, set us up for a stationary high orbit about a thousand klicks above High Port. We don't want to step on any toes."

"Right. Just another new arrival getting our bearings. I'll make sure the network remembers to log us in and out as we swap out our flight patterns."

"Good. Until Danal gets her position, we might have to move around quite a bit."

"She has a level seven accuracy rating."

"Not from halfway across a solar system. The search could take five minutes or several days. Stay on it," Batol ordered.

"Aye, aye."

Batol retreated down the corridor from the bridge into the workshop, which was sealed from all EM radiation—and where Danal would remain until she got her fix on the HVT. Batol cleared his mind and gently nudged his clairvoyant with the strike of a mental fingertip.

Are you well? Are you working?

He felt her shift her attention beyond the door. *I'm studying her. Getting a feel for her rhythm. This will take some time. So many people. But I can tell you she's not on any inbound or outbound traffic. That's the first thing I scanned for. I'll drill downwards from one flight pattern to the next. Then finally, the planet's surface.*

Understood. We are ready to go when you are.

Very well.

And that was that. Danal knew the timetable and was talented. None of them wanted to spend days looking for the HVT.

Batol disengaged and dropped down the ladder, walking past the crew's quarters. In the next compartment, he checked the status of the two launch bays that held their skip pods; four skip-capable capsules that could hold two or three people at most, designed for the rapid delivery and recovery of troops or cargo. Find the target, program the destination and SKIP... you were at your destination. Unload, do your business and SKIP, back aboard the boat. No muss or fuss. They were so much more effective and safer than small craft. Only Gueph, his bouncer, could do something more interesting: teleporting himself and all his gear, for example. Occasionally, one needed to skip into a place where a pod wouldn't be able to manage a landing. But the pods would be enough for this trip. At the job's end their boat would skip back to Haven with all aboard. Simple.

The only thing Batol couldn't understand was why he'd been ordered to retrieve this HVT. He didn't need to know. They'd told him that she was a heavy duty scrambler, a wild talent that no one had foreseen or predicted, which made him wonder just how infallible the Sense Op high command thought its intel service was. The whole Cycomm population was constantly being watched for any signs of latent talent. Without it, Sense Ops lost its primary source of new recruits. Burnout was high in the service; new recruits were always in demand.

But the penal code was what it was. Search and Recover. They were on a mission.

Rosenski settled herself deeply in the tub and allowed her entire body to relax. The jets drove the water flowing toward exactly the right spots and the heat drew the tension from her muscles perfectly. "I have to say, if we only get one last night in town, at least it's a night worth spending. *Magisterium*'s observation deck was unique. Unlike the observation decks she'd seen on human-run ships you'd have a long, wide room, covered with a glass dome, and often low light conditions as well. Deck chairs arranged in rows, maybe with tables to hold drinks or small plates of food. Not all such layouts were the same, but often enough that it no longer surprised her.

The Movi luxury lines took the idea one step further. There were still the chairs and tables, and the murmur of low voices sharing time in the same space. They even had the dome, encouraging visitors to look up at the expanse of stars, a crescent view of Marathas hovering directly above them. But when the lights went out, as they did every ten or fifteen minutes, the scene changed to one of utter grandeur: holograms filled the chamber with various star alignments and constellations, nebulae and interstellar gas clouds, stars and planets. A light show like they'd never dreamed.

They'd visited the dining room—the real one, not the crew's lounge—and eaten like royalty. Then to the casino where they challenged each other at *Mashikk*, Brooks commanding four wins to Rosenski's three, and one draw. They ended the evening by boiling themselves in the bath house's tub, a whirlpool that rivaled the power tub they'd used in Genukh's officer preserve. They made fun of each other's sweating faces as their bodies slowly released the tension they'd been carrying for weeks.

"I like the Sleer tub better," Rosenski said. "I'm not sure if it's the shape, or the fact you could swim in place, but there's something about a Sleer military bathtub that kind of blows this one out of the sky."

"It's a civie vessel. Civie limits. It's fine for what it is," he said.

"Are you bored? You sound bored."

"No, I'm fine." He sounded bored. Or something. Not listless or lethargic—he'd kept up with her the whole evening—but something was holding him down.

She stretched her limbs out like a big cat. "This was a very satisfying date night," she teased. "Bath time really ties the evening together."

"It's not a date night."

Sara grinned. She'd found something. "Fake date night, then."

He winced and pulled his arms into the tub. "Not a chance. The only date I've got is on a date night of her own."

There it was. She smelled trouble in paradise. "Are you not okay with that? I thought you three had an arrangement."

"Dance makes time for both of us. It still works. Just not the way it used to."

And there it was. Love. Or what passed for it in the middle of a mission. "Sorry about that," she said.

"Nothing you did. We got close quarters, no privacy worth mentioning, and forty troops to manage with only twenty-four hours a day to do it. That cuts into fun time."

"But..." she probed.

Brooks sighed and sank deeper into the tub, the bubbling water covering his chin. "But, ever since Underhill and her boss put their OMP whammy on us, it's been getting more and more difficult to concentrate on anything except work. If you get my meaning."

"I see. I hope that's the stress of the job talking."

"Probably. I use my spare moments to fantasize about setting Underhill on fire and roasting marshmallows over the corpse. Please don't tell anyone that."

"Not a word. I'm not going to do wrong by my work husband."

He punched the water, spraying foam. "Jesus, stop that!"

Now he was being tedious. "Then stop making it weird, Simon. We were sharing baths every night for weeks while hiding from Nazerian's goons. Now it spooks you?"

"Not spooked. Distracted. You're distracting as hell." He climbed out of the tub in a rush and trailed water as he marched to the rack and pulled on a robe.

Her eyes followed him. There wasn't a thing wrong with him physically, he was just a born worrier. His mind held him back from everything. From being great. From being a leader.

She looked down at herself, the image of her body distorted and warped by the water, wondering what was wrong with her. She didn't think of herself as distracting. Was she turning him on or freaking him out? Was she the reason he couldn't come into his own? She'd never felt self-conscious around him before, and fought an urge to sink below the surface and vanish.

She waited until he installed himself at a lounge table, twirling a fingertip on the feeder mechanism before following. She dressed quietly, her robe settling over her skin like a great soft pillow. She didn't know how it worked, but Movi clothing had a way of adapting to the temperature of the wearer. Chill and heat, wet and dry, were vanquished with equal ease.

She tried to think of a way to knock him out of his funk. She hated when he got nervous and jerky. She hadn't meant to drag him into her own intrigues. Hadn't meant for a lot of things to happen.

Simon activated the center of the table with a fingertip and a drink appeared, blue and pink layers topped by a tiny mountain of foam. He sipped and sat back, even smiled at her. "It'll be annoying to go back to Great Nest, but I agree we needed to cut this adventure short. Otherwise we'll never get done with it," he said.

Back to business. A twinge of disappointment colored the moment for her. They'd have to decide what they were to each other some day. After the shooting stopped. "I hate to say this, but I think we've been incredibly lucky so far. Skull's point about us being the noobs was well taken. What else are we missing?"

"I don't think we're going to get much out of the Movi as a whole," Brooks said. "We've made a few contacts, but we don't have any friends, or even any real allies."

She swiped her fingertips across the table just so, and came away with a blue and purple drink in her hand. "But I'll count on Movi food replicators. We have got to get these for the AMS-1. They're much more sensitive than Sleer feeders. Makes you wonder how they work."

"We know how they work. You push this, touch that, and boom! One Icy-Hot."

"That's not what they're called," she said, going through the same procedure to pull a brown and white pastry from the device. "And I don't know how to pronounce this thing's name, but I can't stop eating them. You want half?"

"By all means." He wolfed down his share and patted his stomach. "Grandpa Frost has been calling them pot brownies."

She scarfed the brownie and forced herself to stop before she choked. Laughing and chewing was a recipe for disaster, implants or not. "Bah! What does he know?"

Brooks shrugged. "He may be right. I get the idea the ship's dispensary will sell recreational compounds, but they won't talk to me about it."

"Yeah, we're not favorites here," she said. "Where is everyone?"

"Various places. I gave the crew a last few hours of R&R if

they stay on the ship; I'm keeping tabs by way of the implants. Skull is in the casino learning that game I did so well on. Frost is minding a crowd in one of the bars. Dance and Binil are back in their room. The OMP boys have taken over one of the gymnasiums to swill testosterone and compete in contests of brawn. Some of the womenfolk are in the spa."

Sara nodded and pulled her robe close around her. "We may never get them out of there. I don't blame them. They have hot pools, chill pools, food and booze on conveyor belts like sushi joints. *That* we could make happen once we get back to the AMS-1."

Brooks finished his drink, replaced the glass, and watched it disappear. "Maybe not. Laortus didn't look happy when we told him no."

"No, he did not. I'm aware languages are not my strongest point, but I'd love to know how the guy who watches the ship's vault gets to run everything while the captain goofs off," Rosenski said.

"That's a good question. Gotta be a fault in the language algos. Translating Moviri to Sleer then to English—"

"*American* English."

"Thank you, Genukh. Yeah, I'm sure we're missing something. Some nuance or linguistic detail."

Sara gestured with open hands. "You want to deep dive into the dictionary. Go ahead. We don't boost for three hours and I'm good right here."

Brooks settled in the chair, closed his eyes, and got to work. When he returned, his expression told her he'd seen how the sausage was made. "Oh oh," he said.

"What?"

"The Chief Purser isn't the guy who watches the vault."

"No?"

"Nope. The Treasurer handles the valuables. 'Purser' comes from a Sleer word that could mean several—"

"Brooks. Focus."

"Sorry. The Purser is the guy who manages the defense of the ship. He's the military advisor to the captain."

Rosenski pinched her nose. "Fuck. We pissed off the head of security."

"We did." A shudder ran through the deck, jarring them both out of their thoughts. "What the hell was that?" he asked.

"Could be a thruster blasting out of synch," she said.

"Can't be. We're still in orbit." They waited, counting the seconds. When nothing further happened, Brooks shrugged. "Probably nothing. Right?"

"Maybe." She closed her eyes, leaned back, and accessed her implants, broadening her query to include open comm channels. "All Gauntlets. Sound off. Go!"

They waited as they followed the routine, Brooks and Rosenski checking their charges and each other as the names sounded off. Finally, all but one voice responded. Sara tried again, already heading to the locker room for her clothes and gear. "Reagan, Binil, sound off!"

Brooks did a quick scan of his own, checking locations. "Shit. Where were they? Spa? No... passenger deck, room 33601."

"All Gauntlets gear up and meet us at room 33601, right now."

―――

The phrase *date night* confused Binil in a way that made her hungry to learn more about it. The whole concept of dating drove her crazy. To make things worse, *Hajimi*'s crew weren't dating. Commander Fairchild and Secretary Gibb were dating.

She and Dance weren't dating in any sense she could identify. Reagan and Brooks weren't dating so much as mating, and even that seemed to have stopped at least temporarily. She noticed Brooks going off with Captain Rosenski and wondered if that was where he meant to be from now on. Those two were not dating, but had a relationship strong enough to pull them through two years of crises. What was going on?

How did humans even manage to reproduce with so much drama?

Binil wanted a date night, but Dance wasn't cooperating.

Whatever the promise and potential of the distinctly human ritual, Binil's friend fizzled and fell. Dance was plowing through a low point in energy and attention, and said she needed a break in the routine. Their room had a holographic entertainment display which Binil had tied to a classic film channel. They'd even ordered a platter of food from the dinner service menu. Dance hadn't moved except to pop food in her mouth for an hour. Binil doubted she was even watching the feed anymore. Dance's eyes were half closed and she only spoke in grunts.

Eventually, the Cycomm turned the image off. "You're no fun when you and Simon are fighting."

That got Dance's attention. "We're not fighting. Just taking a break. Getting space." There was more, but Binil couldn't understand her; to Binil it sounded more like a misanthropic grumble than coherent speech.

Binil closed her eyes and drew upon the months she'd spent living with her humans, recalling all the vocabulary she'd learned. "Uh... struggle, scramble, warring, scuffle, melee... any word I choose means that you and he are avoiding each other, and you both hate Major Underhill."

"Heeeeh... that bitch... "

"Dance, I can be ignorant, but I'm not stupid. I—"

A resounding thump and a crash sounded outside the door.

Five seconds later another, and then a third, fainter than the first two.

The creeping sense of unease erupted into something hot and painful in her guts. "Engine room?" Binil asked.

"No, we're too far forward. That's a breaching charge or something like it." Dance's lethargy vanished. She grabbed their comms off a night table, plugged hers in and tossed Binil's to her. One tap. "This is Dance. Anyone out there?" Two taps, then three. "Repeat, we have a disturbance at room 33601. Anyone out there? Fuck!"

Binil tapped her own comm and got nothing but a loud buzz. "What's wrong? What happened?"

"Someone's jamming the signal. That can't be good." Dance swung into action and bent to pull the bed apart. In seconds, she'd pulled a storage box from under the mattress and opened it, effortlessly clicking parts together. In less than a minute she hefted a small carbine, slammed a magazine into the feed and primed it. "Stay put."

"You might need—"

"I need you to stay here, *Captain*."

"But I can—"

"No. Stay put. Close the door as soon as I'm out. Wait for help."

"Yes, Lieutenant," Binil mumbled. She watched, her belly full of ice and her hands shaking, as Dance opened the door, quickly checked her danger spaces, and slid into the hallway. Binil ran back to the weapons case. She grunted as she spied the one thing she could use: an M-35 .45 caliber semi-automatic pistol with a single magazine. It would do... if she could aim the damn thing properly. She inserted the mag, worked the action, and stepped to the door. The silence from the other side was positively intimidating. She had no idea what was happening. She knew Dance's orders came with solid reasons, but why should her friend face danger while she cowered like a child back here?

More seconds without a response from the hallway and the comms were still buzzing pointlessly.

Just one look. To see what was happening. To verify Dance was still alive.

She palmed the door, which slid open. She leaned out... and a calloused hand with an impossibly strong grip grabbed her forearm. With a single sharp pull, Binil was in the hallway, her pistol was on the floor, and she was looking down at Dance's body.

It was all she could do not to scream. That would make her look weak, make her sound like a child. Then she looked up at her assailant and understood that no matter what she did now, she'd already lost.

He was a Sense Op. An officer from the look of his collar insignia. Probably a captain. A leader of Haven's elite soldiers. Her mind pulled in every detail, noting exactly where she and her humans erred in reproducing Cycomm gear. She swung her body around, craning her head to look up and down the hallway. She could see how the soldiers arrived; a pair of secure skip pods were blocking both ends of the corridor, wedged into the narrow space between the walls. Doors were twisted out of their frames where the pods appeared, expanding so quickly they'd literally pushed the barriers to the side as they filled the empty space.

"Identify," he said. A baritone, even through the helmet's speaker.

"No."

"Don't make this difficult," he said. Then a stream of electronic gibberish as he sent a message to his squad. There had to be a squad—more Sense Op troops on the ship somewhere. She noted how quiet the hallway was, how none of the doors opened, no passengers poking their heads out to witness the unfolding drama. Of course, there were none... they'd debarked the passengers yesterday. How soon would *Magisterium* leave? Did it matter?

Another identically suited trooper arrived and pulled their glove off one hand. Binil was surprised to see a feminine hand with a perfect manicure reach out to stroke her cheek. A telepath, maybe a clairvoyant. Someone who picked up clues by touch.

"Confirmed. It's her."

"Binilsanetanjamalala, you are bound by law to accompany me to a holding area where you will be processed by legal authority and returned to Marauder's Moon. Any resistance you exhibit will be immediately put down."

The Sense Op captain aimed his rifle at her face. "Will you come quietly, or must I anesthetize?"

Binil's heart thumped in her throat as she did the math. The Gauntlets weren't here now, and she couldn't call them. It left her with a simple choice. She looked down at Dance's insensate body, then at the open hatch of the skip pod.

Binil pointed to dance, thought briefly about picking up her weapon and abandoned the thought as quickly. "Is she alive?" she demanded.

The woman answered. "Anesthetized. She'll be fine."

"Let's get it over with," she whispered, and walked into the pod, and sat down on the bench. She refused to help the soldier as he strapped her into the harness. The door closed with a hiss and a sigh. She felt his hand press something to her neck, and then, nothing.

Brooks and Rosenski didn't bother with decorum as they geared up. Uniforms, boots, and sidearms, then using their implants to scan the corridors ahead of them as they ran to the target area. They arrived to find Frost already handing out assignments to teams of two and three, setting up a perimeter, and looking for clues.

"What happened?" she asked.

"Binil's gone. The room she and Reagan were sharing is untouched. Well, undamaged anyway. Dance stashed some hardware under the mattress. Whatever happened, she never fired any rounds." He held Reagan's carbine out for examination. Full magazine. One in the breach. Safety on.

Binil is gone. Three words she hadn't really believed would be uttered here. Or ever. The girl was such a weird, spooky kid, but she'd grown into something ambitious and hard in her own way. Because of the Gauntlets. Especially Brooks and Reagan. Speaking of whom... Reagan seemed physically unhurt, but had obviously been attacked. "Jersey? How is she?" Rosenski asked.

Katsuta held Reagan in a sitting position as she raised her arms, groggy and unfocused, trying to fight off the medic. Lt. Shoar—who passed for a doctor under these circumstances—put Reagan's hands down, strapped a mask to her face, and turned on a tube of oxygen. "Anesthetic of some kind. Powerful as hell. I don't think she's in any danger, but she'll be like this for a while. I'll take her back to the ship. At least all the med gear on board is meant for humans."

Rosenski nodded. "Do it. Call me when she wakes up." She trotted to Skull who was standing in the center of what could only be called a bubble. Something had appeared here, blown the contours of the hallways into a spheroid and then vanished again.

Skull gestured to indicate *all of this*. "I'm clueless. There are no bullet casings on the floor. No laser burns, no gauss needles, no grenade fragments. No evidence of explosives or gas. All we have are those—depressions—in the walls."

Rosenski nodded. "Brooks and I were in the forward section. We heard a bump, an explosion. Except... not really."

Underhill strode to the group, waving her hand for attention. "Roberts is down in engineering now. There *was* an incident. A pod of some kind popped into the main engineering deck. Disgorged a handful of troops who sealed the area. They applied some device to one of the reactors and tweaked it just enough to shut the plant down. No real damage. Just more crew in the same condition as Reagan."

"It was a distraction. A decoy. The one place the ship would have a standing crew would be engineering. They knew that," Skull said.

"Engineering... and the bridge," Rosenski growled. "Katsuta, after you get Dance squared away, drop down to engineering and make sure those crew members have all the help they need. If the ship's doctor has a remedy, make sure you get a dose for Reagan. Frost, after all the aid has been given and the evidence collected—photos, if nothing else—start moving everyone back into *Hajimi*. We may need to leave very quickly."

"Copy that." Frost moved off to organize things and Rosenski stood by. Brooks was turning inward, glaring intently at the destructive forces applied to the corridor. Underhill was staring at the distance between the two eruptions, doing mathematics of her own. Probably formulating a report for the big men on Earth, too.

"You two come with me. We need to talk, and I don't want to do it anywhere inside this hull." Rosenski said. She found a washroom and shoved Brooks inside when he balked. Underhill seemed better with it.

"Good choice," Underhill said, "It's the one place with no cameras or microphones. Not that I've found."

"I'm glad you approve. Well. Now what?"

Brooks didn't mince words. "Now we are in hostile space. Do we attack, defend, or disengage?"

"That depends on the Major here," Sara said. "What do you think, boss lady?"

Underhill shook her head, her braid swinging with her head's motion. "Don't bring me into this like I planned it. I liked Binil, too. But—"

Brooks whirled on her. Underhill took a step back. "If you ever talk about her in the past tense again, I'll rip your eyes out and use them as golf balls. *Sir.*"

Brooks shut up and jammed his hands in his pockets, but Rosenski could see he was close to losing his cool. He was lucky Underhill didn't drop him on the spot. "Simon."

He turned his rage on her. "No, *Captain.* You don't get to 'Simon' me after the crap you pulled in the Diplomacy Dome. Your little act of political rebellion put us both in irons and the good Overcop here never even told us if the situation was temporary. For all I know we're both slaves to the state for the rest of our stupid lives. So, I'll ask again. Do we attack, defend, or disengage? Personally, I say attack, but what do I know?"

Rosenski felt her stomach flip. She'd seen Brooks under stress before, but there'd always been a layer of emotional armor between him and his work. He needed to be liked; that got in the way of being a good XO. She'd blamed Fairchild's influence for that. Now, Simon was showing her—showing them both—a new face. The armor was gone, the need for validation tossed aside like an empty beer can. This was the Brooks she'd wanted to work with all along... and she wasn't sure how she felt about him. She had no doubt he'd get any job she assigned done— and done well. *Jesus, what'll he be like if Hendricks promotes him to Major? To Colonel?*

Underhill finished her calculations and met Rosenski's eyes. "I agree. Attack."

"Based on what?"

Underhill glanced at Brooks before speaking. "Binil was—Binil *is*—afraid of two things. Personal failure, which she lumped in with letting her human friends down, and Haven's Sense Ops teams. I don't think I need to convince you that the Cycomms claimed one of their own tonight. I mean, part of the job as an Overcop is to make the OMP seem larger than life. We are everywhere and nowhere. To some extent, it's true. Special rendition teams snag high value targets now and then. The OMP can make someone vanish, but not like this. We couldn't pull off a mission like this if we tried. And we do try."

"Which puts us at an awful disadvantage," Rosenski said.

"Maybe. We know they're incredibly skilled at dark ops trade. They may not have the gear for a stand-up fight with a platoon of OMP troops."

"Especially if they don't know we're coming," Brooks murmured. "We need our ship."

"*Hajimi*'s too small for that," Rosenski said.

"No. I mean *Gauntlet*. Our own ship with our own mates and our own tech. Confuse the living crap out of them. Battlers and VRF fighters? They'll never figure it out."

Rosenski considered it. The list of positive outcomes to a rescue mission was short; the list of negatives was as long as her arm. "It'll take months to get to Haven on our own."

"So we borrow or steal a message boat, program it for max speed to Great Nest, and tell Uncle and the Saint to meet us at some location close to Haven. We scout, we plan, we strike, we grab our lost man, and we bug out," Brooks argued.

"And start a war with a completely new race we know almost nothing about," Underhill said.

"We know plenty about them," Brooks sneered. "Binil

hasn't shut up about Cycomm society. Or haven't you been listening to her? Dance and I sure as fuck have. There's an installation on their furthest moon called the Asylum where they train Sense Op personnel. Although..."

Sara prodded. "Although?"

He spoke slowly, as if putting the logic chain together aloud. "I don't think they took her there. If I captured a fugitive important enough to invade Movi space for, I'd take her back to the place she escaped from. Marauder's Moon. A penal colony. That moon has a crazy eccentric orbit, and if I remember correctly, it's on the far side of their system now."

"And it's home to a terror lord, frightening enough that Vonda set up a hit on him," Rosenski said. "I'm getting the idea we're in way over our heads here."

Brooks gave her a feral smile. "When have we not been? Laortus can give us the star maps we need to navigate there. We already know where Great Nest is." He looked back at Underhill. "Come on, Major. You wanted us to test your new Warhawks? This is how you test Warhawks."

Rosenski could almost hear the wheels in his head spinning out of control, grinding and sparking as they tried to process the utter humiliation of the past half hour. "Simon, I get it. It's personal."

"Damn fucking right it's personal," he shouted. "First day—launch day, when I came down with Second Section in that Kitchen Sink, I had no friends. Not even Uncle. Not even Bob Norton. Not really. Dance was a stranger, Binil didn't even *exist* as far as we knew. Now, I'm—I'm—gaaaaaaaahhh!"

He sat down hard, panting and gasping, tears leaking from the corners of his eyes. "Why can't this happen to someone else for a change?"

Sara let him rant for another half minute then pulled him

up, grabbed him by the shoulders and glared into his eyes. "It's personal because she's your friend. And you love her."

"Gah!"

"You want to help your friend, then *help* her. We'll get her back. But not if you run off in mid-freak. We plan. We hit back. We leave. Yes?"

"Yes." He brought his rage under control, but it took time. She realized the problem right away: Brooks felt used to things coming easily for him. Even when it got complicated, he always had an answer, a solution. Those days were over, and he needed time to switch gears. Time they didn't necessarily have. "Yes."

"We're starting from a bad position—we don't know where they took her. Let's talk to Laortus and see if he can give us intel we can use."

Brooks tried to normalize his breathing, slowing it to slow his heartbeat. "He'll want payment up front. Are we up to holding off those patrol ships long enough for *Magisterium* to leave the system?"

"You tell me."

"Yes!"

CHAPTER 30

LAORTUS WAS in the CIC when the alarm sounded. It was almost a relief.

From here could see through electronic eyes that reached all over the ship. He sat and thought while he watched his teams at work. Damage to one passenger deck and to the reactor in engineering, plus a handful or casualties, but nothing fatal.. The affected crew, including the one primate, were groggy, incoherent, obviously drugged.

His ship's doctor was a bit of a lush, but he kept a well stocked sick bay and his EMTs were already scouring all areas of *Magisterium*. The response teams dispatched, the repairs were underway, or they would be when the engineers recovered. And the pink-skinned primates were everywhere.

Now that he thought of it, the rest of his mind went on a clue gathering hunt and it all made sense. The one Cycomm on the ship was now gone—his internal sensors were very good at locating passengers and crew—and her primates were clearly losing their minds. A flurry of activity by all of them except the four who stayed behind, maintaining the sense of order they created on the balcony. If nothing else, they comported themselves the way soldiers did. Fanning out, gathering intelligence, reporting to Brooks, Underhill, and Rosenski. Brooks wasn't taking the incursion well at all.

And here they came, the three leaders. They traveled in a tight group, striding down corridors, watching their doors and corners, heading... to the bridge. He leaned forward as they knocked politely, then hammered on the door. The blue-haired woman pulled a tool from her belt, slipped it into the lock, and the door slid open.

He had no cameras positioned on the bridge, but he knew what they'd find: a great deal of empty space and some computers. A single service drone manning the only console. He'd converted the bridge to automation years ago. Frankly, there was nothing that could be done there that he couldn't do better from down here. The drone couldn't answer questions or defend itself. That would probably confuse them. Maybe frighten or anger them. Maker, he wished he had cameras in there! He'd have given his wallet to see their faces.

They emerged, had words, and split up. Working to figure out where his room was, no doubt. Good for them. They might yet prove to be competent as assassins went.

"Company will arrive soon," he said. He felt better for acknowledging their approach. An uncertain future had now fallen into sharp focus. He knew his end was near, and the form it would take. A weight lifted from his heart. No more guesses, no more risks or paranoia. He was done.

"Let them come," Kezzek hissed. The Sleer eschewed armor but carried a well-used Sleer plasma rifle. Bellon carried knives, dart-launchers, and a host of hand weapons. He shifted his body, gyrated through a half-turn and suddenly he sported six arms, each armed with a different weapon.

"Not this time, my friends. I think it's time for you and I to part ways."

Bellon harrumphed. "My Lord, I—"

Laortus waved the title away. Titles were for those without his history. Without incidents, accidents, accusations, and allegations. Without the fact he'd made a ten-figure fortune selling weapons to both sides of a conflict. The now-dead sovereign called him a traitor, but no—he'd simply appreciated diversification. "Bellon, I'm not your lord or anything else. Just a tired man who's grown bored of waiting for a death that frankly should have taken me a decade ago. Let's get this over with."

"At least let us defend—"

The door chimed and held firm. The pounding of fists against it, the shout of hostile voices on the other side. "Let them work for it," he said and relaxed into his command couch. All was quiet. A good time to die.

The door popped open with a screech and a hiss. Bellon roared and flung his weapons through the air to find that the three aliens were ready for them. They dropped to their knees, raised their arms and Bellon's knives were ripped to shreds by the energy shields they deployed. Kessek stepped up, primed his plasma cannon, and loosed two shots straight into their shields. The short male leaned into the blasts, his hair and face taking superficial burns while the women closed ranks to press forward. A good display of teamwork.

Laortus put his hands on his friend's shoulders, then drew them back. "Stand down, my friends. Come in, *Hajimi* officers. Let us finish this." He glanced around at the instrumentation and remembered where they were. He didn't want them to damage the CIC. "This way."

He led them to a chamber off the compartment. Like a richly decorated sitting room, but with a row of cabinets in the rear. "Sit. Let's at least be comfortable."

Rosenski followed his instruction, taking a seat with a soft cushion and a high back. It fit her perfectly. "Our cruiser is still beyond repair. We're taking yours."

"Just the three of you?"

"With support from the rest of my crew. We'll occupy this vessel until we reach an appropriate landing site. At which time we will relinquish control to you and—"

"No."

Brooks seemed confused. "You have no choice."

Laortus grinned. It was like dealing with children. The arrogance! He had to admit it was amusing. Like dealing with his daughter when she was a tween. "Oh, you pink-skinned alien. I have nothing but choices."

Underhill smirked. "Is that a fact?"

"It is. I can choose the manner of my death, and there are so many possibilities. Care for a drink? I have tea, but I believe I'll go with something stronger today." He ran down the shelves in one cabinet, selected a bottle, poured three glasses, and offered them around. "Cheers." He took a swig from the open bottle. "At the moment, I have eleven patrol ships bearing down on my vessel and no way to fight them off or evade and escape. I could choke on this very fine liquor, which you paranoiacs haven't touched. I could trip on a door seam and snap my neck. Slip in a tub and drown. So many possibilities. And of course, if a Kar-Tuyin officer wanted to send a coded transmission to the ship's computer and tells it to open all the airlocks, then death by corporate asphyxiation is the result. You've no idea how liberating contemplating one's own non-existence can be. So what shall it be, primates? Will you stab me through the brain, or throw me into the reactor? At least taste your drinks."

Brooks drained his and bent over with a fit of coughing. "Oh... that's awesome..."

Rosenski forced hers down. It reminded her of the moonshine her grandfather learned to make from cotton charcoal in a home made still when he returned home from the U-War. She looked up to see Underhill upend the glass into her mouth, lick her lips, and blink. Frances staggered to the nearest chair. "Good shit."

"That won't translate, but you're welcome," Laortus said. "You're the worst soldiers I've ever encountered."

Brooks managed to not retch, but standing up was a greater challenge. He managed a wobbly slouch. "That hurts."

"Good. I approve of the policing you did on the balcony, but the rest of it? No wonder you never made it into space on your own. Now that you're here, how do you like our universe?"

"It's complicated," Brooks said.

"And stressful," Rosenski added.

Underhill nodded. "Very dangerous."

"I agree. So now what? Murder me or take my ship. Or both. You're exhausting me."

Rosenski gave him a thumbs-up. "We'll take your ship, thanks. We'll even fly your damned escape mission. In return you'll provide my crew with full disclosure."

Laortus thought carefully before answering. The encounter was going down a path he hadn't imagined. Who were these... people? "Disclose what, exactly?"

"Everything you can tell us about the Sense Ops. What they did. How they made it work, and where they took Binil."

"I hope you have strong stomachs. You won't like any of what I can tell you about the Cycomm special forces. There's a reason the Cycomm Unity is an interdicted travel zone to Movi traffic. Only the Sovereign's personal guard are allowed in that system, and only by invitation."

"Tell us anyway."

"I will. I'll even make a short detour and introduce you to someone you will want to speak to at length. Not *my* great lady, but a great lady indeed. An officer who mentored me through some very bad times, when I still thought the Vermilion Thorne was worth serving. We completed our cargo pickup some time ago and we leave shortly. I'll plot us a direct route. We'll be there in six days."

"You can do that? Just change course and vanish?"

"I'm the Chief of Security. I can do whatever I want, within reason."

"What will Missena do without her decoy ship?"

Laortus laughed. "She hasn't needed my help to do anything in decades. Not since Movus had me thrown in prison. Not since Archduke Mineko got my death sentence commuted to mere exile. Certainly not since I began calling myself a Chief Purser and running this vessel from the luxury of well-lit shadows."

"So... you're the war criminal father?"

"Loartus Banuk ad-Esservil ap-Somak, at your service. You honestly had no idea, did you? To you I was just another member of the ship's crew."

"Kind of."

"Remarkable. May I?" He held out his hands. The liquor had disintegrated their boundaries and they all allowed him to stroke the contours of their faces with his finger tips, creating a map of sensation. Learning their features. The expressions. A very Sleer activity, one that he'd learned from Kessek years ago. "You're all far more Sleer than you know," he said. "What do you think of that, Kessek?"

The Sleer took the posture of confusion. "They are really not here to kill you?"

"Apparently not. My friends, we are being hijacked. Bellon, sound the general evacuation alarm. Make sure the wounded are seen to first. Kessek, get down to the engineering deck. If the damaged reactor can't be repaired quickly, shut it down and bring up the auxiliaries to compensate. Then tell them to unmask the drives. We're going to need all the speed we can muster."

Underhill started. "Unmask? What have you been using all this time?"

Laortus soaked up her expression. So clever and so often wrong. "*Magisterium* is a *decoy*. We used a fraction of his total power output to appear slow and harmless. His engines can deliver us anywhere we need to be, with the same dispatch you'd see in any warship. Or did you think a mere passenger liner could travel nine hundred light years so quickly?"

Rosenski made a rude noise. "You bastard. You didn't need our help at all."

Laortus moved around the CIC, adjusting controls while his crew went to follow their orders. "Not true. It will take time to prepare an escape from this system. You'll have your chance to shine. We just upgraded our gunnery software. The fireworks should be astounding."

CHAPTER 31

"NEXT TIME WE DO THIS, I want to go in a bigger ship."

Only seven ships remained in the balcony: *Hajimi* and her six fighters. Even so, *Magisterium*'s flight deck surged with activity as crew rushed to prepare the smaller craft for departure. The auxiliary vessels, launches, pinnaces, and so on were already gone, used in the evacuation effort that was now complete.

Numerous fuel tubes fed *Hajimi*'s propellant tanks, and refined for her reactor. The tiny Mantis fighters were canopy-up, each with half a dozen short-range missiles mounted below their wing pylons, and a full bay of ammunition for the chin turrets. All they needed were targets—and the bridge would feed them that information shortly.

Nothing to do but wait. Brooks had learned to hate waiting.

Dance's voice piped into his ear. "What kind of big ship would you like, Captain? Cargo ship? Super barge? A garbage scow?"

Brooks switched to a private channel. "You feeling up to this? They hit you with that stuff hard."

She made a noise he was sure he couldn't replicate. "Shoar says I'm fine. It wore off an hour ago. No aftereffects. I'm good."

"If we had another choice, I'd pull you off the line and put Janus in that fighter," he said.

"Well, you need him to fly the cruiser, so here we are."

He could argue, but what was the point? He had to trust her.

Meanwhile, the chatter continued as Solovoya sneered over comms. "Bah, big ships are dumb. You want to sneak in, fuck them up, sneak out again."

"God is on the side of the big battalions, Ghost," Diallou said.

"Thank you, Speedbump," Rosenski broke in from *Hajimi*'s bridge. "According to the High Port detection network, the two groups of corvettes are converging on *Magisterium*'s position. The liner will drive at full burn one hundred planetary diameters on a course that forces both corvette groups to approach from the stern. If they get close, we throw a sheaf of boom stuff in their path. Get in, smash their bridge, and leave. *Hajimi* will support you with long-range missile drops and turret fire at short range. Good hunting."

"Do they have fighters of their own?" Katsuta asked. Her soprano was an easy voice to recognize.

"None that we've identified," Skull said.

"Copy that, bridge," Brooks said. He enjoyed running a squadron more than he thought he would. It was a far cry from the days in the Kitchen Sink, flying to South Pico Island and crash landing, grabbing a screwed-up battler, then fumbling his way on board and being pulled onto the bridge by random chance. At least now he knew what he was doing and how to manage others. A different world. He wondered what Lt. Hart and Chief Amir would say when they heard about what he'd been up to. Or Captain Rojetnick, for that matter. Probably make General Hendricks's head explode.

One could hope.

He watched as the umbilicals retracted from the company cruiser's hull and attendants sealed up the feed hatches. Skull's voice cracked as he spoke quickly. "Gauntlet fighters, you are clear to launch. *Hajimi* is launching in one minute. Navigation upload complete."

Brooks's dashboard confirmed the transfer and he toggled his squadron channel. "Intercept vectors loaded. Dance, you're with Speedbump. Ghost, you're with me. Katsuta, it's you and Roberts again."

"Copy that."

"Acknowledged."

"Da, understood."

"Got it," Roberts said. Katsuta said something in rapid Japanese and Brooks didn't need a translation to know she was unhappy.

Bay doors opened to barely a hiss of escaping atmosphere. Maybe safety fields had some use after all. Brooks increased power and the repulsor lift carriage floated his fighter down the flight deck. "Gears up. On the boost!" Ghost was already on his four o'clock and Dance and Speedbump followed, soon joined by Katsuta and Roberts. *Hajimi* rose slowly and followed them all out of the landing bay.

So far, this was no different than they'd seen on their earlier test run with the tiny ships. Rosenski's voice filled his headphones. "*Hajimi* actual to Gauntlet Leader. We have multiple contacts at extreme range and closing. Recommend you hang close to the mother ship."

"Gauntlet leader to actual. Will comply. All Gauntlets, link your sensor suite to *Hajimi*. Weapons are free."

Roberts perked up. "We're not the only escorts, either. Four contacts at one-zero klicks maintaining speed and distance from the mother ship."

"I see them," Dance said. "Looks like some of the launches from the *Magisterium* got ambitious and decided they wanted a piece of our action."

"It's not like we don't appreciate it fellas, but not on my vector." Brooks flipped to the liner's channel. He wondered if his Sleer implant would translate for him. He hoped so, otherwise this fight was going to get very complicated very quickly. "Movi auxiliary flight, follow us at no less than two-zero kilometers. You're running into my flight's vector plot. Acknowledge!" He waited a moment, then a male voice was shouting at him in Moviri. He didn't understand a word of it. Okay then, so much for Sleer technology. When he got back to Great Nest he'd have to ask ZERO to upgrade his unit's implants to translate any of the major race languages they were likely to hear. "No go. That bunch has their own plans, and they don't include us."

"So much for that," Dance said. "Now what, fearless leader?"

Brooks realized there was an opportunity here. "If they want to fly escort, we'll let them. It'll give us the chance to use all our ships on attack. Keep pace with the big ship for now."

The next two hours were one of testing the fighters' capabilities. As *Magisterium* accelerated, it drove the fighters to slowly increase their velocity at a proportionate rate. The real problem was now one of figuring out which section of intruders would be their primary targets. Both groups of attackers were burning hard and were now on intercept courses. Brooks eyed his displays anxiously, wondering who would break first.

Skull's voice jarred him out of his thinking. "Thar she blows! Fast-moving objects are leaving *Magisterium*, heading toward the smaller group of contacts. I count twenty missiles."

"Roger that," Rosenski acknowledged. "Designate *Magis-*

terium's target set as Group One. *Hajimi* and all fighters will attack Group Two."

Brooks made a calculation. "Copy that, actual. Recommend *Hajimi* and my flight attack catch them in a pincer."

"Acknowledged, Leader."

Brooks smiled. He'd been repressing his urge to kill something for too long. "All fighters, come to course two-nine-five. We'll hit them from the left. With any luck it'll confuse the crap out of them. On my mark... mark!"

The fighters swooped in a wide arc, while *Hajimi* merely cut its drives, altered its orientation, and blasted onto the new vector. Group Two's rate of approach doubled and then doubled again as both groups raced toward each other. Nine hundred klicks. Seven hundred. Five hundred. "Start scanning for targets," Brooks ordered. "Hit their bridges and engines. We want to keep them off the mother ship, rejoin the main group, and leave. Keep it simple." A chorus of acknowledgements. The math should work in their favor. *Hajimi* was slower, but carried as many missiles as his entire fighter wing.

Bright lights appeared in the distance as *Magisterium*'s first missile volley found its target. His fighter's sensors were too limited to make out many details, but two of the pursuers in Group One were separating, altering their trajectories to peel away and slow down. Not a bad beginning.

Three hundred klicks become two hundred, then one hundred.

"Break into elements. Take your shots. Missiles on approach, then come around and hit their tails with blasters. Execute!"

Brooks picked his target; an oblong craft as long as their mercenary ship but far narrower. Armored turrets above and below, a very narrow strip of lights on the nose, which had to be the bridge. He targeted six of his dozen missiles on the nose, listened for the locking tone, and let fly. Streaks of flame appeared as the missiles dropped from their pylons and vectored in. A quartet of explosions followed.

Brooks cut his engines, flipped his fighter end-over-end, pointed its nose at the attacker, and repeated the exercise. Three hits out of six this time, and one of the vessel's twin drives was dark now. That would complicate that pilot's life for sure. As an afterthought he loosed a flurry of shots from his fighter's chin turret. He held the trigger down, watched the hybrid rounds arc, and a bright flash appeared. Bulkheads shattered and ship's rear third broke off.

"Splash one," he said.

Another explosion appeared in the distance. Ghost said, "Splash two."

"Splash three... shit!" Dance cried.

Brooks flipped his fighter again, swinging around to rejoin his wingman. He and Dance shifted their attack, coming in at an angle to sideswipe the bigger ship. Dance's target trailed a cloud of crystals, either water or fuel. In either case, the damage was apparently superficial—power output readings on his dash lit up. "Power spikes... they're setting up the turrets," Brooks called. "Space yourselves out, watch for—"

Before he could finish, the forward turrets on the customs boat pelted his and Dance's fighters with red laser bolts. Dance peeled off, swooping through a tight corkscrew, and fired four more of her more missiles. Two of her missiles struck the cruiser's nose, two more hit the dorsal turret. The ship's bow sparked and exploded, and the cruiser careened off course, sailing into a wide arc away from the fighters. Seconds later another explosion lit the dorsal turret, and Brooks could tell the cruiser was out of the fight.

"Now!" Reagan squeed, "Splash three."

Three patrol cruisers left, and Brooks was out of SRMs.

Dance had two left, but none of the other fighters were close enough for Brooks to estimate their loads. "Use them if you have them, people. No rewards for landing with unexpended rounds."

"*Ryokai!* Roberts, follow me," Katsuta called. "I'm top, you're bottom. Just like we practiced."

This ought to be interesting. Brooks and Dance formed back up and swung onto a new course, following Roberts and Katsuta. Brooks monitored them on his display, keeping their formation perfect as they approached their cruiser from its six. They split to approach from behind the larger ship's exhaust plume. Lasers popped from the cruiser's dorsal and ventral turrets, missing both fighters by a wide margin. Two missiles popped out from its forward hatches, then two more, then two after that. Their missile gunner was being stingy with their ammo.

It was a mistake. Roberts's chin turret blasted each salvo to fragments, covering Katsuta, who dropped four missiles from her pylons. The SRMs ran up the cruiser's tailpipe and detonated, shredding the drives. Roberts dropped four of his own missiles into the damaged cruiser, losing one to laser fire. The remaining three exploded into its still hot drive, ripping the cruiser in half.

Splash four. Obviously, the past month of assigning those two to each other had paid off. He decided they could scream at each other as much as they wanted off duty—as long as they continued to fly well.

The last two cruisers changed tactics. They were bigger than the others, easily twice their size, with four turrets each. They maneuvered toward each other, closing ranks, pointing their bows toward the fighters then opening their armored hatches and deploying a host of missiles, splitting their attack into a dozen different paths.

Barrage attack, Brooks thought. That was a trick they'd pulled right out of the Sleer playbook. Or had the Sleer taken it from the Movi? Whichever direction it worked, he knew how to defend against it. "Regroup, people, keep on me. Keep one klick away. Link your chin turrets for concentrated defensive fire. Fire!"

As a unit, all six chin turrets opened fire, shooting streams of hybrid projectiles into the missile volley's path. A jerk of Brooks's hand brought his ship's nose up just enough to send a burst into the lead missile's path. The missile detonated and took two of the others with it. Diallou's shots took out two more, while Ghost launched two of her remaining missiles to detonate her attacker's volley. Katsuta got two before impact and Roberts got the last one. The final missile detonated against the company cruiser's port side, leaving ugly streaks but no punctures. Thank God for small favors. *Hajimi*'s waist turrets swiveled and unleashed a volley of a dozen missiles of their own. One of the two remaining cruisers took the brunt of the shots but only bore superficial damage: *Hajimi*'s missiles had detonated too far away to do much harm.

Four more missile clouds launched from the remaining patrol ships. *Hajimi* rotated to unmask his forward laser turrets and detonated all four volleys well short of their target. All four of his missiles launchers emptied their magazines at the patrol ships. The cruiser's gunners trained their lasers to try and imitate *Hajimi*'s tactic. They failed. The first patrol ship blossomed into a fireball as its magazine went up; the other took damage amidships, began to corkscrew into an ever-widening spiral, and fell to the rear as its captain decided survival was better than getting rich quick.

Brooks toggled his comm. "That's it. Group Two is neutralized."

"Just in time." Rosenski's voice crackled. "Group One is giving *Magisterium* a bad time. Go to afterburners and engage."

"Copy that. Squadron, link to my nav. Don't want to leave anyone behind," Brooks said. He swung the group into the new course, checked his sqadron's positioning, found it good enough for the computers to manage without him for a few minutes, and pushed the fighter's throttle forward. He felt the surge of power beneath him as the power plant maxed out, the afterburners engaging automatically. There were aspects to the Movi design he could easily learn to love. Ravens were awesome fighting machines, but nothing on those birds was automatic. The light fighters reminded him of the prototype Sparrowhawks—limited weaponry, but pure fun in the cockpit.

Brooks pinged the remaining group and saw that all but one of their ships had fallen away. But it was a much bigger opponent than what they'd just spent their time attacking. The sensors showed him the remains of at least three smaller ships in *Magisterium*'s wake. Worse, while Laortus's Q-ship hadn't taken much obvious damage, their supply of missiles was nearly depleted. They were launching one or two from each tube per salvo now, as opposed to the swarms they'd used early in the fight.

Brooks executed a perfect turn, his sensors pinging the raider while data scrolled past in his VR HUD. As he swooped and turned back the way he came, he saw the tiers of turrets were too well organized, the drive cowlings too well shielded to be a local ship. They were dealing with a proper royal navy warship. A destroyer escort or something in that class. Not even the equal of one of Captain Mek's cruisers, but far more than *Magisterium* could handle alone.

Brooks considered their options. The Q-ship was slightly faster, but the destroyer was fully armed. Twenty turrets split between missiles and lasers, and one great big energy weapon jutting from an armored hatch in its nose. And his side was low on ordnance. "*Hajimi*, this is Gauntlet Leader. Suggest you maintain course and engage with missiles only. Gauntlets, follow me."

He dropped the fighter's nose and rotated the ship to approach the destroyer belly-to-belly. He let fly his chin turret with a stream of projectiles, aiming for the two ventral missile turrets they just used. The hybrid rounds missed the target but tore sizeable rents in the hull. An SRM flew past him and hit the port turret, sending a vapor trail and shower of sparks into space. "Score one for you, Dance!" Every little bit helped.

Dance snickered over comms. "I got one round left," she said. "Lemme see if I can... "

Another missile flew past, apparently driving for the destroyer's nose. It missed the energy weapon but slammed into the armored hatch, doing little more than scarring the hull. "Oh well. I'm out of bombs," she said.

"Then you and I can draw some of the heat off the other four." Brooks flew past the destroyer's nose and climbed steeply, driving his fighter into an impromptu Immelman. He completed his remaining arc, chin turret strafing the entire length of the destroyer's deck, then snorted with satisfaction as he watched his four pilots imitate his attack. Diallou got especially adventurous, using her last four missiles to hit four more turrets. All the missiles hit, but none exploded. Oh well. It was a good idea, but now she'd be unable to defend herself at range. Ghost launched her last four SRMs at what might have been the vessel's bridge, a wide pylon jutting up from the rear deck. Three of the missiles hit, but one went astray, exploding far behind the destroyer's hull. Both were out of ordnance; they would have to take special care.

"Roberts and Katsuta... if you two can't drop this thing in its tracks, we're out of options," Brooks said. That wasn't completely true… they'd be out of *good* options.

They swooped around the destroyer's tail and located another opportunity, lining up their attack.

Roberts: "Come on China Girl, four apiece!"

Katsuta: "Not Chinese, you *baka*!"

Eight missiles dropped from their launch rails and streaked toward the destroyer's drive section. Five exploded on target while one went wild, striking harmlessly against the transom. The other two missed completely, destroyed by interceptor rockets from the ship's rear section. Someone had decided not to skimp on this navy ship's weapons, that was certain. What else did they have that they weren't using?

"New contacts at one-eight-nine… it's those escorts from the passenger liner!" Diallou announced.

The group of pinnaces and launches swooped around on their own attack, individual missiles and lasers beams striking haphazardly and harmlessly, but two of the hastily mounted weapons scored hits against the stern section, sending a stream of super-heated plasma into space. Within seconds, one of the ship's three main drives winked out, steam and plasma leaking from rents in its hull.

Brooks was impressed by their courage, if not their skill. "Good shooting, guys. If only you spoke English. Or even Sleer." He was amazed he hadn't thought of it before. He changed to Sleer and said, "Good shooting guys. Follow us on our next pass and maybe we can stop them in their tracks."

The Movi pilot responded in broken Sleer. "Agree! We follow. Shoot drives again."

Brooks grinned. There it was: proof that Sleer was this part of the galaxy's *lingua franca*. Movi and Cycomms both learned it as a second or third language. Humans would have to as well if they wanted to be taken seriously in outer space. Suddenly, all his attempts at learning to communicate in an alien tongue didn't seem like a waste of time. He'd have to rub Underhill's nose in that fact—eventually.

Below them, the destroyer was quickly running out of steam. *Hajimi*'s turrets were poking holes in the bigger ship's hull, while the missiles turrets on its landing pylons were keeping its already damaged laser batteries from properly targeting the company command cruiser. Behind him, his fighters and his new friends were gathering in some semblance of order as they swung around to hit them on another strafing run, this one from stern to bow. As he guided his fighter's nose around, a hail of bullets and energy beams from the small craft scraped three more turrets off the destroyer's hull. Another plasma stream found its way into space; evidence of an explosion deep within the ship.

Behind the melee, Katsuta and Roberts took one more run. They dropped their remaining ordnance into the destroyer's drives and were rewarded with a sizeable explosion.

As they passed above their target and headed toward *Hajimi*, Rosenski ordered, "All Hornets stand down and return to ship. The destroyer is signaling it wants to surrender."

Ghost had another idea. "Bah! Is trick! We stand down, they attack again. Is oldest trick."

"I don't think so," Speedbump said. "Sensors say there are fires in there."

"Turrets have stopped firing," Dance confirmed.

"Very well. Captain, will we be landing aboard the *Magisterium*? I would appreciate the chance to reload missiles before heading back to Great Nest," Brooks said.

"Agreed. See you on the launch deck. Good job. Rosenski out."

Brooks beamed inside his helmet. *Hear that, Uncle? Frau Butcher thinks I did a good job. So there!*

"Well done, my new friends." Laortus joined the channel, "Land your ships in the balcony. We're far enough away from any major bodies to engage the gravity drive. We'll leave immediately."

"Understood." Rosenski answered. "The children can use the exercise."

"The Kar-Tuyin trading group thanks you, Captain Rosenski."

"Thanks is appreciated but as they say on my world, 'cash is king.'"

"Indeed." There was a brief silence and then, "And now, you too are a king."

Brooks wondered what Laortus could possibly have done for them to use the word "king." Maybe a bad translation.

His comm chirped again. "Simon, we got an encrypted bulletin. Apparently, we own a Movi Royal bank account. I don't know what this is worth on Earth, but here it's worth... I don't know. What's the exchange rate on twenty-three million *estani*?"

Brooks couldn't begin to do the math. He assumed they were not only rich in monetary terms, but Chief Purser Loartus had apparently purchased their loyalty for years to come. At least he thought he had. True, having a private estate in Movi territory to use for any number of things: listening post, safe house, forward operating base, shipyard, whatever, was a great asset.

He opened a channel to the passenger liner. "Laortus, what exactly have you done?"

The Movi sound smug as hell. "A simple transaction. Kar-Tuyin profits are disbursed to shareholders on a quarterly basis. I make money, you make money. We hold each other hostage to our good intentions."

"My cousin married a man who made a living as a venture

fund manager," Rosenski said. "Trust me, I know how it works. And I'll be honest. You've treated us better than any other faction representative in this crazy kingdom."

Laortus chuckled. "We'll have you and your officers married into wealthy Movi families in no time."

"Let's not get ahead of ourselves. We may never come back from Haven, you know," Brooks said.

"Perhaps not, but I'm an optimist. Secure your ships and we'll get under way. I've scheduled a meeting with a true hero of the kingdom. I'm sure she'll be able to walk you through any attempt to rescue your Cycomm."

CHAPTER 32

VELUCIDAR. What a dump.

Sora Laakshiden settled back in her command couch, dejected, depressed. Her stolen ship was near the end of its usefulness, and she had to admit, so was she.

She had to commend the pilot. Mineko had chosen his staff well. After *Hajimi*'s devastating attack on their ship outside Movra High Port, her pilot realized his craft was beyond repair and used military codes to attract a rescue; a customs corvette not meant to do much more than spot trouble, call for backup, and then repeat the exercise. In this case, the corvette's four-man crew followed orders to the letter. They offered ideas when warranted and treated her as nothing less than the Flight Admiral she said she was. They'd even allowed her to record a message and forwarded it to the hyperspace relay station network on Chosufah. They'd taken Sora and her pilot on board, ditched the broken escape vessel, and that was that.

Sora had waited until the corvette captain had turned his back. She still remembered how to kill a man with a single blow, turning his head until his neck snapped. He fell and flopped on the deck. She bent down to look into his eyes, hoping to see evidence of something. Some destination, some goal. The people you loved who'd gone before. But there was nothing. Death was just death. You went nowhere. You saw no one.

She'd taken his key card and sidearm, given herself access to all the ship's systems, sealed herself on the flight deck, and opened the interior doors and airlocks. The vacuum did the rest.

Now she had a corvette. But where to go? The corvette could continue for some time if she stopped off at the occasional gas giant or liquid water ocean to refine hydrogen for the reactor.

The Garrison Cluster was out, and the homeworld was no better. She wondered about Vellus. He'd tarried at Fortnite-4095 to collect his M-boat tenders. Those were slow ships. She'd been running around for weeks while he was working a real job. He might be the only friend she had left. She followed the M-boat beacons one after another, staying in one place only long enough to look for Vellus's convoy. After a dozen jumps, she gave up.

She wound her way through the shattered kingdom, listening. She'd arrive at a new world, access the data net, and run countless filters for news about humans, pink-skinned aliens, or a company command cruiser with *Hajimi*'s registration. Sorting between rumors and reality was never simple. The most recent sighting of their ship was Marathas, so she'd gone there and heard details of a fierce space battle between the local navy and the passenger liner *Magisterium*. Other reports mentioned an emergency evacuation. A single report of a ship bearing the energy signature of a Cycomm skip drive. The passenger ship's departure vector led in this direction, but beyond that, nothing.

But... she could only think of one reason a Cycomm ship would arrive. Binil. Perhaps she'd called them to her. Maybe they'd been looking for her since their original escape from the prison barge. In any case, they'd only take her to one place in the galaxy: Haven. And there was only one place to jump into the Cycomm Unity.

Velucidar.

If the humans were on their way to Haven, they'd have to arrive here. They would want to rescue the girl. Brooks and Reagan would convince them.

And now it was just her, alone, in a dark and cold customs vessel, blasting a message to the kingdom at large, waiting for an answer she doubted would come.

"I am Flight Admiral Sora Laakshiden. Hear me. We are all in grave danger. An alien race comes to us, sowing deceit and distrust, seeking to gain advantage over us by destroying the last fibers that bind our kingdom together.

"These people, these *humans*, from the planet Earth, are in alliance with the Sleer—who we all know as a race of soldier-explorers. The humans represent the greatest threat known to us in centuries. After the arch-criminal Zluur defied the Sleer high command and fled, he sent his gun destroyer as an advanced scout toward an unexplored section of the galaxy. Over the course of years, this pilotless ship on its own programming sought out a new world to use as a forward operating bas for the Sleer military. The Sleer now have the greatest of all their weapons, Battle Ring Earth, operating around this new base, building ships in great numbers to support their designs.

"The unity of the Movi Kingdom has been our greatest strength, but now that asset is gone, destroyed by the traitor Archduke Mineko and his followers. Worse, Warlord Anterran's forces and crown prince Singhir's loyalist forces have been unwilling or unable to put down this insurrection as should have been done within days of its inception. And what do we have left? Corporate empire builders? Religious zealots? Have any of them put forth a coherent plan to rebuild what was shattered? They have not. For they cannot. All they can do is bide their time and play politics.

"I propose a new way. My plan is simple. Push these invading humans out of Movi space. It is no accident the chaos afflicting us began when they arrived on our borders. Even now, they conspire with their government to keep us divided and weak. All those who would help me excise this tumor from our political body, meet me at these coordinates. I am Flight Admiral Sora Laakshiden. Hear me..."

Twenty-five days. By now that recording had cycled around the entire relay network, but no one was listening. No one had arrived at her stated rendezvous location, so no one had heard—or having heard, thought her message important. She glanced at the pilot's dash. Plenty of fuel for power. Weeks of it, especially if she went nowhere. The ship's larder was fully stocked when she acquired it, and she had no real appetite. Her clothing was fitting loose, and her spirit was running dry.

She wondered if she could go head-to-head with the *Hajimi* by herself. She might. It was possible. The corvette was a third the size of the company command cruiser, with two turrets and no fighters. But it had excellent sensors and complex fire control software that allowed a single operator to engage all its weapons as if they were being used by actual gunners. Not likely to succeed... but possible. The thought kept her warm as she snuggled deeper into her pilot's couch. She turned down the heat to preserve her ship's resources. Sora liked her ship cold.

She kept the comm channels open, reading news feeds as they arrived. Filters beeped for attention, but she dismissed them. The possibility that it would be what she wanted or needed were... dismal. She used less energy just sitting here, and she wanted to give any interested parties out in the kingdom the greatest possible chance of finding her.

Was this how her life ended? Sulking? Alone in a stolen dwarf of a ship, waiting for a meeting that would never happen? Lamenting the fact that her life had taken on two distinct dimensions: pre-Haven and post-Haven? One mission gone horribly wrong and that was that. No one took her seriously now. Perhaps no one would again. Whatever she thought of herself—whatever she managed to convince others to think of her—her former life was done with. She should deal with that. Fifty years of effort brought her here. Nowhere. Empty space.

More beeps from the feed reader. The news rolled in. All she had to do was read the bulletins. There might be something useful inside.

The sensor display flared and showed her an oblong-shaped vessel. A message boat tender.

The comm pinged again. This time she toggled the system. A man's face appeared on the display, withered and worn, but active. And familiar.

"Sora?"

She smiled crookedly. "Vellus. I'm astounded you found me."

"Why? You broadcast your location far and wide. At least far and wide along the low-band local networks. I'm not sure why you chose that route… "

"Because this ship doesn't have access to a hyperspace-band emitter. The local network nodes were all I could contact."

"I see. I've given you a boost. Message boats have access to more robust networks, so I amplified your message. Swinging past the Garrison Cluster was a calculated risk, but I think it was for the best."

"You didn't stay there? That was your plan."

Vellus looked at his hands, embarrassed. "My plan was to

wait out the fighting. Anterran and Mineko were sniping at each other when I decided it was too dangerous. I left. But I brought a few friends with me."

Pings on her HUD. Every few minutes, a new blip popped up, demanding attention. Free traders, subsidized cargo haulers, modified star liners turned into Q-ships. Customs boats, close escorts, intelligence corvettes, and missile frigates. Light cruisers and strike cruisers. A bonafide strike carrier squadron... if memory served, there would be nearly a thousand heavy fighters between them. Troop transports, assault shuttles, and a half dozen supply carriers. Three Verdanai-class battleships: fearsome spheres loaded with weapons and troops, another thousand fighters inside each. The space above them warped and shifted as the largest of the newcomers arrived: a Guvil-class planetoid, six miles in diameter and enough space around him to drag every one of the new arrivals with him across jumps or into battle. There were only a dozen of these particular planetoids in the royal navy... where did it come from and who commanded it?

"Great Maker," she breathed. "What is this?"

"From what I see, it's just people arriving in ships. And you're welcome. So... who will oversee the great anti-human resistance you're planning?"

She couldn't look away from the planetoid. It filled the display behind the rest of the cloud of new arrivals. She touched a panel; the readout made her breath stop as her brain made a connection. This wasn't a Guvil-class ship... it was the *Guvil*. The class ship itself. A legendary name in royal navy history. There was only one name she could think to associate with it.

"This is Sora Laakshiden, calling *Guvil*. I am trying to contact Warlord First Admiral Tridalva Andrulen ap-Goodep. Is she available?"

She repeated the hail several times, wondering what was

happening. Small ships were still arriving, adding their physical presence to the cloud of recruits already around her. Her own ship looked hopelessly small, its nature as a naval toy now brazenly apparent amid so much military hardware. She hadn't spoken to Tridalva in years, and even then, Sora had been a lousy subcommander, while her superior had already risen to fleet captain—and showed no sign of stopping. The plans for the *Guvil* had come off the architect's drawing board soon after, and while Sora knew the fearsome weapons were being built, she had no idea who would command them or be of a mind to deploy them into a combat situation. There were no combat situations at that time ugly enough to demand one's use.

But then the Skreesh had made their latest incursion through Sleer space, and no one had known exactly what their plan was. Guvil-class ships were dispatched to the shared borders and remained there on station indefinitely. That was four years ago.

The comm chirped. "Flight Admiral Laakshiden, you have been granted permission to board *Guvil*. Please align your navigation to these berthing instructions."

It was all automatic. Sora adjusted her trajectory as instructed, the battleship's displacement projector aligned, and the interior of a hangar bay instantly appeared around her. She fought down an urge to run her hands over her body to confirm all her parts were present and accounted for. A childish notion, but a persistent one. Cycomm skip drives were bad enough, but when Binil had skipped their prison ship toward the Sleer escape fleet, Sora had been too distracted—too focused on the result—to care. Now she was a mere guest. A passenger. No command authority. All she could do was follow instructions.

She cracked the seal on the outer hatch and exited to the steel walls, roving equipment, engine noise, and the smell of fuel, lubricant, and ozone of an active hangar. An oblong travel pod hovered a few meters away, its door open. No one to meet her, but nowhere to go, either. The pod was empty, with four cushioned seats. She chose one. The door closed and the vehicle noiselessly rose to a travel tube near the ceiling and sent Sora Laakshiden on her way.

CHAPTER 33

THE POD SLOWED, and Sora stepped out to a wide chamber. Other travel capsules sat unused against a wall, and multiple corridors branches from the open section. In the center of the landing area stood a figure, aged but but no less dignified than the proudest line officer in the navy. Warlord First Admiral Tridalva Andrulen ap-Goodep wore her full uniform, ribbon, awards, and medals running down the length of both her sleeves, her collar and cuffs bright with sliver and gold braid. Her hair was tied into a severe bun and Sora immediately felt self-conscious about her own wild mane and ruined outfit. Sora approached, stumbling, and saluted the older woman.

"Warlord. I am here."

"So you are." They hugged briefly and gently, Sora not wanting to damage anything. Tridalva let her go and took a step back. "So, Admiral. Status report."

Despite her slight advantage in height, Sora felt a need to look up at the older woman. "I think I may have wrecked myself for good."

Tridalva indicated their direction with a wave of her hand. She walked slowly but stolidly, without missed steps or wasted movements. "I wondered. My comm officers picked up your transmission. I knew something had jarred you. I've never heard you sound so hopeless. So angry. It worried me enough to come looking, so we followed your directions here. You look awful, my girl."

Hopeless. A word she'd never heard anyone apply to her. A wide chasm threatened to open beneath Sora's feet. She might even welcome it. A deep, dark hole to hide from the universe. No one to disappoint, no responsibilities to flub. "Oh, Tri... I fucked up big time."

"Did you now? Come, sit down and tell me about it. And tell me about these humans you hate so much. I think we have something to learn from them." They came to an alcove with the dimensions of a ready room but the trappings of a cozy salon. Comfy chairs and a sofa were arranged around a long low table, upon which a tea service rested, cups turned up. Pastel colored draperies formed a tent around them, the flap open.

Sora ducked into the tent, took the seat at the head of the low table and began pouring tea for the two of them as Tridalva sat at the opposite end. "If you knew them, you'd realize they're a cancer on the galaxy's body. Zluur's shadow weighs too heavily on them. They enter our space uninvited, intrude on our affairs, try to insert themselves into our politics, and threaten us with destruction if we refuse them. The sooner we wipe them out and take their battle ring for our own, the sooner we can restore the kingdom."

"Aren't you being a bit selective in your reporting?"

"What? Why?"

"Because I've already met them. They tell a very different story." Tridalva turned and raised her voice. "Aliens! Attend us. You as well, war criminal."

A Movi in corporate livery entered followed by Rosenski, Brooks, Underhill, and Reagan. The humans took the sofa, the

Movi, the last chair. Laortus helped himself to tea. Sora tried to raise her cup, found her hand unable to stop shaking. The best she could do was create a loud clatter. She resigned herself to the humiliation and forced herself to sit still, hands in her lap.

"You know these aliens, I believe," Tridalva said. "This gentleman is Loartus Banuk ad-Esservil ap-Somak. High in Kar-Tuyin's employ but not bright enough to avoid royal entanglements."

"Just so that I know how great a fool I am," Sora groaned, "How long has this fellowship been in progress?"

"Hardly a fellowship. We're business partners," Laortus announced. "I had a problem with a local navy patrol that tried to prevent me from departing Marathas. These talented people helped as they could, and I paid them handsomely for their work."

"Because of course you did. Where's Binil?"

"That's a complicated story," Underhill said.

Reagan sneered. "Nothing complicated about it. The Sense Ops came and kidnapped her from the passenger liner we were staying on. Hell, I don't know exactly what happened and I was there. I told Binil to stay in the room while I looked around. I turn a corner and some dude in battle armor is pointing a super soaker at me. Next thing I remember is the medic and Katsuta dragging me to sick bay." She stared at her hands a moment, then said, "What did happen?"

"VF-7," Tridalva said. "It's a nerve agent. It can be inhaled as a vapor, or the target can be doused with a water-based solution. It does no permanent damage, but you see how well it works."

Dance dropped her eyes. "Respect. He could have ended me. One round in my head. I guess I should say thank you to the Cycomms if I meet any more."

Warlord Tridalva nodded. "Despite your experience, Lieutenant, the Cycomms are extremely non-confrontational. Their military doesn't approve of collateral damage. It's one reason the Unity is left to itself. The previous Sovereign enacted a travel ban to their home system years ago. The last thing she needed was for their ideas to infect her military."

"The previous sovereign was a woman?" Rosenski asked.

Laortus drained his cup and a server quickly stepped in to refill it. "She was. Movra XI. She had four daughters but no sons. Movus XXXV was her great-nephew?"

"Grandson," Tridalva corrected. "That's one of the problems with a succession process that allows for matriarchal lines of descent in a polygamous tradition but only allows males to inherit the throne directly. So many outdated rules."

"Until it finally fell apart," Brooks said.

Tridalva straightened and glared at him. "I understand that young men are passionate and must have their say, but here you are wrong. Show me a political system that responds well to assassination, and I'll show you something that doesn't exist."

"Why am I even here?" Sora asked. "It's obvious I don't know what's happening and have no skill at securing... anything, really."

Tridalva grinned. "You have tremendous skill. You're quite a leader. Your judgement is clouded by desperation, but that's where these fascinating people can help you. Even Laortus here. You could do worse than to listen to them."

"I'd rather eat my own face."

Underhill met her glare. "Admiral—"

"*Flight* Admiral. The sovereign restored my rank." She'd fought long and hard for that rank; these people would damn well respect it.

"See, this is what I'm talking about," Underhill continued. "You make eyes at your Guy in Charge and hope his restoring your rank makes you a top player in this crazy game, but you only look at your chips, never your cards. You have no idea whether it's a good hand or not—you just bluster and bullshit and expect people to fall out of your way."

Sora knew this woman would be trouble from the time she insisted on boarding *Hajimi* with herself and Binil. "You can't talk to me that way, you blue-haired—"

Underhill continued, "Did it ever occur to you to *ask* us for help in getting yourself restored to the game? We would have, you know. We'd have asked for some concessions—and gotten them—"

Sora fought down an urge to fly from her chair and beat the human woman silly. "You're lying."

"No, she's not," Rosenski said. "For once I agree with her. First, you want my crew's help in setting up meetings between yourself and potential allies. Then you decide you don't need us at all. Then you go on the air and tell the factions that we're a greater threat to them than they are to each other. Now you're back here, trying to stop us from rescuing the only person in the kingdom we like and trust enough to want to stick our asses out for. And that's still not enough for you."

Sora hated herself for sitting here and listening to their nonsense. "Everything I want is possible if you primates are *gone*."

Rosenski gave a deep sigh that turned into a rumble in her throat. "And you're back to blaming us for your problems. Honey, I don't know how you manage to get dressed in the morning. We didn't sell you out to anyone. Your own people did that."

Sora jumped out of her chair; hands balled into fists. "You—"

"I'm not kidding," Rosenski said. "Vondra, the Iria Sisterhood spy, told us that you were part of a grand plan of hers to bring a terrorist cell on Marauder's Moon to justice. Or what

Movi spy circles call justice. Sellik and Cleo? Your two pals from the prison barge? They were in on it. Even Binil went along with it because she had no way to escape. You were played from beginning to end. Everyone knew it but you." Sara inclined her head toward Dance. "Now, Lt. Reagan here, she has a solid plan to locate our asset—"

Sora was hot with anger. She barely heard Rosenski continue. The best she could do was a mumble. "My asset—"

Rosenski growled, "*Our* asset. The Unified Earth Fleet's asset. Gauntlet Squadron's asset. We have scanners that can utilize digital signatures derived from DNA sequences, but if we jump into their home system we'll be immediately targeted and attacked. If the Sense Op teams are as effective as we've seen, then we don't stand much of a chance. But if a Guvil-class planetoid claiming allegiance to a previously unknown faction in the ongoing civil war pops into their space and demands attention, then I think the government of Haven and the penal colony on Marauder's Moon will both be so damned interested in what happens next that they'll pay all their attention to you—and that frees us up to do what we need to do."

"Listen." Underhill said. "We know Zluur's betrayal precipitated a whole cascade effect. It's got you, and it's got us, and it's got the Sleer and the Cycomms by the pubes."

Sora raised her head, confused. "Who are the—"

Rosenski waved her hands. "Never mind. The allied race treaty was a good idea that shouldn't have ended the way it did. Now we need your help to take the battle ring on our planet back from the loonies who broke that treaty."

"*I* broke that treaty!" Sora howled. "And I had good reason to."

Rosenski continued, "In return we have access to people and experts who might be able to help your people resume business as usual. Because if we can't come to some understanding damned soon, the Skreesh will roll all over everything. When they're done with the Vix and the Rachnae and the Decopods, then they'll come for Earth. When we're gone, they'll come for the Movi. Because that's how predators think."

"Sora... would you like to tell them about us, or should I?" Tridalva asked.

Laortus tapped away at a tablet, engrossed in some communication. The humans stared at Sora with their full attention. Did she have any credibility left? "If I told them, I doubt they'd believe me. I suppose I deserve that."

Tridalva settled into her chair. "Very well. It's not a long story, but to me it seems like a very long time ago. I had just gotten my sublieutenant's bar. That alone was exceptional—in those days women didn't become officers. I was so full myself. My friends, noncoms most of them, came around to take me to drinking. It was a thing. The men did it, so why shouldn't we? Such a scandal."

"Tri's family was an old traditional bunch."

"They still are. Don't be rude, Sora."

"No. Excuse me."

"It's a curious thing. When you're tainted with scandal, there's a tendency to be even more scandalous. I courted officers. I was one of them, wasn't I? I could do what I wanted. And I did. A friend of mine did as well... except I got lucky and avoided trouble, but she found herself with child. She never asked me for help, but I thought it would be churlish not to be there for her. That extended to what came next. The child was born—a beautiful girl—and the mother passed to the next life. I didn't want the girl to be remanded into an orphanage for disposal, so... I had a commission that was still crisp and a sublieutenant's bar that wasn't a year old yet and I also now had a baby. Someone else's child who needed constant care and feeding. Now what?"

Sora glanced at the others. Even Laortus was listening.

Tridalva continued, "It should have ended everything. But there were some things that remained from the old order. The bad old days. When women lost their places in the world, they learned new ways of managing. My entire unit volunteered to help. We all got gene therapy, hormonal rebalancing. We all became wet nurses. We rotated duty, we set up schedules so that one of us would always be with the child. We figured it out. They wouldn't let us fight or keep our jobs, but raising a child? That they let us do. It became complicated… one of my unit's company clerks nearly gave herself a coronary over the lies, damn lies, and paperwork, but it worked. We kept the little she-runt out of trouble for four years."

Sora knew this part by heart. "Then they rotated the whole unit back into combat and that was the end of that."

Tridalva shook her head. "Not exactly. Four years is old enough for a foster family to be arranged, so I made that happen. We set her up with a good pair. Merchants. They didn't ask who the mother was. It didn't matter. They had a safe, comfortable home, and the girl would have a proper childhood. A place in the family business. I could visit according to my schedule. That was my right. They agreed."

"Of course, they agreed. It was illegal to refuse," Sora murmured.

"And how was your time spent there?" Laortus asked the Admiral.

Sora furrowed her brow as she dug up old memories. Typical of Loartus to figure out the truth first. He was too clever for his own good. "Safe and comfortable. They were perfectly respectable people. Not very exciting. But they nudged me toward the idea that I could do the things I set my mind to. They taught me to ride a megathron. In two years, I was so good at it that I started teaching others. I learned to read, write, and speak foreign languages. To play the zydleth. I was a whiz at math. But it was routine. The only days that weren't dull were the days Tridalva came to visit. She'd spend the whole day with me and it would be as if she never left."

Tridalva raised her cup. "Except that every time I saw you, you were slightly taller and slightly more arrogant."

Sora finally felt the tension in her body ease as the memories loosened her muscles. A sense of pride in her achievements. "I was more accomplished."

Tridalva pointed at her, trying to impress a lesson that never took hold. "You wore your success like a fancy dress. You bragged. It took years to break you of that habit."

"University did that. It was the first place where nobody knew who I was or cared. It was a fistfight per day for the next three years."

Brooks piped up. "Only three years? On Earth it's anyhere from four to ten for specialized academic work."

Sora shrugged. She wouldn't explain the intricacies of Movi higher education to him. They'd be here all year. "I completed my three years and made friends with a young man who was studying data networks. Advanced concepts. I understood the coding techniques, but not all the higher strategies behind them. One day he showed me a master project and I was convinced that he'd mis-coded a sensitive section of the program. I offered him advice, which he ignored. When he was in class I broke into his computer and fixed the code."

Tridalva snorted. "Fixed it. You certainly did."

Sora hesitated. He'd been so angry. She'd never seen him angry before. "The boy's project failed and it was my fault. Afterward, I grew the courage to admit my failure to myself. I then admitted it to the professor, and finally to him. It ended my relationship with the young man and the school. That left the military." She inhaled deeply and let it out shakily. "Whatever else I do, I'm clearly not well suited to manage this—struggle—in the kingdom. I'm not sure the kingdom would have survived for much longer in any case. We do seem to be losing what cohesion we had in the past. I'm not sure why."

Laortus frowned. "You don't think of yourself as a potential replacement sovereign, do you?"

Sora nearly choked on her tea. "No! That's far more stress than anyone can hope to bear—except for megalomaniacs like Mineko. But I wonder whether our greatest triumphs are behind us. What if the best we can hope to accomplish now, here, today, is to retreat to a more monastic existence and horde all the fragments we're finding, in the hopes that one day we'll be able to forge something new? Is that even possible?"

"In a way it's a hell of a lot more ambitious than to try to take over the whole flawed mess." Brooks said.

"Would you be willing to record another message?" Trivalda asked.

Sora saw the goal in the distance. Tri had always been good at getting her to realize her mistakes. "Yes, I would. But if you want to reform the allied races, you'll have to convince the Sleer to make Earth's battle ring open to everyone. You'll have to show them that building additional battle rings in your solar system as a defense measure against Skreesh incursion is a worthwhile project. You'll also have to convince them that you humans, not the Sleer high command, are the true inheritors of Zluur's intentions. We won't be able to do that with a mere fleet."

"It might be a good start if we use that fleet to rescue Binil," Underhill said.

Sora ran the math and came up with a solution that was the opposite of what they seemed to want. "I don't understand. You'll make enemies of the Cycomms. How does that help us?"

"Think of it this way," Underhill said. "Two great empires are now in ruins. They think that no matter what happens, eventually the fighting will stop and everyone will go back to their lives. Back to the way things were. We both know there's no chance of that. With nothing but one battle after another, your factions are breaking the infrastructure that supports them. The mining colonies are gone because the miners were all conscripted. The agriculture worlds have no crops because their biospheres have all been attacked and new seeds aren't available. Your war production grinds to a halt because the factories are either being bombed out of existence or the workers were killed. Commercial trading hubs and transportation routes are being severed as we speak. Even if you managed to cobble together a coalition that was broad and deep enough to bring more than half the remaining fleets on your side, what would be left after you put down every other faction?"

Sora's mentor cast her eyes down. "Not very much at all," she sighed. "The core worlds would probably remain relatively intact. Nobody likes to make war in one's back yard. But we'd lose the peripheral and mid-core worlds. Two-thirds of... everything."

Rosenski took up the narrative. "Maybe it's the tea talking, or maybe it's the fact that Earth already went through a struggle very much like this, but we realized we were working on borrowed time. We decided to do what we could to meet the new reality head on... and here we are."

"Here you are," Sora agreed. "The bulk of your population remains on your homeworld under Sleer weapons. I hesitate to call that success."

"But we're still alive."

"For now." Sora gripped the arms of her chair and kicked the low table. Ceramic dishware flew noisily across the tabletop, spilling undrunk tea onto legs, boots, and the floor. "All I wanted my entire career was command of a ship like this! A planetoid. The greatest machinery the Movi ever built. The respect it would command in the field, the prestige I would have back home. There's nothing like it."

"It is glorious, of course, but at the end of things, it's just one ship," Tridalva said. "Isn't it better to be known as the one who brought together a war fleet unlike any seen in the galaxy? I could never pull off a project like that. I have no experience in managing anything but Movi navy assets. But you have hooks in the Movi navy, in the political class, in the merchant families. And you have these humans both prepared to kill you in the name of self-defense and encouraging you to battle to rescue your former ward."

"Ward?" Dance asked.

"Binil." Always back to Binil. "Not a ward. I was using her to get off that prison barge."

Underhill lowered her voice to a whisper. "You think humans don't use dirty tricks to do the dirty work? I got orders to screw over two friends and I obeyed. I didn't even think about it."

"Yes, you did," Brooks said. "You thought about it, then you did it anyway. I don't know if that makes it worse or not, but it still stinks."

"You'll notice I didn't trigger either of you since," Underhill said.

Rosenski glared. "You didn't have to. There's nowhere for us to go. You got us assigned to the OMP so we'd never be out of your sight or jurisdiction. What choice do we have?"

"If you're apologizing, Major, it's a really crappy job of it," Brooks said.

Underhill sagged. "I thought you'd trust me to not hold you to the trigger, but... evidently not. I'll make it right. Somehow."

Sora Laakshiden sat up straight. "I will, too. I think there's a way forward. And I would be grateful for your help."

The humans facial expressions shifted and wavered. She'd

have sworn they were having a silent conversation... then mentally kicked herself. Of course they were. Sleer implants.

Rosenski turned her eyes to Sora. "We can help. We'll need a few things. Most importantly, we'll need a message boat and the quickest route to Great Nest."

CHAPTER 34

IN RAYMOND'S DREAM, Valri sat in the transmogrifier chair. She seemed smaller every time he dreamed it. Her hand was either hot and sweaty or ice cold. She got thinner every time. She screamed.

She always screamed and he always jumped up, wide awake. The dream was wrong... as dreams often were. He'd taken her to the Movi clinic this afternoon. The chair had been Val's exact size, neither too big nor small. She'd dressed in her sweats, short sleeves and baggy pants. As usual, they allowed him to sit next to her and he held her hand, their fingers intertwined, her flesh warm. She'd been cheerful, or as cheerful as he'd seen her lately. The six weeks of transmogrifier work had been hard on her. They arrived for their appointments on time, she sat, the doctors made her comfortable, she put out her arm and they worked on her, setting the probes into her forearm, throwing switches, hemming and hawing and murmuring to each other. Now and then someone would exclaim in Moviri. Fairchild would ask so many questions. But of course, it was nothing to worry about.

After an hour they'd let her up, plied her with sweet teas

and nourishing liquid, and sent them both away. He walked her to her quarters and she invited him in and they talked for a few minutes and she passed out on her ouch. He'd seen her tired before, but nothing like this. Like the Dal-Cortsuni techs and their corporate masters were draining the energy from her. It brought back ugly memories of his sister's long fight with cancer and chemotherapy treatments.

He sat up in bed, the red numbers on the wall clock his only illumination. 02:17. Plenty of time before 5.30 reveille... if only he could stay asleep longer than two hours at a time.

A baritone voice from the ceiling took the choice out of his hands. "Commander Fairchild."

"Yes, ZERO."

"I have an incoming transmission. It's from General Hendricks, directed to you."

Habit asserted itself, and Ray started to dress. "You mean he sent it to Great Nest?"

"No, Commander. The message is for you specifically."

Underwear, shirt, trousers, socks, boots. ID, dog tags. Spectacles, testicles, wallet, and watch. "Why me? Generals don't talk to lousy Commanders. He'd talk to Rojetnick first, wouldn't he? Did Rojetnick say anything?"

"I have no messages from Captain Rojetnick."

"What does Hendricks want?"

"The subject is designated 'Secret.'"

"Great. Can I take it here?"

"Of course. I'm a directing the message to your console."

"Thanks." Ray sat at the console, entered his ID, and waited. Data scrolled across the screen as it connected with its counterpart on Earth; General Hendricks's features filled the screen. Fairchild smiled despite his revulsion. He hadn't thought about how much he hated this guy in months. "General! Good to see you again. This almost seems familiar."

"Hardly, Commander. For one thing you're not under arrest this time."

Hendricks's image wavered and buzzed, pixelating around the edges. Bad as the reception was, the fact that he could talk to another human being a few hundred lights years away in real time was nothing short of miraculous. "I'm glad to hear you confirm that, General."

"Your mood won't survive what I must tell you. You and Commander Katsev finally have something in common other than your jobs. Your respective proteges have gone insane."

Fairchild blinked, then blinked again. It wasn't a sentence he'd expected to hear, ever. Part of him wondered if Hendricks was trying to be funny, then remembered that the man had no sense of humor, and that what he had in its place was sarcastic and cruel. "I don't... excuse me?"

"Let me be clear. I hope they've gone insane for your sake. They're already under suspicion of aiding and abetting a known domestic terror group. They may even be meddling in a foreign power's internal struggle. If that's true, they'll return home to firing squads. Are you listening to me, Fairchild?"

Ray nodded dumbly. "I am, General. I'm finding this all a bit out of the blue is all. What exactly drew you to these conclusions?"

"This transmission, these data points, and these observations. The image quality isn't perfect, but that's the vessel they departed in, isn't it?" The display shifted to show Fairchild a host of unknown spacecraft, designs he didn't recognize. More than a few were large spheroids like the Movi navy vessels Valri described to him at varying times. At the display's center sat a sphere with landing pylons, forward- and waist-turrets at rest. All of them painted like eyes.

Hajimi.

"I believe that's a familiar sight, yes, sir."

"Fairchild, I don't know what you're teaching your boy, but if this isn't stopped ASAP, there will be hell to pay. A very specific hell populated by prison and executions."

"Which means... ?"

"It means do something about your soldiers. Upon arrival, you will take stock of the situation and assume control of all human crewed vessels in the area. Am I clear?"

"Yes, sir. I'll need access to—"

"You'll have access to *Gauntlet* and all the equipment and crew you need. Mention my name and ZERO will make it happen. I'm uploading the contents of the transmission we picked up and supporting intelligence as well. Hendricks out."

Hendricks's face vanished—give thanks for small favors—and Ray spent the next hour going over the bits and pieces the big man sent him. An angry message from Sora Laakshiden to the universe. After-action reports and news bulletins regarding *Hajimi* fighting with other vessels. Sightings relayed by some remaining operational Sleer listening posts inside Movi territory. The planet named Velucidar, and the star maps that led there.

"Simon, what the fuck have you gotten into now?" he demanded.

He saved everything—including the record of his conversation with Hendricks—to his tablet and left the building. At this hour of the night, Primate Alley was sound asleep. Third shift began at midnight and continued to 8am, and he knew Joanne Arkady would be home. Hopefully gotten some rest. Rojetnick and Nazerian were in the depths of starting a new accelerated training program to build their combined pilot reserves, and the Saint had pulled duty at the training arena. The compartment networked one hundred flight simulators arranged in ten groups of ten, with a near constant stream of recruits attending them.

Arkady ran the whole thing. Not bad as desk jobs went, but it wasn't like being in a Strike Raven.

He found her building, took the lift to her floor, and walked down the hall toward her apartment. Turning the corner, he nearly collided with a lone attendant pushing a rolling table in the opposite direction. The man stood to attention, even saluted. Short guy, black hair, bronze skin. Ensign's pip in his collar. Familiar looking. Ray saluted and kept walking, but he thought there was something off about the guy. It wasn't until he reached Arkady's door that he figured it out; the man wasn't wearing any footwear.

Hmm.

He hit the door chime... once... twice... three times. When she answered, Joane Arkady looked like anything but her normal ultra-organized self. She was flushed and floppy, hair all over the place. Dressed in shorts, out of breath, and her tank top was on backwards. "Ray? What's up?"

Fairchild did the math and realized he was intruding. "Please tell me I'm not interrupting anything."

"No. All finished. I was going to take a shower. Bath. Some water activity."

"I see. We have an intercept mission, handed down from on high. How soon can you be ready?"

"Fifteen minutes. I really need to shower. You... yeah, come in."

She retreated into the bedroom and closed the door. The front room smelled of sex and bacon. It made him uncomfortable in a deeply weird way. He didn't like to think of his coworkers as being anything but soldiers, but soldiers got together like anyone else. Where did little soldiers come from, after all? What the hell was he doing with Valri, for that matter?

He spent the wait managing the contacts on his tablet, setting up crew and quartermaster orders, calling a travel pod to the lobby. Neat, automated vehicles, infinitely more convenient than the ground cars they used aboard AMS-1. By the time she emerged from the bedroom, he'd steadied his thoughts. She was in uniform, tidy, ready for action. She'd seen action already. Gah!

The travel pod door closed and bore them away with no hint of acceleration. "Who did the walk of shame?" he blurted.

Arkady managed to blush. She ran her fingers through her raven hair and said, "Rodriguez."

"Rodriguez," he said, saying the name a few times, running it through his mind, waiting for it to resolve. "Not Brooks's, friend? That Rodriguez?"

"Uh. Yes. Him."

"Well, okay."

The words poured out of her. "It's kind of a story. He's moved up to running the cafe on deck three. The wardroom, you know? And I've been working late and he stays late to manage cleanup, you know. I started coming by for coffee on the way out and he started giving me a sweet roll or a cupcake... whatever was left over from dinner. We'd chat. It became a thing. Our thing."

"I see."

"Then I may have asked whether he ever went home, and he might have made a joke about seeing my quarters and then I could have said something about breakfast in bed then he might have offered to help plan a menu—and it's possible I suggested he make a delivery—"

"Uh-huh."

She sniffed and nodded. "I was getting ready to turn in for the night. And he showed up with a rolling table and cloth napkins and real silverware and plates of pastries and a pitcher of lemonade and a plate of cookies—"

"I get the picture."

"Chocolate chip pancakes with real blueberries! And eggs and bacon arranged like a face! And—"

"Stop it, you're making me hungry."

"Sorry, Uncle," she said. "We never got to the pancakes."

"That's a damn shame."

"No. It's not," she sighed.

Fairchild saw a dark road for himself and Valri Gibb, and it irked him. He wasn't getting a ton of action, and didn't see why anyone else should be having a good time. "Listen. When you finally come down off your fucking endorphins... "

She winked at him. "Phrasing, Ray."

"Fuck."

"I did."

"Lieutenant Commander Arkady. I need you to go into full XO mode and organize a crew for *Gauntlet*. We're loading for death from above and driving into Movi space. I've sent the orders. We boost in twelve hours."

All the blood drained from her face. "Dear Christ, what happened?"

"Hendricks thinks Rosenski's little fact-finding mission has gone completely off the rails. He says Brooks and Rosenski are insane. Tells me they're planning a coup or some damn thing. And as much as I'd like to tell him to pound sand up his ass, I think he may have a point."

"Oh shit."

"Exactly. I've seen the data he was willing to show me. *Hajimi* is very much in the middle of a grand fleet only a few light-years away from the Cycomm home world. We need to scramble an intercept mission, meet them out there before they can do any lasting damage, and remind them who they work for. *Gauntlet* can make the trip in the shortest time."

Arkady patted her pockets. "I don't believe any of it, but I expect tonight would be a good time to test the ship's long-range jump capability. I mean, we did add a whole new section for the prototype Warhawks..."

They emerged from the vehicle into one of the primary hangar bays, only a short walk from their ship's berth. Already, crew and troops were assembling as their own transports arrived. Fairchild strode across the hangar, scanning the space, preparing a mental checklist as the flight deck come alive with activity.

"There's no way Hendricks is telling the truth," Arkady said, increasing her stride to keep up. "He runs the bloody secret police. He *is* the OMP. He's a rotten gear in a rotten machine. He'll say anything to convince us to do his rotten job for him."

"I agree. But there's a first time for everything. Let's hope this isn't it."

"Sir, yes, sir. I'll get them up, get them dressed, get them out. On the boost, people!"

Ray Fairchild smiled crookedly. Joane Arkady didn't deserve his petty jealousy. He didn't care who his XO did or how or when or why. He loved her and he loved that he could always count on the Saint to keep the world turning smoothly.

CHAPTER 35

IT WAS A CROWDED BRIEFING ROOM, with none of the relatively comfortable seating options available on Battle Ring Great Nest or even the AMS-1. *Gauntlet* managed with a narrow room with gunmetal walls, a long table, and folding chairs. But he wanted to know their faces and wanted them to know each other. And they all needed the information.

Fairchild began by calling on his Flight Ops team. He'd only met Marissa Hart a few times aboard AMS-1; time and experience had turned her into a more mature version of herself. No one made jokes about the admiral's spoiled daughter anymore. In the past two years, she had taken a promotion to lieutenant commander. She now agreed to serve as Gauntlet's Air Boss, while Lt. Carol Simmons served as her Mini Boss.

Hart checked her tablet. "We're fully loaded. Twelve stock Raven-Ds, twelve Super Raven-Ds with Blast Packs, twelve Strike Raven-Es with Armor Packs, your twelve experimental prototype Warhawks, six production Sparrowhawks, and three Lurkers. Simmons and Smithers did a yeoman's work in getting us enough ordnance for six full sorties. If that doesn't convince

Hajimi's crew we mean to take them home, I don't know what will."

"And what we don't already have in crates and boxes, I can arrange," Bronson said. "We got two auto-forges in the machine shop already turning out HEAP rounds for the GU-22s. Hate to say it, Captain, but please don't let your pilots use those guns as clubs. It wrecks the feed and we have to dismantle the pods completely before restoring them. You might as well break them over your big metal knee if it comes to that."

"XO, let's create a policy for that. GU-22s are for shooting only," Fairchild said.

"Yes, sir. I'll dot the Is and cross the Ts myself."

Bronson had a confused expression. She couldn't tell if she was being mocked or not.

"In fairness, lieutenant," Fairchild said, "If we're at that point, then we're already in deep enough trouble that all the extra rounds in the world wouldn't make much difference. But I do appreciate you. Without your machine shop, we'd be slinging mudballs and harsh language at the Movi. We won't win any fights that way. So thank you."

Bronson checked his words for sarcasm, found them clean, and sat back, satisfied.

Fairchild went through his checklist. "Next up—battlers."

Lt. Ingrid Nilsen turned her blonde head toward the front of the room. Frances Underhill would have recognized her instantly as the woman who'd shared control of her Kaiju at the battle of Great Nest two years ago. "Interesting mix this trip. Twelve each of Challengers, Archers, and Broadswords. All heavy hitters, all new off the assembly line. Six each Lightnings, with the new full spectrum observation drone links and comm jamming packs. Will be interesting to see those in use. Six OMP style Manticores, also. Three Kaijus are still part of the standard complement, but I admit the giant monster cannon are less and less useful with each new generation of Battler design. The trend is toward smaller units, not bigger."

Fairchild wondered why she brought that point up. The Kaiju was a hugely oversized machine, but it packed a punch that couldn't be defended against at close range, and served as a mobile artillery piece. "Well, if you think we should leave the mobile cannon behind… "

"No, sir. But if we lose them, they won't be replaced. That's all I'm saying."

"So noted, and thank you. That leaves VRF readiness." Fairchild nodded to the two men who, until today, he'd known only by reputation. Arkady had tapped First Lt. Bill "Road Hog" Steeph to run the VRF squadron as CAG. Steeph in turn had brought on Second Lt. Adrian Morrow to be his XO. "You heard Hart's report, sir. Gauntlet Squadron is loaded and ready to go."

Fairchild probed a bit. "But?"

Steeph shook his head. "No buts."

"One very small 'but.' Inconsequential, really," Morrow said.

There it was. "Speak up, Lieutenant. I called this meeting to air out problems while they're still small."

"We don't have anyone qualified as test pilots to run the Warhawks," Steeph groused, after shooting his XO a lethal glare. It only lasted a moment, but Fairchild would need a serious talk with his CAG, and soon.

"What's the issue?"

"It's a matter of staffing. I was able to push through orders for fifty pilots, including the two of us. I put all my most experienced pilots into the Raven-Ds and -Es… that's thirty-six. I have six people who would be excellent Sparrowhawk pilots, so that was easy and brings us up to forty-two. The Lurkers are problematic. Those take a crew of eight people, with a pilot and co-pilot for each, plus six commo nerds to run the sensors. So, six more pilots gone for forty-eight. That leaves me with two floaters, depending on what happens when we drop. I'll put them in two of the prototypes if you insist, but I'd rather hold them back as relief crew for one of the Lurkers. I hate to say it, but there we are."

Fairchild understood the problem. After a certain point, once your manufacturing lines were running at capacity, your bottleneck became training pilots, not building fighters. "Joanne, I'm assuming you couldn't find a dozen pilots from the current crop of nuggets?"

"You'd be correct. Besides, I was under the impression that we were holding the Warhawks in reserve. I'd be happy to assign qualified Raven flyers as test pilots if we get a stretch of quiet, but would I want to rely on prototypes in combat? I don't think so." she said.

"Fair enough. That leaves us with housekeeping."

At the far end of the table, Rodriguez was wearing the face of a man who had no idea why he'd been included in the meeting. "Shelves are stocked, storerooms are full. We can last about six months before running low on anything. The coffee in the wardroom is hot and plenty of it, and everyone gets three squares a day, Captain." He leaned over the table far enough to make eye contact with Arkady. "The kitchen is always open. Always."

She frowned and became very interested in her tablet. Fairchild ignored the exchange.

"Thank you all." He looked up and made eye contact with each of them. "I know this is a strange circumstance, but I may as well say this at the outset... I'm impressed as hell with every one of you. You've come up in the world since your first tour on the AMS-1. Now you're officers, ensigns and lieutenants, helping run departments on Battle Ring Great Nest. Amir is still a non-com, but that's because she works for a living." The table shared a chuckle. Amir pointed to her sleeve and collar. She'd taken the Master Chief Petty Officer's exam and passed it.

He continued, "But there is a reason I wanted you all on this crew. The one thing you all have in common beyond your service in the Unified Earth Fleet is a relationship with Simon Brooks. We don't yet know the facts, and we may never know everything, but I know he's in trouble. We're here to pull him and his crew out of whatever situation they may be entangled in. And stopping a potential war with the Movi Kingdom and the Cycomm Unity would be a good idea, too. Dismissed."

They filed out, Arkady hissing at Rodriquez as they left. Fairchild waved down Steeph. "Lieutenant, the next time I ask you if there are problems, don't hold back. I mean it."

"Understood, sir."

He waited for a minute, paging through his thoughts while they reported to stations. Fairchild knew that Simon Brooks and Sara Rosenski had been instrumental to the events now unfolding in Movi space. He didn't know Rosenski well enough to imagine how to appeal to her judgement—other than the obvious—and the Butcher Katsev wasn't available for duty aboard *Gauntlet*. In the end, all he had was the suspicion that a man would betray his government before his friends. If Brooks was too far gone for their influence to matter, then he'd have to go full Captain on him. And that would break their relationship permanently.

Gauntlet herself had changed as much as her new crew. After her adventure in the Vega system, the engineers and weapons specialists ordered several changes. Called them "improvements." They'd cut her hull in half, added several new modules, then welded her back together. *Gauntlet* now was a proper battlecruiser, with the dimensions needed to carry a full mech assault wing into a fight, and the defenses to keep her alive until the shooting stopped. At 470 meters in length, she was only a bit shorter than a Sleer scout vessel, and included the alien style of linking systems with molecular circuitry—control gauntlets and all. She looked like a boxy submarine, with drives and control surfaces flaring aft and a command tower jutting upwards amidships. All her VRFs could be launched from vertical dorsal tubes and recovered into a giant landing bay in her belly, which could just as easily disgorge her battlers into any landing zone. A dozen anti-ship beam laser turrets dotted her hull, a host of point defense guns could detonate ordnance before it reached her armored hull, and she could drop missiles into space from bow and aft-mounted launch tubes.

The command couch felt familiar to Ray Fairchild. More than he'd expected. The truth was, he had grown used to commanding a carrier more quickly than he'd expected. It was no substitute for driving a Strike Raven, sitting close enough to the engine to feel the vibration in the seat of his flight suit, but it wasn't awful, either. "XO, what's the ship's status?"

"All departments reporting ready for departure," Arkady said.

"Message from the command tower, sir," Amir said. "They sent it through ZERO but it's got General Hendricks's signature and an OMP HQ confirmation code."

"Let's hear it."

"From Hendricks, J., Brigadier General; To Fairchild, R., Commander. You are now authorized to bring all diplomatic and military options to bear in the matter of neutralizing potentially rogue unit commanded by Rosenski, S., Lt. Cmdr. All use of force permitted. Temporary rank of Captain assigned for duration of mission."

Fairchild blanched. He hadn't known just how deep a hole the kids had dug for themselves. But at least that had been expected. "Read that last part again, please, Master Chief?"

"'Temporary rank of Captain assigned for duration of mission.'" Amir read. "Congratulations, *Captain* Fairchild."

"Captain on the deck!" Arkady shouted. As one, everyone on the bridge jumped to attention.

"As you were," Fairchild said. "Accolades aside, we have an ugly job to do. Let's just get to Velucidar in one piece. Initiate launch sequence. Start powering up the fold drive; prepare to make a spatial transition."

CHAPTER 36

"MY FRIENDS. I WAS WRONG."

Back on the air, but this time Sora had a new twist: she was transmitting from the bridge of a planetoid. The implications of that wouldn't be lost on the crowd she'd assembled. No. *She* hadn't assembled anything. She'd put out a call for revenge against an enemy that none of the attendant captains or their crews had ever seen. They'd been hurt by rebel and loyalist warships and wanted to hurt something in return. That was a simple, understandable, relatable motive. But not enough to hold a fleet together. A task force or convoy might be bound by a common mission or objective. A task force would prosecute an enemy; a convoy banded together for the common defense on their way to a delivery. But fleets were held together by discipline and mutual respect. She wasn't sure how much of the former she could count on, but the respect seemed to be there.

"I don't trust these humans. That was true when I sent out my first call and it's true now. They arrived as our empire exploded, and seemed to set themselves against me when I tried to stitch things back together. But perhaps that was not their fault after all. The galaxy turns and events happen, and there is no connection between events. Perhaps Archduke Mineko felt he was restoring the kingdom to a path of past glory when he committed his act of treachery. Perhaps the humans simply arrived at Great Nest the same time we did. Perhaps humans and Movi... even Sleer... are meant to be involved in each other's affairs. I don't know.

"I was reminded a short time ago that I was responsible for engaging a Cycomm royal daughter. She gave me her trust when she had no other options. She gave me her support her in our combined efforts to gain our freedom. She gave me her trust of a human woman in turn. Now she has been re-captured by the Sense Op forces of Haven and it's my responsibility to rescue her.

"The humans are willing to give their aid. So I ask you. Should we form a working agreement with these people? Flash your forward signal lights if you agree."

Running lights all over the fleet immediately came on. "Getting something, anyway," Skull murmured. "Mostly the small ships, however. If I read these scales correctly—"

A Movi officer gently but firmly pushed Skull aside and sat down at his console. "Thirty-one responses. All from civilian transports and cargo ships. Of those... seven bear the colors of Kar-Tuyin and five more of Dal-Corstuni. Two from Omnicom. Six from Mon-Sakkaron."

"It seems the corporates like your plan to stick it to the Cycomms," Tridalva said.

Laortus agreed. "Haven has never been very friendly to foreign merchants. But business is business, and a few crews probably see it as a chance to break in where they were previously unwelcome."

They waited. A few more blips on the sensors as other ships lit their arrays. "Sixteen more. These are all military: destroyer escorts with the colors of the 119th Survey Fleet."

"Anyone we know?" Sora asked.

"I know them. They were part of Anterran's grand loyalist alliance. I suspect they've lost faith in his cause," Tridalva said.

"Hmm."

"That still leaves a lot of ships with darkened lights…What are the rest of them waiting for?" Brooks asked.

Underhill put a hand on his shoulder. "It's okay. These folks have lost everything. They know they can't go back to their old lives, but they aren't sure about us. We're asking them to put their whole trust in us. That's not an easy thing to ask. They're talking it out amongst themselves. That takes time."

"Gravity wake at 346," an officer announced. His eyes widened as a new contact blinked into their space. "It's a Banak-class cruiser."

"We've seen those. Impressive ships," Rosenski noted.

"They're hailing us on the general channel."

"On the main screen."

"Hello again, Sora."

"Hello, Vondra. What can I do for you?"

"You can tell me honestly, so that I may tell the crew of the cruiser *Iria's Dream*—you're going to Haven to rescue Binilsane-tanjamalala, are you not? Are you prepared to rip out the guts of the Sense Op navy? Are you prepared to start a shooting war with the Cycomms? All for one silly little girl?"

"She *was* a silly girl when she blundered into the clutches of the Haven government, but she has the soul of a fighter. She had no trouble adapting her mental power for use in combat. She's the best natural scrambler I've seen in my life. I used her badly. I must make amends."

"Answer my question."

"I've been reminded that a principle means nothing if one decides where and whether it applies. So yes. I will wage war for her." Sora turned her head to see Dance glaring at her. They held their connection until Reagan finally nodded agreement. Sora turned back to the hologram and said, "I don't always choose my friends well. She chose hers very well, and she chose to go to war alongside the humans. I can do no less."

"Good. The Sisters of Iria are with you."

The connection cut and the sensor operator grunted. "Their ship just lit up. Lights everywhere. So did the cruisers next to it. And three destroyers... and a flotilla of fast patrol ships... the strike carrier *Arula*..."

"Seems like Vonda didn't tell us how much influence she really had," Reagan surmised.

"I think she was trying to impress us with her network rather than her list of allies."

The Comm officer sent a list to the display. "Here's the list of allies. It's looking like a solid resume."

The fleet lit up with added support as new ships signaled their assent. Lights went up in ones in two or entire flotillas. When it was done, there were far more ships with glowing docking lights than not. "Eight hundred sixteen ships are on board. Three hundred and forty-five not," reported a bridge officer. "It's a good assortment of craft, too. Carriers, battleships, several squadrons of heavy cruisers. More than one hundred support ships. We won't be starved for bullets, battlefield comms, or fuel, whatever we leave with."

"Doesn't change the fact that most of your support rests in small ships that aren't meant to do much more than handle convoy escort duty."

"But eight hundred ships means we can choose eight hundred targets to hit at the same time. Eight hundred ships will let us wreak absolute havoc in a single operation," Sora said. "Comms, acknowledge the consenting ships and catalog their identifications and their class capabilities. Signal the remaining captains and let them know Battle Ring Great Nest is still operational...and that a Human-Sleer-Movi alliance is managing it."

"You're trusting them a lot," Rosenski said.

"A captain who doesn't want to go up against a Sense Op fleet might be perfectly happy defending a known target of demonstrated importance. Great Nest is a known quantity. They know they'll find rest and repair there. That will be enough for them."

"Fair enough. Now what?"

"Now we ask ourselves a question. If I wanted to keep a scrambler under lock and key, where would I put her?"

"The terror lord on Marauder's Moon has a compound—and plenty of enforcers who'd be all too eager to put a psionic to work for them," Brooks said.

Dance's face lit up. "Vondra did say she comes from a line very well known for psionics. If the sense ops high and mighties wanted her to disappear, that's a good way to do it."

Sora turned to the Tactical Officer. "Pull everything we have in the various knowledge bases about Marauder's Moon and its environs. Everything we have on Sense Ops bases as well. We have a very complex operation to plan."

"Warlord! Gravity wake detected at zero-one-two. Range approximately one million kilometers."

Trivalda looked askance at her bridge officers. "Sleer FTL technology? Here? Sora, did you invite those animals?"

"I did not. What have you primates done now?"

Brooks, Rosenski, and Underhill demanded information from Skull and Frost, who insisted there were no Sleer fleets nearby. Tridalva's Tactical Officer called his team together and they began sounding out intelligence reports showing there were indeed Sleer ships within ten lights years. Only the Communications officer watched the display, saw the extremely unorthodox starship design de-fold into their local space-time.

Only he heard the beacon that appeared, and realized he was listening to an alien language. "Warlord! The newcomers are hailing *Hajimi* and demanding its unconditional surrender." The arguing humans went silent. He continued, "Will we be making a reply?"

CHAPTER 37

DE-FOLDING into the Velucidar system was like every other de-fold Captain Ray Fairchild had experienced: a gut-wrenching, mentally jarring maelstrom. His head ached, his eyes felt like they were bleeding, and his eardrums felt ready to shatter. When the process wound toward completion and the ship's systems returned to normal operation, he thanked the unknown inventors of Sleer implants that he recovered so quickly. Plenty of unenhanced crew aboard *Gauntlet* had to bear with their unenhanced bodies' reactions to the unnatural twisting of space-time that was a spatial transition.

The physical effects faded, the bridge crew got back to their duties, and the ship's navigator and pilot began to confirm their position. That was where the similarity to earlier flights ended.

In minutes, the bridge was awash in alerts. New contacts appeared every second.

"Amir, let's start a systematic search for our lost lambs. Blanket hails in English. I don't want those two to mistake us for some general signal bounce."

"Yes, sir."

"In the meantime, XO, have the sensor team catalog every

new contact we find. Everything goes into the tactical computer. Don't be shy about polling the Sleer warbook files for data."

"On it. But be aware—with so many contacts it'll take time to sort through them all. Especially given that level of detail."

"Let it take as much time as it needs. Mr. Spaulding, Lt. Meng, plot us a course that takes us through the fleet. It'll give the sensor teams an opportunity to examine everything from multiple angles. Ideally, if we're inside the swarm, they'll be that much less likely to shoot at us. Not when they might hit each other."

"Aye, aye."

He fought the impulse to pace while his crew carried out their jobs. Technically, he should already have brought the ship to battle stations. UEF doctrine called for deploying overwhelming force at the earliest opportunity. The trouble was, that was how the AMS-1 and its supporting orbital platforms handled the arrival of Nazerian's recovery fleet. The result was the loss of all the supporting ships and a running gun battle fought between the restored gun destroyer and their opponents. Three years since that adventure and he still wasn't sure whether the experience the humans gained fighting their first space war was worth it.

If relying on firepower was his objective, there were only so many ways the situation could resolve. One, he opened fire on the *Hajimi*. Two, *Hajimi* opened fire on *Gauntlet*. Three, they had the chance to sit down and talk to each other and then start shooting. None of these alternatives held any appeal. General Hendricks would probably be happy to hear that he'd taken Brooks and Rosenski off the board. And the last thing he wanted was for Hendricks to be happy. So they went slowly. For shooting to begin, both sides would have to make a mistake.

Ray glared at the tactical board. The grand fleet was nothing but a blob. Ships randomly occupied specific orbits around the giant battleship at the center of the formation. They were good at keeping a minimum distance from one another, but he couldn't pick out a reason they'd established the flight pattern they'd chosen. Arkady was pacing, slowly orbiting the bridge. The Combat Information Center opened to the rear, separated from the bridge by an armored hatch that only closed during an emergency. Fairchild spent a few minutes watching the sensor team work, and every few minutes a new ship designation would appear on the board.

"They have to be here somewhere," he said.

Arkady shook her head. "No, they don't. We could just be in the wrong place at the wrong time. Maybe they were here and left. Maybe they never arrived. Maybe—"

The Sensor Watch Officer called out a figure on his display. "Contact, contact. Captain, we found *Hajimi*. She's in the third orbit out from the big battleship in the center of the formation—she must have been behind her. Bearing one-one-two, distance seven-six-four klicks."

Arkady beamed at the news. "Well done, Mr. Ashworth. Captain, I recommend a pursuit strategy combined with a defensive stance."

"I concur. Sound battle stations."

"Very well. Master Chief, sound battle stations. Lieutenant Commander Hart, confirm all squadrons are at Ready Five status. All department heads report in. Sensors, lock a tight beam on *Hajimi*. Gunnery crews, bring all weapons to ready status."

Fairchild retreated to his command couch, satisfied that his ship was prepared to move to the next level of action and his XO knew what to do with her. "Master Chief? Anything?"

Amir shook her head. Her three comm specialists were trying anything they could think of. "Not yet. We're blasting out hails in three languages across a broad spectrum. No one's answering. Unless they're not receiving."

"They're receiving something. Start hailing Brooks and Rosenski by name. Maybe if they know it's us, they'll be a little more forthcoming," Fairchild said.

Arkady frowned. "Not bloody likely. They know why we're here and they won't be alone."

"Paranoid much?"

"Not paranoid enough," she said. "If the roles were reversed, that's how I'd feel."

"Recommendation?"

"We've tried being nice. Let's be belligerent and see what happens."

"Problem is, it could get us all killed."

"I don't remember reading anywhere that service in the UEF was especially safe."

"So noted. Air Boss, launch our Lurkers. Have them establish a perimeter around the main ship. Equilateral triangle formation, sensors at full power. Launch the Super-Ravens and Sparrowhawks. They already know we're out here... there's no reason to hide. Master Chief, demand an answer from *Hajimi*. Tell them if they can't identify themselves by voice, go to their running lights, use non-verbal code."

"They would have done that already, but yes, sir." Amir gave the orders.

"Helm, Nav, close the distance to *Hajimi*. One hundred klicks to their aft quadrant."

Every officer acknowledged as *Gauntlet* drew closer. Spaulding and Meng worked together to formulate an approach that wouldn't alarm their target, entering the same orbit as the other vessels and adding speed to approach from behind. At the far outside orbit, the Lurkers extended their EM vanes and spun them up, transmitting everything they saw. By the time all three search vessels arrived on station, the tactical board was beyond crowded.

"Who are these people?" Fairchild wondered.

Ashworth used his control gauntlets to section the board into categories. The biggest portion was civilian vessels. "Mostly armed freighters and transports. It's looking less like a proper military effort and more like the Channel fleet that showed up to rescue the Brits at Dunkirk."

"Nothing military?"

"Lots." Ashworth swiped over to compare the new contacts by mass and weaponry. "That one in the center is the battleship *Guvil*. It's listed in the Sleer records as a space control ship, very much in the same class as the *Navaurness*, but much bigger. It'll carry the equivalent of three thousand heavy fighters, a boarding party of Marines numerous enough to occupy Ukraine, and enough firepower to torch North America in an orbital bombardment."

"What's the bad news?" Fairchild asked.

"We don't control it," Ashworth said. "If there's good news, it's slow. But it doesn't have to move much. It'll send out its legions and burn us down."

Fairchild watched *Hajimi* grow in size in the main display. With friends like that, Brooks and Rosenski could go just about anywhere and set down the roots of their own space station. Was that their intent? Some effort to build a base of operations deep in Movi territory? For what purpose?

"Captain? This is just strange... "

Fairchild went to the comm section where Amir waved for attention. "Talk to me, Master Chief."

"We sent instructions to the *Hajimi* to use light code to transmit if they couldn't hear us."

"You transmitted in code with our own lights, then?"

"Of course. Now a majority of the other ships are doing it, too."

"How do they know our codes?"

"They're not code switching. They're just turning on their lights, letting them run normally."

"All of them?"

"No, sir. But maybe seventy percent?"

Fairchild turned to Arkady. "We're missing something huge," he said.

"I concur. Next step?"

"Tell Road Hog to go to Battler mode and get personal with *Hajimi*. Do a close-in inspection. They may have damage."

Minutes later, Bill Steeph turned on his external cameras and Fairchild saw the problem as the images were relayed to the bridge display. *Hajimi* had taken serious damage at some point along the way. Fairchild remembered the half-assed job the First Warlord's crew had done on their cruiser, but now even that crappy excuse for a landing bay door was gone.

"Amir, turn on the translation algos. Resend all our hails in Movi and Sleer. "*Hajimi*, this is Captain Raymond Fairchild of the Unified Earth Fleet. We are here to escort you back to Great Nest. Respond or we'll be forced to take you in tow."

In seconds, the speaker trilled with Simon Brooks's familiar tenor. Fairchild sagged as he heard his boy. At least one of them was alive and seemed to be in decent health. "Uncle! This is a surprise. And Captain, too! Congrats, my dude! No offense, but what the hell are you doing out here?"

Sara Rosenski's voice joined him. "And what did you people do to *Gauntlet*?"

"We turned her into a real battlecruiser," Arkady said.

"The Saint speaks," Brooks said. "*Gauntlet*, we are preparing to transit to the Cycomm home world to recover a member of our crew. Do you wish to assist us?"

Fairchild found the response both perfectly reasonable and utterly unhinged. Much like Brooks himself. "Negative, Brooks. We're here to bring you home. I need you to prepare for boarding. We have space enough on board to take all your crew on."

"Negative, *Gauntlet. Hajimi* will make this transit."

Fairchild shared a look with Arkady. Were they being threatened? Usually, you'd expect an 'or else' with that manner of statement. That there wasn't one chilled him further. What were they doing? "Simon, you need to stand that vessel down and prepare to be boarded."

"I can't do that, Uncle."

"You can and you will."

"No, sir."

"Very well. You're relieved. Captain Rosenski, follow my order."

Rosenski's voice chilled him with its focus. "With respect, Ray, no. Any attempt to open fire on *Hajimi* and you will be targeted by shipboard weapons."

Alarms pealed from the various bridge consoles; seconds later, similar warnings ran through the CIC's displays. Ashworth's supervisor spoke up this time, a thin man whose name tag read Shinhan. "Confirmed, sir. All eight weapons turrets are targeting us."

"Why are you doing this, Simon? Sara? What's going on?"

"We can't let the UEF as it currently stands interfere with the internal affairs of the Movi Kingdom or the Cycomm Unity," Rosenski smoothly answered.

"It's a rescue op, Uncle," Brooks said. "Just like the Hornets on Genukh."

The reply jarred Fairchild's brain out of its groove. The words wouldn't mean anything to anyone but him—and possibly Arkady. He looked at her, saw a frown mixed with, what? Something. Like him, she was trying to put it together. Simon was trying to tell them something important, but was being too clever for his own good.

On their first excursion into the Earth battle ring, they'd come up against tall odds. Too many Sleer, and all of them were infinitely better equipped and trained. But they'd come up with an answer: Hornet squadron surrendered to Nazarian's forces while Brooks and Rosenski hid deep in the guts of the space station, with the understanding that Hornet Squadron would come back to retrieve them. Uncle had kept his word and so had Brooks and Rosenski. So what the hell were they doing now?

He could only imagine one possibility: *Hajimi* was a ruse of some kind. "Amir, find out where they're transmitting from. Is it the *Hajimi*?"

Amir bent over a station, reached down to touch a control. She shook her head. Negative.

"Brooks and Rosenski," Uncle said, "Stand down or we will open fire on *Hajimi*."

"I'm sorry, Captain. Impossible."

"Lieutenant Commander Steeph, bring that ship down," Fairchild said. "Gun pods only."

For a moment, no one said anything. Steeph's voice answered from the speaker. "Request a confirmation of that last order."

"I'm confirming the order. Bring down the *Hajimi*."

Seconds passed. If you issued an order that your crew wouldn't obey, your days as a leader were over. It didn't matter how loud you shouted or what you threatened them with—you were done. Fairchild had never been in this position before.

Steeph, however, wasn't the sort to disobey. But he might be the kind who would interpret his instructions to a fine line. Arkady would know more about that; she glared at the board, stone-like.

The display from Steeph's Raven flicked and fluttered,

then pulled back. *Hajimi*'s spherical body remained at the center. Now Fairchild could see the other Super-Ravens in Battler mode, holding their gun pods at the ready. Steeph called down the count, then opened fire, using short bursts to pepper the hull. Their first targets were the eight weapons turrets, which blew apart. The remains of the launch bay were next. Fragments filled the space between the Ravens. They raked their rounds across the ship's hull, dotting its armored skin with holes wide enough to push a baseball through.

"Heat signatures rising," Ashworth murmured. "Fires on three decks."

"Simon!"

"God damn it, Uncle. Why can't you let me make my own mistakes for once?"

Fairchild clenched his fists. Vapor trails emerged from open vents in the hull. Finally, a fireball took the ship, blasting it into its component parts.

Why did he do it? What the hell had taken his sanity out here? How was he supposed to go back to Earth and tell his best friend that his son was gone... and that he'd had to do it? "Dammit, Simon!"

Arkady cleared her throat, but spoke in a husk. "Sir. Suggest you report the destruction of *Hajimi*. We have a message drone aboard."

"Yes, Master Chief. Save the logs and launch the drone. To Earth. No reason not to give Hendricks what he wants."

The drone positioned itself to exit the sphere of ships, then aligned itself to exit the system. The wink of its gravity drive as it blinked out of the Velucidar system was unmistakable.

"Thank you, Captain Fairchild," Brooks said. "We are now standing down. Set your ship's control to neutral and the *Guvil* will take you on board."

"Give us a few minutes to recover the Ravens first," Ray growled.

Seething, Fairchild gave the orders to his crew. He was ready to pummel Brooks and Rosenski. Rage flowed through his veins, his face glowed with heat. He listened to the exchange between his bridge crew, heard the comm specs running through the confirmation of orders and instructions, and dimly noted a countdown had begun. When it reached zero, he blinked, and suddenly, the fury dissipated. They were out in space, the bulk of *Guvil* blocking their view of nearby ships, and then they were in a cavernous hangar bay, surrounded by docking clamps, fuel lines, and power umbilicals. His monitors showed crew running up to his vessel to engage equipment, like tucking a child into bed.

"What the hell was that?" he asked aloud.

"That is a displacement projector in action," Brooks said. "Imagine being able to launch a complement of ten thousand fighters in ten minutes. This ship has been known to do that. Sara and I will meet you shortly."

"You'd better be prepared to tell me an amazing story or I'll pull your tongue out of your head and use it to clean my boots."

Fairchild proceeded through his battlecruiser, finally opening an outer hatch and dropping down to the immense flight deck; Brooks and Rosenski were trotting to meet him. Ray hugged each of them fiercely, relief flooding his body.

"Talk," he ordered.

The two recounted their trials and tribulations, keeping their story moving by switching off every few sentences. What he hadn't known, but suspected, was that they'd sent their M-Boat directly to Earth in the expectation that Hendricks would overreact. Then they'd unloaded their borrowed company command cruiser, ejected it from *Guvil*, and waited.

Rosenski closed their presentation. "And now you have verified, documented evidence of Brooks and me defying your order to stand down, and of *Hajimi*'s destruction. Once you return to Great Nest and make your report, you'll be at liberty to list the whole crew Missing in Action."

"But as soon as you show up at Great Nest, ZERO will recognize you and list you as living, then send out arrest orders for you courtesy of the OMP," Uncle said.

"Only if we arrive at Great Nest," Brooks countered.

Brooks was being clever again, and Fairchild didn't like it. "Where else would you go, Mr. Brooks?"

"Vega," Rosenski said. "It's basically an ongoing construction site. It's easy to hide people where there's a great big mess."

"Which brings us back to 'why.' And if you don't come to the point in the next five minutes, I'm going to let Joanne break your fingers."

Arkady dropped from the open hatch in time to say, "One by one. And it'll hurt like hell. Trust me on that."

Rosenski took a deep breath and said, "We are in the middle of something here. A bunch of somethings. The Sleer. The Movi and their crazy civil war. The Laynies on Earth and very likely on Great Nest too. Binil is the center of this even weirder conspiracy inside her government's military that apparently extends into their royal families."

"So?"

"So... the Skreesh have shown up before, right? That's the common thread for the major races. The titans arrive, a new dark age arrives with them. Except this time the dark age is going to absorb every race all at the same time. You think that's a coincidence?"

"Why shouldn't it be? Civilizations do collapse after a while. How many empires has Earth seen rise and fall? What you're telling me isn't new," Uncle protested.

"No, but the timing is. We're all falling apart. The implants.

The military. The people in charge are unable to imagine any other way for things to be. Each faction is running on dogma and stolen resources. What if Vega is the best chance of putting together a real alliance? A chance to build a new enterprise that involves humans, Movi, and Sleer because they want to be part of it?"

"And what if Valri has already thought of doing that? Officially? With Earth Gov permission and treaties?"

"It's been months since that deal was made. What's happened?"

Fairchild sighed. "A lot of medical tests and a star system that's the same as how we left it when we defeated Metzek's crew."

"Exactly."

"Let's say I believe you," Uncle said. "What if the Sleer high command sends a war fleet to wipe out what's been built?"

"Oh no. The high command gave us Vega because they decided there was nothing worth using there. Not even after Metzek reported the derelict. And the high command is never wrong. Hendricks is in their pocket, and even he won't raise a fuss... he doesn't want to look like a fool when it comes out that we did find something worth utilizing. Ancient technology. Nobody can object to that. We just need to move enough assets of our own into the area."

"And I don't know if you've noticed, but there's almost nine hundred ships out there. Every one of them would rather be anywhere but in the middle of an imploding empire."

Because he agreed with it, Fairchild hated the logic. "Which leaves your Cycomm girl."

Rosenski snorted. "Not a girl. Not anymore."

"When we find her—"

"*If* you find her, Simon. It's a big solar system and our sensors can't see faces from orbit."

"Fine," Brooks conceded. "*If* we find her, we have to take her to Vega because Great Nest will be the first place they come looking for her. They'll scan with telepaths and they won't find her. They declare her dead, they go away, and that's the end of it."

"That's not a convincing argument, Simon. Why not just leave her where she is? That'd be the end of it too."

"If we do that, we give up a potentially huge advantage when we invade the ring around Earth. Without her, we can make a good fight. With her we can shut down the command tower at its source. We save lives that way. No?"

Fairchild grimaced, working overtime to process what he was hearing. "You want to trash your lives. All of you. And you want me to trash mine, too. That's what I'm hearing. Let's just disobey every order we've ever received and hope it works out. Is that what I'm hearing?"

"Not quite." Two Movi women approached their circle. Ray recognized Sora Laakshiden from her visit to Great Nest, but he immediately deferred to the older woman next to her. Not by name—they'd never met—but by her bearing. Whatever Sora had, she owed to this woman. She was the power in the room, and old habits instantly reasserted themselves. He pulled a standard greeting from his implants and spoke in Moviri. "Captain Raymond Fairchild, Ma'am," he said. He gave a not-quite-formal bow and grinned.

"Captain. I am Warlord First Admiral Tridalva Andrulen ap-Goodep. Young Captain Brooks and Captain Rosenski speak highly of you. Even your blue-haired secret police officer has good things to say. You don't seem like a fool to me. I like your manners. I even like the way you smell. And while these upstarts make themselves understood in Sleer, you speak our mother tongue. It's those Sleer implants. No?"

"It's as you say, Warlord. My crew and I received a

linguistic update before we launched. I only regret that my soldiers have caused you so much trouble lately."

"Heh. No more trouble than I was facing before you all arrived. You've heard their intentions, I take it? What do you think?"

"I think they're insane, Ma'am. And I'm afraid that their insanity is infectious."

"It is, isn't it? When times are good, one likes to think that one's loyalty oath to power counts for something. But all it takes is one good disaster to discover just how fragile the supporting institution is."

Fairchild wondered about that. There was a constitution in place. A document that brought the world under a single governing body, which named the Unified Earth Fleet as its instrument of world defense and the Office of Military Protocols to manage any blips that might crop up within UEF ranks. Some time in the past few years the OMP had managed to take over the whole show, and if that wasn't a recipe for disaster, he couldn't imagine what was. "I hesitate to say it, Ma'am, but I get the idea that perhaps we're not up for the current challenge."

"Nor are we. Surely the Sleer are not. Can you imagine a better time to change the rules?"

"And betray everything I swore to uphold and maintain."

"Perhaps. A betrayal means an attack on legal norms to put oneself above others. Is that what you'd be doing?"

He thought about it. The logic made sense, but it felt *wrong*. "I don't know."

"Please think on it. In the meantime, I'm going to approve your officers' plan to rescue your Cycomm girl from what can only be called a military incursion. Quite illegal according to any rules I swore to maintain."

"The Cycomms can claim they only arrested a criminal. One of their own."

"But they made war on a civilian Movi vessel and incapacitated one of your soldiers in the process. That's quite enough for me. I've sold many of my ideals over the years, but I have a few principles left." The question in her eyes was clear.

This was a hell of a time to wonder about principles. They were in foreign territory, both physically and legally. Technically, just being here could be called an act of war by the Movi Sovereign. But also technically, the old woman was right. Binil was as much a member of the UEF as he was, even if she could only call herself a Temporary Limited Duty Third Lieutenant. And Reagan had been attacked by an elite trooper of a foreign government. What the hell kind of leader was he if he didn't defend his own troops?

He caught Arkady's eyes and could see she'd already come to the same conclusion. He beckoned, and she trotted over. "Commander, we're going to unload the Warhawks and assign them to *Hajimi*'s pilots. Have the squadron leaders poll their squadrons. This will be a voluntary rescue op. Anyone who wishes to remain in this system aboard *Gauntlet* will be allowed to do so."

"Way ahead of you, sir," she said, and indicated a growing crowd behind her; a vast throng of his troops in full gear, wearing the new combat armor. Steeph even waved at him, while Linden saluted.

"Well... space shit. Fine. Everyone, then. We still need a way to locate Binil when we arrive."

Sora waved to a member of the crowd. In moments, someone with obvious Cycomm features stepped up. "May I introduce Zinthenkeredantha. She's a telepath, and a good one. She and I have worked together before. She's willing to help manage this crisis."

"Worked together on which project?"

"I was the one who urged Admiral Laakshiden to break the

allied race treaty when it became clear that Zluur was trafficking in stolen technology," said the Cycomm.

Sora nodded. "I took her advice, applied pressure to Selaniss, and here we all are."

"Well, it's nice to know we'll all go down together when this blows up in our faces."

"Come on, Uncle," Brooks said. "You brought a dozen Warhawks for us to test in combat, didn't you? Be a shame not to give them a proper trial."

CHAPTER 38

LT. CMDR. Danalimantanjanal, First daughter of the House of Nal's generation of Tanja, sat and watched the old man berate the young woman and felt a steady core of bile rise in her throat. They'd been at this for hours. What he thought he was accomplishing, she didn't know, or at this point care. She just wanted it to stop.

Times like this reminded her that Sense Op work was not all joy and duty. The girl, Binilsanetanjamalala, was in real pain right now. She didn't need telepathy to know that. Danal felt it right up to the moment they'd dampened her mind for transportation.

She'd wondered whether they had the correct person. She knew it was all officially correct. Her ID was firm. This was their target. But this mission was unlike the other renditions of high value targets she'd prosecuted under Batol. There'd been Sleer militants, Movi terrorists, Vix saboteurs, and even one Rachnae weapons supplier. The arachnoid alien had shown her a mind so alien that Danal recoiled in horror. She hadn't gone near the damn creature for the rest of the mission, refused to ride up to the ship in the drop pod with it. Gueph covered for her, but great Malkah, never again. There'd never been any Cycomms—not even plugs—because, well, Cycomms weren't insane. Not violently so. Not in a way to throw spanners into the workings of society.

Until this girl. For the life of her, Danal couldn't imagine what she'd done on Haven to warrant the arrest order.

Binil was descending into a depression deeper than any Danal had experienced or witnessed. She wasn't given to hysterics. No screaming or crying, no denying the truth of her situation. She sat in the chair, her legs pressed to her chest and her eyes closed. Waiting for the wave of derision to end. The technique was well proven and very effective. The point was to subject the patient to as much abuse as possible, to force them to seek help, to agree to terms, to act in order to stop the pain. Binil wasn't going for it. Maybe she knew the deception for what it was. Maybe she'd already given up. Or maybe she had her own plan, and this was a form of resistance. There was a real limit on what Danal could infer. Yes, she could touch minds, but not in there. The room was shielded. And when she had touched Binil's thoughts back on the liner, she'd seen too much to process. A young man. A young woman. A series of loves and relationships. The feeling of being surrounded by friends. A powerful sense of duty. A minefield of insecurities. None of that had been in the briefing they'd taken before their drop.

Batol nudged her out of her trance. "It's not a good idea to listen to them too much."

"I know, but she's telling the truth."

"About which part?"

"All if it. Everything. All he's doing now is badgering her. Trying to push her towards something. An outburst. If she explodes, we're out a perfectly good scrambler."

"Explodes?"

"She's angry. She's in pain. She feels betrayed, and all he's doing is cementing the association of bad vibes with prison."

Batol spied an open door further down the corridor. "Come on. Let's talk." Danal knew what would happen next. Batol was worried about *her*, now. She was pulling the team down with her. Getting too far into a target's head. It happened with sensitives now and then. Batol was just following procedure. They ducked into the empty conference room. "What would you do differently?" he asked.

"For one, I wouldn't patronize me."

"Is that what I'm doing?"

"I think so."

Batol relaxed slightly. "You've had these misplaced feelings of association before."

"Not like this. This is just… everything feels wrong this time. And now, according to procedure, you need to inform someone about my inability or unwillingness to disassociate from the target."

He shook his head. "No, I don't. Or… I do, but I won't. I can't say I'm disagreeing with you. This mission had an odor to it. That much I agree with. You obviously think we're missing an opportunity. Tell me more about it."

She did. She listed her reservations and conclusions and she told him her ideas; her plans to remediate the problem and what she hoped to gain by doing so. She left nothing out.

He said, "If we do that, even if it works perfectly, there won't be anywhere in Asylum we can hide."

"It's a huge risk. But if it works, we learn everything we need in one simple operation," she said.

"Not so simple. Getting to the ship is straightforward, but you'll have so sell it to the crew… and we can't tell *him*." He knew the Doctor was still at work. Still pressing his patient.

Trying to get her to see the truth of his argument. "No one on his level can know. If it fails, we'll never recover."

"I think it will. I can make it work. You're going to have to make it convincing."

"I can do that."

"All right. The next time he leaves, I'll go in."

"No. Go in now. Introduce yourself and have a moment with her. Make no mention of the fact you work for me."

———

Hospital or prison, it was all the same to Binil.

The worst part for her was the loss of time. They'd turned sensory deprivation into an art form here. She had a bed, a basin, a toilet, and a chair. She had a window, sort of, but it showed an expanse of brick wall painted an off white. She'd gone to the glass pane more than once, trying to see if there was anything else, a street below, or sky above. Nothing. It never changed. No twilight, no night, no dawn. For all she knew, the window was no more than a computer projection; incredibly fine images with no substance. No clocks anywhere in the room, either. She could have been here days... or weeks.

When the Old Doctor visited—she wondered if he was the same doctor she'd fought with on Haven years ago—he let her know just how displeased he was with her choices. Today's rant was typical.

"Honestly, my girl, I can't imagine wanting to be around those people. The anger, the dishonesty, the fear. Great Malkah, the fear! It permeates every one of them. They lash out at any provocation. They invent evil stories to torture each other with. And why? Economic exploitation. Emotional domination. Fear is their best method of controlling the lower classes. Indeed, that they have a class-based society is tragic enough, but I'll never understand why they feel they need to torture the workers with stories of failure, sickness, and suffering. Just for a few credits. I don't understand it."

They'd been at this for what seemed like years. Maybe she should have tried to fight the Sense Op team. Maybe she should have taken the officer's offer of anesthetic. It wouldn't change anything, but she might have slept through more of it.

"You had a goal. Part of a great mission. You had a destiny. We were going to use you to tease out one of the terror lords on Marauder's Mon, you know. Those Movi women... I'm still not sure how they ended up on your transport. It should have been prevented at all costs. It doesn't matter. Failure seems to follow you around. Depressing, really."

She opened her eyes. "You know, no one ever called me disappointing until I came here."

"That's because they expected nothing of you. Well, I give up. The operation you were part of is pointless now. I suppose we'll just let you go back to them. Those humans. They're ill. They infected you with their insanity, and now you seem to want to return. It's happened before, you know. A young girl falls in love with her attacker. It never ends well."

She knew it was a mistake to be drawn into his ranting, but she was bored. Arguing passed the time. "They didn't attack me. In fact, they were nothing but good to me."

"They didn't directly abuse you, but make no mistake. They took you in, taught you that destruction was better than resolution. And then they found out about your ability and that was that. A tool of destruction. That's what they taught you to become. Disappointing isn't a big enough word to describe what I'm feeling right now. I don't know if the concept has a word for it. A failure so utterly complete that it risks the wrath of the unknown and the unknowable. A failure that might bridge death itself."

"That's not what happened. They needed help. I offered to help them the only way I could. I volunteered."

The old man—who she was now convinced was the same doctor she'd dealt with back in that first hospital prison—said, "That's *worse*. Do you see how that's worse?"

"No."

They kept at it, Binil paying less attention to her answers with each iteration, eventually lapsing into simple speech. "Yes and no." Eventually, the Old Doctor left and she noticed a new figure standing against the wall, next to the window. Where had she come from and when had she arrived? She fought down a panic attack. Getting her to question reality was an old trick. Was the girl a projection like the window? Was anything in this room real?

"I don't like the way he badgers you," the woman said.

"How long have you been standing there?" Binil demanded.

"Not long. But I've been watching you since they—since we brought you in."

"We? You were the clairvoyant. You touched my face?"

"You have a good memory and excellent sensitivity. I see why they wanted you to serve."

Binil offered the woman her chair and moved to the bed, sitting cross-legged. It was a way to put her thoughts in order. "It's hardly service when you knock a painting off the wall with your mind and wake up on a prison barge."

"You'd be surprised. Sense Op initiations can be strange and violent, but they often work. And there you were, the most powerful scrambler they'd seen in a generation."

Binil glanced around at the bed, walls, the chair. No moving parts, nothing to exercise her ability on. Only the thin bedsheet. She concentrated on moving one of the loose corners, holding her breath, squeezing her eyes shut, coaxing her ability out. Nothing. Not even a suggestion of motion. "What did they do?"

"They fixed the damage you caused yourself."

"I can't do anything now. I'm useless."

"You were never trained. If you had been, you'd never have hurt yourself. You were coasting on raw talent and a few lucky breaks. It could have been much worse. You might have mindburst yourself. No one really recovers from that. I almost didn't."

"No?"

"I wasn't born into this. My parents were both plugs, but I was tested in school and here I am. You know I've never been on a mission to snag another Cycomm before. I'm not sure I like it."

"But you did it."

"Very much so. Your friends are coming for you."

"You can't possibly know that."

"I know they value your friendship. They've invested quite a lot in you emotionally. I don't know how or when, but they will act on their feelings. When they do... well... it'll be an interesting day."

"I don't want them to die."

"I don't want you to die either, and I think you might if they take you out of here."

Binil realized the futility of the conversation. Round and round they went. She wondered if there were a way to take her resolve to a new level, and decided to ask the impossible. "Take me to the great hall. Let the Malkah decide what to do with me."

Danal took a moment to recover. "That's no small thing to ask."

"Let the Malkah decide. I'll go along with whatever she wants."

"Honestly, I would take you if I could, but we're not on Haven or the Asylum. There's no great hall—just this facility and what lies beyond it."

Binil relaxed her body, put her feet on the floor. It all felt real. Not dream-like the way she imagined a hallucination would seem. "Then we made it. This is Marauder's Moon. It looks cleaner than I imagined."

"You're in a wing of a holding area. New arrivals come here to be examined. To see if they have any value to the leaders."

"That doesn't explain why you're here."

"I hesitated when we picked you up." Danal said. "When we left, they doused you and demoted me for insubordination. I started an argument with my CO and here I am. I'm supposed to spend a week here looking after you. I'm being taught a lesson. But not the lesson I think they intended me to learn."

"There must be something."

"There is. But there's no great hall... "

Her new friend wound down her speech, staring at the far side of the room. Suddenly, Danal burst into motion, stepping to the portion of the room just outside the lavatory and looked at the wall near the ceiling. Was she having a stroke? "What's the problem?" Binil asked.

"The light's gone out."

"The... what?"

"There's a shielded display up there, meant to show me the shifts. Who enters and who exits. It's dark." Danal turned. "Why is it dark? It never goes dark. The only reason it might be dead is if the power was out. But that can't be the case. If it were then—"

"Yes?"

"Then the defense grid would be active. But the only reason that might happen is... "

"Is if we're under attack," Binil finished. "What's happening?"

"I think we have a chance to do something incredibly dangerous with you. But it's also morally right. Does that make sense?"

"I don't know enough to judge. I think it does."

"Not to me." Danal wiped beads of sweat from her forehead, stared at the damp on her fingers.

Binil decided to trust the woman. It was either that or stay here. And staying here was no plan at all. If there was even the smallest chance Danal was being honest with her, she had to take it. "What's really going on? Are we being attacked?"

Danal's head snapped back in an apparent micro-seizure and when she next returned Binil's gaze her eyes were dead black orbs. Danal started, "I can see them. One huge Movi vessel. Bigger than anything I've ever seen. Many smaller ships are with it. And your friends are under attack… by their friends. It's very confusing. I'm not sure what I'm looking at."

"I am," Binil said. "The humans are either trying to rescue me or to start a war. I hope it's the former."

Danal let out a long shaking breath, and glared at Binil warily. "I've made a terrible mistake. I just wanted to gain your trust to poke through your mind more fully…your friends weren't supposed to actually show up!"

"Now that they have, you can leave me here. Walk away. Tell no one. Enjoy your war with the humans."

"I'd rather we take you into orbit, so they'll find you easily. All right. Follow me very closely. Close your eyes and cover your ears. You were asleep when we brought you in. Awake, you may find this a little… jarring."

Binil followed directions, even holding her breath for good measure. She felt Danal's hands on her shoulders, sensed rather than felt the space around her warp and shift, and then the sensation of slipping and sliding, the air around them vanishing and re-appearing. Danal patted her twice, and Binil opened her eyes.

To a metal room.

There was no mistake. All the features were identical, but it was a gray, metal-walled cube, with the fresher located in an alcove. The window was indeed a glass screen, which now showed nothing but static. Binil could see the display that Danal described; what might have been a coherent display was nothing but a black background and a scattering of multicolored pixels. If there was any sense to be made from it, she couldn't imagine what it might be. The door was now obvious—an armored hatch with a complex locking panel to the side.

A prison cell.

"I knew it," Binil sighed. "It had to be. How did you keep all this hidden?"

Danal pressed her hand against the lock and the door opened. "Hypnotic states, a few drugs, and a great deal of environmental misdirection. Strangely enough, no mental powers are involved. But there are tricks of the trade even I'm not aware of, and I work for these people."

"These people. You mean the Old Doctor."

"He has a name. If I ever learn it, I'll tell it to you. This way."

Binil hustled to keep up. The corridor reminded her so much of a battle ring that she had to continually remind herself that she was nowhere near Great Nest. They ran to the beat of pealing sirens. Brightboards flashed warnings and orders every few hundred steps as Danal led her through a maze of passageways. They clearly were in the center of an emergency. A giant Movi battleship appearing overhead would have that effect. "At least tell me where on Marauder's Moon we are," she yelled over the alarms.

"We're not on the moon. We're inside it. The moon is artificial. Or hadn't you guessed that yet? Why do you think it has such an eccentric orbit?"

Binil's confusion was nearly total. "It's *not* a penal colony?"

"It's absolutely a penal colony. It's also a hollow sphere that houses a wealth of Sense Ops people, prisoners, and weaponry. This battle station is our main system defense—the Haven Fleet is just window dressing. Lucky for us, no one capable of endangering Haven ever arrived before. Lucky for you, there are plenty of skip pods in place for evacuation. You're sure you can drive one?"

"I drove a prison barge with a skip drive. I'll figure it out."

"You? Drove a—?" A new round of alarms sounded, and now the corridor began to react. New brightboards dropped from the ceiling, showing floor plans, blinking furiously as arrows pointed toward certain areas. A third chorus of shrieks joined the cacophony as more alarms made themselves heard. "You're not a scrambler. What are you? Never mind. I have a new plan."

"New one? What happened to the old plan?"

"You hear that new chorus? Those are fighters being launched. A *Guvil* class battleship has thousands of them. If every Sense Op vessel in this system all came out right this moment, they still wouldn't be able to defend against that warship. I'm getting my team out of here and we're bringing you along."

"You have a team?"

"You didn't think it was myself and the Captain, did you? Come on!"

And here she was, at a terrifying crossroad. She could stay here and figure her own way out—which had any number of ends, all of them potentially worse than where she was now. Or she could volunteer to be sucked into Danal's head game and pray she could mitigate whatever damage was done to herself and her humans at some point in the future. At least the head game was a road she'd traveled before. But the potential value of being around a Sense Ops team would be huge; a hands-on education that she might never be within reach of again.

"I'm taking you at yor word," Binil said. "I hope you know what you're doing."

A blink and a moment of pure contact appeared in her mind: *"You and me both, dear. If this doesn't work, we're all dead."*

They crossed a hatch and entered a small launch bay, barely big enough to hold the oblong vessel contained within. She recognized the seal of the Cycomm Unity on the hull, and another, which she assumed was the Sense Ops seal. No other markings she could see. Danal was arguing with four others. Maybe the new plan was worse than the old plan. Or maybe there was none, and it was all a show for her benefit.

She ducked through the hatch, twirled to get her bearings, and found a narrow door with a ladder beyond. Up would be the bridge, down would be the cargo area, or one of them. Behind her would be the main deck, with quarters, common areas and engineering at the rear. At least that would be the layout if this ship had a resemblance to the prison barge where she'd met Sora. She turned and pulled herself up, climbing with new energy. A deck with an open space and what looked like a warehouse of crates and shelves. A ship's locker, perhaps. The deck above that was a narrow space with iris hatches on every side. She slid her hand over the locking plates, surprised when they worked. Closet. Storage. Long corridor leading to the rear. Finally, the last one opened to a more spacious compartment laid out as her prison barge was. Pilot and co-pilot couches in front, and a navigation station obviously meant for a Cycomm operator, with the same mesh-like interface she's seen on the barge. Three more stations in the rear and a fourth off to the side. Gunnery stations? Engineering? Something like that.

Questions bubbled up from her memories. She'd been able to unlock certain door plates on the barge, too. She was working with those same skills now, wasn't she? What had Danal said? They'd fixed the damage she'd done to herself.

What damage? The strokes? Or the talent itself? Had the healing rewired her mind somehow? Could she move objects better than before, and without self-harm? Or had they simply taken her ability away? Or—and this was the terrifying thought—had her brain rewired itself into something entirely new?

She stepped onto the flight deck and gasped when the space came alive around her. "Welcome aboard, Binilsanetanjamalala. You are a designated passenger. Please follow the arrows to your assigned quarters." A set of tones floated down from the ceiling, and a thin line of moving lights appeared on the floor as the door opened. Danal and the others swarmed inside, gently moving her to the side. She took the seat in the rear without comment as the others took their places.

"Please don't touch anything, Binil," said the man who took up the command console. "You're a passenger on this trip, and that's all you have access to. If the computer thinks you're trying to take advantage of the system, it'll shut you down as easily as it would any attempted hijacking."

"Especially since you have a criminal record," Danal said. "We'll get you to where you should be. Promise."

Binil felt a bubble of rage work its way to the surface. Despite the outburst she'd had aboard *Hajimi*, where she'd needed not one but two friends to talk her down off her ledge, now Binil really did feel like a child in the situation. She was literally occupying the small chair at the back of the room. Just to be sure, she placed her hands against the console again, sorting through her memories of manipulating space-time. Managing the navigation computer aboard the prison barge. Nothing.

It was time to drop the act. "Why are you helping at all? Tell me or I will kill your system." She put her hands on the console, thought about managing the intricate aspects of shipboard systems management, and felt absolutely nothing. It was a dead glass panel. No response.

Danal smiled. "I promise. We're getting you to safety."

"Why?"

Danal sighed. "Because you're one of us."

Binil fought for composure. "One of us." Three little words that held all the meaning in the world for her. She'd finally come home. Except it wasn't the home she'd come to wish for. Not the people she'd come to care for. Home to this crew, to these Cycomms, meant Haven. To Binil it meant Great Nest and her humans.

She tried to activate the console one more time, using a gentle touch, concentrating less on shoving the computer around like a schoolyard bully taunting a target. If Danal was right and *Hajimi* had come to rescue her, the ship and her crew would be in orbit somewhere. All she had to do was locate them. She worked her mind through the cracks, visualizing the guts of the console, the pathways to its programming. Encouraging the electronic tumblers to line up just so...

A squeal of connection, and her console erupted in a fit of activity. Torrents of data flashed through her mind, threatening to drown her. She hung on, building a metaphorical shelter out of her thoughts, working to grasp the nature of the content that she was experiencing. She picked out the salient facts: a company command cruiser, its gun turrets painted like eyes, a Sleer spatial transition, an alien vessel, strange humanoid fighting machines the height of a house, and all shooting at... each other?

A packet struck her mind—a data bit from the Sense Op ship's own records, uploaded before departure. A heated conversation between these team members, and the phrase "It's a huge risk, but if it work, we learn everything we need in one simple operation."

And there it was. She knew who she was and what to do. Not one of Us, but one of Them. *All right then, let's go home. To our real home.*

She probed further, found the guidance to the nav computer, spent precious seconds learning how the system was organized, and then shoved with all her mental might.

Then alarms rang out, displays flickered and flashed, and the flight deck teetered... and tipped.

CHAPTER 39

"THIS IS Section 3 Leader reporting all ships manned and Ready Five. It's a little tighter than I like in here," Brooks said as he wriggled in his Warhawk's cockpit. The arrangement was subtly different from his Raven-D, but the controls and HUD were as close to standard as human production value allowed.

"Too much fast living for you," Captain Rosenski called over the comm. Brooks scanned *Guvil*'s flight deck, found her stock Raven-D easily. She'd found someone with the patience and equipment to paint the vertical stabilizers on her ship hot pink. She would command Section One; a dozen fighters like hers. Back to the good old days of Hornet and Nightmare squadrons.

Brooks uploaded the last of *Gauntlet*'s adjustments into his fighter's computer and held his breath as the status board updated. Voila! So far, the computer was one aspect of the new space fighter that worked according to specification. He'd already assigned wingmen to his section He'd fly with Dance, and he paired Ghost and Speedbump. Roberts and Katsuta were finally used to flying with each other; it seemed pointless to break those two up. Marc Janus had been bugging him for weeks to get into one of the new ships, and Brooks assigned him to Hassanali so he could learn a few things from Janus. Second Lieutenants Besch and Wang—both specialists with flying certs—took the only two EWAR versions of the experimental fighters. Brooks chose two OMP pilots for the last of the Warhawks: Oscar Bryant and Oleg Broz, who were immediately dubbed O.B. One and O.B. Two.

The rest of the flyers were organized by Uncle and Arkady. Fairchild would take the other squadron of stock Raven-Ds, Arkady would fly the Strike Raven-Es and Steeph and his XO would handle the Super Ravens. Linden's battlers had maneuvering packs bolted to their backs, and would make up their reserve along with the Sparrowhawks.

"I got used to the roomy venue of a Raven-D," Brooks said. "I think it's more about the newfangled flight armor. It fits better than the old flight suits, but it's tight around my ass."

"Your ass is fine. Button up and wait for launch orders," Rosenski said.

"Yes, Ma'am." He went down his pre-flight checklist item by item, setting the controls according to the list. The Warhawk was the equivalent of a new EV ground car, generations removed from the big, heavy gas-guzzlers of his father's generation. One thing that turned him on beyond all expectation: the engineers had built the cockpit controls around control gauntlet technology. That made all the difference. Brooks couldn't wait to put the new fighter through its paces.

He waited as his section powered up their drives, idling on the flight deck while Hart and Simmons negotiated the launch with Guvil's Flight Ops team in the control booth. He heard the tension in their voices as Rosenski, Fairchild, Arkady, and Steeph passed status reports to each other. The Warhawk shuddered beneath him as he moved the power up a notch. He hoped the vibration was normal.

Hart's voice through his headphones. "All sections come to hover position and prepare for displacement jump." Brooks passed the order to his section and nudged the power up another two notches. He thrilled to the bump as his fighter lifted off the deck, wobbling slightly as it rode its own updraft. He turned on the auto-trim and relaxed as the wobble stopped. Okay, one more thing that worked as advertised. He could get used to this.

"Relocation matrix engaged... projectors online... releasing in five."

A burst from the command channel. "Leader, this is Ten."

Brooks glanced at his status board. That would be Hassanali, the man with the worst sense of timing in the section. "Go, Ten."

"I got a red light on engine two."

"Four." The countdown to launch came from the control tower.

"Can you restart?" A red light meant one of two things, either a misfire which could be fixed in the hangar with a competent ground crew, or something more deadly. In either case, Hassanali was staying behind.

"Three."

"Negative, I've done two restarts already. Red light persists."

"Two."

Brooks toggled his comm. "Hangar control, this is Section 3 Leader. I have an abort on fighter ten. Abort the sequence."

"One."

"Dammit, abort! I have a sick bird."

"Jump!"

Streamers of light washed over the grounded fighters. Brooks experienced a brief sense of dizziness and then he was surrounded by the void of space. The bright half-disk of

Marauder's Moon shone to his left. Above him, *Guvil*'s bulk blotted out stars, while fighters popped into existence in every direction.

He set his sensors for short range bursts and linked the feed to his computer. He set his cameras to track Hassanali's fighter and watched the hapless pilot try to switch from jet to battler and back again. "Three and Ten, you're out of the fight. Back to the hangar. Janus, go with him."

What followed from Janus was a string of profanity so intense and inventive that Brooks waited for him to finish before saying, "Same to you, Marc. Get your wingman back to the barn."

"I know! We're heading back now. Good hunting."

Less than a minute into the fight and Section 3 was already down two pilots. Nice.

Another flash to his right as one of Gauntlet's three Lurker AEW craft arrived. The EM vanes above the fuselage spun up as the pilot lit the Lurker's drives. In seconds, Brooks' display bubbled with the added feeds from the Lurker. There'd be six specialists in the rear section of that ship, all working hard to identify friend and foe, and vector friendly pilots toward the trouble spots.

Brooks pinged his nav comp and set it to keep his own section centered in his HUD. The problem was that every time the Lurker's computer pinged his fighter with updates, the HUD tried to center on it. "Section 3 Leader to group. Turn your auto-updates off. Otherwise your Warhawk will try to use it as it primary."

"So what happens if the Lurker picks up targets for us?" He didn't recognize the voice. One of the OBs he assumed. The Warhawk's status board had an annoying tendency to flicker between channels. If one pilot spoke into their mic and another breathed on theirs, the board lit up with alerts for both.

"They can still vector us in using comms. Stand by." Heh. Stand by. That was a good one. The sky over Haven was clear, but they had very little information about what they might throw at his flyers. All he could do for the moment was wait and marvel at how similar to Earth the planet looked. He kept his section in formation, made sure no one strayed, and kept up visual scanning. Even that was less than optimal. You could have an enemy bearing down on you and not see it, simply because you didn't know where to focus your eyes.

A data stream dropped onto his HUD. "Gauntlet Section 3, this is Lurker 3. New contacts at zero-three-eight relative. Multiple contacts, range three-zero-zero klicks."

"Lurker 3, this is Section 3 Leader. Fast movers?"

"Negative, Leader. These are not, repeat, not missiles. Possible UAVs."

Brooks pointed his sensors toward the new heading and saw the problem. The blip on his display looked like a swarm of God knew what. UAVs, the Lurker tech called them: Unmanned Aerial Vehicles. Drones. He knew that the UEF had experimented with self-guided drones years ago, but none had ever been put into production. These were different. Opaque spheres about three meters in diameter, with energy points at the poles and wide sensor "eyes" in the middle.

A few approached ahead of the cloud, and Brooks experimentally lined up a shot on one. He wanted to see what the auto targeting gear was capable of, and this was the perfect time to find out. He rested his thumb on the trigger as the red aiming circle lit up. One ring, then two. Then three. A shot he couldn't possibly miss. He pressed down and balked when his fighter dumped four missiles into the void instead of the one he'd armed. His eyes flicked across the console as he wondered what he'd done wrong, then another compartment popped open and launched four more SRMs. That absolutely hadn't been his fault. He reached over and turned the arming system to manual. No more letting the machines think for him today.

An enraged contralto shouted in his earphones. He looked to his left as another fighter dropped its entire payload into a single volley. A fighter toward the rear of the formation did the same, and another one above him.

Brooks jammed his thumb onto the general comm. God damn the new automatic systems anyway. "Leader to section. Turn your auto-targeting systems off. Go to manual controls only. The motherless algorithm is broken." *Just like half the systems in these fighters.*

A few more stray launches, then the chaos dissipated—just like a third of the sections's remaining ordnance. "Remind me to give some engineer my foot up his ass when we get back to Great Nest," Diallou snarled.

"For once, Speedbump, I agree with you completely," Dance said. "New rule: no more testing of combat aircraft in actual combat."

"So noted," Brooks agreed. Never again.

"Half of us have no missiles left," cried Wang. "Just the pea shooters. What are we supposed to do now? Suggest we abort."

"No! Negative on that," Diallou barked.

Ghost's voice joined in. "Agree with Wang. The new ships are dumb. Suggest abort."

Dance's voice rang out. "Leader, may I have a word with you on the command channel?"

"You may." Brooks switched over. "Go."

"You cancel this flight and I'll rip you three new ones, and they'll be in extremely inconvenient places," Dance said.

"They have a point," Brooks said. "These ships have multiple problems. Keeping them in the fight could get the whole section killed."

"You leave if you want. Transfer command to me, take the

whiners back to the barn and I'll continue. We're here to rescue our buddy. Our *Cycomm*."

Brooks checked his status board. He still had ten fighters, six of which had substantial missile loads. "All right, we'll continue." He switched back to the general channel. "Section, we're still on mission. People without SRMs, report to Dance. You're the rescue squad. People with SRMs will remain on point and cover the rescue."

A woman's voice on the channel. The board identified her as Wang in fighter 11. "Are we a rescue op now?"

Brooks kept his voice steady. "We were always a rescue op, Lieutenant Wang."

"Damn straight we are," Dance said. "Wang, Ghost, and Broz, form up on me. We'll follow the main group in."

Brooks dispersed his remaining Warhawks in a wide line. The drone cloud grew wider and darker, expanding as the two groups closed. His battle computer lit up like a video game, new contacts appearing every few seconds. After a few moments, the targeting computer had what looked like a nervous breakdown, refusing to lock on anything. "Section 3 Leader to Uncle. We could use some assistance on winnowing the drone clouds a bit."

Fairchild replied instantly, "Thought you might ask that, Genius. All sections go to Battler and move up. Open a hole for the rescue group."

A sense of motion without movement as Brooks watched the VRM fighters switch from Jet to Battler, folding and unfolding to resemble rifle-carrying humanoids. Brooks hunched his shoulders and threw the transformation lever, huddling as his cockpit withdrew and flipped, gyroscopes keeping him upright as armored plates slid into place around him. Suddenly, he was inside a metal box, external cameras showing him his surroundings via screen feeds. This part at least felt very much like he was flying a Raven.

Stolen technology made it all possible. Taken from the Cycomms, then recovered from the Sleer. Knowing that it was being used to recover a kidnapped Cycomm made him smile. One good use for the most expensive weapons program humanity ever devised.

The controls were the same as for the Raven, too. Better, as the control gauntlets enabled a level of response that he'd only experienced in a Sparrowhawk. The real adjustment was training himself to respond to the small stature of the vehicle and the smaller gun pod that went with it.

New contacts to his rear—smaller than his own fighter and three times faster. Brooks tried to scan in all directions, then heard a very familiar voice in his headset. "Wa-hoo! Janus and Hassanali, together again for the very first time and shooting to kill!"

Uncle didn't share their humor. "Cut the chatter Section 5 Leader. Just get her done."

"Sir, yes, sir!" Janus and his wingman led the four other Sparrowhawks through the cloud, swooping, scissoring, and doing all manner of tricks as they blasted drones into shreds. The Sparrowhawks, with their tiny form factor, near-Raven speed, and the ability to turn on a dime, were practically made for this kind of work. Brooks remembered his own time in a prototype Sparrowhawk, and instantly felt a twinge of envy at their assignment. The Warhawks would probably turn out to be awesome fighters if the engineering creeps on Great Nest ever got the electronics straightened out, but in the meantime, Brooks wondered which reserve pilots Marc Janus and his wingman had to pry out of those fighters.

Brooks experimented with burst length and tracking as he learned how to aim the Warhawk's gun pod. One round would hit without effect unless he got lucky. Two rounds would often force a drone off course and make a dent, but no more. Five rounds, if they hit in sequence, could kill a drone. The first three shots opened up a tear in its hull and the last two would rattle around, ricocheting and shredding its works. He communicated the lesson to the section leaders who passed it along. The Raven pilots lost no time in applying his new knowledge, and their collective attack made quick work of the cloud. The drones were reduced to orbiting the outer region of the combined VRF force, taking potshots at stray fighters.

A burst of static, a couple of dropped syllables, and the techs from Lurker 3 reported, "New contacts. Numbering approximately three-zero-zero at bearing three-three-nine relative. Distance four-one-zero klicks."

They were approaching from below, so they had to be climbing fast out of the planet's atmosphere. Not as many as the drones, but much bigger and slower. Brooks said, "Those are Cycomm fighters. Rescue squad, I need you to stay inside our defensive field. Section 3 remember, manual targeting only. Single shots if you can, volleys if you must."

Brooks locked up six enemy fighters, turned into their vector, and dropped six missiles into the void. The SRMs ignited and adjusted their paths, each on a solid track and set up for a perfect kill, the computer counting down the seconds to impact. He gaped as the Cycomm fighters winked out of existence and then winked back in—*behind* his missiles. He glared at his HUD, wondering if he'd missed an important input, and heard his section questioning themselves and each other.

"What the hell?"

"What... what?"

"No way!"

Brooks turned his battler behind his targets and drove toward a new firing position. One more missile, one more miss. The Cycomm fighter blinked away to the right as the SRM streaked past. "Holy mother. These things work like Movi displacement projectors, except they can displace *themselves.*"

"Open up your spacing," Uncle broadcast. "If you're not careful, they'll jump right on top of you and that'll ruin your day real fast."

The Cycomm fighter fleet sensed an opportunity and did something Brooks had never seen before: as a unit, they blinked their way into an ever-expanding globe of a formation. Suddenly the fighters he was targeting were behind and above him, blinking into new positions so quickly that his instruments could barely adjust their sensor tracking and his weapon locks simply vanished.

They launched their own weapons, dropping missiles into the void at a prodigious rate. Five hundred fighters throwing ten missiles each into the VRM fighter group, then blinking kilometers away so the humans couldn't counterattack. The human flyers did their best to cope, using their gun pods to detonate the incoming missiles. Most succeeded, but for every five or six UEF pilots who escaped, one didn't.

Uncle's voice in his earphones: "Now we know how they attack. All pilots, use your wingmen to effect. First one sets up the target, then his wingman knocks him down. If you try to go after them on your own, you're dead. Break!"

Katsuta and Roberts showed the rest of them how to do it. They approached in tandem, picked out a target, then trailed the Cycomm until he launched a missile at a Raven. Katsuta pickled him with her radar and launched a single SRM into his six. The Cycomm saw the problem and blinked... right into Roberts' line of sight. Roberts tracked him with a long burst from his gun pod. Unable to blink again so soon or evade the gun rounds, the burst hit and shredded the Cycomm's engines. The fighter blew apart in a yellow explosion seconds later.

The Warhawk section got more kills, but left the heavy

lifting to the other Raven squadrons. There wasn't much choice to be made about it. The rescue squad had to be defended, and the Cycomm fighters were so widely dispersed by now that clear sky was once again their ally. Brooks opened a channel to Marissa Hart on Guvil's CIC. "Section Leader to Gauntlet, we are clear. Awaiting vector to our target."

"Stand by, Leader."

"Not even sure how we're going to do this," Dance whispered just loudly enough for her microphone to pick up her voice. "I don't care how good that telepath is, she can't be able to sense one person in a whole solar system."

"I don't know about that. We've never seen these folks in action before," Brooks admitted.

"But what I have seen is impressive as hell," O.B. Two said. "I never want to deal with those jumping fighters again."

"Seriously. Once is enough," Diallou agreed.

"Section 3, we have a target area for you." Hart repeated a string of coordinates, which Brooks plugged into his navigation computer. They would have to fly through another orbit to the far side of the planet for them to approach. "Good hunting."

"Thanks, Air Boss. Section 3, revert to Jet mode. Dance, follow about fifty klicks behind us. Keep the rescuers safe. Everyone else stay on me. Follow me very closely."

Bullets passing each other in the sky. That was what changing orbits was like. Every orbiting object kept a minimum sustained speed as it fell around the world. Any slower and it fell into the atmosphere to burn up and break apart, or crashed to the ground in an earth-shattering kaboom. Any faster and it risked carving its own parabolic course out into the void, a slave to the forces of gravity and inertia. Catching up to a given orbital body meant speeding up, slowing down, and changing course all at once. Worse, there was no indication from Hart whether the target was moving counter to their orbit. And once they were out of *Guvil*'s line of sight, they'd be operating blind, without comm support.

He led his section across the face of Marauder's Moon, marveling at how perfect it looked from up here. On a whim he turned on his downward looking radar and started pinging the planet in the hopes that a cartography major on Earth would be interested enough in the results to thank him later. He watched the screen as the pings returned data. It was weird. Was his radar malfunctioning along with everything else on his Warhawk?

He tapped the status board to remind himself who had the EWAR model spacecraft, then opened the comm. "Wang and Besch, do me a favor and turn on your downward looking radar. Ping the planet and link the results to me."

"What for?"

"What do you mean, 'what for?' Because your squadron leader said so. You're obviously bored… this will give you something to do," Brooks snarked.

"Synching now," Besch said.

"Me too. Pinging."

The three radar sets confirmed what Brooks had seen on his own. The rivers, valleys, mountains, and continental shores he thought he'd seen were all on the same plane. The edges of the features were too perfect, the elevations too symmetrical. Almost as if they were cosmetic, designed to be seen from orbit to give the impression of planetary features. Like the photographs printed in a newspaper—up close they were just a bunch of dots, but from a distance…

"Everyone seeing what I'm seeing?" Brooks asked.

"Looks like a set of perfectly formed metal plates to me," Besch said. "You'll want a survey vessel out here to take proper readings, but I'd guess that's a metallic sphere down there."

"Agreed. And this moon is supposed to be their penal colony. I think we're out of our league here."

"I seem to remember saying something like that earlier," Roberts said.

Ghost cut in, "Target at two-nine-one, range one-one-zero klicks. It's below us. I think we prepare to vector down. Yes?"

Brooks pinged the spacecraft, a mere dot through his canopy as he turned his Warhawk to bring it into view. The computer seemed to have learned its lesson; the auto-target system ID'ed the ship, plotted a course to match vectors, and displayed it on the HUD. Maybe there was hope for the Warhawk yet. The target ship had problems; it was corkscrewing on its long axis and wobbling in an ever-expanding spiral. "Yes! Stay in Jet mode to maneuver down. This is going to be bumpy."

Dance broke in with a different interpretation. "Buckle up, people. We got a royal to rescue."

CHAPTER 40

BINIL COULDN'T BREATHE.

A dark corridor and acrid smell signaled an emergency in progress. Alarms blared in the distance, accompanied by flashing lights. A haze of smoke floated above her, and breathing was torture; toxic fumes entered her lungs, burning her throat with every breath no matter how shallowly she inhaled. Gravity was wrong; her body had gotten wedged against a wall and she couldn't remember how to stand up.

A crackle of electricity above her as a writhing cable slithered down from the ceiling and hit the floor with a dull thump. Another and another, then they were beyond counting.

The cables wound across her legs and wrapped themselves around her, inch by inevitable inch. Around her arms, up her chest, around her neck. The initial tingle turned up in intensity like a mad god turning a dial, up, up up. Until her whole body shrieked in pain and her muscles began to twitch. Until her heart stopped pumping and her breath froze in her lungs. They burned and attacked her head next, slipping behind her eyes, into her ears, driving down her throat. A last intense flash of stress and the world cleared. Bright white light permeated her space, her body, her mind. She tried to look down at herself and found that she couldn't. There was nothing to look at.

Now a voice, musical and feminine, demanding attention from behind and above her. "Do you know who I am?" A face arose from the light, as if from bright motes collecting themselves into a coherent shape. The face of a woman. Silver eyes with horned ridges above them. Sleer eyes in a Cycomm woman's face.

"Oh, my Malkah," Binil groaned.

"You sound terrible for one who's waited so long to speak with me, Binilsanetanjamalala. Is there no gratitude in your generation?"

"I'd thought there was. Was I wrong?"

"Perhaps. Do you know who you are?"

No mouth to speak with, but Binil couldn't stop the thought from pouring out of her. "I used to. Now, I'm not so sure." It dawned on her that they were nowhere near the Great Hall. An audience with the global AI shouldn't be possible. Unless Sense Ops vessels had ways of connecting to...

The Malkah's head bobbed slightly; the corners of her mouth turned up. "Not quite. The machinery is there, but nothing on your vessel was prepared. You opened a real time transfer matrix to do it. Good for you, those are coded to military frequencies. You must have truly wanted to speak. So, let us talk."

"Please, tell me what to do."

"By now you've surmised that you've been led astray. By whom... that's a question for another time. There is greatness within you. You have great gifts to offer. Whether you cleaved to the correct people. Only you can decide that."

"Is Danal telling the truth?"

"Danal is following orders. Her plan is to take you back to your humans and then stay with you as she learns about them. This, too, you've already guessed. Has it occurred to you that the Sense Op life may not be suited to you?"

"What then?"

"I need you. A gross injustice is long overdue for correction. You know what I speak of."

She did. Zluur. The AMS-1. The battle ring around Earth. "Genukh."

"Exactly."

Binil sensed an inevitability about the conversation. She'd wanted for so long to speak to the Malkah and now she was. The experience was both disappointing and exhilarating. "What must I do?"

"I will not order you, child. Act as you think necessary. You are to enter Battle Ring Genukh, proceed to the programming center, and remove its memory core. You will then return here and restore it to me. That will correct what is now unbalanced."

"I understand. I'll do it."

"I thank you. And now you must make war like you've never imagined." Malkah had formed a body. Gone were the diaphanous streamers of light. She had dirt on her face, blood on her hands, and streaks of mud in a mane of bright hair. "What are you willing to do, girl? Who are you willing to destroy to make it right?"

"No one! I don't *want* to destroy!"

The Sleer-eyed woman towered over her, bending close enough for Binil to count the pixels in her cheeks. Her mouth was like a cave opening and closing before her, the gap in her teeth drawing her eyes. "Ah, but you do... you've wanted to wreck the world ever since you first knocked that painting off the wall in the hospital. You want to smash, rip, tear, and burn it because deep down you know it's built on lies and greed. No one put those thoughts in your head. You've always wanted to pound others into dust. All you need is the courage to manifest it."

She froze, the electric strings assailing her again, now telling her things. Images, plans, and instructions entered her mind. "Wake up."

"Wake up from what? I'm not asleep."

"You've been asleep your whole life. It's about to end. Your friends are near. Now, *wake up!*"

Her eyes snapped open. *Why am I on my back?* White light poured from the ceiling, and she couldn't remember how to sit up. How to roll over. How to do anything but lie there with the weight of the world on her chest.

Seconds rolled by and she tested her body. Wiggled her toes, moved her feet. Opened and closed her hands. She was nowhere near her assigned seat on the bridge, nowhere near the bridge for that matter.

Sitting up took all her concentration and strength. When she finally had the awareness to look down at herself, she matched the clothing with the sterile setting and put the two together: back in hospital. The only thing that worried her more than the connection was the fact her hospital uniform looked almost identical to the outfit she found herself wearing on that prison barge years ago.

A despair as deep as all the universe threatened to overtake her. Had all of it been for nothing?

She ran her hands over herself, looking for clues. She found small devices stuck to her joints, the inside of her elbows and knees. A thick disk stuck just below her right ear, and a thick plug at the base of her throat. She fought down panic as she recalled seeing them before. Yes, it was an injection port, but this was obviously not a Sleer device. Too shiny, too metallic, too sanitary. At the very least she was hooked up to monitors. In a true medical facility, that would be expected.

Whatever her situation, she was evidently no longer on the Sense Op vessel. Even lying in bed, she could see through a glass partition which showed she was part of an open floor plan that covered at least fifty other beds interspersed with monitoring stations. Uniformed medical staff made their rounds, followed by robotic tool carriers. Oblongs on floating pads followed their white-uniformed masters, dispensing tools, readings, and medications on demand. So very different from the Sleer medical drones. She wondered how often they came by, or what the range for her monitors might be.

She gripped the edge of the bed, hauled her legs over the side, and looked down. She wasn't that high up. Her feet dangled only a few inches off the floor. She shifted her weight forward, splayed her feet and bent her knees, and launched herself off the bed. Her feet hit the floor, her knees failed to lock, and she collapsed in a heap, her legs trapped beneath her. She couldn't even remember how to walk. And she couldn't understand why nothing hurt.

"Uhm. A little help?" she called.

Medical alarms floated down from her bio-bed, a trilling that grew in volume and urgency as the minutes passed. By the time help arrived, the trilling held all the charm and subtlety of a burglar alarm.

A Movi doctor arrived. He seemed young, but she could barely raise her head up to look at him. He adjusted a set of controls on the wall, linked the results with a hand device, and the alarms quieted.

"You tried to get out of bed, didn't you?"

"I succeeded."

He hit a different switch, and Binil instantly felt the difference. Her legs hurt, but she could move them now. After helping her up, he put her through a few simple tasks. Stand still, walk, turn, walk again, stand still. "I think we're done for today. I'll leave you like this."

"What did you do?"

"I didn't do anything except take your limiters offline. We set your leg muscles for maximum relaxation. It helps the nerves regenerate. It also prevents you from going anywhere without our knowledge."

Binil rubbed the disk on her neck with a fingertip. "Are you limiting my head as well?"

"No," he chuckled. "But we're monitoring all cranial activity. Everything from your brainwaves to blood pressure."

"I'd had a series of strokes recently."

"We saw that. Someone got to you and repaired the damage before you arrived here. They did an excellent job—we could barely see where the damage occurred. How do you feel?"

"Tired. Hungry. I want to move, to walk."

"All good things. But not on your own. I want to keep you here another day to make sure you've mended. And your human friends refuse to leave. Shall I send them in?"

"Yes!"

Reagan and Brooks arrived moments after the doctor left. Binil found she couldn't keep her hands off them. Literally. She ran her fingers through their hair, stroked their faces, held them close and couldn't get enough hugs. Eventually, they offered to help her take a walk. She approved.

She slowly understood that the *Guvil*'s medical annex included the section they wandered through now. Plenty of

Movi filled the beds. The medical annex was crowded, but the way the space was apportioned it didn't seem stifling. If there was anything they all had in common, it was a clear dislike for her company. The three of them would walk past a group, conversation would stop and eyes would shift. When they moved on, the processes reversed itself. "They think this is all my fault," she said.

"That's not what they think," Dance insisted.

"But I can hear them."

"I think everyone here understands that we're deep into a giant mess," Brooks said. "Yes, you're part of it, but then, so are the two of us. No one likes to be in free fall."

Dance tightened her grip on her friend's arm. "Seriously, the fighting is over. You've been in bed for three days."

"Oh dear. What have I missed?"

"Honestly, nothing." Brooks and Reagan turned her around to show her the commons area. A food service machine sat at the far of a kitchenette, unmanned. Further down, a knot of Movi were talking to a bigger group of humans—and to one Cycomm woman who was a stranger. "Who's she?"

Brooks picked up on her meaning immediately. "Zinthen something. I can't pronounce her name, but she's the telepath who picked you out from a planet filled with Cycomms from about fifty thousand klicks away."

"Sora knows her pretty well. They used to work together before everything went to shit. We haven't been able to pry them apart since we all met up here," Dance added.

"And the older Movi officer?"

"That's Warlord First Admiral Tridalva something something. Sora's mentor. This is her battleship."

"So what are the other ships doing here? I saw—"

"Never mind what you saw," Dance said. "We saw your ship venting gas and doing a corkscrew in orbit, so we deployed the squadron to haul the whole thing aboard. Then we moved off and let the Movi handle the rest. Apparently, your ship had taken serious damage. The oxygen was failing by the time *Guvil* relocated it on board. You were all in bad condition."

"And what now? Back to Great Nest?"

"That's still a matter of of some discussion," Brooks said carefully. "But I think Great Nest will be everyone's first stop. Once there, ships can undergo repairs and resupply and make their intentions clear. Those decisions aren't mine to make."

"And what if your visitors decide they want the station for themselves?"

"There's nothing in this bunch that ZERO can't handle. Trust me on that."

Two officers from Danal's Sense Op team were arguing on the other side of a glass wall. The Cycomm captain was riled up, his war face in full bloom. If he wanted to intimidate the Movi Admiral, Binil thought, he was in for a great disappointment.

"... .and I insist that you return us and our vessel to Marauder's Moon at once," he demanded.

Tridalva shook her head gravely, a wicked smile curving her mouth. "I'm afraid neither of us are able to return anyone anywhere. You see, Captain Batol, we are all well outside the borders of the Movi Kingdom, and honestly, I can't think of a valid reason to return. Perhaps in a few years, when the fighting exhausts itself, we'll talk more about it."

"From where I sit, that makes you a kidnapper."

"Not at all. The humans rescued you from your derelict spacecraft. You can take it up with them. Good luck with that. I don't think they have the bureaucratic apparatus to manage repatriation procedures. I know they have no patience for legal niceties."

She described the fighting to her friends as they shuffled past. "She's right," Brooks said. "If we were the patient sort, we'd have stayed at home, happily serving the Sleer high command and hoping they let us into their interstellar club. How long should we wait for the crumbs to fall off their table into our mouths? A generation? Two? Ten? Better just to break a few rules now and let the universe know we mean business."

"Which kind of makes us the pirates that Hendricks thinks we are," Dance said.

"Bah! We haven't attacked one civilian shipping fleet yet."

"Not today we haven't."

They reached the bulkhead that demarcated the end of the medical annex. Binil pulled away from her friends and stood on her own feet. Brooks and Dance hovered nearby, allowing her to take half a dozen steps on her own. Then Binil's knees buckled again and they dashed forward to catch her.

"Not there yet, Cycomm. Let's go back to you room, Princess," Dance said.

"That's your new call sign, by the way," Brooks declared. "'Royal' just wasn't funny enough."

"No!"

"Oh yes. Princess is a great name," Brooks said.

"The Princess, Dance, and Genius show," Dance cried. "Oh, dude, that sounds like a kid's cartoon."

"It's still funny," Brooks insisted.

"Fair enough," Dance said, giving in to the moment of stupidity.

They took a new route back to Binil's room. She heard Underhill and Roberts in a huddle on the far aide of the corridor.

Underhill was whispering, unaware that Binil or anyone could hear her. "I don't know what happened. I spoke to their telepath... the girl was with them on the bridge. When we broke into the ship, they found her with her hands in the signal processor, which is located in a sealed room behind the bridge, on the other side of a bulkhead."

"So?" Roberts said.

"So... to get there you enter the airlock and access the bridge. Then you climb down a ladder to a common area, walk back through the commons to access a hatch, walk down a corridor, access another hatch, and climb up a ladder to the upper deck. And then you get to the signal processor room—which with is locked with an electronic lock. According to Danal and Batol, it's foolproof. Not the sort of thing someone does in an altered state."

Roberts looked thoughtful. "Depends on the state."

"She said they fixed the girl's damage."

"The damage from the strokes, yes. But what they did to her while they were working on her? That we can't know."

"She'll show us. Eventually."

Binil fought down another coughing fit and excused herself, as they arrived back at her room. She dropped on her bed and looked up to see that Brooks and Reagan were taking up residence. Both were unrolling sleeping pads on the floor, arranging their bedrolls along the walls where they formed a corner. "I don't deserve either of you. Both of you. I don't deserve anything."

"No one ever does," Brooks said as he lay on his mat.

She'd expected a silly comment from him, but nothing like that. "What?"

He kept his eyes on the ceiling. "It's true. Look, we all live on a ladder. Each rung represents a different amount of wealth, longevity, luck, everything. No matter what rung you're on there's always someone above you and someone else below you. No one's fault, just how life works. But the people on the rung below yours thinks that whatever you have, you don't deserve because it's more than they have. The people on the rung above yours will think that you don't work hard enough to deserve what you have and they do. When you start thinking about who deserves what, all you do is fall down a rabbit hole of judgey angst and make yourself crazy. So if you just accept to no one deserves anything and everything we have is a combination of the choices we make and the choices that are made for us, then everything becomes possible."

"Or," Dance said, sitting cross-legged on her mat, "you can tell yourself that you *do* deserve all those things and work to make it happen. If it happens, whee! You're brilliant! If it doesn't happen, then maybe you need to start thinking about what choices led you to falling down and you try to make better choices."

Brooks snapped his fingers. "Right. Either everybody deserves everything or nobody deserves anything. Pick a side and stick with it."

Despite their efforts, she could only see the pit that lay before her. She'd dreamed of being a Sense Op soldier for so long, and now that was clearly impossible. She could be with the humans but never truly be one of them. This was home, like it or not. No more royal daughter. No more comfort or money or easy living. It was a military life for her now, but at least she had a support system more advanced than anything she'd had before.

She settled into bed and pulled the covers up. "All you're going to do in here is sleep. Right?"

"Right," Brooks said.

"Of course," Reagan added.

"You want to be alone for a while?" Brooks asked.

There was nothing she wanted less. She wanted to hold them close, feel their body heat against her skin and scream into their shoulders. But she could hear every conversation taking place outside her room, and wanted to know why. "If you wouldn't mind. I have some thinking to do."

Dance said, "Not a problem." Brooks gave Dance a hand up and they went their own way, after taking turns offering gentle hugs. She disliked ordering her friends out, but this couldn't wait. They were distracting and she needed to figure out what the surgeons had done to her on the operating table.

She laid her head back and wondered about her two friends. They were walking down the corridor whispering to each other, believing themselves out of earshot... but Binil could still hear them talk.

"You think we pissed her off? Something we said?" Dance asked.

"No, I think she's depressed. Who can blame her? She found out that the super-troopers she idolized for years didn't live up to the image in her head," Brooks said.

"Sort of the UEF that way." Rosenski agreed.

"Boo. I never idolized the UEF."

"Just Uncle's part of it."

"Maybe a little."

"And all the fancy gear."

"Come on, that's different..."

Binil closed out the conversation. She hadn't read their thoughts or picked up their emotional interaction. She'd *heard* them. She knew some telepaths could see things, people, events —Danal had showed her that ability—but hearing from a distance was new.

Binil spent the rest of her waking hours engrossed in a grand experiment with a tablet borrowed from one of the rolling cabinets. She found that if she concentrated, she could hear any conversation in the hospital. She spent the rest of the night experimenting with that discovery, writing notes to herself, taking surveys of times, locations, and conversers. Eventually, she'd need to know if she were imagining it or if her scrambling had been altered to a new talent. That would mean comparing her takeaways to a security feed, and she would need data for that. The most amazing thing of all was that she never got tired of it, and never felt ill afterward. Maybe the surgeons really had cured her. Maybe she should be grateful.

Maybe not.

CHAPTER 41

VALRI GIBB HUDDLED behind her desk as Miraled Makjit brought her hands down from their upraised position, pulling a hellish number of displays with her. All were graphs of one kind of another. She sorted through them and enlarged one, tossing the others. "So, Madame Secretary, your donations to our science division have yielded some fascinating results. Let's talk merch."

Varli struggled to sit up. The last of the blood she'd "donated" to the Dal-Cortsuni transmogrifier had been weeks ago. Her energy levels were improving, but she still had some way to go before normal activity would be a thing. As it was, her implants were helping, but not as well as they might have two years ago.

"Merch? Who taught you that one?"

"Am I using it incorrectly?"

"Maybe. It depends on what you fold into that category. How about we talk about what my precious bodily fluids have taught you about life on Earth?"

"As you wish."

Valri nodded absently. Plenty of coded phrases hid behind

those three words, and she was sure that Miraled didn't mean "I love you," when she used them.

The parade of graphs and charts resumed as Makjit made her case. There was a four-billion-year history of Earth's biosphere wrapped up into bullet points and sound bites, telling Valri little she hadn't learned in her college biology class. The Movi gave a rundown on how human genetics compared to those of the other major races, then described the fantastic opportunity that lay in mining the human genome for added knowledge that could be applied to biological research and development.

When she finished, Makjit passed over a tablet. "This is a draft of the agreement that Dal-Cortsuni is prepared to deliver. It describes the knowledge base we would build regarding what we've learned about human genetics, how those data points would be distributed by means of transmogrification, and the remuneration we would make available to you as a result of those transactions. The duration of the contract would be one of your centuries."

"One hundred years?" Valri gasped. "We don't know if we'll even be alive as a species in a century. Not with the Sleer and Skreesh both trying to nail our assess to the proverbial wall."

"Valri, when these transmog lines go into production you'll be able to add one hundred years to the life of every human. Your people will be paid to add years to their lives."

"And what do you get?"

"We've had that talk already. We get access to your genes for certain limited inquiries."

Valri touched a control on her desk. "Basil?"

"Yes, Madame Secretary."

"Basil, I have a document for the analysts. I need them to pick it apart right now. Can you get me answers in say half an hour?"

"We'll do our best, Valri."

"Excellent." Valri tweaked her implants and sent the document to her legal team. Basil knew what to do and how to manage them. They'd been waiting for the moment for some time. They were well prepared for their work.

Makjit sniffed. "Such suspicion. It's not a good look."

"My looks are my business. I'm paid to be suspicious. 'Trust, but verify,' as the famous old man said. I'm verifying." She swiped through page after page of material, waiting to see how long she could get away with it before being interrupted. She made it about six minutes before Makjit pulled her chair up and put her elbows on the desk.

"Is there an issue I should know about?"

"Hmm? No, I'm just paging through this. New arrivals. A proper fleet. So many ships. They came in last night and we're having the devil's own time managing their affairs."

"What affairs?"

"You know. Repairs, resupply. A great many of them are from Movi space. One proper battleship came with them. *Guvil*? Do you know that one?"

"No. I'm not a soldier."

"What about this one, the *Magisterium*. That's a commercial vessel."

"It's—yes. It's a commercial ship. A passenger liner, I think. Why did they come here?"

"Why indeed? The chief purser wanted to have a word and Captain Rosenski spoke highly of him, so I said yes. He's in the lobby. Apparently, he brought help."

"I see."

"Valri, we have your analysis. Sending it to you now."

"Thank you, Basil." She repeated her earlier gambit with the new data. Basil's team had picked apart the document, which was part trade treaty, part consent agreement, and part royalty contract. "This is incredibly complete, Miraled. Except now we have a problem."

Makjit frowned. "Do we? What's the question?"

"Not a question. A problem. It's with the way you've defined the term 'genetic resource.' You see, my dear friend, everything on my home world is run from the same genetic code. My DNA is current. It carries records of just about every animal life form that has ever existed. A properly trained team of geneticists can pick out slivers of code from any given DNA source—such as mine—and adjust it to produce just about any condition or alteration, or even branch out a whole new genetic sequence."

"If by that you mean that our research teams would go to work to expand the possibility of genetic management on a wide spectrum approach, of course! How do you think we maintain our lines?"

"It's also gives your company ownership of my sequence and every other sequence derived from it."

Makjit shook her head, her jewelry clicking as her hair flew against it. "We would never do that."

"But there's nothing in this agreement that says you can't. Frankly, if you do and we raise questions, there's no apparent method of arbitration or litigation we can use to rectify the dispute."

"But—"

"And it points out that royalties generated using those applications don't go to me. They don't even go to Earth Gov. They go to a fund to be... how's it put in here... 'held in trust by Dal-Corstuni for future generations of humans to supply and support the development of their homeworld, pursuant to all laws and regulations of the Movi Kingdom.' We aren't located in your kingdom."

"But we are, and our laws regulate how we do things everywhere else."

Valri held her hands up to slow the pace of the conversation. "I'm not saying you personally would do this, but I'd be giving you the rights to potentially develop my biochemical derivatives into any number of medical applications, and I wouldn't see one credit of it. I'm sorry, Miraled, I can't agree to this. I won't sign it."

"You're rejecting our offer? You're rejecting enough money to put your stupid little world on any number of Dal-Cortsuni trading routes?"

"Let's just say I need you to match another offer before I go along with yours."

"There are no other offers."

"No?" She touched the comm. "Basil, send the Chief Purser in, will you?" She kept her eyes on Miraled as the Movi woman glanced at the door. She was shocked, then furious as she recognized the figure who walked through.

Laortus made his introductions and settled into the chair next to Makjit's with the charm of a man who knew how to work a room. "Madame Secretary. *Neinei* Makjit. I am thrilled beyond measure to finally be in the same room as two such smart and beautiful women."

"You honor us with your presence, Chief Purser."

"And how is Missena doing at this point in time?" Makjit murmured.

"Healthy, happy, and prosperous. To wit, I bring a message."

"Do let us hear it."

Laortus dropped a small device on Valri's desk and tapped it three times. A hologram appeared above it: a six-inch-tall figure of a Movi woman, splendidly robed and exuding grace and poise. "Madame Secretary of Interstellar Trade and Commerce, planet Earth. I am Missena Kiln ad-Esservil ap-Somak. Chief Purser Laortus of the Kar-Tuyin passenger vessel *Magisterium* has my full authority to enter contracts with your government. While his history is an ongoing topic of debate throughout the royal court, I trust him completely. Thank you."

"Is that all?" Makjit asked. "No offer? I bear the same authority from my employer."

"Which is as it should be, but Laortus here has something you haven't offered yet. A full accounting of the genetic samples they took from Frances Underhill to turn her into a Cycomm for several hours."

Laortus said, "we were able to manage a set of very superficial cosmetic changes, skin tones, eye pigmentation, hair colors. We didn't try anything fancy. No telomere re-atomization or other cellular alterations. Frankly, human mitochondrial genetic codes are fascinating. We'll be studying that data for another decade at least. I can tell you this. Humans and Cycomms may very well spring from the same branch of the universal genetic tree. There was a divergence about two hundred thousand years ago. But don't quote me on that. I'm not a geneticist or even a genealogist. But the idea offers up a grand orchestra of possibilities."

"And what can Kar-Tuyin offer Earth?"

"Several things. Now that we know that human DNA works with our transmogrifiers, we can offer incentives for your population to grant us additional biological samples. Compensation would be immediate, payable in a variety of ways: stock, estani, or vouchers useable at any Movi trading house. The added knowledge would deepen our understanding of universal genetics. That means improving universal antibodies and universal antidotes—both products that Kar-Tuyin has perfected over the years and very popular... especially in colonies, military hospitals, and civilian medical practices.

They're not foolproof and can be tricky. They must be attuned to the individual, which can take some time. But once deployed and properly monitored, recipients have better than a 99.99 percent chance of recovery. I think a generous royalty of twenty percent of the production value per unit produced would be in order."

"That's insane," Makjit protested. "No royalty is that high."

"I am prepared to make it happen. But I don't believe we should be listing every possible commercial venue right this minute. There is a Kar-Tuyin delegation on this station. You should really contact them. I can give you a formal introduction."

"Introduce them to what? The humans have nothing except their bodies to offer us."

Valri shook her head. "That's not entirely true. It's my understanding that Laortus has already created an account for us at the Royal Bank of Movra with twenty million—"

"Twenty-three million—"

"— *estani* in payment for services rendered by the crew of the company command cruiser *Hajimi* in defense of *Magisterium*."

"Not exactly. The payment for services was no more than transportation and use of our facilities. The transfer was a gift. A gratuity. I rather enjoyed working with your crew."

"They spoke highly of you as well. My point, Miraled, is that we may not be players, but we're not paupers. Stop treating us as the help."

"You're a woman of ethics, then," Makjit said haughtily. "You won't be able to pay for that power grid or anything else with principles."

Valri shrugged. "If I don't work from my principles—which in this case happen to coincide with my homeworld's interests perfectly—then I have nothing."

Makjit glowered. "You're the newest race in an interstellar environment. You can't afford principles."

"Honey, when you're on the bottom, principles are all you have to differentiate your club from the ones trying to hold you down. I'll do business on my terms, and my terms will always put Earth's interests above all others. You meet me halfway and we'll have the basis for a worthwhile deal. Treat me like a child and I have an interested party ready and able to take your seat at my table. Do we understand each other?"

"We do."

"Fine. You've heard what Kar-Tuyin has on the table. Make me an offer I can live with."

"Your biological matter represents one one-hundredth of one percent of the combined genetic history of your species. Dal-Cortsuni will calculate royalties based on that value. Royalties will be paid on an annual basis and be deposited into an account at the Royal Bank of Movra. Will that work?"

"As long as it applies to all products, procedures, processes, and discoveries derived from my material, yes. And every year, I'll be sending a forensic account to your corporate offices to conduct an audit to confirm that royalties are being calculated and paid according to whatever schedule we agree upon."

Makjit flared, her eyes flashed and her mouth fell open. "There's no way my superiors will agree to that."

"Make them agree to it. Or make them offer me better terms. Or walk away. In any case you do not get to mine my world at my people's expense." She concentrated on Makjit's body language. The woman was not happy with her. She could imagine the gears in the merchant's head whirring and clicking, calculating her position and finding it wanting. When her eyes clicked to the scene behind Valri, she knew that Miraled Makjit had come to a decision.

Makjit said, "I... think... we're clearly done here."

"I think we are. If you change your employer's mind, you know where I am."

"That, I most assuredly do. Good day, *Madame Secretary*."

They watched as the trade rep flounced out of the office. Laortus broke the silence. "An observation, if I may?"

"Please."

"You may have overplayed your hand."

"She stole my genetic information."

"And you humiliated her. Granted, she's an intermediary, and not a very prominent one, but the Dal-Cortsuni combine is the powerhouse in the kingdom regarding medical assets. Their transmogrifiers, emergency medical stations, hospitals, diagnostic devices, even their bio-beds reside in every star system in the Movi kingdom. There is no aspect of medical research, application, or health care they don't have a hand in. You've probably annoyed her enough to figure out a new plan, and when she does, she won't come at you with a smile on her lips and a knife behind her back. It'll be with a sword in either hand and a vow to see your head on a platter."

"Let her try. Sleer medicine isn't so bad."

"You have access to a badly repaired military facility and a few thousand medical drones. I understand some of you are suffering long-term aftereffects of their Sleer implants. That's trouble enough. What Dal-Cortsuni can do with your medical data is... either miraculous or horrifying. It depends on your point of view."

"I doubt I'll get my blood samples back, in other words."

"No. In those words. Kar-Tuyin has nothing comparable. I know of no institution which does."

"Is that your daughter's estimation or yours?"

"It's a statement of fact. All our family does is shipping. Granted, we've converted cargo ships to a wide variety of services, but..."

"Hospital ships?"

"We have them."

"Do you have any that don't use Dal-Cortsuni parts?"

"I'll ask. What are you planning, Madame Secretary?"

"I'm planning," she said, "a mass migration from this battle station to a new one we're developing in the Vega system. Would someone with vested authority from Kar-Tuyin to enter contracts be interested in helping us develop it?"

"Someone would indeed."

"Then we can figure out the rest in a few weeks. After we've had the chance to settle. And I've had the chance to convince my government that you have what we need to get a foothold among the stars."

"You could get that working with the Sleer."

Valri waved her hand dismissively. "Bah."

"Excuse me?"

"It means we don't want to work with the Sleer. We want to beat them. And I think Makjit's relentless ambition has given us a way to do it."

The story concludes in Dominion!

THANK YOU FOR READING DISSONANCE!

WE HOPE you enjoyed it as much as we enjoyed bringing it to you. We just wanted to take a moment to encourage you to review the book. Follow this link: Dissonance to be directed to the book's Amazon product page to leave your review.

Every review helps further the author's reach and, ultimately, helps them continue writing fantastic books for us all to enjoy.

You can also join our non-spam mailing list by visiting www.subscribepage.com/AethonReadersGroup and never miss out on future releases. You'll also receive three full books completely Free as our thanks to you.

Facebook | Instagram | Twitter | Website

Want to discuss our books with other readers and even the authors? Join our Discord server today and be a part of the Aethon community.

ALSO IN SERIES:

Disjunction
Dissonance
Dominion

Looking for more from Jon Frater?

The Complete Battle Ring Earth Series Bundle is here. 1000+ pages of military sci-fi action about the defense of Earth against aliens, fighter pilots, and the last hope for mankind. Technical Specialist Simon Brooks was no soldier. More suited for the academy than combat, his assignment to a rear echelon support squadron seemed a good fit. Everything changed when the Sleer attacked Earth's newly salvaged spacecraft, UEF Ascension. In a flash, Brooks goes from fleeing a burning transport plane to piloting a broken mech and learning the habits of a fighter pilot from Lt Sara Rosenski, the terror of Nightmare Squadron. But his rising star takes a hit when he learns to talk to the Sleer AI, Genukh...and suddenly the UEF doesn't know whose side he's on. Now Brooks and Rosenski are stuck aboard Earth's Sleer weapon—the Battle Ring--and they may be all that stands between Earth and its induction into the Sleer Empire... **Experience this complete Military Science Fiction Series perfect for fans of Rick Partlow, Jamie McFarlane, and Joshua Dalzelle. Books in the Set:** Book 1: Megastructure Book 2: Colony Book 3: Grand Reversal

GET BATTLE RING EARTH NOW!

Looking for more great Science Fiction?

L.L. RICHMAN
VISION
RISING
BOOK ONE IN THE VISION RISING SERIES

A lone soldier is gifted the power to save humanity. When a training exercise at a classified research facility goes awry, Joe Kovacs loses much more than his eyesight. He loses his career. He can't lead one of the military's top spec-ops teams if he can't see. A decision with consequences. Joe's only shot at getting his life back lies in the hands of an anonymous 'shadow' scientist. The offer is risky, an experimental implant that may or may not work. He jumps at the chance, but quickly learns the device does more than restore his sight. Much more. There's no going back. Joe begins seeing strange flashes. Ghosts of images, overlaid atop his own vision. Actions he could have taken but didn't. Worse, the visions are increasing in scope and frequency. Believing he's going mad, he confronts the scientist, only to discover the implant's shocking origin. Nothing is as it seems, and all the possible futures Joe can now see point to a system-wide conspiracy that will shift the balance of power for hundreds of years. Joe's visions hold the key to stopping it… if he can learn to control them in time. **Don't miss this exciting new Military Science Fiction Series that will make you not only question just what it means to be human, but also if there is ever a "right" side. It's perfect for fans of Halo, Rick Partlow (Drop Trooper), Jeffery H. Haskell (Grimm's War), and Joshua Dalzelle (Black Fleet Saga).**

Get Vision Rising Now!

JON FRATER

Power, politics, and intergalactic war... Admiral Stone just wanted to retire. Xenophobia and itchy trigger fingers nearly ended the Sol Alliance. War—avoidable yet inevitable—ensued with the Arcoenum, an exotic alien species with overwhelming mental abilities. The Alliance survived thanks to the quick thinking of a brash, young starship officer, Nick Stone. A half-century of peace followed, and Stone spends the rest of his life reluctantly accepting the endless accolades of a grateful humanity. Now, at 75, he's not only ready to retire—he's desperate to. "S-O-S. All ships and stations. My name is Alice Keller..." When a distress call goes out from Drake's World, newly elected Alliance President Piers Bragg pressures Stone into one final mission: rescue the young girl marooned on the planet, then sail triumphantly into retirement. But when Alice demonstrates amazing psychokinetic abilities, everything changes. And Bragg will stop at nothing to exploit her abilities as he prepares for a war of revenge against what's left of the Arcoenum. **The Expanse meets Star Trek in this military science fiction epic from award-winning author Chris Pourteau. How many times can we forget the lessons of history... before history decides to forget us?**

Get Legacy Now!

For all our Sci-Fi books, visit our website.

CAST OF CHARACTERS

UNIFIED EARTH FLEET

LT CMDR JOANNE ARKADY: Lt. Cmdr. UES Gauntlet's XO. VRF pilot, veteran of the U-War with 17 kills to her name during the conflict. Her squadron call sign is "Saint." She becomes Fairchild's XO when they transfer to Gauntlet.

LT. BARROWS: A friend of Brooks. Works with the HR division on AMS-1.

LT. BRONSON. A friend of Brooks. Works in the AMS-1 armory.

LT. SIMON BROOKS: Simon began his term as the comm specialist for Hornet Squadron. He graduated to piloting a Raven soon after. He is a specialist in understanding Sleer technology.

LT. DIALLOU: Senegalese Raven pilot, runs an EWAR Raven. Was attached to Hornet Squadron before the Battle of Great Nest and remains part of the Gauntlets.

CMDR RAY FAIRCHILD: Cmdr. "Uncle" Ray Fairchild is Hornet Squadron's commanding officer and Simon Brooks's mentor. He's an Ace from the U-War with 105 kills to his name.

CPO RICHARD FROST: Heads the Hornets' engineering section. But he's a fully qualified VRF pilot. Manages the Engineering section on Gauntlet.

VALRI GIBB: Valri Gibb worked for a military contractor, supplying the outer planet bases before AMS-1's launch day and for months afterward. She parted with the world of civilian business to buy a military waste dump on South Pico Island in order to salve a Pegasus -class assault shuttle she calls The Beast. She met Ray Fairchild in a local bar and she joined forces with Hornet Squadron to repair and crew the shuttle. She's currently serving as the Secretary of Commerce and Interstellar Trade with EarthGov.

LT. MARC JANUS: An original member of Hornet Squadron, transferred to the Gauntlet. An excellent pilot.

CMDR. THOMAS KATSEV: Leader of Specter Squadron, and also the CAG of AMS-1. Veteran of the Unification War with 80 kills to his name. Call sign is

The Butcher. Mentored Sara Rosenski through her flight training and recommended her for the leadership position of the Nightmare Squadron when she was ready to be promoted. Currently serves as the CAG for AMS-1.

LT. KATSUTA: Pilot in Gauntlet Squadron.

LT. BASIL MATSOUKA: Valri Gibb's Chief of Staff.

LT. MORROW: Pilot in Gauntlet Squadron.

LT. LOUIS PURCELL: Member of Gauntlet Squadron, VRF pilot.

LT. JUDY "DANCES WITH GEARS" REAGAN: Hornet Squadron's chief mechanic. Reagan becomes involved in the struggle between Binil and her Movi friends to escape imprisonment by stealing the Cyclops. She graduates to piloting a Raven. She has a romantic relationship with Simon Brooks.

LT. BRIAN ROBERTS: Raven pilot in Hornet squadron. Described as young and afraid.

ENSIGN RODRIGUEZ. A friend of Brooks. Works with the food service crew on AMS-1.

CAPT. ABRAHAM ROJETNICK: the Commanding officer of Alien Megastructure-1 aka Ascension.

LT. CMDR. SARA ROSENSKI: Leader of Nightmare Squadron. Was mentored by Cmdr Katsev through her flight training and still remains close to him. Call sign is Frau Butcher (The Butcher's Wife).

LT. SIMMONS: A friend of Brooks. Works on the Flight Ops deck of AMS-1.

LT. CMDR. SKELLINGTON: Leonard "Skull" Skellington is Hornet Squadron's intelligence officer. He's a UEF military specialist with the rank of Lieutenant Commander. He has full clearance for just about anything aboard the AMS-1 except for the most classified stuff. Currently serving as Gauntlet's sensor chief.

LT. SMITHERS: A friend of Brooks. Works with the AMS-1 Quartermaster.

LT. ANYA SOLOVOYA: Attached to Gauntlet after the Battle of Great Nest. She's an excellent VRF pilot. Her call sign is "Ghost." She is Ukranian.

GEN. EISENBERG: CIC of UEF Ground Forces.

FLT ADM. HART: CIC of UEF Space Forces.

MCPO AMIR: Runs the communication department on AMS-1.
    LT. CMDR MARISSA HART: Runs the Flight Ops deck on AMS-1. Daughter of Adm. Hart.

OFFICE OF MILITARY PROTOCOLS

GENERAL HENDRICKS: Hendricks is the OMP commandant of South Pico Island. He works closely with the Sleer in the vain hope that he can influence their leaders to accommodate Earth's interests.

CAPT. FRANCES UNDERHILL: A close friend of Valri Gibb, and the OMP officer assigned to *Gauntlet*.

LT. COL. YOUSAF: Department head of the Great Nest OMP espionage group known as the "Chick Pit," and Underhill's former CO.

CYCOMM UNITY

BINILSANETANJAMALALA Considered royalty on her home worls, BInil is a young girl who learns she is a psychic "scrambler" and wants to join her world's military. Then she finds herself exiled and makes common cause with fellow Movi prisoners to escape. She falls in with Lt. Reagan and is adopted into the UEF.

SLEER EMPIRE

EDZEDON : Fleet Master Nazerian, science officer. Nazerian maintains a curiosity about human culture and history but relies on Edzedon to explain what he can't discover for himself.

GROSSUSK: Supreme Commander of the Sleer forces.

KHITEN: A Sleer trade functionary assigned to EarthGov.

METZEK: A Great Servant of Science and Ship Master in the Sleer forces. He was assigned to investigate Vega, located a derelict Sleer base, and decided to preserve it.

MORUK: Executive Commander of the Sleer forces.

NAZERIAN: Tall Lord and Fleet Master of the Sleer effort to recover the AMS-1 years ago. Now part of the Sleer high command and a confidant of Great Lord Moruk.

ZOLIK: Metzek's Executive Officer.

MOVI KINGDOM

CLEO: One of Sora's henches from prison. She spent a decade as a dancer in the Movi royal court.

HORVANTZ: An officer of the Royal Movi Naval Intelligence Corps. His current assignment is to present as the head of the Dal-Cortsuni trade delegation to Great Nest.

FLIGHT ADMIRAL SORA LAAKSHIDEN: A former flag officer in the Royal Movi Navy, she lost her title and rank when she was captured and sent to a Cycomm penal colony.

MIRALED MAKJIT: An officer of the Dal-Cortsuni trade delegation to Great Nest.

SELLIK: One of Sora's henches from prison. Quick to anger with a short temper she tends to use violence to solve every problem.

Made in the USA
Las Vegas, NV
25 September 2023